Sara Sheridan was born in Edinburg College, Dublin. As well as writing Bevan Murder Mysteries, she also w novels set between 1820 and 1845, in which was shortlisted for the Wilbur Smith Award. Fascinated particularly by female history, she is a cultural commentator who appears regularly on television and radio. In 2018 she remapped Scotland according to women's history and the resulting book was included in the David Hume Institute's recommended reading for 2019. In 2014, she was named one of the Saltire Society's 365 Most Influential Scottish Women, past and present.

Sara tweets about her writing life as @sarasheridan and has a Facebook page at sarasheridanwriter.

Praise for the Mirabelle Bevan Mystery series

'Mirabelle has a dogged tenacity to rival Poirot'
Sunday Herald

'Unfailingly stylish, undeniably smart'
Daily Record

'Fresh, exciting and darkly plotted, this sharp historical mystery plunges the reader into a shadowy and forgotten past'
Good Book Guide

'A crime force to be reckoned with'
Good Reads

'Plenty of colour and action, will engage the reader from the first page to the last. Highly recommended'
Bookbag

'Quietly
Shots

The Mirabelle Bevan Mysteries

Brighton Belle

London Calling

England Expects

British Bulldog

Operation Goodwood

Russian Roulette

Indian Summer

Highland Fling

Highland Fling

A Mirabelle Bevan Mystery

Sara Sheridan

CONSTABLE

CONSTABLE

First published in Great Britain in 2020 by Constable

A CIP catalogue record for this book
is available from the British Library.

ISBN: 978-1-47212-712-9

Typeset in Dante by SX Composing DTP, Rayleigh, Essex
Printed and bound in Great Britain by Clays Ltd, Elcograf S.p.A.

Papers used by Constable are from well-managed forests
and other responsible sources

Constable
An imprint of
Little, Brown Book Group
Carmelite House
50 Victoria Embankment
London EC4Y 0DZ

An Hachette UK Company
www.hachette.co.uk

www.littlebrown.co.uk

This story is for the thick and
thin of us – those who have
seen me through with generosity
and kindness. Thank you.

Highland Fling

Chapter 1

It is best to avoid the beginnings of evil

Wednesday 22 January 1958

Mirabelle checked her lipstick in the small mirror fixed to the maple-wood door. The train jerked and she put out a hand to steady herself. Through the window she could just make out London as it whizzed by, shades of grey in the driving rain. 'The weather from here only gets worse,' Superintendent McGregor had said solemnly as they dashed from the taxi into the station past two boys selling newspapers, one on each side of a large board that proclaimed 'If Khrushchev wants a shooting match, let's give it to him'. *The Times* was feeling punchy.

'It's beautiful up north but there's no disguising it's colder,' McGregor continued.

Mirabelle rolled her eyes. 'And wetter. And every other Scottish stereotype.' She liked teasing him.

'It's geography,' he insisted. 'There's no stereotype about it. It's a shame it will be dark as we go through Edinburgh. I'd like to have shown you my home town.' She had thought that was particularly sweet of him. Once they'd found their cabins, McGregor had discreetly left her to unpack.

Mirabelle hung up her tailored, mustard-yellow coat. Shrouded in brown kid gloves, the engagement ring made her finger look lumpy, but she decided not to remove the gloves. Above, the uplighter on the wall glowed orange, casting peachy light on to the plush velvet seating, which would later be converted into a bed. She had an overnight case, but until the bed was turned down it seemed odd to take out her things, so now there wasn't anything else to do except watch the vague grey shapes of the buildings as the train sped north. The rap on the door saved her.

'Yes?'

It opened and a young steward in a white jacket stood in the frame. 'Miss Bevan? Mr McGregor asks if you'd like to join him in the Pullman car?' She must have looked eager. The boy grinned. 'It's four carriages along.' He pointed, his greased-back hair glistening in the diffused light from the foggy windows.

'Thank you. I'll come directly.' Mirabelle scrabbled in her handbag, sprayed a mist of L'Air du Temps in front of her and stepped into it. She replaced the tiny lid with its swooping doves, dropping the bottle back into her bag and closing it with a satisfying click.

The Pullman car was only half full. She counted three tables occupied by men dressed in various muted shades of tweed, all nursing tumblers of whisky and smoking cigarettes. Two were mostly shielded from view by the *Financial Times*, the entire front page of which was dedicated to the possibility of Russia's missile superiority over America. Mirabelle sighed. Khrushchev's attempt at nuclear one-upmanship had been going on for months. Everyone was exhausted by it. It was, as Mirabelle's friend Vesta had commented, 'Worse than the bleeding Blitz.' Potentially, it was certainly more dangerous. Schools organised drills. City councils considered reopening wartime bomb shelters. Only last week an alarming public information leaflet had been posted through Mirabelle's door advising her to remain calm.

McGregor smiled from the table near the bar. Beside him, a bottle of champagne was already on ice. He got to his feet and kissed her on the cheek as if they hadn't already come up to town on the Brighton Belle and shared a meal of steak and sautéed mushrooms followed by inky, bitter coffee in tiny cups. The bartender popped the cork and poured two crystal saucers, which frosted immediately. Mirabelle watched the bubbles clinging to the side.

'To us.' McGregor lifted his by the stem.

Mirabelle toasted, clicking her glass against his. 'Our first proper holiday,' she said. 'Not just a weekend.'

'I can't wait to get away.'

'We are away.'

'You know what I mean. I'm as tired of dead bodies as I am of politics.' McGregor's eyes flashed with wry humour as the bartender pretended he hadn't overheard. 'It'll be good for us – fresh air, a bit of exercise and no grievous bodily harm,' McGregor said. 'You're going to love Scotland.'

'How long is it since you saw your cousin?'

'It was before the war – '37, I think.'

'Is he like you?'

'A little. My mother always said he was the big brother I never had. He's six years older. He won't have changed.'

'What do you mean?'

'Bruce's been the same since we were children. He's the closest family I have.'

Mirabelle let the icy champagne slide over her lips. She was glad McGregor didn't come with a full platoon of brothers and sisters, nephews and nieces. Family felt as if it would be an encumbrance to their relationship. She had nobody left on her side and was slightly relieved that now she and McGregor were engaged, she didn't have to drag the poor man around the country introducing him to a succession of relations. Still, the prospect of a holiday was pleasant. He'd promised open fires and games of cards. When she'd asked if they might hear the bagpipes, he had laughed and said, 'I'm sure we can manage that. We won't be far from Inverness and the pipes are almost mandatory in that neck of the woods.'

She put down her glass. 'It's very nice of your cousin to invite us.'

'I think it's because he got married so recently himself – they tied the knot a couple of years ago; a quick wedding at the register office in Edinburgh. I had no idea, but weddings make you think about family, don't they? He hadn't been in touch, but when I rang him to tell him about our engagement, it poured out. Her name is Eleanor. I think she must be younger than he is – he said she's changed the entire household.'

'There must be something in your family that makes the men wait so long before asking the question.'

'In Scotland we call that canny.'

'Maybe that's it.'

'You are happy, aren't you Belle?'

It was a question more than one person had asked over the last few days. An engagement was supposed to be an occasion for celebration but Mirabelle, quite honestly, felt that they had done what they ought to do. Perhaps that was harsh. It might be kinder to say that she and McGregor were meant for each other, not in the airy-fairy, romantic sense portrayed in books and at the cinema, but in the way that their lives dovetailed, that they could trust each other and that they already had a life together. They were a team and, after all, that was the nature of marriage. Mirabelle was too old for romance – these days all that seemed foolish. She'd had an affair of the heart many years ago and one or two dalliances since. There was no doubt that she loved McGregor, but you only had the magic of first love once. And Jack was long dead. 'I'm happy. But I'm not eighteen again, Alan. Even getting engaged isn't going to manage that.'

He reached for her gloved hand and pulled it to his lips. 'I knew the moment I saw you,' he said.

'In the graveyard at the Church of the Sacred Heart?'

It had been after a funeral. McGregor had been chatting up another woman, as she recalled, who was visiting her husband's grave. The woman had offered to cook him dinner, which was more than Mirabelle ever had.

'Was it the graveyard? That's too grim. It can't have been.'

'It was the graveyard. You told me to keep my nose out of your case.'

He relented. 'It sounds like me. Did you ever dream you'd end up with a policeman?'

'A detective? I could only have hoped.'

McGregor refilled the glasses. 'Here's to us,' he said.

By Peterborough it was dark outside. Neither of them was hungry after the steaks so they nibbled bar snacks and drank more champagne. Mirabelle regaled him with the tale of the day she'd told Vesta about their engagement and Vesta had screamed so loudly that the staff from the next-door office came bursting in to see what was the matter. 'We made tea and one of the girls from Halley Insurance fetched biscuits,' Mirabelle reported. 'It was fun. Everyone was talking about dresses.' She didn't tell him that after the insurance girls had gone back to their own office, Vesta had asked if Mirabelle was happy and that she had given the same answer she'd just given McGregor. 'And you won't give up work?' Vesta had checked. Mirabelle had duly promised she wouldn't dream of it and no, they hadn't set a date, but they were going to Scotland to visit McGregor's cousin and were considering buying a house. Barely restraining her excitement, Vesta had managed to restrict herself to an excited squawk. 'About time,' she pronounced. 'If you need help with the house, you know where I am.'

Vesta was a far better housekeeper than Mirabelle had ever been. She had a knack of putting things together. 'And the dress,' she'd added. 'Count me in on that shopping trip.' The bloody dress. You'd think the whole thing was about the dress or, if not the dress, the ring, though in the case of the latter, three days after she'd accepted his proposal, McGregor had surprised her with an unusual pale pink, emerald-cut diamond of just over two carats, mounted in yellow gold and nestled in a dark blue velvet box. It was an unexpected choice and she loved it.

The beds had been turned down when they stumbled back along the corridor, swaying with the motion of the train and dizzy from drinking the entire bottle of champagne. McGregor was booked in the next-door cabin. 'That isn't necessary,' she'd said when she saw the tickets, but he had insisted. Always considerate, he hadn't wanted people to judge her. Now they kissed as Mirabelle opened the door and pulled him into her cabin.

'We'll never both fit on that bed,' McGregor said, nuzzling her neck. 'I bet when we get there, Bruce will put us in separate rooms and we'll have to sleepwalk. Let's wait.'

'You quitter.' Mirabelle took off her gloves and undid the top button of her blouse without taking her eyes off his. Her satin brassiere gaped as she leaned forward. 'Don't think

I'll let you off that lightly, Alan McGregor.' She pushed him against the door of the wardrobe. He tasted of champagne and salted almonds as she kissed him, running her hands over all the places a nice girl would never dream of.

'Well, I'll be damned,' he murmured.

She liked feeling his arms around her – his strength. She liked the intensity of his stare as she stepped back and let her skirt slip over her hips on to the floor. He tipped her on to the mattress and it wasn't too small after all.

Later, the train uncoupled somewhere in the pitch black and Mirabelle was shaken awake naked. McGregor had gone. Her discarded clothes lay in a tangle on the floor, and on the air the faint aroma of aftershave mixed with the tang of sweat and tussle.

In the morning, they changed trains at Inverness. The atmosphere was damp and the air felt heavy as they stalked down the platform and on to a local service. 'Newspaper, sir?' the porter offered, his breath clouding ahead of him in the freezing air. McGregor shook his head. 'We're on holiday,' he replied by way of explanation as the porter loaded their cases and McGregor solemnly tipped him. 'Enjoy your trip, sir.' Mirabelle marvelled at his voice. McGregor's accent was mild by comparison. He laughed as the man left. 'Your face! You know everyone speaks like that up here.'

'Did you used to?'

'I haven't lost my accent,' McGregor objected. 'I'm from Edinburgh, you ninny. Up north they're right teuchters. Aye,' he said, hamming it up. 'Up here, we're closer to Stockholm and Oslo than we are to London. Don't you know that? And you're just a pretty wee Sassenach.'

'Are you saying the Scots are Vikings?'

'Some of us. Not me, obviously. I'm far too civilised.'

It was a short train journey and even the weather couldn't hide the beauty of the scenery. The sky was like an oil painting – dark as slate with a froth of white cloud, and as the train continued, a slash of breathtaking blue. Patches of snow peppered the peaks. Mirabelle hovered in her seat, her eyes on the bright window. 'What do you love the most up here?' she asked.

McGregor peered through the glass. 'I think it's the morning,' he said. 'The air feels different – green. Clean. I don't know, maybe it'll have changed. I've certainly changed since the last time I was up.' He squeezed her hand.

The station was in good order, Mirabelle noticed, as they pulled in. The window boxes were planted with heather. McGregor was keen to disembark, rushing her towards the door before the train had fully stopped. On the platform, a couple was waiting with a porter in tow. The woman, a strawberry blonde, looked like a magazine model, out of place on the slick cobbles. Her lipstick-lined mouth opened in a sunny smile as she spotted them through the window and raised her hand to wave. The man moved forwards.

'Al!' he said as McGregor stepped down. They shook hands. 'I'm so glad to see you.'

'Me too. It feels like coming home.'

'That's as it should be. We should never have lost touch. And this is your fiancée?' he said. 'You're welcome. I'm Bruce Robertson. This is my wife, Eleanor.'

'Gee, your coat is wonderful,' Eleanor grinned and kissed Mirabelle's cheek. 'I love the ochre.'

'You're American? Alan didn't say.'

'Yeah. The Yanks are here to stay. Woo-hoo! You must be exhausted after a night on the train.' Eleanor threaded her arm through Mirabelle's and guided her out of the station as the men directed the handling of the baggage.

The car was parked directly outside – a Jaguar Mark IV. Eleanor opened the door. 'We don't have a driver,' she said, 'but luckily we both like taking the wheel. The roads, of course, are terrible.' Mirabelle's eyes were drawn to the view. Beyond the station entrance a huge hill loomed. It was like walking into a painting – rock plummeted into gorse and heather. 'Wow,' she breathed.

'Have you been here before?' Eleanor asked.

'Never.'

'I loved it on sight. The Highlands are kinda dramatic. They feel free. It's hard to explain.'

Mirabelle laughed. 'I'm sure you're right.'

'Bruce said you're only staying for ten days but please feel free to stay longer. We love having people around and this time of year the sky is getting lighter and there are some glorious days. In the wood near the house there will be bluebells before we know it. Right now, it's all snowdrops – they seem to last for ever. January, huh? Do you like whisky? I can arrange for you to see the distillery if you like.'

'I do. My guess is that you mix cocktails?'

'Yes! Oh thank God. I was worried you were going to be stuffy. Well, if you like cocktails you'll definitely like what's on offer at the cashmere mill. There are no shops. Well, none to speak of. But the mill and the distillery make up for it.'

'Alan didn't say.'

'Oh, they make for everyone. I have a friend – another Yank – she's here at the moment, buying for a terribly chic boutique in New York. That's how good it is. It's the Scottish water – the best in the world, and it just rolls off the hills for free. We had a buyer from Paris last autumn and he went

9

potty about it. *Formidable. Incroyable,*' she said with a flourish, imitating the man, with, Mirabelle noted, a passable Parisian accent.

The porter appeared, wheeling the cases on a rickety trolley that bumped over the uneven footpath. The air felt so clear, it was as if she'd get cleaner by simply walking through it. Mirabelle smiled as she noticed that Bruce and Alan were exactly the same height, with their shoulders jutting at identical angles and their hair growing in the same shape at the napes of their necks. Old Mrs McGregor had been right – they could have been brothers. Bruce tipped the porter and got into the driver's seat while Alan slid in next to him. A decade old, the car had seen better days. The leather fittings were worn and inside it smelled faintly of cut grass. Eleanor continued.

'If you like walking, it's paradise. They say the queen loves hiking when she's here, all round Balmoral. The Cairngorms are a bit further south, of course. Anyway, we have maps you can borrow if you like that kind of thing.'

'Eleanor, let Mirabelle settle in. I'm not sure you're a walker, are you my dear?'

Bruce cast an eye over his shoulder at Mirabelle's shoes. The heels ran to two inches.

'I brought a pair of stouter shoes,' she said, amazed at the curl of annoyance she felt that he had judged her. She'd been brought up properly. She knew what to wear in the country.

'I stand corrected. Quite right.' He started the car.

'The thing is that Bruce can't imagine a woman might have more than one face, or, for that matter, function. I'm educating him that I can glam up for the Highland Ball *and* deal with tenants.'

'Oh, you've done it, darling. I'm convinced. Eleanor is down-right wonderful with the tenants and the staff and the chaps at the distillery. She's reorganised everything.' Bruce sounded jolly despite his wife's criticism. 'She's started a crowd making tweed along the Firth. You won't know the old place, Al, honestly. It's a hive of industry. The old mill that used to turn out horse blankets? It's the height of fashion these days.'

'I'm looking forward to seeing it all. It's been too long,' Alan chimed in.

Mirabelle wondered about the tenants Eleanor had mentioned. She'd been expecting a farmhouse. Alan's stories, such as they were, had included childhood memories of lost lambs and summer picnics that were rained off, not of extensive grounds or anywhere that might have supported tenancies. Eleanor elucidated. 'I like being hands on. I can't stand the idea of being a lady of the manor. It sounds ghastly – sitting about all day ordering people around and never doing anything yourself. We're in the countryside and we should be making things – be useful. That's what I think.'

In a slice of the rear-view mirror, Mirabelle caught the expression on Bruce's face. She thought she'd never seen a man look more proud.

The car turned off the main road and startled a flock of crows that ascended from a field in unison. In the distance the hills looked as if they had been torn from a slab of rock, the dark crags disappearing in a deathly plunge into frost-fringed fields on the lower ground. The patches of snow were so perfect that they could have been applied by a landscape painter. Between the crisp white shards, the colours were amazing. It was strange how much difference a few hundred miles could make. Brighton at this time of year was grey, but the colour of the place was essentially bright – vivid pastels, light and without texture. Mirabelle loved the clear winter mornings when the terraces of Georgian stucco shone blinding white against the blank, blue sky. Here the hills were muted, with patches of green and grey in contrast to the inky black of the sodden granite cliffs and the gentle undulation of the lower slopes.

'In summer we have days when it looks like the Caribbean,' Eleanor said, as if she could read Mirabelle's mind.

'Are there beaches?'

'I'll say. I'll take you up to the Firth. I love the ocean. I was brought up near the water, just outside New York. There's nothing like salt on the air. Tell you what, we can take a picnic. Picnics aren't only for the summer, don't you agree? We'll have a Thermos of soup and watch the tide. You can see for miles. It's a bit of a drive but it's worth it.'

'How long have you been here?' Mirabelle asked.

Eleanor thought for a moment as if she was counting it. 'Since we got married. Three and a half years,' she said. 'But we leave sometimes,' she added with a giggle. 'Don't we darling?'

'Eleanor loves the sea. She goes on her own sometimes,' Bruce said fondly. 'I think it speaks to her.'

He turned the car on to a track, leaving the engine turning over. 'I know you want to,' he said to McGregor. *'Druim a 'mhadaidh* has missed you.'

Alan opened the door as his cousin cut the engine. The men glanced at the women in the back seat.

'Come on,' Bruce called.

Mirabelle looked blank.

'It's Wolf Ridge. You need to change your shoes,' Eleanor said.

Twenty minutes later they had hiked up a stony path and caught the first of the view. The road was shielded so the landscape looked as if it was completely wild. High above, three large birds swooped, gliding on the breeze. Alan's eyes were bright. 'We used to come here as kids,' he said. 'It's not bad, is it?'

Mirabelle found herself out of breath. 'Bad?' she said. 'It's breathtaking.'

They stopped to take in the view.

'Don't you love it? Feeling so small,' Eleanor gasped.

It was true. Nature here humbled you, miles from everything. In one direction there were more hills and in the other the view dropped below the ridge, the sky clouded with the misty promise of the sea far in the distance. 'At home you get the hills or the beach,' Eleanor breathed, her skin pink with the exertion of climbing, 'but here there is everything within reach. Right there.' She walked right to the edge of the precipice. 'Beautiful!' she shouted. 'Beautiful!'

Alan stepped next to her. He threw back his head and howled like a dog. Eleanor clapped. 'It echoes,' she said. 'Do it again.'

He did. Mirabelle found she was laughing. She'd never seen Alan like this. Perhaps, she thought, we'll go wild up here.

On the way down they spotted movement in the gorse. Bruce raised his arm, as if he had a gun. 'Rabbits,' he said.

Eleanor sniffed. 'It smells like carrion.' She set off, carefully picking a route through the undergrowth, looking back at the others as a weak growl emanated from near her feet. 'It's a fox, Bruce.'

'Is it injured?'

Eleanor nodded. She picked up a stick and parted the jagged stems. 'It has two broken legs, I think. Nasty. He must have had a run-in with a cow or a horse, or something.' The growl deepened.

Bruce followed his wife up the incline to take a look. On one side the bone had broken through the skin. He shook his head. 'Nothing to be done. It must have been up here a while.'

'Bruce, could we—' Eleanor started but Bruce dismissed her.

'Nobody would thank us for bringing a fox down to the village.'

'Poor thing,' Eleanor sighed.

'Nothing of the sort! That,' Bruce indicated the fox, 'is a hen killer.'

'Well, he's suffering,' Eleanor objected.

'True. He'll starve to death up here. Want to step down?' Eleanor backed on to the path. On the other side a crow alighted on a boulder.

'Shoo!' Eleanor chased it.

'You might want to turn around,' Alan whispered, laying a hand on Mirabelle's arm, but she declined as Bruce picked up a rock and dashed it into the fox's skull. The injured animal made a shrill, squealing noise as it died and the smell of hot blood hit the air.

'Sorry,' Bruce apologised. 'It would have suffered if we'd left it.'

Eleanor wiped a tear from her eye. 'I'm silly. I know,' she said, staring in the direction the crow had flown. 'But the countryside is absolutely vicious. Sometimes I can't bear it.'

Fifteen minutes later, the car turned through a pair of grand stone gates three or four miles from where they'd been walking. Bruce drove slowly up the twisting driveway banked by sparse woodland on both sides. Then, as he made a final turn, the vista opened and parkland rolled into view.

The house was set in the lee of a peak they'd seen from the summit. Constructed of granite, it was grand in style, though Mirabelle felt glad it wasn't as huge as some of the houses she'd visited over the years. A black poodle sat at the threshold. Three horses fitted with green oilskin blankets grazed in a paddock. The whole place felt curiously domestic compared to the wildness of the landscape around it. The animals ignored the car as Bruce parked at the doorway, stopping dead and abandoning his vehicle. He peered through the windscreen.

'Where is everyone?' he said.

Eleanor got out and searched her pockets as she moved towards the fence. The horses began to show an interest. One walked casually towards her as she drew out some sugar cubes. He hauled his huge head over the fence and whinnied before taking the treat. The poodle got up and fell to heel. Eleanor put out a hand absentmindedly to pet him.

'This is Jinx,' she said. 'Just ignore him.'

'What a lovely spot,' Mirabelle declared.

On the lower ground, mist rose from the grass. She felt a spit of rain on her cheek but nothing like the lashing there'd been as they left London.

'January is the cruellest month, isn't that what the poets say?' Eleanor smiled. 'Or maybe that's April.'

Bruce was standing at the door as if he was mystified. He clapped Alan on the back. 'Well, they can get the bags later, I suppose,' he said, turning the handle.

Inside, the hallway was wide with smooth stone columns set into indents, one on either side. Beyond these, the reception area opened into a high stairwell flooded with light from a cupola.

'This is very odd,' Bruce said. 'It's like the *Marie Celeste*. They knew we were coming back.'

'I want coffee,' Eleanor declared. 'It's my only luxury,' she confided in Mirabelle, a fact Mirabelle immediately questioned, what with all the talk of whisky, cocktails and cashmere. 'My cousin sends me bags of beans from the States,' Eleanor continued. 'That and letters jammed with his noxious views on Eisenhower.' She shrugged. 'The coffee's roasted in Brooklyn and it's good. Thank God! Honestly, over here it's all dishwater.' She wrinkled her nose as she walked airily through the mahogany double doors and into a drawing room at the front of the house with Jinx behind her. The room was decorated in shades of pale blue. Eleanor pressed a brass bell next to the fireplace. On one side there was a stack of wood, on the other a small mountain of peat. 'Make yourself comfortable,' she said. 'You must be pooped.'

The dog climbed on to a chair and Eleanor languidly pulled him on to the floor, where he settled.

'Bruce's right. You've changed the old place,' McGregor said. 'For the better, I might add.'

Eleanor grinned. 'I couldn't bear all those stag heads and everything so dark. It felt as if we should be feasting off bloody meat the whole time and stealing virgins from the nearest village. Whatever Bruce did to that poor fox, it's not entirely barbarian round here.'

'The decoration isn't the only thing Eleanor changed.' Bruce sounded jocular. 'Not by a long shot. They're costly items, new wives, Alan, I tell you. I had to put my foot down in the end. I kept some of the stags' heads in my study. And the old furniture. A stand for tradition, eh?'

Eleanor poked the logs burning on the fire with a brass implement. 'Tradition,' she said. 'That dreary old desk!'

'And the gun cupboard,' Bruce added.

Eleanor rolled her eyes. 'Well, I suppose you're allowed some say. There,' she said, putting down the poker.

Mirabelle took off her coat and sat on a low sofa as the fire began to crackle.

'When I was a kid we used to play hide and seek in here,' McGregor said. 'Do you remember, Bruce?'

'I do. We had visitors' cake in the afternoon.'

'Visitors' cake?'

'We didn't have it if there weren't visitors.' He laughed. 'Why do you think I liked having you to stay?'

Alan turned to Mirabelle. 'We're going to relax here, darling, aren't we?' His shoulders had dropped and she realised she hadn't thought once about the nuclear threat – not since they'd turned down the morning papers. Standing at the fireplace, Eleanor checked the slim gold watch on her wrist. 'Relax! At the moment I can't even seem to secure us a pot of coffee.' She rang the bell again.

Quite quickly then, a fresh-faced young girl appeared at the door. She was wearing a brown woollen dress and a pink flowery apron. She bobbed an odd, awkward curtsey without coming into the room. Her hands were trembling, Mirabelle noticed, though Eleanor didn't seem to have taken that in. 'Susan. I didn't expect you. Where's Gillies?'

The girl sniffed. Then her face twisted. She pointed back up the hallway, her finger jerking. 'Miss Orlova,' she managed to get out.

'Well, if Nina's here, bring us all some coffee and tell her we're in the drawing room.'

'Nina is El's American friend. Very smart,' Bruce explained. 'She's in fashion. In New York.'

'She's been staying down at the lodge,' Eleanor added.

'She's here for a fortnight and I thought it would be nicer with only us in the house. Family.' The maid at the door heaved a sob.

'Susan? What is it?' Bruce asked.

'It's Miss Orlova, sir. She's dead. Gillies checked for a pulse but there wasn't one, so she went to fetch the police from the village.'

There was a moment's stunned silence. Bruce let out a shocked sound – more a puff of air than anything else. Eleanor stood by the ornate mantel, her hand over her mouth. McGregor got to his feet. Jinx looked as if he might follow but, having checked that Eleanor wasn't going, he rested his head on his paws.

'Show me,' McGregor said.

Susan didn't move. She pulled a crumpled handkerchief from her apron and started to cry. 'I can't go back there, sir,' she said. 'I can't.'

Mirabelle got up and touched the girl lightly on the arm. 'Mr McGregor is a police detective.' She kept her tone comforting. 'I know it must have been a terrible shock, but I think you should show him where the poor lady is lying. She needs to be looked after. Mr McGregor will know what to do.'

The girl stifled another sob. She seemed to take this in, then she nodded and set off down the hallway. Bruce and Mirabelle got up to follow, but McGregor shook his head solemnly. 'Let me look first,' he said. 'The fewer people the better, before the local constabulary arrive.' He left the room. Bruce sank back on to the sofa. 'My God,' he said. 'Poor Nina.'

'Tell me about her?' Mirabelle couldn't help herself.

'She's the cashmere buyer,' Eleanor explained. 'She was Russian, really. I mean she was born there. Wonderful eye.'

'Did you know her well?'

18

'Not really. She's a friend of a friend. You know how New York is. They're here for a fortnight—'

'Oh God. I forgot about the girl,' Bruce said suddenly.

Eleanor sat down with a bump. 'I hadn't thought of that,' she said. 'Poor Tash.'

'What girl?' Mirabelle enquired.

'Nina brought her goddaughter. Tash.'

'A child?'

'She's seventeen,' Eleanor waved her hand in the air as if swishing away something troublesome.

'Her age is irrelevant, darling,' Bruce said. 'This will be a terrible loss for her. They're close. Nina brought the child up – her parents were killed in a car crash. We have to look after her, El. I mean, has anybody even told the poor thing? And that chap they have, the steward?' Bruce got up without another word and left the room, striding up the hall in McGregor's wake.

'I was seventeen. Almost eighteen,' Mirabelle said. The words seemed to slip out.

'Well, we all were.'

'I mean, when my parents died.'

'I'm sorry. I didn't mean to be flippant.' Eleanor put her hand on her stomach.

'Bruce said the girl was brought up by the dead woman?'

Eleanor gestured. 'Nina stepped in when Tash's parents passed away. She never married, you see, but she was close to Tash's mother. It was a brave thing to do – a woman on her own bringing up a friend's child. Not that they discuss that kind of thing round here. The village is fearfully old-fashioned. People probably just assume Nina was the girl's mother.'

'Poor kid,' said Mirabelle.

'It looks like you managed.' Eleanor gave an apologetic smile. 'How did they die? Your parents?'

Mirabelle felt her cheeks burn. Eleanor was American and that explained her directness, but she hadn't ever talked about what had happened. Not in all the years. Not to McGregor. Not to Jack. 'It was an accident,' she said. 'Unfortunately it was the same year my grandmother died. She was terribly old. It left me rather suddenly with nobody – I didn't have godparents, you see. But this poor girl – it'll be awful for her. A double loss.'

'What kind of accident?' Eleanor asked. 'Your parents, I mean?'

Mirabelle pursed her lips and tried to smile. Eleanor was easy to talk to, but there were limits.

'I'm not sure why I brought it up,' she said, closing the subject.

Chapter 2

Courage is the quality that guarantees all others

The police arrived five minutes later in a rickety car that looked as if it had seen better days. The women heard it before they saw it, the bell ringing intermittently as it approached. It pulled up in front of the drawing-room windows and Eleanor went to the door to let the men in. When she returned she placed the guard in front of the fire. Jinx got to his feet.

'How do you feel about going to the kitchen?' she said. 'It's not the form, but at least I could make us coffee.'

'Thanks,' said Mirabelle. 'That would be nice.'

The coffee was strong and Eleanor found shortbread in the pantry. Mirabelle slid on to a bench that ran up one side of the scrubbed pine kitchen table. McGregor had mentioned this table – or at least the hearty bowls of broth that had been served there with thickly buttered bread at lunchtime, the stuff of childhood memory.

'The police will want to speak to Tash, I imagine,' Mirabelle said.

Eleanor slumped into a chair. 'God.'

'I wonder how she died.' Mirabelle peered out of the kitchen window. She tried to figure out where the body was located. McGregor had not been clear about the layout of the house in his reminiscences. Through the glass she could see a kitchen garden, a stretch of lawn and, beyond that, more hills.

'Perhaps she had a heart attack,' Eleanor said.

'Maybe,' Mirabelle sounded doubtful. The prospect of natural causes hadn't occurred to her. McGregor, she realised, was right about them needing a holiday. She sipped her coffee and the caffeine assailed her. Eleanor pushed the biscuits across the table. At length a policeman knocked on the door and put his head round.

'Mrs Robertson and . . .' his voice trailed into a silent question mark.

'Miss Bevan,' Mirabelle confirmed. The man took a note.

'I just want to confirm. You got back from the railway station and entered through the front door. You haven't been to the orangery?'

'Is that where she is?' Eleanor sounded horrified.

'Yes.'

Mirabelle piped up. 'Might I ask, officer, what you think happened to the poor woman?'

'Oh it's murder, miss. She's been strangled.'

'Murder?' Eleanor put her hand to her mouth and Mirabelle noticed her perfect, white teeth digging into the flesh of her finger.

'Yes, Mrs Robertson. The laird is there with the English policeman now. They're talking to the sergeant. They all agree. It can't be anything else.'

'Superintendent McGregor is from Edinburgh,' Mirabelle explained.

'I see.' The man looked at his notepad but didn't write this down.

Mirabelle continued. 'In answer to your question – we arrived from the station at around 11.30. We went directly into the drawing room. Mrs Robertson rang for coffee and when the girl came she told us that she and the housekeeper,' here Mirabelle flicked her eyes towards Eleanor, who nodded, 'had found the body and the other woman had gone to fetch the police. Superintendent McGregor insisted on seeing the scene of the crime. Mr Robertson then went to find Miss Orlova's goddaughter. Mrs Robertson and I waited in the drawing room for a few minutes before coming here. Neither of us have seen the body. I have never met Miss Orlova.'

'Thank you, miss. Most efficient.'

Mirabelle nodded. There was no point explaining how she knew what he needed.

'And Mrs Robertson, when did you last see Miss Orlova?'

'They came the night before last for dinner. We had beef en croute. There was a crowd of us. Neighbours and so forth.'

'Did you see Miss Orlova yesterday at all? Or at any time since?'

Eleanor thought for a second. 'No,' she said.

The constable took a note. 'You seem very self-possessed, ma'am.'

Eleanor became flustered. She half rose from her seat. 'Well, it's such a shock,' she said. 'I'm not sure what to do.'

Mirabelle was about to ask a question about the crime scene when there was the sound of steps approaching up the hallway and the policeman sprang out of the way to allow a tidy-looking older woman with a black coat and a felt hat pinned in place to come into the kitchen. Behind her a tall, dark-haired girl slipped into the room. She was swathed in a tartan woollen rug that kept falling off her shoulders.

'Tash, darling.' Eleanor got to her feet and threw her arms around the girl, who, Mirabelle noted, wore a glazed expression. Her cheeks were oily with tears as she nestled in Eleanor's embrace, with her arms curled around her own body as if she was protecting herself. Meanwhile, the woman removed her hat and coat and went into the rear of the kitchen, reappearing as she tied on a well-starched linen apron.

'Neil Gordon,' she said. 'Do you need a cup of tea?'

'That would be very kind, Mrs Gillies,' the policeman replied.

'How many of you are there?'

'Just me and the sergeant.'

'Only two of you? One of the laird's guests has been murdered.'

'They're sending more men from Inverness.'

'I should hope so.'

'If this is the lady's goddaughter, I need to speak to her,' the policeman said sheepishly.

The girl looked up as if his voice had come out of nowhere.

'What's wrong with you, man?' Mrs Gillies snapped. 'The bairn's only just been told. Have you no decency?'

'But . . .' the policeman started. Mrs Gillies, however, cast him a glance that halted further dialogue. 'I'll bring a tray,' she said.

The policeman hovered for a moment and then disappeared. The redoubtable Mrs Gillies straightened her apron and put the kettle on the range. The girl sank on to the bench along from Mirabelle. Her lashes were so long, Mirabelle wondered if they could possibly be real. Tash gasped – a tiny gasp like a baby who can't quite catch its breath or an animal that has been hurt. She squinted and sniffed. Shock, Mirabelle diagnosed silently.

'Tash, this is Mirabelle. She's a cousin of Bruce's by marriage,' Eleanor said.

Mirabelle smiled. 'Hello there. Actually, we're not married yet, so I suppose I'm not really a cousin. I'm so sorry to meet you in these circumstances.'

The girl kept her eyes trained on the floor. She gulped in another breath, this time as if she had been half-drowned. More than anything, she reminded Mirabelle of bruised fruit. Mirabelle remembered that feeling – an ache and a numbness at once. Under the table, the poodle laid his head on the girl's feet.

'We're going to look after you, sweetheart. Don't worry,' Eleanor said sagely. 'Gillies will move your things up to the house, won't you, Gillies, and we'll make all the arrangements. You won't have to do a thing.'

Tash made a keening sound and Eleanor put a comforting hand on her shoulder. 'There,' she said. 'That's right.' As if making the child cry was some form of progress.

'I'll take you to your room, shall I, miss?' Gillies cut in, her tone making it clear that there would be no further examination of anyone's feelings. 'I'll fetch a brandy for the shock and then I expect it would be good if you could manage a nap.'

The girl nodded and got up, folding the tartan rug around herself as if it was armour. She was crying quietly now – quite a beauty, even in pale grief, as she shuffled out of the room behind Mrs Gillies like an obedient puppy.

'I don't mind helping,' Eleanor said as she moved the kettle off the boil and poured the water into the teapot that Mrs Gillies had left warming on the side. 'I mean, it's all hands on deck at a time like this.'

'Jinx is very good. Calm, I mean,' Mirabelle said.

'Oh he's deaf, dear thing.' Eleanor put her hand on the dog's collar. 'Aren't you?' she raised her voice. The dog didn't move. 'He's a sweetheart and you're right – very placid. I sometimes imagine what it must be like for him – living in absolute silence. I mean, he's no idea what's going on.'

Mirabelle sipped her coffee. She had wondered about Jinx the minute the policeman had intimated it was murder. Most dogs would have woken in the night if they had heard a tussle. Most would have barked at least.

'Strangulation is a violent crime.' She heard the sound of her own voice. She couldn't help herself. 'I mean, the constable said she'd been strangled – murdered. That suggests rage to me,' she continued. 'A fight.'

'Rage?'

'I mean, not cold-blooded. It's a hands-on way to kill someone, not like shooting or poisoning. The victim dies in front of you. Comparatively, it takes a long time. They pass out quickly, but to kill someone you have to continue restricting their airflow. You have to really want them gone.'

Eleanor laid two mugs on a small tray, adding a jug of milk and a sugar bowl. 'I suppose, as a policeman's wife, you probably know a lot about this kind of thing. But if Nina's dead, I don't think we should dwell on it. What's the point of worrying about whether it was poison or strangulation?'

Mirabelle held back from repeating that she and McGregor weren't married. She wondered if Eleanor's assumptions might mean she and McGregor would get to share a room. Then she chastised herself for thinking so selfishly at a time like this. 'I'll take in the tea if you like,' she offered and, before Eleanor could object, she had picked up the tray and slipped out of the kitchen in the direction of the orangery or, at least, the direction in which the policeman had disappeared.

Eleanor, it seemed, had decorated the whole of this floor. Mirabelle passed through a day room freshly done in plummy, gothic tones with heavily fringed furnishings and dark family portraits in gilded frames. Beyond, the orangery glowed with light. It looked onto a garden and a small orchard of old fruit trees with lichen dotted over their gnarled branches. The sky was brightening now, the clouds blown away. A bank of wicker chairs with comfortable canvas cushions, festooned with fashionable, geometric designs in black, orange and khaki, lay between Mirabelle and the men crowded around the body of the woman on the tiled floor. Peroxide blonde, slim and dressed in a smart red tailored suit, she looked out of place in the surroundings – as if she had been overlaid on to the scene like some kind of strange découpage.

'Mirabelle.' McGregor stepped into her sight line.

'Eleanor sent tea for the uniformed officers. Would you and Bruce like anything?'

Bruce had been crying. He shook his head. 'No,' he said. 'I'm fine. Thank you.'

McGregor motioned to her, and Mirabelle laid the tray on a small wooden table beside a tropical plant with huge glossy leaves. 'Nina's goddaughter is here. The housekeeper took her upstairs to lie down. I think she hasn't quite taken it in,' she said.

'She was a wonderful woman,' Bruce cut in. 'Seeing her like this is a travesty. She was so full of life.'

'Perhaps, sir,' the sergeant said, 'you might like to join your wife. She must be shocked too. After all, Miss Orlova was a friend of hers.'

Bruce clearly hadn't thought of this. 'Oh yes,' he said. 'Are you all right here, old chap?' he asked McGregor.

'You never entirely get used to it,' McGregor admitted. 'But I'm fine.'

Bruce walked out of the room like a man in a trance. The policemen picked up their tea and moved off, discussing arrangements quietly as they gazed out of the long glass panes, glancing back now and again at the body.

Mirabelle peered. The woman had undoubtedly been beautiful. There was something of the film star about her, even in death. Her elegant legs were splayed in their heels, her lipstick still perfect, though she had clearly bitten her tongue during the death throes and her face was swollen. Mirabelle tried not to ask the question but she couldn't help it. 'Do you know what she was strangled with?'

McGregor indicated a slip of fabric, which had been folded into a square and placed on a side table. 'Her scarf. It's Italian – real silk. It was on the ground but the officer picked it up. Looks like she broke a nail as she struggled to get it off her neck.'

Mirabelle shuddered.

'It's rather macabre,' McGregor admitted. 'Sorry.'

Mirabelle ignored him. 'But they can't have known,' she said, eyeing the scarf, which was embellished with a fashionable pattern of red roses.

'Known?'

'Yes, the murderer can't have known she would wear a scarf. I mean, it can't have been planned, can it?'

McGregor's eyes widened. 'You think it was a crime of passion? Spur of the moment?'

Mirabelle nodded.

'I suppose,' McGregor conceded. 'Yes.'

Mirabelle peered through the doorway behind her. Bruce had gone. The policemen were on the other side of the orangery. She lowered her voice to a whisper. 'It seems so intimate. You would need to be very close. You don't think your cousin was involved?' she asked as she thought of Bruce dashing the rock into the fox's skull.

Alan laughed. 'That's a leap, Mirabelle. Bruce is a sentimental old fool but I think he adores his wife – are you postulating an affair gone wrong?'

Mirabelle considered this. 'No,' she said uncertainly. It worried her that she cared so much. Eleanor was lurking in the kitchen – you couldn't have paid her to come into the orangery, and that, in truth, seemed more normal. But then Mirabelle had never been normal.

'Well?' McGregor was waiting.

Mirabelle shrugged. There was no point in taking the theory only halfway. 'It's just that there isn't anybody here. Two house staff – both women a million miles away from this lady's world. Her goddaughter, who reminds me of Bambi more than anything else – hardly a murderer. And Bruce and Eleanor. I suppose there might be a gardener or something. How close is the nearest house? And what on earth could the motive be? I mean, she'd only been here a week.'

McGregor's eyes twinkled. 'You just imagined a motive,' he pointed out. 'It wasn't a very good one. Who knows what the woman was up to, in here, in the middle of the night? The police will have to investigate.' McGregor folded his arms and then, realising that this conveyed his unwillingness to talk about the murder, he unfolded them. 'Look, we're on holiday. This isn't our responsibility. I've secured the crime scene. I've talked to the officers and offered my professional opinion. The first thing they need to do is place everybody in the vicinity. And that's what they'll get on with, I imagine. Given you and I were on the overnight train, there's no need for us to get involved. We're supposed to be getting away, darling. Frankly, I could do with a proper drink.' He checked his watch. 'I wonder if Bruce might make an exception. It's a little early for spirits.' He got to his feet. 'You'll let me know time of death?' he said to the sergeant.

'Yes, sir. The doctor and the rest of the team will be here from Inverness in the next half an hour.'

McGregor guided Mirabelle into the hallway. He laid his hand casually in the small of her back. Through the open door to the kitchen, they could see Mrs Gillies slicing a cucumber with the efficient movement of a woman who did not appreciate her schedule being interrupted. At the table the maid, Susan, was sitting with a large handkerchief pressed against her mouth. She was heaving gulps of air through the cotton as tears ran down her pink cheeks. Mrs Gillies looked up. 'They're in the drawing room, sir,' she said.

'Mrs Gillies,' Alan greeted her. 'Nice to see you again. It's been a long time. I'm sorry it has to be on such a difficult day.'

'Yes, sir,' Gillies said. 'I understand congratulations are due.'

Mirabelle stepped through the threshold. 'Excuse me, Mrs Gillies,' she said brightly. 'Might I ask a question?'

Gillies came to the end of the cucumber. 'Sandwiches,' she replied. 'Instead of lunch. Mrs Robertson said to bring them to the drawing room and you'd help yourselves.'

'It wasn't that. I just wondered why you didn't ring the police? There is a telephone here, isn't there? When he was arranging our trip, Mr McGregor rang his cousin several times. But you went down to the village to fetch the police officers. Is the line out?'

Susan stared at Mrs Gillies as if this named her the guilty party. The housekeeper remained completely calm. 'I rang to the police station, miss, but there was no reply. Davina McCrossan's baby is due and I thought the boys must be assisting. So I walked down to the village to report Miss Orlova's death.'

'Instead of ringing 999 and asking for another station?'

'Mrs McCrossan is alive. Miss Orlova was not. Dialling 999 would not have changed matters.' Gillies stared sternly. 'There are only two policemen between here and Inverness on any number.'

'And was Mrs McCrossan in labour?' Mirabelle was not deterred.

'Andrew and Neil – that is the constable and the sergeant – were busy with another matter when I got down.'

'Really?' The village, Mirabelle realised, sounded like a hotbed of crises. 'What were they doing?'

'One of the dogs had injured a sheep. They were seeing to it.'

'Seeing to it?'

'Shooting it, miss. Or making sure that the farmer did.'

McGregor cut in, pulling Mirabelle by the arm. 'Thank you, Mrs Gillies. Ham, is it?'

'We have ham and cheese, sir. And I thought I'd make some with cucumber in case anybody was feeling delicate.'

'Marvellous,' he said.

'Well, somebody had to ask,' Mirabelle spat in her defence as he guided her down the hall, his hand firmly on her arm. 'It didn't make sense.'

'And you thought that old woman was somehow involved?' McGregor kept his voice to a whisper. 'She's in with the bricks, Mirabelle. She's worked here since I was a child.'

'Someone here did it,' Mirabelle hissed. 'You said it yourself – we need to figure out everybody's whereabouts.'

'The police do. The boys in blue.'

Eleanor and Bruce were seated on either side of the fire. Jinx had settled at Bruce's feet and appeared to have gone to sleep. Bruce nursed a glass of whisky. Eleanor was staring blankly into the flames. The burning peat, with which Bruce had stoked the fire, reminded Mirabelle of the smell of Laphroaig.

'Help yourself,' Bruce nodded to Alan, motioning in the direction of the drinks tray as they came in.

'Mirabelle?' McGregor offered.

'I won't. Thank you.'

'Nasty business. I can't imagine who would want to hurt Nina.' Bruce's voice sounded hollow.

'We need to focus on her goddaughter now. God, poor Tash,' Eleanor said. She reached over to a side table and languidly removed a cigarette from a silver box, lighting it with a spill directly from the fire. 'That was your instinct, Bruce. And that's what we ought to do. I guess we should call somebody.'

'Do you know if she had relations?' McGregor asked.

Eleanor glanced apologetically in Mirabelle's direction, as if mentioning a lack of relations was some kind of dig. 'Smoke?' she offered. Mirabelle shook her head.

Eleanor continued. 'We were more acquaintances than friends. I think she had a brother. I know who to ring, though – friend of a friend. It's almost time to get up in New York. What were you two whispering about in the hallway?' Her eyes twinkled with curiosity. 'Lovers' tiff?'

'I asked Mrs Gillies why she hadn't used the telephone to call the police,' Mirabelle said.

Bruce sat forward in his seat. 'That's a good point.'

'Alan didn't want me to bring it up,' Mirabelle admitted.

'It's so unpleasant, isn't it? All this.' Eleanor drew deeply on her cigarette. 'We just need to get through it.'

'What did old Gillies say?' Bruce asked.

'She said she rang but nobody picked up. Somebody is expecting a baby and she thought the police must be helping with the birth.'

'Martin and Davina McCrossan's first child. It's late,' Eleanor said. 'They run the bar in the village.'

'As a result, Gillies didn't ring 999. She said she didn't want to distract the police from the living towards the dead and decided to walk to the village herself to make the report.'

Mrs Gillies cleared her throat as she appeared in the doorway with a tray that contained a tidily organised platter of sandwiches and another pot of coffee. She laid it on the side and began to unload the contents on to a satinwood table behind one of the sofas.

Bruce got to his feet. 'I'll find us a bottle of wine, shall I?'

'Miss Orlova had been dead for a while, madam, since you're discussing the matter,' Mrs Gillies said, and Mirabelle shifted uncomfortably at having been overheard.

Eleanor blew out a cloud of smoke. 'Really, Gillies? How on earth do you know?'

'It was before your time, Mrs Robertson, but I was a nurse during the Great War. As a girl.'

'Gosh. I had no idea. At the front?'

The housekeeper's gaze fell coldly on Mirabelle. 'Near the front, ma'am. In Serbia. Miss Orlova died, by my estimation, early this morning. Certainly well after midnight and before breakfast. I was also able to determine that she had been garrotted. Strangled, that is. With a ligature. I saw the marks when I examined the body.'

'He used her scarf,' said Bruce. 'The police found it. On the ground beside her.'

Gillies didn't speak for a moment, as if she was scanning

the crime scene in her memory. 'I didn't notice that, sir. I simply examined the body.'

'Did you allow for the temperature in the orangery, Mrs Gillies, given the glass?' Alan asked.

'I did, sir. You're right. It's colder by a degree or two – more at night, though we keep the electric stove on for the plants. It takes the edge off.' Gillies turned to Eleanor. 'I gave Susan the afternoon off, ma'am. She is shaken.'

'Of course. Yes.' Eleanor stubbed out her cigarette and picked up a sandwich. She extracted the ham and offered it to Jinx, who snapped it up eagerly. 'It feels like an age since breakfast,' she said.

'We only had a cup of tea on the train,' McGregor admitted. 'Both of us slept in.'

Eleanor smiled indulgently. 'Honeymooners,' she said as Bruce arrived with a bottle of red wine.

Behind him, Mrs Gillies disappeared out of the door as he poured four glasses. Mirabelle relented from asking more questions and helped herself to a cheese sandwich. It tasted good. Gillies had taken the trouble to add chives to the butter. Mirabelle was hungry. The steak and mushrooms in the dining car had been quite some time ago. She took another sandwich as the enamel and ormolu clock on the mantelpiece struck the half-hour. One thirty.

'This wine's Italian,' Bruce announced. 'Dad used to only buy French for the cellar, but I've taken to investing in Italian wine and Spanish sherries. Some people won't buy from places that fought alongside the other chaps – but I think some of these vintages are terribly good.' He handed Mirabelle a glass. To say it tasted like nectar would be only a slight overstatement. She wondered if it was the fresh air that had given her such an appetite. It seemed impossible that only earlier this morning Alan and Eleanor had stood on the summit of the hill and screamed into the wind.

'The Spanish were neutral,' she said. 'In the war.'

Bruce smiled. 'Yes,' he replied, raising a fist to reinforce his point. 'But the French were on our side. I suppose that's their reasoning. People are funny, aren't they? I was down in London last year and drinking vodka these days is practically seen as treason because of the Ruskies.'

'This is delicious, Bruce.' McGregor smacked his lips.

'We don't do too badly,' Bruce grinned.

'I never knew Gillies was a nurse,' Eleanor said. 'I suppose when the men joined up, some of the girls must have gone as well, though I haven't seen any of their names on the war memorial in the village.'

'Nurses? They don't put nurses on war memorials, dear.' Bruce sounded bluff.

'Well, why ever not?' Eleanor objected. 'Really. This country.'

'Are things different in the US?' Mirabelle asked.

Eleanor shrugged. 'Yes. And no,' she admitted. 'Some ways. I'm going to speak to Reverend Wood about it – the war memorial, I mean. If women from the village died in the theatre of combat they ought to be commemorated. Alongside their male comrades.'

'See,' Bruce said fondly, 'she's changing everything.'

Chapter 3

There is nothing insignificant in the world

Upstairs, Eleanor and Bruce put them in separate rooms but on a discreet corridor at the end of an otherwise deserted wing. The rooms were side by side, both decorated with oriental wallpaper and velvet furnishings, one in shades of yellow and green and the other in yellow and blue. Mirabelle's cases had been left in one and Alan's in the other. There was some debate about whether they ought to be moved to the other side of the house as the view from the windows took in the corner of the orangery, though not the area where Nina's body lay. In the end they decided against it.

'The guest rooms on the other wing aren't as nice,' Bruce said. 'And it's more private here.'

'More policemen have arrived,' Mirabelle announced as she peered through the window. A constable was smoking under one of the apple trees. She supposed he was keeping an eye out. For miles beyond, there wasn't another soul – only rolling hills bathed in bright sunlight as clear as an iced glass of water. Even from inside, Mirabelle shuddered at her insignificance in the face of the scale of the landscape.

'This room was where my mother used to stay,' Alan said. 'You haven't decorated it, have you, Eleanor?'

'Upstairs was much better than down and, besides, Bruce insisted I stop spending money! I love this old paper, don't you, Mirabelle? I think it's hand-painted.'

Mirabelle turned back into the room. 'I think it is.'

'If you need anything, just ring, won't you?'

'Does Gillies live in?' Mirabelle ventured.

Eleanor nodded. 'Both of them do. Despite what you saw today of her, Susan is actually very practical. She fixes things and touches up the paintwork and she is astonishing with the laundry. She can iron practically anything. We're lucky to have them. The gardeners come up from the village and we have a cleaner some days. For larger house parties we use this wonderful agency in Aberdeen who find you bar staff or jugglers or, well, anything you want.'

'Two house staff. It's nothing, is it? When we were young there was a squad of them, but that's the reality these days. Well, we'll leave you two to settle in,' Bruce said. 'Dinner will be at seven thirty. You'll hear the gong and if you want anything, just come and find us. I'll be in my study and Eleanor . . .?'

'I guess I'll try to get hold of someone in the Big Apple. You know, about the body.'

Once they were alone, McGregor tutted loudly. 'Who lives in? Who was around in the middle of the night, you mean. Who's on the suspect list?'

'Well,' Mirabelle retorted, 'we need to know.'

'That man will know.' McGregor pointed out of the window in the direction of a police officer. 'In an area like this they'll know everybody who lives in a twenty-mile radius and probably have a good idea where they were last night.' He kissed her on the cheek. 'I'm going to unpack.'

He stalked out of the room and Mirabelle heard his

door open and close. She surveyed the adjoining door and slowly removed her lockpicks from her handbag. It took less than twenty seconds to spring the catch. McGregor laughed as she turned the porcelain handle, joining the rooms into a suite.

'Well,' he said, 'at least you're putting your skills to good use.' He laid down the shirt he was unpacking and wrapped his arms around her. 'It's lovely here, isn't it?'

'Apart from the murder.' She smiled.

'Why don't we get changed and walk to the village? I can show you my childhood haunts.'

'I'd love that.'

Outside, the air still felt crisp and cool but the greyness had disappeared. The bright sunshine was at odds both with the temperature and the enforced quietness of a murder scene. Walking down the drive felt like an escape. It was strange to be in flat shoes, but the road was uneven and Mirabelle knew it would only get worse beyond the estate. On the ride from the station she'd been distracted by the scenery, but Eleanor was right – the roads were terrible. She pulled her woollen coat around her and took McGregor's hand. 'How far to the village?'

'A couple of miles further down the road we drove in on,' McGregor said. 'Eleanor's got the measure of the place. There's nothing there apart from the pub and a shop. From memory the shop doesn't sell a lot. Some boilings, milk and newspapers.'

'I haven't had a boiling in years.'

'What do you like? Aniseed balls? I bet you're an aniseed ball kind of girl.'

'Certainly not. My favourite is lemon sherbet, I expect.'

'You don't know your favourite?'

'I always keep my options open. You'd better remember that.'

McGregor smiled. He liked that she kept him on his toes. It was one of the things that made him want to spend his whole life with this woman.

'If we go cross-country, we'll see more,' he gestured. They began to climb a small hill that ran up the side of the road. 'It feels like an escape here, doesn't it?'

Mirabelle smiled. 'I love it,' she said. 'Except . . .'

'Yes. The murder. Sorry about that. Look, you can make out most of the estate from here. There are a couple of farms.'

'Sheep?'

'Mostly. Sometimes when I was a kid we were here for the lambing. I suppose it must have been Easter. I recall the weather being good. They just tipped Bruce and me out in the morning – we were like little savages, on our own in all this. Other times it was shearing season. They sent the bales of wool down south on the train, packed on a horse and cart to go to the station. It seems so quaint – I bet they use a motor now.'

'It's very isolated.'

'When we were little, I never thought of it that way. It felt safe because we knew everyone.'

'I always think of you as a city boy.'

'I am. Do you know, I can't remember being sad in this house. Not till today, and we didn't really know her, did we?'

'Bruce and Eleanor seem happy – together, I mean.'

'I'm glad for him.'

'I wonder where they met?' Mirabelle tried to picture it. 'They are quite different.'

'I suppose that's what attracted them. I mean, when it

happens, it happens, doesn't it? They literally met four years ago. A shorter time than us, and they're married already.'

'Do you think we're different from each other?'

'No. We're similar. If I was in your situation, I'd do just what you do.'

'But you're always warning me off when you're working on a case.'

'That doesn't mean you aren't useful occasionally.'

'Useful!' She punched him playfully on the arm. 'You know perfectly well that there are times I've solved the whole thing.'

From the higher ground, the view spread like a roll of carpet, but there was a nasty wind. Mirabelle's ears ached as she strained to make out the footprint of the house. She spotted a roof terrace with a long wooden bench, which she decided to explore later. On a clear day like today, it would be a pleasant place to sit. Beyond the house, in the glen, she could just make out one of the farms and, beyond that, the village nestled in a dip.

'Where's the lodge?' she asked.

McGregor pointed down the hill. 'On the other side of those trees. It used to be the main entrance to the old place but it's been out of use for years.' He watched as she strained on tiptoe. 'Do you want to have a look?'

Mirabelle nodded.

'When we were kids we thought there were fairies in those woods.' McGregor's cheeks were whipped pink by the breeze.

'Who lived there when you were a boy?'

'It's like Bruce said. There used to be more staff. I can't remember whose place it was – but someone who worked on the estate. The old house was quite posh in those days.

There was a butler, but he was about a hundred, even then. I expect he's been dead for years. And two footmen. And a cook and an army of maids. The war did for the family finances, though. It's a good thing Bruce's fallen for a woman who's prepared to roll up her sleeves.'

Far off, the sound of shotgun fire echoed on the air. Mirabelle arched an eyebrow.

'It's the countryside,' McGregor berated her. 'Don't go seeing murder and mayhem everywhere.'

'All right,' she said.

They trooped downhill and the light changed as they hit the lower ground, where the air smelled of wet grass and the slope provided shelter. McGregor took a few deep breaths and his stride widened. 'You don't get this in Brighton. Not even on the Downs.'

The wood had different kinds of trees. A path had been cleared and lined with chipped branches. Mirabelle could understand how children might believe there were fairies between the holly, the silver birch and the long-needled firs. There was something magical about stepping on to the track. The air smelled green and, above them, she spotted a robin flitting between the branches. She took McGregor's hand. 'I'm half expecting it to be a gingerbread house.'

McGregor laughed. 'Nothing so continental.'

Turning back towards the hill, she noticed the curtains were closed in one of the bedrooms on the first floor of the main house. That must be where Tash had been put to bed. It was unlikely the girl was sleeping but it might help to lie in the dark. She remembered closing the window of her own bedroom when her parents died. The noise of the traffic had suddenly seemed overwhelming.

A police constable walked around the side of the house and stationed himself at the front door. They would probably start searching the grounds soon, combing the grass for signs of anybody prowling in the night or making an escape cross-country. After dark, she imagined, it must be absolutely black here, miles from any artificial light. She tried to remember if there had been a full moon last night but she couldn't. A few steps further and the house was completely masked by trees. In these woods you could ignore the order of things, she thought. You could be private.

McGregor pulled her behind him. 'Come on,' he said. 'You wanted to snoop.'

The lodge house was situated beside an old gate, chained shut and sealed with a mass of rusted metal and rosemary growing in between. The old place must be dark inside, Mirabelle thought, with all these trees. It was pretty, though – a good-sized, double-fronted stone cottage with a slate roof and a patch of partially cleared ground at the front that served as a garden. Wild roses grew in a tangle on both sides of the path and there was the faint smell of thyme. McGregor pushed open the front door. Inside, there was a countryside theme with pretty, patterned wallpaper that featured posies of flowers. A brass umbrella stand stood next to the door, with several black umbrellas bunched inside like flowers in a vase. To the left there was a sitting room furnished with large chairs. A skylight meant it was lighter than she had expected. On the oak table beside the simple fireplace, there were offcuts of cashmere in different colours scattered across the wood. Mirabelle ran her fingers over the wool. It felt luxurious. She pulled a small square of turquoise material between her fingers. 'This one's nice,' she said.

McGregor opened the doors as he moved ahead. Straight on there was a kitchen. To the right a bedroom with a comfortable-looking bed, its plump mattress swaddled in pink blankets with a satin quilt on top. The ashes lay piled in the grate from the night before. 'They must have hated this,' Mirabelle said.

'Oh, I don't know. I think it's got a certain old-world charm. If you were American, you would definitely think so. The rooms are quite large for a cottage, don't you think?'

He opened the wardrobe. At the bottom there were two leather suitcases and, above, neatly stacked piles of clothes ordered by colour – red mostly. A couple of dresses hung on the rail but several hangers and two shelves lay empty. Mirabelle thought that they must have contained Tash's clothes, which Gillies would have cleared to bring up to the house while they were having lunch and seeing to their rooms. She ran her palm across the carefully folded woollens left behind – all good-quality, high-gauge cashmere. Nina had had a good eye.

'That's a bit gruesome, Belle. Sorting through her things.'

Mirabelle stopped for a fraction of a second as her fingers found a small leather notebook between the cashmere folds. Alan had moved to the window, one hand on the curtain. He wouldn't let her read it, she thought. And when the police found it, they'd whisk it away. So, in a split second, she hid the book in her hand and moved smoothly to the bed. On one side there were two cheap novels – an American romance, *Broads Don't Scare Easy* by Hank Janson, and *From Russia with Love* by Ian Fleming. 'These must belong to the girl,' she said, bending down as if to read the covers as she slid the notebook under the bedside cabinet. She could come back and read it later before handing it to the police.

'Where's the bathroom?' she asked.

McGregor turned back into the room. 'You're going to love this,' he said as he gestured her to follow him through to the kitchen and out the back door. There was a good-sized hut a little way off, half-covered in claret-coloured ivy. The walls were freshly painted in soft blue and a single window had been fitted with opaque glass etched with small stars.

'Really?' she laughed. Lots of places still had outdoor toilets, but she knew that – for American tourists from New York – the prospect must have been horrifying.

'Don't you dare postulate that the poor woman killed herself to avoid having to come out here in the middle of the night. It's rather nice, I think. Sneaking out, under the stars. There's a big enamel bath, if my memory serves me.'

Mirabelle adopted a stern expression. 'I've never known you to be flippant about a case, Alan McGregor.'

'It's not my case,' he said.

She opened the door. There were two oil lamps on either side of the bath and a geyser for the hot water. Around the sink there was a scatter of lipstick and a small mirror in a wire frame. The air smelled faintly of orange oil and bergamot.

Back outside, Mirabelle sank on to a wrought-iron bench beside the kitchen door. A scatter of cigarette butts littered the ground. 'She did sneak out under the stars, didn't she? And not for a bath. Assuming Mrs Gillies was right about the time of death.'

'I doubt Mrs Gillies has ever been wrong about anything.'

'Well, then out she went, in the middle of the night. In her red woollen suit. Of course, there's something wrong with that, for a start.'

McGregor looked concerned. 'She was American,' he said, as if this explained everything.

'She was Russian and she was a fashion buyer, Alan. She might not have been dressed for the country, but she should have been dressed for dinner. That was a day suit. It was business attire.'

McGregor sighed as he sat down. He laid a hand on her leg. 'I wish you'd let it drop, Belle. We're here on holiday – a ramble through the view and some pints in the pub, which I, for one, plan to particularly enjoy. Bruce and I used to have to sit outside with a bottle of pop each – you know, with a straw.'

'I'm not buying that you had an underprivileged childhood. Not here.'

'You're right. I'm privileged. In every way.'

Her eyes flashed. 'And yet, so unspoiled. I'm finding it interesting, squaring all this with you. You don't seem to come from a place like this.'

'I didn't. This is my mother's family home. We didn't live this way in Edinburgh. We had a bungalow. Tiny by comparison and in the suburbs. There was football in the street and a three-mile walk into town.'

'And your father?' Mirabelle was aware she'd hate it if McGregor questioned her this way. But he didn't seem to mind the intrusion.

'Dad didn't like it here. I suppose he was a townie, but he let Mum and me come for holidays.'

'He let you come?'

'He was fine with it. My guess is that he got to kick up his heels in Edinburgh while we were away. We weren't rich people, Belle, but we had more than enough and, honestly, now I'm grateful – a house like Bruce's is a huge responsibility. I was lucky to come here sometimes – and I always got on well with Bruce. Not every kid in my class at school learned to ride and shoot.'

'Or stood on top of hills howling.'

He laughed. 'Come on,' He got to his feet and pulled her after him. 'Let's go down to the village.'

'For that pint?'

'Well, a gin and IT for you.'

They climbed over the stone wall and on to the road. It was remarkably empty. The countryside around Brighton always had an inhabited air, with its intermittent brick houses and cheerful, brightly painted front doors. The hedgerows brought everything down to scale. Here the landscape juddered like a modernist painting – dramatic angles and high contrast tones – and there was nobody about. To call the place murderous was a step too far, but the crags and vicious winds could certainly harm someone who wasn't prepared. Mirabelle smoothed her skirt. 'Do you think this is what it'll be like after the bomb?'

McGregor grinned. 'The bomb?'

'You know, if there's an attack,' she said. 'It feels so empty up here – like we're the last people in the world.'

McGregor squeezed her hand. 'We were briefed at the station. I didn't want to tell you about it. The truth is, I'm not sure we'd want to survive. At least if we were up here, we could hide in a cave and light a fire. I don't know what we'd eat but there'd be something. I'm sorry – I've brought you on holiday and it's made you maudlin, what with the murder.'

Mirabelle laughed. 'I don't usually have the time to dwell on it,' she said. 'Did it surprise you that Bruce cried?'

McGregor shook his head. 'About Nina? No. He's not a hardened professional like me. Or a hardened amateur in your case. He isn't used to it. And he knew her.'

'Do you think he'd seen a corpse before?'

'Maybe not a dead woman. He enlisted when the war broke out. He was in logistics, I think, but he saw a bit of action. We've never discussed it.'

'And you were in Edinburgh?'

'That's right. I didn't pass the medical.' McGregor always bristled when the subject of the war came up. Mirabelle looked at him striding out. He seemed perfectly fit.

They crossed an old bridge, one side of the stone pocked with a scramble of yellow lichen and lush green moss. Mirabelle peered over. Below, the water was clear enough to make out the riverbed and she had a sudden urge to take a drink. 'It's a pretty stream,' she said.

'That's the burn,' McGregor corrected her. When she turned, he was watching her. 'And you're the pretty one,' he said. It seemed, when Mirabelle had time on her hands, she thought about Cold War disaster scenarios, but, given the same luxury, McGregor was developing a line in romance. 'I think we should set a date for the wedding,' he said.

Mirabelle smiled, 'You'll have to wait. I don't carry my appointment book with me on long country walks.'

He put his arm around her shoulder and kissed her once more. 'OK,' he said. 'We'll do it later.'

The pub was warm compared to the brisk, cold paper-cut of the January Highland air. Flames from the fire licked the stone grate. An old man with a ragged beard sat smoking a pipe at the bar. McGregor greeted him as Mirabelle took a seat and, eyeing the superintendent warily, the old man slowly knocked out his pipe, downed the last of his pint and left. As he closed the door a heavily pregnant woman appeared.

'Hello,' she said. 'You'll be the laird's cousin.'

'And you'll be Mrs McCrossan.'

'Davina,' the woman shook his hand. 'They're saying there's been an accident up at the big house. What with all the police cars.'

'Who's saying that?'

'Susan MacLeod was half-hysterical. She came past on the way to her mother's. She hardly made sense.'

'And she said it was an accident?'

'No,' Davina McCrossan admitted. 'She said it was a murder, but I wouldn't like to repeat that without knowing it was true.'

McGregor hesitated, then relented. 'There's a body. A dead one, I'm afraid. Another guest of the laird's and poor Susan is right – it looks like murder.'

Davina McCrossan crossed herself. 'My God,' she said. 'That's terrible. Was it one of those smart ladies who had been up and down to the mill?'

'It was. What makes you think that?'

'Only that they were strangers. Was it the mother or the daughter?'

'The mother – or the godmother, in fact – but I expect it's not something for a lady in your condition to go into. It's a distressing business.'

Davina crossed herself again. 'God rest the poor woman,' she said. 'They're already saying, of course.'

'Saying what?' McGregor asked.

'Oh, the Green Lady. You know, the ghost up at the hall. She's a tangled soul. It's a tall tale but you know how people are.'

A smile played around McGregor's lips. 'Ah,' he said. 'Tell me, did Miss Orlova ever come in here?'

'Yes, the two of them did. They took out a bottle or two. Off-sales. They were far too smart to sit in.'

'Well, Mrs McCrossan, I hope we are just scruffy enough.' McGregor smiled.

'Oh sir. I didn't mean . . .' She sounded distressed.

'Not at all. I'm only teasing. We'll have a whisky and a gin and IT, please.'

Davina McCrossan poured the order and laid it on the bar. 'I'm going to sit in the back,' she said, supporting her back with the palm of her hand. 'I'm overdue.'

'Perhaps I shouldn't have mentioned anything . . .' McGregor started but she stopped him.

'Actually, I was saying only yesterday I could do with something to bring it on,' she smiled. 'My husband says if this business with the Russians and Americans wanting to kill everyone isn't giving me enough of a scare, he doesn't know what will. Not that I was wishing for something like this.'

'Of course not.'

'Just call if you need anything.'

The fire crackled again. Mirabelle felt her stomach rumble. It must be the country air. The cold made you feel curiously alive, she realised, as McGregor brought over the drinks.

'The Green Lady?' she said.

McGregor shook his head. 'My great, great, great grand mother. Maybe even more greats . . . the original chatelaine of the manor. She died young and is said to have been beautiful. She kept away from the village, so this story started that she'd walled herself in or her husband locked her up, or some-such. You know how people are. A hundred years from now they'll be calling Nina Orlova the Red Lady. Villages thrive on gossip.' He took a pack of cards from his pocket. 'This might not be the holiday we planned, but I promised you peace and quiet and a decent hand of rummy and, by God, I'm going to make good on that at least – murders and hauntings aside.'

He was different here, she thought as he shuffled the cards. Brighton had contained him somehow. She wondered if she was different – it didn't feel that way, but then she wasn't coming home. Mirabelle never thought much about having a home, but if the McGregor she came to live with was a little more like this fellow, she thought she might like it.

'You'd better watch out. I'm very good at rummy,' she said as he dealt the cards.

Chapter 4

*The death of a beautiful woman is the most
poetical topic in the world*

From their vantage point in the pub, they watched as the sun sank fast, bleeding across the vista in a pool of rich oranges and reds like a bloodbath. Mirabelle tried not to think of it as an omen. Once it was dark, the locals flooded into the pub. Conversations struck up between those who had seen Nina Orlova at one time or another, passing in a car or walking into the village – the local gossip mill getting to work. 'Was she Russian? Do I have that right?' one man asked.

'No. American. She spoke like those fellas during the war,' another corrected him, and then they lowered their voices, glancing guiltily at McGregor and Mirabelle, as if they were somehow involved.

When they left the pub it was half past five and had been dark for over an hour. The temperature had dropped dramatically and a piercing wind whistled along the main street of the village. The sky was cloudy, obscuring the light from the moon, which had only just risen. Mirabelle wondered how clear it had been the night before, when Nina Orlova had set out from the lodge in the middle of the night.

Just as she and McGregor stepped out of the last pool of streetlight and into the dark, they heard a pounding sound. Ahead, high above, trees were silhouetted against the sky at the top of the hill. Mirabelle felt her skin prickle.

'What's that sound?' She reached for McGregor's hand.

'I don't know,' he said. They froze as the pounding drew closer until out of the darkness two shadowy horses pulled to a halt just ahead of them, their hooves clicking on the tarmac as they stepped on to the road.

'Hi,' said a woman's voice, out of breath. Mirabelle peered. Eleanor's skin looked translucent in the wash of low moonlight. It struck Mirabelle she had forgotten the size of horses – from a stand at the Brighton racetrack, they looked like toys. Here, she could smell the sweat on their hide and they seemed huge and utterly unpredictable. Her heart was pounding. 'You gave us a fright,' she said. 'We couldn't see you.'

'Sorry. We had to get out,' Eleanor apologised. 'It's late to ride but they've got eyes in their heads.' She patted her horse.

Bruce was wearing jodhpurs and a tweed riding jacket. He smiled as he walked his horse forward and leaned down to offer Mirabelle a hand. 'Come on,' he said. 'We'll ride home together, pigeon pair. Climb up.'

McGregor helped her to mount and then climbed behind Eleanor and they set off up the hill, trotting at first and then speeding to a gallop across the open ground. It was exhilarating. It had been a long time since Mirabelle had felt a horse move beneath her and the slap of freezing air on her face – the adventure of not being able to quite see ahead. She could only just make out McGregor and Eleanor a few feet away thundering up the hill beside them. She heard Eleanor unleash a shrill laugh and wondered what McGregor had said or whether it was the thrill of riding at speed that had made her cry out. Ahead, Bruce moved as if he was part of the animal. She'd forgotten the strength you needed to ride – the sheer force of will as she clung on to Bruce and squeezed her thighs against the horse's flanks. In conditions like this, any moment they could be thrown, but she trusted Bruce's competence. He'd lived here all his life. He knew the landscape and the animal. At last, the house came into view, its warm yellow windows a beacon.

They dismounted and Bruce took the reins. Then in her peripheral vision she saw a movement and swung round just as a man stepped forward from the portico. He was ungainly, as if his limbs did not fit in place.

'Mr Robertson?'

'Yes.' Bruce squinted into the light. 'Ah, Murdo Kenzie, isn't it? What can I do for you?'

'It's what I can do for you, sir.'

Eleanor let out a sigh. She was right, Mirabelle thought, this was a cheesy start, whatever Mr Kenzie wanted. His accent, she noticed, sounded craggy compared to the soft brogue of Alan and his cousin.

'I work for the *Inverness Courier*, sir. They sent me to cover the story of the woman's murder. People are saying all sorts of things.'

'Are they now?'

Eleanor took the reins from her husband and made to lead the animals back into the paddock while Kenzie continued. 'Given that I know you . . .'

'Know me?'

'That I'm from here . . . I can help, I think. I can keep the heat off. We're going to run the story on tomorrow's front page, if you'd give me an exclusive . . .'

Bruce advanced. 'Someone has died in my house . . .'

'She was murdered, sir, and the public are curious. If you could just see your way . . .' The man took a notebook and pencil from his pocket.

Bruce looked as if – had he still been on his mount – he would have run the fellow down.

McGregor stepped in. 'Mr Robertson has nothing to say except that everyone is trying to deal with this tragedy and we'd appreciate you not imposing—' he said.

'Mr Robertson has more to say than that,' Bruce cut in. 'He says get off my land, you animal. Go on! Your father must be ashamed of you. You should be ashamed of yourself.'

'But, sir,' Kenzie pleaded, 'every paper in the country will want the story . . . if you let me cover it . . .'

'You can sell it, is that what you're after? Christ almighty! Go on! Off with you!'

'You think nobody is going to care about a dead American on our soil? Or was she Russian? This is a story of international significance, Mr Robertson. Given the political situation . . .'

Bruce let out a roar. His eyes were lit now. Kenzie stuffed the notebook in his pocket and backed off the portico as Bruce advanced.

McGregor moved quickly. He held back his cousin and the reporter disappeared down the driveway, into the darkness.

Eleanor returned. 'Is that Dougal Kenzie's son?' she asked. 'The schoolteacher's boy?'

'It is,' Bruce replied. 'Bloody intrusion!'

'I put the horses in the paddock but I can't—' Eleanor started.

'I'll see to the tack,' Bruce told her. He patted McGregor on the back and went to see to the animals. The others stamped their feet on the doormat and gratefully bundled inside. Mirabelle caught a flash of herself – skin pink and eyes bright

– in one of the hallway mirrors. Her cheeks felt like blocks of ice. Her ears ached.

'Do you ever lock this door?' she asked, as she relaxed into the relative warmth of the hallway and the ease of electric light.

'No.' Eleanor dropped her riding crop on a Georgian mahogany carved chair. She removed her hat.

'Not even at night?'

'It's always been like that,' McGregor confirmed. 'We used to nip out for midnight assignations – biscuits under the stars, Bruce and I. In those days my uncle had three basset hounds. They followed us everywhere.'

That meant anyone could just walk in, Mirabelle thought. Though Mr Kenzie hadn't gone that far.

'Cute – midnight feasts,' Eleanor commented. 'Well, we'd best dress for dinner,' she said and made for the stairs.

In her room, Mirabelle fell on to the bed.

'I bet that made your heart pound.' McGregor slid his hand around her waist.

It had, but she pushed him away. 'I was going to have a bath,' she said. He wandered away to lay out his evening suit as she set off down the hallway.

The bathroom was mostly taken up with a sea-green enamel tub. The window was frosted with the same starred, opaque glass as the hut at the lodge, though the upper panes were clear. Mirabelle turned off the electric light and lit three candles on the windowsill, so she could watch the dark sky and its pepper of stars. Then she turned on the taps and swished her hand through the water to check the temperature. On the walls, paintings juddered in the candlelight. She recognised the hill they'd climbed in a watercolour signed DBMc, and she wondered who the artist was. Then, as the bath filled, she slipped out of her clothes, tied up her hair and stepped into the steaming water, soaping herself with a square of hand-cut soap that trailed the scent of lavender. The heat felt as if it was sinking bone-deep into her, an antidote to the piercing chill. As she floated, she ran over the events of the day: the body in the orangery, the diary she'd squirrelled away and the story of the Green Lady, as haunting as the landscape. This place was beautiful but it was making her jumpy. In the candlelight it was easier to believe in ghosts, she thought, as she stepped, soaking, on to the mat. And besides, there was a murderer here, or nearby. Somewhere.

The peach towels on the heated chrome rail were vast. Eleanor had an eye for quality, Mirabelle thought, as she gathered her clothes and sneaked back along the corridor, dismissing the idea of a green ghost in the shadows. In her room she surveyed her wardrobe. She had packed four evening dresses and chose one with a fitted bodice and flared skirt in burnt orange taffeta. Quickly, she dressed her hair, put on her diamond earrings and carefully applied red lipstick before stepping into a pair of tan, ostrich-skin high heels that she'd been wearing for over a decade. When she was done, she gazed out of the window at the low moon.

The gong sounded. As the echo faded, McGregor knocked on the interconnecting door. Silently, he held out his hand and they walked downstairs. On the last run of steps they heard music – something by Fanny Mendelssohn. They followed it. The dining room was off the main hall, opposite the drawing room. The double doors lay open and, inside, the walls shimmered silver in the candlelight. A vinyl record moved on a turntable, catching the light as it spun. Bruce and Eleanor stood at the fireplace, both turned away from the door, nursing champagne glasses and talking quietly. Bruce, like McGregor, wore black tie, while Eleanor had slipped into a floor-length pale pink gown with a diamond brooch pinned to the swooping neckline. Her hair was curled in a chignon. McGregor coughed politely and Bruce swung round.

'Come in. It's only us tonight. Just family.'

'We're having duck,' Eleanor said. 'It's your favourite, isn't it, darling?'

'I bagged them myself. I'll shoot again tomorrow if you fancy, Alan. We might get some pigeon if we're lucky. Will you join me?'

'Why not?'

Mirabelle thought it was extraordinary after all that had happened that they were discussing food. But then there wasn't much else to do in the country. She recalled riding for hours and afterwards lurching from meal to meal in her younger days, when she used to get invitations to house parties. 'Is Tash coming down?' she asked.

Bruce shook his head. 'Gillies took her a tray.'

'Shock,' Eleanor added.

The champagne was delicious. Eleanor swayed in time to the music. Behind her, Mirabelle noticed the ornate mantel, its swirls carved out of moss-coloured, polished granite with veins of white-flecked grey. Her heart lurched at the sight of a figure on the threshold. A shadowy apparition – a woman in green. She let out an involuntary squeal and everybody turned. 'Are you all right?' McGregor asked.

'Sorry,' Mirabelle apologised.

It was Tash. The girl stood absolutely straight. Her deportment, Mirabelle thought, was marvellous. She had fixed her hair in a glossy bun with trailing wisps and wore long pearl earrings, which swung like tiny lamps as she walked into the room. Mirabelle noticed her hand was trembling. Poor thing. It had taken guts to come downstairs.

'Darling,' Eleanor breathed. 'Are you sure you're up to it?'

Tash shrugged. The dress was astonishing. A perfectly fitted sheath of green satin hung in folds around her slim frame, setting off her jade eyes and milky skin. As she sashayed towards the fireplace, the fabric glistened in the low light, moving like a pool of tidal water. She seemed quite different from the weeping wreck in the kitchen, though as she moved into the light it was clear the girl's eyes were puffy from crying. 'I didn't want to sit up there by myself,' she said, her American accent stronger than Eleanor's. Momentarily she looked as if she might cry again, as if she was sculpted entirely of water and might dissolve into droplets.

'Just look at you, you could be a model,' Eleanor kissed her on the cheek. The words seemed to pull the youngster together. 'Is that dress a Schiaparelli?' The girl nodded. 'Well it's beautiful.'

'Thanks. I read somewhere that when someone you love dies, you're supposed to wear sackcloth. But sackcloth isn't going to make you feel any better, is it?' she said, her voice breaking.

Eleanor took her hand. 'You're being very brave, darling,' she said. 'And just for the record, we all feel different shades of lousy tonight. But you are the main thing. We're all here to look after you.'

Tash smiled weakly. Bruce poured her some champagne.

Tash paused. 'I've spent all day thinking about Nina. And crying. It's just been . . .' she gestured, 'feelings, I guess. It doesn't seem real.'

'I'm sure that's quite normal, dear. Did you sleep?' Eleanor asked.

The girl's eyes flickered and she bit her lip. 'Not really. But it was probably good to rest. I'm still jet-lagged. It's been more than a week but I can't seem to get over it and now this . . . Anyway, I thought I'd come down. Is that awful?'

'Not at all.'

Tash sipped her champagne. 'I expect it's the shock,' she said. 'The way I was this morning, I mean. Waking up and being told and then feeling it was a dream. My parents died when I was only five years old. I don't remember much, but I got through it. I suppose I will get through this too.'

'Nina was a wonderful woman,' Bruce said. 'So clever.'

Tash wiped away a tear. Her voice was breaking again. 'It's not what most people will remember her for. I'm glad you said that – not just that she was stylish or beautiful, though she was those things too. But that she was clever. She always said the Orlovs were doomed to tragedy.'

Tash began to cry quietly and Eleanor handed her a cotton handkerchief.

'Whatever do you mean?' Mirabelle asked.

'Their history,' Tash sniffed. 'Nina came out of Russia in 1917 as a baby – she and her mother and brother fled to Paris with my family. Thinking about it, that must have been far worse than this.'

'And Nina's father?'

'Same as my grandfather. The Reds put him in prison and later we found out he had been shot. He was only a baron, which is the lowest there is, but they shot anyone who didn't get out.' The girl shivered. 'Nina talked about St Petersburg all the time when I was growing up. She was only a few months old when she left, but it was as if the life her family had in Russia was real and everything since has only been . . .' Tash parted her lips and puffed. 'Of course my generation

59

feel differently. I was born in America. Still, if the Revolution had gone another way, I might have been a princess, I guess. Just think of that.' Tash looked like a princess, Mirabelle thought. She could certainly have carried a tiara with ease. Bruce refilled her glass and used the opportunity to change the subject.

'Nina's brother is coming. Eleanor managed to get hold of him. He should be with us by tomorrow evening.'

Tash sighed and crumpled her handkerchief into a ball. 'Oh God,' she said. 'Uncle Niko. He'll say it's the Reds.'

'The Reds?'

'As if they're still after us. Niko inherited the title. He's Baron Orlov. Not everybody uses their titles these days, but he is terribly keen on the whole thing. Both he and Nina are neurotic about the Reds. But it's not as if we were the Romanovs, for heaven's sake. "It's ridiculous – you like red. It's your favourite colour," I used to say,' Tash sighed. 'She wore red all the time. You'll see – it'll be the first thing Niko says. It's the Reds. They'll never give up.' Another tear slid down Tash's cheek. 'I'm sorry,' she said. 'I feel as if I'm leaking.'

'Well, I'm looking forward to meeting Baron Orlov,' Bruce said. 'That's one more for dinner tomorrow so we'd better bag a brace of pigeons in the morning, Al.' He tried to sound cheerful.

Tash sniffed. 'If you're shooting, can I come? Once in Montana, Nina was buying furs for Nieman Marcus and we stayed on a ranch. I swear I was only twelve but I bagged a buffalo.'

Eleanor laughed.

'I know it's awful,' Tash said. 'But I need to keep busy. I can't just sit around crying like this.'

'If you like, we could go to the cashmere mill?' Eleanor offered.

Tash shook her head. 'I'd prefer to kill something.'

'God help those pigeons.' Bruce grinned. 'I'll look out a shotgun for you.' He gave a little bow as Gillies appeared at the door with a tray.

'Ah – lobster cocktail,' Eleanor announced. 'We always have fish towards the end of the week.'

Gillies had excelled. The lobster was succulent. When she cleared the plates and brought in two roasted ducks, Bruce got to his feet to carve them. Tiny white onions scattered across the china in a sea of burgundy sauce. Mirabelle thought it was an elegant meal – more than she had expected. Tash hardly touched a bite, pushing the food around her plate and sipping her champagne. You couldn't blame her – food in grief, Mirabelle knew, lost all its flavour.

Afterwards, the men wanted to smoke cigars and stay at the table. The women elected to retire to the drawing room where the long blue velvet curtains had been drawn and the fire set ablaze. They settled on the sofas. Jinx was already asleep, curled around the edge of a chair.

'Archaic, isn't it?' Eleanor said indulgently as she plumped the cushions. 'But I don't mind some of these traditions. Girls together.'

Gillies brought in coffee. When the door closed behind her, Eleanor got up and switched out the lamps, making the fire glow seemingly brighter in the darkness.

'What are you doing?' Tash asked.

'You'll see.' Eleanor paused dramatically at the window before pulling back the curtains as if revealing a stage. 'Look,' she said. Through the glass, the night sky was peppered with acres of stars and the low, bright moon, which was not quite at its fullest, the clouds patchier now. 'I find it soothing. It's difficult to believe anything can go wrong, looking at this. All the wickedness in the world and yet such beauty. I thought you'd like it.'

Tash sank on to the sofa and stared at the view as if it was medicinal. The moonlight bathed the fields in an eerie, translucent blue. A flash of snowdrops by the curve in the drive flashed luminous, as if stars had fallen out of the sky and scattered across the dark grass. Inside, the women's faces were lit by the fire. Mirabelle was reminded of camping as a child, with the girl guides, somewhere near Hampstead Heath.

'Being close to nature,' Eleanor said. 'That's what I love here. When it rains sometimes I rush to the orangery to listen to it hammering on the glass.' Suddenly, she stopped. 'I'm sorry. Of course, I won't do that any more. Bruce said that we should tear the thing down.'

'Don't be silly,' Tash insisted. 'You can't demolish a place just because somebody died there. There'd be nowhere left.'

Mirabelle picked up her coffee. The darkness had brought a kind of intimacy and, it struck her, both Eleanor and Tash were extraordinary. British women would never talk so frankly. Not even if they were family. 'Do *you* think it could have been the Reds who killed your godmother, Tash?' she asked.

Tash laughed. The question had caught her unawares. 'I never met a Red, not a single one. They're just vilas. Bogey men. They're newspaper headlines and, yes, right now Khrushchev has it in for Eisenhower. No doubt about that. But for Nina? Baron Orlov's daughter in exile? After all this time? It's a kid's story – easy to say, that's all. White Russians love an excuse. Something goes wrong – it's the Reds. There's an accident – it's the Reds. That's what they said when my parents . . . you know. That the motor had been tampered with. But my father was driving too fast, that's the truth. As far as I can see, the Reds don't care about us. Why would they? They won. But for us – the Russians who lost everything – it's different. Uncle Niko would be back in St Petersburg like a shot, reclaiming the Orlov lands – the dacha by the sea, the townhouse and the farms. He still considers them his.'

'And you don't?' Eleanor sounded intrigued.

'I wouldn't go back to Russia if you paid me. I'll marry an American, you see if I don't. A very nice, very rich American.'

'Oh really, Tash!' Eleanor put down her cup.

'Are you saying you didn't marry Bruce for his money?'

'I certainly did not. In fact, if anything, people assumed he'd married me for mine. Because I'm a Yank, of course, and they think we're all loaded, which we're not. The judgement was palpable, let me tell you. I was broke, of course. But money isn't what it's about for either of us.'

'Well, he has quite a lot of money for something that wasn't a consideration.'

'I'm not saying we're not comfortable, but it's Bruce I love. Besides,' Eleanor continued, 'taking that position plays straight into the worst things men think about women – especially women as beautiful as you. Gold-diggers every one. How will you feel if your future husband is simply looking for a long pair of legs and nice eyes?'

'Well, what if he is?'

'But you're so much more than that. You're intelligent and talented.' Eleanor looked to Mirabelle to back her up. 'Tell her, Mirabelle. You chose Alan for himself, didn't you?'

Mirabelle found herself laughing. 'I have money of my own. We're quite modern, I expect, though we're not starry eyed. I chose him because he's a good man.' As she said it, she realised it was true.

'Well, I'd like a rich, good man,' Tash insisted. 'And for the record I hope he likes my legs and my eyes and all the rest of me too.'

The ash in the fire shifted and a shower of sparks tumbled into the grate. It broke the conversation. Jinx raised his head and settled down again. Outside, Mirabelle thought she saw something glint in the moonlight, as if something was moving up the hillside. She told herself to stop being jumpy.

'It's nice to hear laughter,' Eleanor said. 'I thought we might never cheer up.'

'I cried for hours upstairs,' Tash admitted. 'I'm over-wrought, I guess. We've been living like night owls, Nina and I. Neither of us was able to adjust to the time difference. And it gets dark so early here – it's kind of beautiful, but disconcerting.'

'So you didn't notice your godmother had gone in the night?' Mirabelle asked.

Tash shook her head sadly, as if she had only just realised. 'It's a terrible thing to say, but no, I didn't.'

'And you last saw her, last night?' Mirabelle kept pushing. 'Late?'

'It must have been about three. I went to bed and she said she was just coming. I told the police.'

'Was she wearing her red suit when you retired?' Mirabelle checked.

Tash sniffed. She was crying softly again but not so much she couldn't answer the question. Her face was all shadow in the darkness. 'No. Even in the lodge, just the two of us, we'd always wear something nice for dinner. Not necessarily full length, but it's fun to dress up. Nina could cook. I don't know where she learned. And we played cards and read by the fire. It was old-fashioned. She ordered every glossy magazine she could think of to keep us amused. I think she was put out about being in the lodge, but I loved it. I thought I'd miss American television but I don't. I've been sketching, actually, and reading. You're right, Eleanor, the countryside is special. I watched a rabbit the other day, in the garden at the lodge. I sat on the bench outside and watched him for half an hour.'

Mirabelle detected a note of tenderness in the girl's voice. She thought of the cigarette butts beside the bench, and of Tash, sitting there smoking. 'The thing is, Nina's outfit seemed odd to me,' she said. 'The red day suit.'

Tash shrugged. 'If she was planning on going out, I suppose it made sense. It was warmer than what she wore for dinner. She must have changed once I was asleep – maybe she wanted to walk.'

Suddenly, Eleanor jumped up from the sofa. Her coffee cup tumbled on to the carpet and the saucer smashed. Jinx jerked to his feet and licked the liquid.

'Are you all right?' Mirabelle picked up the broken crockery.

Tash put an arm around Eleanor. 'What is it?'

'I thought I saw something outside,' Eleanor said. 'There was talk of a wolf a few weeks ago.'

'Are there wolves up here? I didn't know that,' Mirabelle said.

'It's a silly rumour. That's all.' Eleanor sat down again.

'Well, it's a good night for a wolf.' Tash grinned. 'That big old moon and the sky so clear.' She let out a whoop, a lame kind of wolf cry, not a patch on McGregor's howl at the ridge. Then she laughed. 'Ha! I'm hopeless.'

Mirabelle laid the broken saucer on the tray. 'Would you like another coffee, Eleanor?'

'I've probably had enough.'

Then they all jumped at the rap that emanated from the glass. Eleanor let out a squeal, rather than a scream. At the window a dark shadow tapped once more. The girl squinted. 'Gregory!' she shouted and flung open the double doors, flooding the room with light from the hallway. Eleanor snapped the lamps back on. 'I knew I'd seen something,' she said.

Tash returned with a black man in tow. He was tall and broad and his clothes were so dark, it was no wonder his figure hadn't been clear on approach. Mirabelle thought he had the air of a boxer, as if he was ready for a fight and wasn't the least afraid. 'Ma'am,' he said, nodding in Eleanor's direction, his voice like American honey slowly dripping from a spoon. 'I only just got back. They told me what had happened in the village. I understand the police want to speak to me.'

'Well, they aren't here at this time of night,' Eleanor said testily. 'You gave us quite a fright sneaking up to the house like that.'

'I came to check if Miss Natasha was OK. When she wasn't at the lodge, I assumed she was with you.'

'I'm fine, Gregory,' Tash replied smartly. 'I'm just shook up, is all.' She poured him a whisky from the tray beside the door. 'Here,' she said. Then her eyes filled with tears and she began to sob. Gregory put down the glass and held her as her body shook with grief. Mirabelle felt a tug of relief that Tash was with somebody familiar. She'd put up quite a front. Gregory withdrew a handkerchief from his pocket and helped the girl to sit down. She glanced shyly at the other women. 'Sorry,' she said. 'Losing it like that.'

'Darling, don't be silly,' Eleanor perched on the edge of a footstool in front of her. 'We all understand. Everyone here has lost their mother – Nina brought you up.'

'Were you ladies sitting in the dark?' Gregory asked, looking around the room.

'We were stargazing. Like schoolgirls.' Tash giggled. 'Mirabelle, this is Gregory. He's our steward.'

'Mr . . .?' Mirabelle was certain that Gregory was not the man's last name. Everyone was so casual here, but it seemed wrong not to address him properly.

'Just call me Gregory, ma'am. Everybody does.'

'Well . . . Gregory. If you don't mind me asking, where have you been?' Mirabelle's voice sounded like cut glass, she realised, amid all these soft American tones. Next he'd encourage her to call him Greg, she thought, or something equally awful.

'Ma'am?'

'Miss Bevan is Mr Robertson's cousin,' Tash explained. 'Her husband is a detective.'

Mirabelle decided not to elucidate. 'It's only you said you just got back,' she said. 'I wondered where you'd been?'

'Glasgow.' His accent made the city sound foreign, almost exotic.

Tash sniffed. She gesticulated towards Gregory. 'He went to speak to an exporter about shipping our cashmere. The mill can do it from here, but Nina thought we'd be better to have our own guys. She sent him yesterday morning in the hired car.'

'What happened?' Gregory asked gently. 'In the pub they said it was murder.'

'Miss Orlova was strangled last night,' Mirabelle said. 'I'm sorry.'

'Where?'

'Here. In the orangery.'

Tash began to cry again. Everyone shifted. It was beginning

to seem cruel to talk like this in front of her. 'Come along, dear, I'll take you up,' Eleanor said.

As Tash followed willingly, Gregory's gaze followed her. Then the dining-room doors opened and Bruce and Alan crossed the wide wooden boards on a tide of post-dinner jollity, cutting into the sombre atmosphere. 'Goodnight,' Bruce called to the women disappearing up the hallway. 'Ah, Gregory,' he said, as if he'd temporarily mislaid the steward and only this second discovered him under some papers on his desk. 'The police asked where you had got to.'

'I'm a suspect?'

'We're all suspects. I hope you have an alibi for last night.'

'I was in Glasgow. In a bar. And if I wasn't there, I was asleep, and if I wasn't there I was at the docks early this morning.'

Bruce snorted. 'You're doing better than I did. At least you stand a chance of witnesses in town. Today when they asked me where I had been, all I could say was upstairs and not a soul had seen me.'

'I thought Eleanor was with you,' Mirabelle objected.

'Yes. But we were asleep,' Bruce pointed out.

'Where did you sleep, Gregory?' Mirabelle asked.

'At the Central Hotel, ma'am. I rose early and drove to the port at Greenock.'

'Business go well?'

'Lady, I don't think they had ever seen a black man.'

Bruce smiled. 'Oh, I doubt that, old man. It's a port. Though they might not be used to doing business with one.'

'This wouldn't have happened if I had been here.'

McGregor stepped forward. 'What do you mean?'

'If I was here, I'd have been able to protect her.'

McGregor took a moment to process this information.

'I don't doubt your abilities, but Miss Orlova would appear to have left the lodge in the middle of the night and come up to the house alone. Even if you had been here, you probably wouldn't have been with her.'

Gregory nodded. 'Maybe you're right,' he said. 'But it's my job.'

Bruce poured himself a coffee. He flung a piece of tablet in the direction of Jinx. It hit the dog on the side of the head and the poodle snapped it off the carpet. 'Sorry old man,' Bruce apologised. Then he gestured towards McGregor, offering coffee. McGregor declined. 'There's nothing you can do tonight,' Bruce continued, putting a piece of tablet into his own mouth. 'You'd best go down the hill and get some sleep. The police will want to speak to you in the morning.'

Gregory carefully put down his glass of whisky. He hadn't tasted it. 'Yes, sir,' he said. 'I guess they will.'

Later, on her way up to bed, Mirabelle overheard Alan and Bruce talking. The men had retired to Bruce's study but the door was open. A huge pair of antlers, mounted on the wall, cast fingers of shadow on to the long planks of oak that floored the hallway.

'Do you think he could have made it there and back in time?' Alan asked.

Bruce considered. 'Glasgow's a good five hours – what with the roads, it might be more. And in the dark. Greenock's perhaps another hour on top.'

'They'll find witnesses, if anyone saw him. He's black – they'll have noticed him at the Central Hotel if he really stayed there. And I suppose, in the bars. We don't know the time of death yet, that's the thing.'

Mirabelle hesitated a moment before stepping through

the door frame. The men sprang to their feet but she waved them back to their seats.

'I couldn't help overhearing,' she said. 'When we were talking by the fire, Tash said she went to bed at three last night. That means Nina was alive at three and in evening wear. It at least shaves a few hours off Gillies's time-of-death estimate. She would have had to change and get up the hill. I'd say the earliest she could have been here was 3.30, and Mrs Gillies said she must have been dead "before breakfast". When is breakfast?'

'About nine,' Bruce replied thoughtfully. 'Though Gillies probably consumes hers at some ungodly hour.'

'It gives a shorter time frame,' McGregor said slowly, figuring it out. 'Well then, yes. Gregory could have done it if nobody saw him in town. He could have come back from Glasgow after closing time and made it down again to check out of the hotel. A sleepless night, but he could just about do it. It depends what times he was seen.'

Bruce knocked back his whisky. 'I can't see who else could have,' he said.

Mirabelle crossed her arms. 'And you think he somehow arranged to meet Miss Orlova in the orangery in the middle of the night, even though she'd sent him away on business?'

'They're on New York time. Tash said so,' Bruce chimed.

'Four in the morning is only eleven at night across the pond. Sure. But why here? If she wanted to see him for some reason, he could have called at the lodge. It doesn't make sense – she'd just sent him away. Where is he staying?'

'He has a room in a boarding house outside the village. It's a farm, really,' Bruce said. 'You're right, of course. There was no reason to send the chap away and then call him back.

I'm not even sure she could have – and if she'd left him a message at the hotel, there's bound to be a record. The police will find out.'

McGregor nodded. 'Yes.' He got up and stood beside the window. 'Maybe the police will find evidence of a prowler. There's always the chance it was a random attack.'

'Lucky,' Bruce said. 'I mean, out here. A prowler. First of all, not knowing where they were going, one presumes, and second of all not knowing if anyone would be up. Especially given, well, you know.' He nodded towards the mahogany, glass-fronted cabinet beside the fireplace. That side of the room was dark, but Mirabelle could make out the vertical lines of shotgun barrels stored tidily in a row. 'Mind you, the chap would have a fighting chance,' Bruce continued. 'By the time I got downstairs and unlocked the damn thing—'

'Don't joke,' McGregor cut in. 'You don't want to end up on a self-defence charge.'

'In my own home,' Bruce objected.

'You can't shoot people for coming inside, Bruce.'

'It might have been better for poor Nina if I had.'

Mirabelle peered through the glass. The guns were in good condition. The barrels had been oiled. They glowed in the low light.

'They belonged to my father,' Bruce continued. 'Made to measure. Luckily Al and I are more or less the same dimensions in the shoulder. The two on the left belonged to my grandfather. They're out of date now. We'll see how you take to them tomorrow, Al. My guess is that Dad's will fit you like a glove.'

McGregor grinned. 'It's good you have them locked up.'

'Grandad always had a proper cabinet. Even before you had to.'

Mirabelle turned back into the room. 'If it was a prowler, are you sure nothing was taken? It occurs to me that the whole thing still might have been a burglary gone wrong.'

Bruce was adamant. 'There's nothing missing. Not at all.'

After midnight, Mirabelle found herself craving the darkness and the cold. She pulled on a coat and sneaked some sugar cubes from the sideboard. Her steps echoed in the hallway now everyone had gone to bed. Outside, the darkness swallowed her. The horses hardly stirred. 'Hey,' she said, coaxing them with the sugar. 'Here.'

One woke and sauntered over to eat from her outstretched palm, his breath hot on her skin, the smell of hide and hay wafting around him. Above, the sky went on for ever. She shuddered as she imagined Nina walking up the hill, glad to get inside the house – so much warmer than out here. Then she turned, hoisting herself on to the fence to stare back at the mansion, the windows dark, the silence absolute. This was how it had been last night – the murder just under twenty-four hours ago. Her heart quickened. She was vulnerable out here alone, she realised suddenly, with a murderer somewhere. It felt different from the usual run of things. A town. Streetlights. Officers on patrol. She jumped as the door opened, casting round for a weapon, about to get off the fence and pick up a rock from the ground to defend herself in the darkness as a shadow moved across the threshold. If she screamed everyone would hear her on this side of the house, but could they come quickly enough? She took a breath, letting it out slowly in relief as the light from the moon revealed the figure as McGregor. He helped her down, his hands firm on her waist.

'You OK?'

She laid her head on his shoulder. 'We are so small,' she said, 'aren't we?'

She had never been so glad to see anyone.

Chapter 5

Better three hours too soon than a minute too late

Mirabelle had never seen rain like it. She woke in the morning to the sound of hammering on the window-pane. It seemed impossible that such a deafening clatter could follow the stillness of the night. They had made love when they came indoors and this time so tenderly that she felt as if there was no space between them. Now the morning light fil-tered blearily through the curtains as her eyes adjusted. Susan was standing in the middle of the room staring as Mirabelle sat up.

'Miss.' The girl dropped her eyes.

Mirabelle smiled. McGregor was asleep next to her. If she woke him, he'd be mortified. 'Thank you, Susan,' Mirabelle said quietly, nodding towards the fire that was kindling in the grate. 'You can leave the curtains.'

Susan walked smartly out of the room. McGregor turned over and snored as Mirabelle laughed softly at the girl's shocked expression at finding two unmarried people in bed. She wondered if Susan would tell Mrs Gillies – the shame of it. It wouldn't be the first time in a house such as this, but unmarried love was ever the scandal.

As she turned over, the details of Nina Orlova's death came

back to her. Sleep was usually a good way to work things through but this morning the murder remained stubbornly inexplicable. Gradually, the sound of the rain intensified. Mirabelle thought it must sound like being under fire – not that she ever had been. Still, the noise woke McGregor. He shifted blearily and reached for her, kissing her neck, hauling himself out of bed and padding along the hall towards the bathroom. The lock on the door clicked behind him.

Mirabelle got up and pulled the curtains. The sky was overcast. Below, there was movement in the orangery. The police must hardly be able to hear what they were saying, she thought. Such heavy rain on glass would drown out normal conversation. A large, grey puddle, the size of a small lake, had formed in the middle of the lawn. A little way off, three black-and-white milk cows sat under a tree. From the bathroom she could hear the pipes sing as McGregor ran a bath. Mirabelle slipped into the seat at the dressing table and fixed her hair. It seemed impossible that the men would go shooting in this weather. She had hoped she might walk up the hill again today. She always thought of herself as a town mouse. It surprised her that she was enjoying the country. Still, the wild landscape had granted her a reprieve from the world of wedding dresses, and standing outside with McGregor, holding each other in the darkness after midnight, had been the best part of the day. Getting up, she pulled a tweed skirt and a sweater out of her wardrobe and tied the laces of her sensible shoes. She'd leave him to his ablutions.

Downstairs, Bruce sat alone at the breakfast table, reading a newspaper. 'Morning,' he said, bobbing up and down as a matter of courtesy. 'You're the early bird.'

Mirabelle helped herself to scrambled eggs from the

warmer and smoked fish poached in milk. She was surprised she was hungry – most days she skipped breakfast, but the Highland air or the holiday spirit seemed to have endowed her with an appetite.

'We're headline news.' Bruce pushed the newspaper towards her. *American heiress murdered at midnight in local estate* – the article took up the whole front page and featured an out-of-date picture of Nina Orlova in an old-fashioned dress, which must have been obtained from a press agency. 'It's only the local paper – that idiot, Kenzie. Of course, she wasn't really American and she survived midnight. The fool didn't get anything right. His father sent a note this morning, apologising.'

Mirabelle poured a cup of tea and added a lump of sugar and a splash of milk.

'We'll hide it from Tash,' Bruce said, pulling out a copy of *The Times* and laying it on top of the *Courier*.

'I've been wondering,' Mirabelle said, 'why the orangery? I mean, what is it usually used for?'

'We use it all the time,' Bruce sounded bluff.

'When?'

'Afternoon tea. Sometimes we have drinks there before dinner – in the summer when it's light. And Eleanor reads there. She says it's away from the bustle of the house.'

'Quieter, she means?'

'I suppose.'

Mirabelle considered this. If Nina Orlova had arranged to meet somebody, the orangery was certainly out of the way. An argument in the drawing room might be overheard, she thought, even at night, but to the rear, close to only the guest bedrooms, which were empty on the night she died, you had the least chance of being either overseen or overheard,

76

despite all the glass. Eleanor was right – the orangery was out of the way.

'It's too wet for shooting, I suppose?' she said, taking a forkful of eggs.

'Probably. But it's ideal fishing weather,' Bruce said cheerfully. 'They say there's no bad weather in Scotland, only the wrong attire. The river's on our neighbour's land, but we have an agreement. I'll look out gabardines and Al can join me. It'll be salmon en croute for dinner, if we're lucky.'

'Are the neighbours far?'

'The Dougals? Not really. They're the nearest proper house. Ten miles, I suppose. Ah, good morning dear,' Bruce said, as his wife came into the breakfast room.

'You're down?' Mirabelle had expected Eleanor to eat in her room. It was the usual way for a married lady.

'Yes,' Eleanor said as she helped herself to a pile of toast and pulled a dark pot of plummy jam towards her. Mirabelle admired Eleanor's forest green cashmere twinset. She had adopted the best of Highland style, and no mistake. 'I'm engaged in a stand-off,' she admitted. 'For the first three months of our marriage, Gillies delivered a tray to my room and I brought it to the table. It was round one and I won it. However, she downright refuses to make coffee for breakfast. Round two. We'll get there.' Eleanor bit into a slice of toast and sipped reluctantly on a cup of tea. 'I was just thinking,' she continued, 'how marvellous it is that Tash has broken free of her family's past. She's remarkably open-minded, don't you think?'

'She is coping well, all things considered,' Mirabelle agreed.

'To be able to give up all that stuffy privilege and not care about her uncle's title. Well, I think that's fabulous.'

'You never know what's going on under the surface,' Bruce

told her, sagely. 'When I was in the forces, chaps coped, of course, but there was a price. Al has come through rather well, I think.'

'Al?' Mirabelle heard her voice say his name. It seemed to hang in the air.

'Yes,' Bruce continued. 'After what happened. He's the kind of chap that it might have stuck with. Not being able to get everybody out.'

Mirabelle stirred her tea, though the sugar cube had long since dissolved. It was as if a chill had settled. The table lapsed into awkward silence. Bruce peered at her. 'Oh lord. He hasn't told you. I'm sorry, Mirabelle. I assumed you knew. I mean, you must have wondered about the scar.'

Mirabelle felt herself blush. McGregor had always been silent about his wartime experiences and she'd been grateful for that – she didn't want to talk about hers either. Now, she looked mournfully at the pink diamond single stone on her engagement finger. It didn't sparkle this morning – the light was too low. Instead it looked as flat as glass. She knew she had to ask. 'Scar?' she said. 'What do you mean?'

Bruce and Eleanor looked at each other and then Eleanor laid her hand on top of Mirabelle's.

'Oh my dear,' she said. 'We assumed you two would have . . . you know. Enjoyed the fruits of love. I mean, that's why we put you in that wing, all on your own.'

Bruce squirmed in his seat. 'Really,' he said, 'Al ought to tell you himself.'

'Tell her what?' Alan came into the room, scenting the air with lavender. 'There is no way we're going to bag any pigeons in this,' he said, nodding towards the window. 'Though who wants sodden, miserable pigeons anyway? Bloaters.'

'I thought we could drive over to the Dougals' and fish

instead. Until it clears,' Bruce sounded bluff. 'But I have a couple of things to see to first.'

Eleanor jumped to her feet with a slice of thickly buttered toast still in her hand. 'I really ought to help you with that, darling,' she said.

They disappeared as, unhurried, McGregor perused the warming trays and piled a plate with scrambled egg. 'Sleep all right?' he asked.

Mirabelle waited. Her heart wasn't exactly pounding but she could feel her pulse. Every noise in the room seemed amplified – the serving spoon on the porcelain plate, the scrape of his chair as he sat at the table. She felt horribly flustered. 'Alan,' she said.

'Hmm?'

'I think it's time we talked about what you did during the war.'

McGregor turned over the paper. 'Oh dear,' he said. 'We ought to keep this away from Tash. Look, they got the times wrong and that's a terrible picture of the poor woman.'

'I mean it. If we're going to be married, we have to be open.'

McGregor put back the newspaper and laid down his fork. 'Right,' he said. 'And are you prepared to be open too?'

He had a good point. Mirabelle had never talked about what she'd done during the war. Not to anybody. Her war had mostly been spent in Whitehall and she'd never lied about that, but she had signed the Official Secrets Act and there wasn't a lot she could talk about – not that, in truth, she had any inclination to. And then there was Jack. Darling Jack. She had loved him through the conflict and after it, despite the fact that he was married. He had been the love of her life and quite suddenly, after everything he'd been through – naval intelligence and a stint at Nuremberg – he'd died of a cardiac arrest in the street. And for a long time she'd wanted to die too. Some things, she thought, were best not shared with the man you intended to marry. 'Is what you did secret for a reason?' she asked quietly. 'Is it secret for the public good?'

McGregor cast his eyes to the ceiling. 'Not even close,' he said. It's difficult to talk about, Mirabelle, that's all.' She kept her eyes on him. 'I kept thinking that you were bound to notice and that we would talk about it then.'

'Notice what?'

McGregor sighed. He got up and closed the door. Then he put his foot on to one of the chairs and, with awkward fingers, pulled up his trouser leg to reveal a patch of uneven skin on his calf. It was a painful-looking scar about the size of Mirabelle's palm. Her heart lurched. How had she never noticed? How?

'There was a fire,' he said quickly, without meeting her eyes. 'Actually, the fire was my fault. It didn't happen at the port in Edinburgh where I told you I was stationed. I was in Glasgow at Clydebank before that – early in the war in '39. When the bombing started our bond was hit. The Clyde was a target – with all the shipyards. By the end of the war the whole place was just rubble, but then, well, I was supposed to be in charge. It was only for a few months – I was due to go into the navy but they wouldn't take me after what happened and well, this took a long time to heal.' He indicated his leg. 'The warehouse blew up. Several fires broke out – in the offices and some of the stores. I didn't get everyone out – we had a procedure, but I wasn't prepared and I gave the order too late. I went in to try to save people but they were beyond . . . I got oil on my leg and it set alight. That's how this happened. They said I was lucky. Lucky! I didn't care about my stupid leg. All that mattered was the women in there.' His eyes were hard now. He was trying not to cry. 'They all died.' He couldn't look at her. 'If you want to call off our engagement, I'd understand.'

Mirabelle touched his skin, tracing the scar with her fingers. The livid craters on the surface felt dead. It did not seem part of the man she thought she knew. She suddenly remembered a performance of *The Tempest* at the Garrick when she was at school. The actor who played Caliban had crawled across the stage, twisted and ugly. 'I never noticed,' she said. 'Is it sore?'

He shook his head. 'It's not a part of the body one generally spends time on.' He looked guilty. 'The truth is I didn't want you to notice. I didn't want to have this conversation. I left my socks on. I got up in the mornings and fetched you a cup of tea or went into another room. I made sure the light was out,' he said bitterly. 'It's so ugly. And worse is what it means – I'm marked for life by the night I let everybody down, Belle. I thought I was so smart – freshly qualified in a spanking new uniform. I was so young.'

'Qualified in what?'

'I was an accountant. That's why they put me in charge of the place. I was supposed to keep an eye on procurement.'

'We're engaged to be married, Alan. Did you think I was so shallow, I wouldn't love you because of a scar?'

'Of course not.'

'Did you think I'd never see it?'

'I should have told you. But you're so beautiful. I watch you sometimes when you're asleep. It never seemed the right time to admit—'

'That you're not perfect?' She managed a slim smile. 'It must have hurt.'

'I walked with a stick for a while. I know it's monstrous. Every time I see it, it reminds me that it's my fault fifteen women are dead. Can you forgive me?'

She took a moment. When she thought of the things she loved about McGregor, it was his bravery she admired most. And he had proved himself brave – four years ago he'd taken a bullet that had probably saved her life. He'd put hundreds of criminals behind bars, including members of his own force. But he hadn't been brave about this. He hadn't trusted her. 'It's not the scar. It's the lie,' she said. 'I think I've always known you were holding something back.' She tried not to cry but tears were threatening to spill.

McGregor's face twisted. 'I was just a kid. All the emphasis was on not panicking. Keep calm, you know. If I'd been a minute quicker . . . Even if I had saved one person and it was fourteen dead or thirteen or twelve. And instead all that was on my mind was productivity. I weighed the risk wrongly. If only—'

'You can't torture yourself with maybes,' Mirabelle cut in. 'Especially not about the Blitz.' If there was one thing the war had taught her, it was that. McGregor had always seemed so honest. And this was important. This had formed him. The question wasn't whether she could forgive him, but whether she would be able to trust him again. Did she know him at all, if this had been on his mind all these years and he'd never said a word?

'I recuperated in Edinburgh,' he continued. 'There was hardly any bombing there. They should never have let me near responsibility again, of course, but they were short of men at the docks and I was no good for fighting. So they gave me a second chance and, after that, I moved to the police force. I'm sorry, darling. It got to the point where I should have told you and I hadn't. I didn't know how to.'

'I need time to think,' she said, her voice matter of fact as she rose from the table.

Momentarily, she touched his arm. It was difficult to square this. He'd never lied before and she'd known him for more than seven years. He was a good officer – too careful, if anything, but now that made sense. This had been between them all the time. Was McGregor's secret the reason she had found it so difficult to commit?

'I'm going for a walk,' she said.

She left the room. When she glanced back through the open door, he was sitting at the table, wide eyed and devastated. She felt like a fool that she hadn't noticed the scar. How could she feel as close to him as she had last night and not have known? This, she realised, defined so much about him. The cold menace that she caught a glimpse of now and then, just below the surface, as if he was angry. Well, he was. He was angry with himself. Did all the times he'd tried to stop her getting involved in his cases, hark back to the women he hadn't protected? No wonder he was always trying to keep her away from his investigations.

In the hallway, she picked her yellow coat off the hook and grabbed an umbrella from the stand. Outside, the rain was running in rivulets off the driveway and pooling on the grass. There was no point in putting up the umbrella – the wind was too strong. It was like standing under a waterfall. Mirabelle cut in the opposite direction to the one she'd taken with McGregor the day before, striding behind the house on to a laneway pockmarked with puddles that reflected the slate-grey sky. As she rounded the corner, the plants in the orangery were vivid blurs of green through the glass. There was only a single policeman now. They couldn't search the grounds in this weather and a storm like this would destroy any evidence. The world was washing itself clean.

Mirabelle kept going. Along the muddy lane she discovered a complex of old stables that had been converted into storerooms and a garage. The umbrella was useless but she held it aloft anyway. As she progressed she felt droplets of rainwater dripping off her hair, slipping down her neck and under her clothes. Beyond the old stables, there was another building across a cobbled yard. Blurrily, through the glass, she spotted Eleanor and Bruce sitting on opposite sides of a desk. As Mirabelle passed, Eleanor jumped up and appeared in the doorway. 'Mirabelle!' she called.

Mirabelle wanted to keep going but she was freezing already and she didn't want to be rude. She stopped but couldn't quite bring herself to fake a smile. 'Oh for heaven's sake,' Eleanor exclaimed as she ran across the cobbles on to the lane and grabbed Mirabelle by the arm, pulling her inside. It felt warmer under cover. Mirabelle put down the umbrella and a pool of water formed on the floor. The weather had suited her confusion, and now she felt becalmed. Though indoors again, she realised that walking off on her own might not be the best idea. After all, there was a murderer abroad.

Bruce stood self-consciously in the hallway as his wife ushered Mirabelle inside.

'Umbrellas are no use in this. It's wellington boot and gabardine weather,' Eleanor said with a smile. She had not taken her own advice and had got soaked in the seconds it had taken to pull Mirabelle indoors. 'Come in,' she gestured kindly.

Beyond the small entrance hall, there was an office. An old oak desk dominated the room; on it a large Bakelite phone and papers scattered about. A single electric bar glowed in a freestanding heater. Behind the desk, open shelving housed several folders and a few books about sheep farming and distilling and some with Latin titles, which must have been about the law. Beside the shelves, there were a couple of modernist paintings. 'I co-opted the estate office,' Eleanor said as she tidied away the newspaper. 'I mean, Bruce has his study, don't you darling? The holy of holies. And I didn't want a silly day room with a sewing box. So I came out here. That's a Patrick Heron,' she gestured towards one of the paintings.

'It makes me feel itchy,' Bruce said with a grin.

'I love it,' Eleanor cut in.

Mirabelle removed her coat. Beneath it her clothes were damp. She wasn't sure what to say.

'Look at us.' Eleanor laughed. She opened a door that led into a lavatory and came back with two small hand-towels. 'Here.' She gave one to Mirabelle. 'It's not love's young dream, is it? I'm sorry. We didn't know that he hadn't told you. Bruce feels terrible. It would have been better if Alan had done it in his own time.'

'Do you think he would have?'

Bruce shrugged. 'I'd hope so,' he said.

Mirabelle half-heartedly dried her hair and wiped her hands. She sank into a green tweed chair on the other side of the desk. It niggled her that Tash had apparently taken her godmother's death better than she was taking this news about McGregor. 'I know it's spoilt of me,' she said. 'But if there was one thing I had to say about Alan, it would have been that he was always honest.'

'He's ashamed, I suppose,' Bruce replied.

'About the disfigurement or what happened?' Mirabelle

realised that she had used words that excused him. She'd said 'what happened' rather than 'what he did' and what McGregor had described was entirely his own responsibility.

Eleanor smiled kindly. 'Go on,' she chided her husband. 'We girls will be fine.'

Bruce got up. 'If you're sure,' he said. As he closed the door, Eleanor leaned in, her hands flat on the desktop. 'I admire you, saving yourself like that. For marriage, I mean. I certainly didn't.'

Mirabelle's throat opened and she let out a sob. 'I didn't save myself,' she wailed. 'I didn't at all. I knew he was holding something back and I wondered if maybe I didn't really love him. Because he's not my first. I mean, at my age! And all this time I can't believe that I didn't notice. Everybody says I'm so observant, but I didn't notice this one bloody thing. Not at all.'

Eleanor sat down with a bump. Behind her the windows were foggy with condensation. The figure of Bruce had disappeared. 'How?' she asked.

'The scar's on his calf and I suppose it's not a part of the body that gets all that much attention,' Mirabelle said. 'It was mostly dark when we . . . you know. He usually keeps his socks on. I knew there was something. I feel like an idiot.'

Eleanor let out a giggle. 'Socks,' she repeated.

Mirabelle felt her heart lurch and then she found suddenly that she was laughing too. 'I know it's ridiculous,' she heaved. 'But he always got up before I did. He used to fetch me a cup of tea.'

'How long has it been?'

'Years. It's been years. I mean, it's just awful.'

'But you don't live together?'

'No.'

Eleanor put her hands up to her face. Her eyes sparkled.

'Well, what I say to Bruce when something comes out, is "that's one to tell the grandkids."'

'What do you mean "when something comes out"?' Mirabelle sniffed.

'Oh, honey.' Eleanor reached into a drawer in her desk and extracted a bottle of spirits and two glasses. 'I got the distillery to make vodka out of the potatoes from the back field. It's good stuff, though Bruce won't drink it. Well, he thinks he doesn't drink it, but I mix Bloody Marys. They're all the rage in Manhattan.'

She poured two small glasses of clear liquid.

'Slainte,' she said. 'That's chin-chin in Gaelic.'

Mirabelle knocked back the vodka. It was smooth but it made her throat burn. Still, she didn't feel cold any more and the taste was sweet and buttery. 'Now that's breakfast,' Eleanor said good-naturedly and refilled the glasses. 'Welcome to Scotland. I hope you can forgive Alan McGregor and become my cousin-in-law.'

Mirabelle gave a half-shrug. 'I don't know,' she said.

'Does it really change the man you thought he was?'

'Maybe. Do you know what happened? Exactly what happened?'

Eleanor took another sip. 'Bruce told me the family stories – you know, when we first met. Then when we knew you were coming up, he reminisced a bit.'

'Where did you two meet?' Mirabelle asked. It struck her that perhaps Eleanor and Bruce's courtship could offer guidance.

Eleanor refilled the glasses. 'London, believe it or not. I was reporting for an American paper and I ran into him. Four years ago this spring.'

'Ran into him?'

'I was curious. I wanted to understand privilege, real, old world privilege, so I took myself lots of places. Westminster, of course. The Albert Hall and the Victoria and Albert Museum. I strolled past Buckingham Palace because you can't go in without an invitation. And then I came to The Ritz.'

Mirabelle laughed. 'You went to The Ritz to understand privilege?'

'I was fierce. And furious, actually. I mean, here was this country that had set up the health service – that's what I was reporting on. I mean, what a wonderful thing, right? Helping everyone – but mostly helping the poor. Changing lives. And yet, elsewhere there was all this privilege and that didn't square. So I was in The Ritz, just walking through the hallway, and out on Piccadilly there was a demonstration. People were shouting and the police had formed a cordon. Of course, in the hotel everyone was ignoring it, except this one guy.'

'Bruce?'

'Bruce. He put down his paper and stared out of the window. And then, he waved, Mirabelle, at one of the protesters. So I went over. "Excuse me," I said. "But do you support that cause?" And he was horrified. "Oh no," he said, and he pointed through the window, "but that young fellow is the son of a friend of mine, and he does." I thought it was the most wonderful example of, well, Britishness.'

Mirabelle started to cry.

'Oh dear.' Eleanor found a handkerchief in her pocket. 'It's rather damp, I'm afraid,' she said as she handed it over.

'So you fell in love?'

'Not then. I thought he must be the most fearful snob. But we got talking and he took me for dinner and he was charming. Then about a week later he asked me up here for a long weekend, and that's the thing. I mean, there's The Ritz and Westminster and all of that, but here he is, making things happen – looking after this place. He's not just living off it like some feudal lord. Truth is there isn't all that much money, though nobody would believe it.'

'He says you're the one who makes things happen.'

'Well, I geed things up. I brought the place into the twentieth century after we ran away together and tied the knot.'

'Where did you get married?'

'Edinburgh. There was literally nobody there. We were in a rush and we didn't want any fuss. Afterwards we came home here and got started on what I think of as our real life.'

'Attracting American business to the cashmere mill?'

'That one hasn't worked out so well, has it? But the French came and that resulted in pretty good orders. And I geed up the distillery and helped make the farms more profitable – looking at yields.' Eleanor raised her glass. 'And I started the tweed collective.'

'It's a collective?'

'Yes. I read about collectives – they're a good idea, don't you think? Bruce can't expect to make money out of everything. I mean he owns part of the distillery and the mill and he gets the farm rents too, so I got him to stick in a few hundred towards the collective – to put something back. I think it's important that people have ownership. The papers are so gloomy about everything. I mean, if they drop the bomb, they drop the bomb. What are we going to do? Hide under the kitchen table? I don't think so. We just have to do our best with the small things. Everyone has secrets, Mirabelle. Every marriage has them. Alan is a good man. I don't suppose anyone knows him better than Bruce. Bruce adores him and I trust my husband's judgement.'

Mirabelle blew her nose. Across the courtyard the blurred figure of Susan dashed towards the office, her apron flying in the wind. She burst through the door, her mousy hair two shades darker on account of the rain.

'Mrs Gillies said you hadn't had enough breakfast, ma'am,' she said, and withdrew a Thermos flask and two plastic cups. 'She made you coffee.'

'Thank you, Susan. It's a terrible day.'

Susan looked confused. 'Miss Orlova died yesterday, ma'am—'

'I meant the weather,' Eleanor cut in. 'Of course, today will not be so terrible as yesterday. Even if we have a hurricane.'

Susan opened the Thermos flask and poured two servings into the plastic cups. Steam rose in thick curls as she reached into her pocket and brought out a container of milk. She seemed, Mirabelle thought, agitated.

'Thank you,' Eleanor said. 'Make sure to get warm back in the kitchen. You're soaked.'

The girl loitered, moving from foot to foot. 'I had hoped to talk to you, ma'am.'

'Yes?'

'It's a private matter.' Susan's eyes slipped towards Mirabelle, and Mirabelle wondered if she intended to complain about her and McGregor – houseguests bedhopping in the night. It seemed faintly ridiculous, especially now.

Eleanor's eyes danced. A slender smile slipped across her lips. 'Might it wait until after Miss Bevan and I have finished? You seem most exercised, Susan. If you are still agitated about yesterday you may, if you wish, go home to visit your family. I know the events of the last twenty-four hours have been difficult.'

Susan's cheeks flared. She bobbed a kind of half-curtsey. 'Yes, ma'am,' she said, and disappeared out of the door.

Mirabelle wrapped her fingers around the plastic cup, which felt comfortingly warm. 'Do Susan and Mrs Gillies live over the yard?'

'Right above here. Two bedrooms, a sitting room, a bathroom and a galley kitchen. I did it out when I arrived. It was positively Victorian but now it's quite cosy.'

Mirabelle noted that meant that the women were on the wrong side of the house to see anything in the orangery. 'I don't suppose the police are making much progress,' she said.

'I don't suppose they are.'

'There won't be any evidence left now. On the ground.'

'I don't know how we're going to get over this.' Eleanor sighed. 'I can't bring myself to go into the orangery. I feel as if there's some kind of presence. I mean, I hardly knew Nina, but it's so ghastly. What would you advise?'

'Me?'

'Yes. I can tell you've lived through things. What's the worst thing you ever saw?'

Mirabelle sighed. 'Nuremberg,' she whispered. 'The trials.'

'You were there?'

'I assisted one of the prosecutors. It was horrible.'

'And I'll bet you haven't told Alan.'

Mirabelle shook her head. 'It's still classified. I shouldn't say anything. But you're very easy to talk to, somehow.'

'Do you get nightmares?'

'Not for years.'

'Well, that's it then. I'm going to stop being such a baby going on about Nina after what you must have seen. I mean one dead Russian! One! What was I thinking?'

Mirabelle managed a smile.

'That's my girl,' Eleanor said, and she stared out of the

window. Raindrops were bouncing off the surface of the laneway as Susan disappeared through the back door and the car drove past, raising a wave as it cut through the puddles. 'That's the boys off fishing. They'll be gone most of the day. Your Mr McGregor will have time to think. And so will you.'

Chapter 6

Happiness was born a twin

Mirabelle curled up in the drawing room alone for the rest of the morning. The fire shifted as it burned in the grate, and outside the window the whirlwind of grey provided a counterpoint to the glowing embers. She watched the rain lashing down and the sky slowly lightening as the downpour gradually softened into drizzle. At midday Tash came down and, with a languid 'Good morning', installed herself on the sofa opposite. 'I missed them, didn't I?'

'There was no shooting,' Mirabelle said. 'The rain was too heavy. They went fishing instead.'

Tash wrinkled her nose. It seemed that fishing did not fulfil her requirement for violent release. The *Inverness Courier* had been removed, but she picked up *The Times* and, skipping past the headlines, turned to the arts pages.

Mirabelle was grateful the girl didn't want to engage in conversation. She held a book open in front of her but she wasn't reading. Instead she ran over everything McGregor had said that morning and the occasions when she might have noticed his leg or have asked about his war. His revelation seemed to call the whole of their relationship into question.

Mirabelle had always been intrigued by scars. Her father had taken a bullet during the Great War. He'd let her touch the scar once, running her tiny finger over the indent between his ribs until her mother had pulled her away and said it was too morbid. Her parents never discussed her father's four-year absence from her childhood, and Mirabelle had been too young to remember anything except the excitement the day her father came home. He had a tan. 'India,' he'd said, and it hadn't seemed odd to her because she was too small to have expected him to be fighting in France. Besides, her father was a hero, wherever he'd been – he had the medals to prove it. The world was simpler in those days.

When it came down to it, it wasn't McGregor's injury that troubled her. It was the secret he'd withheld. What would it be like, she wondered, making love to him in the light now? Knowing all of him – a man who had misjudged his duty and spent the rest of his life atoning for it. What would it be like to kiss him? It surprised her that she was prepared to consider it.

'I think I'll go down and see my cow,' Tash announced out of the blue, folding the newspaper and getting to her feet.

'Your cow?' Mirabelle found herself smiling.

Tash sighed. 'Well, she's not mine, but she is magnificent. She's one of those Highland cows. You know, with the horns.'

'You can't go on your own,' Mirabelle said, thinking of how she had chided herself for setting off along the back lane earlier or standing out in the darkness last night. 'I mean, we don't know who could be out there.'

Tash nodded. 'Do you think it's safe if we both go?'

They pulled on wellington boots from a collection under the stairs and tied matching green silk squares over their hair. Mirabelle mentioned to the police officer that they were going for a walk. 'We're proper countrywomen now,' Tash said as she slammed the front door and set off down the hill through the thick grass. She looped her arm through Mirabelle's. The ground was soft and the air was fresh. The last of the downpour fell in a drizzle as fine as a cobweb and a calm silence overtook the landscape as they tramped onwards. Mirabelle scanned the vista – it didn't seem threatening. It was daytime. Still, it was never as quiet as this in Brighton because of the sea. The sound of the tide washing back and forth on the pebbles woke her almost every morning. It should have felt more restful here, she thought, in such silence. But not today. 'Nina said this weather was good for the skin,' Tash said stoutly. 'There are places in Russia where it's wet all the time and the women are known for their beauty.'

'I suppose it must be good, when you think about it,' Mirabelle replied. 'All that moisture.'

Tash cut across a field at the bottom of the driveway and Mirabelle followed. The ground was uneven, random blades of grass spraying water droplets like diamonds. At a wooden fence, she climbed up and perched on the planking, beyond which a huge Highland cow stood, completely sodden. The animal's coat had darkened in the rain to a deep tan, and drops of water flew from the ends when she moved. Mirabelle thought she looked annoyed, though she realised that was an assumption based on how she would have felt if she'd been caught out in such bad weather. The field was entirely treeless. 'Isn't she gorgeous?' Tash said, her cheeks shining.

Mirabelle agreed. The cow stared at them as if the rain had been their fault.

'Nina said there are black ones, but I like this brown colour. It has . . .' the girl searched for the word, 'texture.'

'You seem better today,' Mirabelle said.

Tash shrugged. 'He's still out here, isn't he? Somewhere. But what else are we going to do?'

Mirabelle laid a comforting hand on the girl's arm. 'They'll find him.'

'When I woke up this morning, I didn't remember what had happened,' Tash said. 'When I did, it was as if my stomach was flattened. I told myself, at least it was quick. It was probably painful, but it was quick, right?' She sniffed and then wiped her nose on the sleeve of her jacket, waiting for Mirabelle's reply.

'Yes – it would have been,' Mirabelle reassured the girl, though she knew that speed was relative. Cutting off her air supply meant that Nina would have lost consciousness in a few seconds, but it would have taken a few minutes for her to actually die. She decided against filling Tash in on the medical reality – nobody knew what the victims of strangulation were aware of as they lay there, apparently out cold. Instead she elected to push for more information. 'Tash, can you think of anyone who would have wanted to kill your godmother?'

Tash shifted her position. The cow looked at her as if this was a personal insult, then slowly turned and sauntered to the opposite corner of the field. 'People were jealous of her in New York. Her family got out with money. Not all the Whites were so lucky.'

'White Russians, you mean?'

'Yes – the opposite of the Reds – thousands of families got out in '17 and '18 and most of us penniless. There are duchesses who've become seamstresses. Actually, Nina employed a couple at one point. There are princes hanging around the Waldorf Astoria on Fifth Avenue, hoping to pick up an American heiress. My grandfather was lucky – so was Nina's. They changed their roubles to American dollars before the currency devalued, so our families had something at least. They couldn't have known. It was terrible for most people. They brought out their roubles too late and couldn't change them. Even if they got out diamonds – the market was flooded. You can still buy Fabergé for a pittance because there was so much for sale. In the end, people stopped trying to sell it. What was the point? There are broke, old Russian women, sipping borscht in Brooklyn, who are just covered in Fabergé. So people were jealous of Nina and Niko, for what they had. And that they made more too. Nina made a lot of money. She had a great eye.'

'And Niko?'

'He made his mint in transport. He bought a firm that runs a fleet of trucks and grew it. Hundreds of people work for him now – drivers and mechanics. His great-grandfather made money investing in the railways in the old country. I guess this was Niko's version of the same thing.'

This, Mirabelle realised, was interesting, but not specific enough to be a motive. 'I know it's horrible to consider, but can you think of anyone who actually wanted your godmother dead – a single person? Can you think of any arguments she may have had? Something more . . . precise?'

'We'd only been here a week when she died. The people at the cashmere mill loved her. I mean, she swanned in and she bought. She sweet-talked them about ply widths, for heaven's sake. Apart from that, we hadn't seen anyone except for Eleanor and Bruce and their friends.'

'Which friends?'

'We had dinner one night – Tuesday, I think. It was fun, actually. It was just the locals – the neighbours. One couple had driven from Inverness. Eleanor mixed cocktails and a few people stayed.'

'Bloody Marys?'

'They were good. How did you know?'

Tash wiped her eyes – a tear or two. Then she jumped down from the fence and began waving, as if she was signalling an aircraft. Mirabelle peered. On the other side of the field a figure cut to the east. He moved quickly given the unevenness of the ground. 'Gregory!' Tash called, jumping up and down. 'Gregory!'

In the distance, Gregory either didn't hear or he ignored her. He disappeared into a patch of trees. Tash seemed downhearted. 'I wonder where he's going.'

'You're fond of him.'

'He's all I have of home,' she replied, though Mirabelle wondered if it was more than that. The girl wasn't as hard-headed as she seemed, talking about marrying a rich man and then doting on a family retainer. This worried her. If his alibi proved unsound, Gregory was the most likely murderer, as Bruce had pointed out the night before.

'He's certainly attractive,' she said doubtfully, wondering if this had played a part in events.

Tash waved off the comment. 'Muscle,' she said vaguely. 'Mirabelle, I know it's creepy but I have a favour to ask. My books are at the lodge and I don't want to go on my own to fetch them. It seems chicken to have someone else do it. Would you come with me? Do you think it's safe?'

'Yes. Of course,' Mirabelle replied. 'The two of us together.'

They walked down the hill and through the trees. The air smelled of crushed pine cones, and where they could see flashes of the burn it was swollen into a torrent. Bunches of twigs – detritus of the storm – clung to the bank.

'You said you liked staying down here,' Mirabelle said.

'The main house is fancier, but it was fun – Nina and I living in a cottage in the woods. Like a fairytale. And that funny bath in the hut outside.'

'Yes, I wondered about that.'

'There was something great about it. Like camping. One evening I left the door open so I could see the stars. Then every day we'd tramp down to the village to fetch supplies. They make this bread – bannock, they call it. It's good. Truth is, it's the most time I'd spent with Nina in ages.'

'Didn't you spend time together at home?'

'She was always working and I have my friends.'

'I had the impression you were close.'

'We are! We were. God, just walking down here is giving me goosebumps.'

'You said Nina didn't like the lodge?'

'She would have preferred to stay in the big house.'

'That's our fault, I'm afraid. Eleanor had this idea that we should be on our own up there, like a proper family.'

Tash shrugged. 'I guess we got to stay alone – like a proper family too.'

The lodge remained unlocked. The two leather suitcases from the wardrobe had been packed and lay in the tiny hallway. Tash stood frozen on the threshold. Mirabelle gave her a moment and then touched the girl's arm. 'All right?'

'We were talking right here, you know, Nina and I, that last evening, sitting in those chairs. We had a discussion about what to do if the bomb dropped. I mean,' she rolled her eyes, 'what *can* you do, right? I said I'd go out, into the fields and watch it coming, and Nina just said, "God,

I can't imagine dying in this hole." And in the end she did, of course. Not right here, but not in New York. She would have wanted to go in New York. In the Stork Club. Wearing a marvellous frock.'

Mirabelle squeezed Tash's forearm. 'I'm sorry.'

'Well, I guess all we can do now is clear up. Gillies said she'd have Susan see to Nina's things,' she said. 'She's a very good servant, isn't she?'

'And your books?' The bed had been stripped and the bedding removed. The bedside cabinets lay bare, the drawers open. The police had been here, Mirabelle thought. They'd searched the place. Of course they had.

'I suppose they're airing everything,' Tash said. 'Oh lord. Susan must have packed my books with Nina's stuff. Let's leave it. It seems gruesome to sort through her things.'

'Why don't you check the hut?'

'The books won't be there.'

'Check all the same.'

As Tash wandered through the cottage, Mirabelle retrieved the notebook she'd hidden the day before. Then she clicked open the suitcases. Tash's books were on top. Expertly, she removed them and checked the rest of the case, running her hands down the side. Then, quickly, she tried to shift the tiny lock on Nina's notebook with no success, until, hearing Tash coming back, she tucked it inside and clicked the case closed again. This would at least get it back to the house. She could retrieve it another time. 'Here,' she said, handing Tash the novels. 'Someone will come and get the rest of it, I'm sure.'

'Thanks. You're a honey. Let's get out of here, shall we?' The girl gave a little shiver, her eyes misty.

They walked back up the hill. The grass was slippery after

the storm, the bloated mud swelling through the green. On the other side of the glen the sky was clearing, and a long patch of blue had appeared. Mirabelle found herself unexpectedly out of breath as she climbed towards the house. At the top, Tash turned to take in the view.

'I won't go down there again,' she said.

Eleanor sat alone at the table with *The Times* propped against a pair of Georgian silver candlesticks when they returned. 'I wondered what had happened to you two. I feel we need to keep tabs on everyone for safety. We rang the gong for ages. Then the constable said you had gone for a walk. I said to Gillies that at least you were together. I'm glad you're back. We might as well cheer up this rotten day,' she said, and headed for the drinks cabinet and the silver cocktail shaker.

Tash downed a martini in one. Eleanor laughed. 'That was obviously required,' she said. 'I know I promised you a trip to the cashmere mill, Mirabelle, but it's not on today, is it? Not now.'

'We can go another time.'

'I want to come,' Tash said firmly. 'I need to finalise Nina's order. We can't let the boutiques down.'

Eleanor put her arm round Tash and gave her a squeeze. 'You're such a good girl,' she said, as if she was speaking to a puppy. Then she handed her another martini. After the second glass, Tash disappeared down the hall in search of the lavatory.

'Feeling any better?' Eleanor asked.

Mirabelle toyed with the stem of her glass. She was grateful for Eleanor's discretion in not discussing what had happened in front of Tash. 'I keep going back to conversations we've had, or things he's done and seeing it in the light of this,' she admitted. 'I know it's silly – I mean, look what Tash is going through.'

'Not at all. If there's anything I can do . . .'

'I feel as if I hardly know him. Apart from anything else, I always thought he was a city boy.'

'Oh, he is. Alan wasn't brought up out here – Deidre, his mother, was. She was the eldest by a year, I think, though daughters don't inherit in families like these. I don't approve. She must have been spunky. She married against her father's will. McGregor's father, Thomas, came to survey the bridge over the burn and ran away with the laird's daughter. I suppose the family would have seen it as marrying beneath her, though who on earth a girl brought up in the middle of nowhere was supposed to marry, I'm not sure. Anyway, it was a love match – must have been.'

Mirabelle stared at her ring. How would the Bevans have taken to Deidre McGregor, she thought? She knew her parents would have considered Mirabelle marrying a policeman beneath her. They would have preferred Jack – a naval officer, whose family was at home on the smart side of London. But then, if she'd married Jack, he would have had to divorce his first wife, and her parents wouldn't have liked that at all.

Eleanor continued. 'As I understand it, Bruce never met Alan's father, or at least not that he can remember. But his mother used to bring Alan here for holidays. You can just see them, can't you? Two boys rambling about the estate – up and down to the village.'

'Bruce is an only child?'

'He had a younger sister, but she died as a baby.'

'Do you want children, Eleanor?'

'It hasn't happened yet, but there's still time. Do you?'

'I think that's passed.'

'So you want a man who's devoted? It's the trust, huh?'

Mirabelle nodded. Eleanor was perceptive.

Tash clattered back down the hallway. 'That martini has gone to my head,' she said and flung herself on to the sofa.

'That martini was two martinis,' Eleanor pointed out. She moved towards the window. 'Oh look,' she said. 'A taxi.'

'What?' Tash sounded as if she was half-singing the word.

'The nearest taxi is in Inverness – who'd be coming from there?'

The taxi pulled up a little away from the house and a man got out. He was tall, wearing a well-tailored navy coat with a black shearling collar and a homburg.

'Oh god,' said Tash, standing as if to attention. 'That's Uncle Niko.'

'He made smart work of the journey. All the way from New York inside of twenty-four hours,' Eleanor said, checking the clock on the mantelpiece doubtfully, as if it wasn't possible. 'Bruce said he'd be in tonight at the earliest.'

'Oh, that's Niko for you,' Tash replied. 'That's exactly what he's like.'

The driver removed two suitcases from the car and followed the impressive figure to the door. Eleanor glanced in the direction of the back of the house as the bell rang. 'We'd best leave it to Gillies,' she said, suddenly standing on ceremony. They waited uncomfortably as they heard Gillies walking down the hallway, then she opened the drawing-room door with the man's coat over her arm. 'Baron Orlov,' she said, and sniffed, as if she couldn't believe the words she had just uttered.

Nicholas Orlov swept past her. He was greying and extremely handsome, with a tidy moustache and dark eyes.

He bowed formally. Eleanor offered her hand and he kissed it. Mirabelle simply nodded. Then Niko threw his arms around Tash and said something in Russian. Tash hugged him and when she stepped back there were tears on her cheeks again.

'Everyone here speaks English, Uncle Niko,' she chided.

'My apologies.' When he spoke English his accent was American.

'Oh please,' Eleanor waved away the formalities. 'You must have had a ghastly journey. Have you eaten? Can I offer you a drink?'

'Thank you.' He clicked his heels, as if he was in the military. 'A drink would be most welcome.'

Eleanor reloaded the cocktail shaker and iced more gin. Niko smacked his lips. 'This is excellent. Thank you,' he said. 'Most refreshing.'

'You got here quickly.'

'I came at once. I want to see her, of course.'

'Nobody gets the boat any more,' Tash sighed. 'I mean, it's so old-fashioned. With these new planes, people will be able to get anywhere in a few hours. Well, rich people, anyway.'

'I'm afraid the police have removed Nina's body,' Eleanor explained.

'Have they caught the man who killed her?'

'That's rather foxing them. It's foxing everyone.'

'Well, if I can't see the body, I want to see Gregory.'

'He's staying in the village. We can send word.'

'Where was he when it happened?'

'In Glasgow on business. Nina sent him.'

Niko let out a low tutting sound, as if this was an unacceptable development and his sister's murder was only to be expected in such circumstances. 'He was to stay with her at all times. It's too close,' he said.

'Close?'

'Uncle Niko means to Russia,' Tash cut in. 'Geographically, we're very close to Russia.'

'In Scotland?' Eleanor was incredulous.

'The Reds,' Niko said. 'I told Nina it was dangerous. I said she could go to Southern Europe. But here it's so far north – an easy journey by sea from Moscow.'

'Moscow is landlocked.' Eleanor sounded confused.

'I mean the orders come from Moscow,' Niko brushed off her comment. 'If the Reds were ever to expand their territory, this would be an easy target.'

'An invasion? In Scotland?' Eleanor's tone continued disbelieving.

Tash sighed loudly. 'I told you,' she said. 'The Reds. Everywhere.'

'What do you know? You weren't there,' Niko fumed.

'You were five, Uncle Niko,' Tash stood up to him.

'Everyone knows how dangerous they are. These terrible atomic weapons and now Khrushchev is threatening America! Next door in New York, the Humbolts have dug a shelter in their garden.'

'I'm surprised you haven't followed suit.'

Niko put down his empty glass. 'I apologise,' he said coldly. 'Family feuds are so tiresome for onlookers.'

Eleanor shrugged this off. 'It's great you feel comfortable enough to speak openly,' she said. 'Gillies has prepared a room. The police haven't said when they will release poor Nina's body but you are welcome to stay as long as you'd like.'

Niko clicked his heels again. 'Thank you.'

'I'll show you upstairs,' Tash offered. 'No point in standing on ceremony.'

'Would you, dear?' Eleanor smiled. 'And in the meantime, I'll see if we can rustle up Gregory. You can speak to him in my husband's study, Baron. I'll have Gillies let you know when he arrives.'

Niko and Tash trooped into the hallway as Eleanor rang the bell for service. A moment later a disgruntled Mrs Gillies arrived.

'Could you send to the village for Gregory, please?' Eleanor asked.

'I can't find Susan anywhere, madam,' Gillies said.

Eleanor paused. 'Oh, I told her she could go home,' she remembered. 'I should have passed that on. She seemed upset this morning.'

Gillies loitered. 'I can't run everything on my own two days in a row, madam, what with the extra guests.'

Eleanor sighed. 'Sorry, Mrs Gillies. I thought I was being kind, but I wasn't very kind to you, was I? Perhaps you could send for Gregory by telephone? Baron Orlov wants to see him.'

Mrs Gillies did not look hopeful. There were only two telephones in the village – a box outside the shop and one at the police station. 'I'll do my best,' she said.

'Thank you. And I want you to know I appreciate everything,' Eleanor gushed. 'I expect this month Mr Robertson will see to it that you receive a bonus.'

Gillies's expression made it clear that money was not the question. It was a matter of principle. 'Youngsters just don't have the grit,' she said, turning to leave the room.

Once she'd gone, Eleanor flopped on to the sofa. 'Oh dear,' she said. 'I'm not sure we'll be able to buy the old girl off. Though I don't agree with her about Susan not having the grit. Anyone who makes it down to Inverslain in this morning's weather deserves a medal.'

'Inverslain?'

'The village she comes from, further along the track. I just can't seem to crack this "lady of the manor" thing, Mirabelle. I hope all this isn't going to spoil your holiday.'

Mirabelle couldn't help but smile. A murder, grieving relations, a revelation about McGregor and a staffing crisis was hardly what they'd had in mind when they decided to come. 'Oh, not at all,' she said.

Eleanor let out a giggle. 'You're so English.' She smiled. 'I love it!'

Chapter 7

Belief is a wise wager

Mirabelle heard the car coming along the lane at the rear of the house at the end of the afternoon. She listened as the engine cut out and the sound of the doors slamming echoed on the damp air like gunshots. A few minutes later, McGregor walked into his room. He knocked on the adjoining door and hovered sheepishly in the frame, his cheeks ruddy.

'Did you catch anything?' she asked.

'Dinner is secure. The fishermen returned with three handsome salmon. Well, Bruce did, anyway. We also picked up company – the Dougals will be eating with us. I can ask Gillies to make you a tray, if you'd prefer? I'd quite understand if you don't want to come down.'

Mirabelle shook her head. 'I'm all right.'

'I'm not,' he said. 'I can't get you out of my mind. I'm so sorry, Belle.'

Mirabelle stared. It felt as if McGregor was a locked box, but then, she realised, perhaps she had liked that about him. What was wrong with her? People changed, after all. People learned. But to keep a secret for this long was a kind of betrayal – except, of course, she had secrets too.

'I feel like an idiot,' she said. 'I'm supposed to be so perceptive.'

McGregor's gaze fell to the carpet. 'The last thing I want is to make you feel foolish. I'm the stupid one. You're the most honourable woman I know.'

She shook her head. 'I've done plenty of things I'm ashamed of.' There were a lot more than fifteen skeletons in her closet.

McGregor shook his head. 'I'm glad Bruce told you. You'd have found out sometime.' He got down on his knees. 'Can you forgive me?'

Mirabelle's heart lurched. She hated the past intruding on them like this. 'God, it was a hundred years ago, Alan. I wish you'd told me. I don't like that you think of yourself as bad. I know all the good you've done.' She dropped to her knees on the floor beside him. 'It's just a shock. You've been racked with guilt for years and I didn't even notice.' She wanted to ask him to promise not to hide anything ever again, but it didn't seem fair when there was so much she had left unsaid.

McGregor smiled weakly. 'Some holiday I brought you on.'

'Oh, I don't know. I like solving murders . . .'

He laughed. 'You want to solve it. Of course you do.' He wrapped his arms around her. 'You and me both.'

'Well why not? We're good at it. Perhaps it would distract us.'

'A busman's holiday, you mean.'

She laid her head on his shoulder. Outside, the sky was darkening. A pale streak of purple flared across the sunset as the moon rose. This was how she kept her guilt at bay, she realised – by finding justice for people like Nina Orlova. They had that in common – it turned out it was McGregor's technique as well.

She was about to say something but the gong sounded for

109

dinner. McGregor jumped to his feet and held out his hand. 'We'd better get dressed,' he said.

The moment was gone. Mirabelle pulled a red satin sheath from her closet and disrobed untidily, stepping into her evening shoes and applying lipstick at the same time. Red had always suited her – just like Nina. It was a colour you could wear like a disguise. She chose a pair of diamond-drop earrings, like tiny stars. Then she surveyed herself in the mirror. Next door, McGregor fumbled with the buttons of his evening shirt. 'You go down!' he called. 'If we arrive flustered, they'll assume – you know.'

Mirabelle checked in the mirror once more. She didn't look in the least flustered. Maybe, she thought, we can just decide not to dwell on it. The war was over.

Jinx sat regally at the foot of the stairs, as if he was an ornament. Mirabelle petted him as she passed. The music on the air tonight was jazz, and there was laughter coming from the drawing room.

'Mirabelle!' Bruce hailed her as she appeared in the doorway. 'You look lovely.'

Eleanor was mixing more cocktails. The baron and Tash sat together on the sofa, Tash tonight arrayed in a demure, silver-grey cocktail dress. Her hair was fixed to one side with a circular diamanté clasp. Beside her, a grey-haired man with a long moustache sprang to his feet.

'This is our neighbour – Willie Dougal. Lord Dougal, but we don't stand on ceremony.' Bruce made the introduction and then turned to a woman Mirabelle hadn't immediately noticed, who was standing beside the window wearing a full-length, midnight-blue velvet dress that camouflaged her against the curtains. A wire-haired terrier wagged its tail at her feet. 'And this is Lady Dougal. Gwendolyn.'

'How do you do.' Mirabelle shook the woman's hand. 'Am I correct that you were here last week for dinner – with Tash and her godmother?'

'Four-and-twenty families.' Willie Dougal grinned. 'Just as in Jane Austen, Miss Bevan. That's the whole county. We dine together endlessly.'

'We've known each other since we were children,' Bruce explained.

'Not me,' Gwendolyn said. 'I met my husband at a house party. I'm from Argyll – an incomer.' She rounded the sofa and sat down opposite Niko and Tash. 'It's a terrible business. You must be devastated, Baron Orlov.'

Niko nodded. 'I spoke to our man this afternoon. I hold him responsible.'

It was, Mirabelle thought, quite common for the victim's family to seek to apportion the blame as quickly as possible, but the baron was being unfair – Nina had sent Gregory away.

'Do you mean the black man?' Gwendolyn Dougal's clipped west-coast accent dripped with enmity. 'I heard he helped deliver the McCrossan baby today. That's a curse on the poor child.'

'A curse?' Mirabelle's tone was incredulous.

'A black fairy at the feast.'

'Well at least Davina has had her baby. A lovely little girl,' Eleanor smoothed the water. 'She's lucky Gregory was about. He fetched the doctor who was out on another house-call – he got the man there within twenty minutes, I heard.'

Mirabelle remembered Gregory running through the trees on the other side of the field before lunch. He must have had some day, between that and the police interrogation he would have undergone and the pub landlady's waters breaking. 'Did you have a chance to speak to the police about Nina's funeral?' she asked.

Niko lit a cigarette. 'They said we'll get my sister's body back in a few days. We'll bury her at home. The airline is making the arrangements.'

McGregor strolled in, debonair in his evening suit. 'Am I the last?' he asked as if surprised. 'I apologise.' He shook Willie's hand and they clapped each other on the shoulder.

'We're wiser as well as older, I hope,' Willie said.

McGregor kissed Gwendolyn's hand. 'Lady Dougal.' Gwendolyn did not invite him to use her first name.

'I hear the fishing was a profitable endeavour.' Willie launched into conversation as McGregor eschewed the cocktail tray and poured himself a whisky with a dash of soda.

'I've missed it, if I'm honest,' McGregor said.

'Catching vagabonds on the south coast isn't a patch on the Highland air and a rod in your hand.' Bruce sounded delighted.

Gwendolyn Dougal sighed, clearly bored by countryside pursuits. She turned away from her husband and addressed Niko. 'I liked your sister tremendously,' she said. 'This kind of thing is abominable. We haven't had a murder here since historical times.'

'That's not quite right, darling,' her husband chided. 'During the war . . .'

Gwendolyn ignored him. It seemed clear she considered whatever had happened during the war irrelevant. 'I feel so sorry for dear Nina. This is the kind of thing that happens,' she said, 'when women go out to work.'

Tash coughed as if she had choked on her cocktail.

'This is the kind of thing that happens when there's a prowler on the loose,' Eleanor objected. Gwendolyn's terrier barked and Gwendolyn smiled indulgently. Mirabelle understood suddenly why Jinx had stationed himself at the bottom of the stairs – the tiny dog was as much of a bully as his mistress.

'What do you think, Alan? You're a policeman,' Eleanor said with the air of somebody calling in the cavalry.

Alan sipped his whisky. 'It's not my case. But there's been no evidence to suggest a prowler. And,' he nodded towards Lady Dougal, 'Gregory has an alibi. Quite a good one, actually, from what I understand.'

Bruce cut in. 'Yes. Well. My guess is that everyone's alibis are checking out far too well. As far as I can see, the police have no idea. There was nothing at all on the poor woman's body, no footprints at the back door and no note arranging a lover's assignation or any other. It's a mystery.' Tash stood up and walked over to the fireplace. 'I'm sorry, my dear,' Bruce apologised. 'Perhaps we shouldn't talk about it.'

'I'm OK. It's only, if it wasn't a prowler, then it means it was somebody here. Somebody in the house,' Tash said.

An awkward ripple of discomfort shuddered around the company. Nobody had, as yet, said this out loud, though, Mirabelle thought, they must have each considered it.

'Why don't I speak to the inspector?' McGregor offered. 'As a detective, I'll see what I can get out of him.'

'That would be helpful,' Bruce said.

'Well,' Eleanor cut in, 'I think it's time we went to the table.'

After the meal, the women formed an uncomfortable company in the drawing room. Eleanor played jazz records loudly. Mirabelle felt grateful for the music – she didn't want to speak to Gwendolyn. Lady Dougal had continued to be unpleasant throughout dinner, airing her views on a range of subjects including tenants' rights (she was in favour of fewer) and sanctions against Russia (she wanted more), which set off Niko Orlov on an anti-Red tirade that included five full minutes on Eisenhower's ineffectiveness and the tragedy of Senator McCarthy's death the previous year. Now, as the jazz music tailed off, they sipped sweet Spanish sherry and Lady Dougal exuded disapproval as Tash talked about New York – her friends, her career and, ultimately, the space left now her godmother was gone. Mirabelle felt grateful when Willie appeared in the doorway and suggested he drive his wife home.

'You're welcome to stay,' Eleanor offered, but outside, Willie packed Gwendolyn into the passenger seat with the terrier at her feet. 'Are you sure, old man?' Bruce said. 'You've had a skinful.'

'There's nothing on the road this time of night,' Willie insisted.

The blue clock on the mantelpiece struck midnight as every-one waved them off. The car's tail-lights disappeared down the drive in a relatively straight line given the amount of alcohol Lord Dougal had consumed. Coming back inside, Niko flung the last of his cigar onto the fire. 'Interesting woman,' he said.

Tash's brow furrowed. 'You're so old-fashioned, Uncle Niko. I'm going to bed.'

Niko checked his huge gold wristwatch. 'It's not late in New York.' Tash shrugged, waved a cheery goodnight and disappeared up the hallway, crossing paths with Jinx who, with the terrier out of the way, climbed onto a chair by the door and then, in response to Eleanor's aghast expression, dropped stoically back to the floor. 'Jinxy,' Eleanor patted the dog fondly. 'That's better.'

Niko waited until Tash had gone upstairs. 'Actually, I have something to ask,' he said.

'Shoot.' Eleanor grinned.

'I was wondering if I might go to the orangery. I didn't want to upset Natasha.'

'What do you mean, old man?' Bruce asked.

'Nina died there at night. I want to see what it was like in the dark.'

'That's a bit gruesome.'

Niko looked mournfully at his feet. 'Perhaps,' he said.

Mirabelle slipped her arm through his. 'I'll go with you,' she offered. 'I'd like to see it too.'

'Next it'll be bloody ghost tours,' Bruce grumbled. 'All right. We'll all go.'

The five of them trooped through. The fires hadn't been set on this side of the house and the air was colder, though the stove in the orangery glowed on a low setting. 'Don't turn on the main light,' Niko instructed as Bruce put his hand to the switch. 'I want to see what it was like for her. It must have been dark. She was found with the light off, wasn't she?'

'We don't know.' Eleanor loitered at the door. 'She might have turned on the light and the murderer turned it off again.'

Niko brushed her words aside. Inside, the orangery was lit by the moon – eerie blue light filtered through the glass and played on the wide, dark leaves of the tropical plants. Beyond, the hills loomed like enormous voids behind the orchard.

'I still don't understand why she came up here,' McGregor said.

'It must have been an assignation,' Mirabelle cut in. 'What I don't understand is the fingerprints. Did the killer wipe their prints from everything once she was dead? It was quick thinking if he did. And why didn't he remove the body? He could have dumped her miles away. She wouldn't have been found for ages. But he just left her and ran.'

The bamboo sofa creaked loudly as Eleanor sat. 'Oh, this is just maudlin,' she said, her eyes avoiding the area where Nina's body had lain.

'I'm Russian. Forgive me,' Niko dismissed her. 'I want to feel it.'

'Well wherever Nina is now, let's hope she's at peace,' Bruce said.

Niko ran his fingers across the long stem of a tall palm. 'Oh no,' he said. 'I don't think so. Nina won't be at peace until we catch him. Not until he hangs. My sister was a fighter. She would demand vengeance. Nina always got to the bottom of everything.'

Mirabelle felt suddenly queasy. The orangery seemed isolated in the dark, more part of the world outside than of the house – a place of contained darkness. The cool air was like silk but you wouldn't meet a lover here, she thought. It was too cold even with the stove alight. You'd meet a lover inside. Quietly, by the embers of the fire, where you could curl up and whisper and throw on a log to burn. The orangery was somewhere you'd meet someone if you wanted to talk. If you were planning to argue. If you didn't want to spend a lot of time. It was an odd kind of room when it was blacked out. There was something alien about the jutting plants and the wash of pale moonlight through the glass. 'Where does Jinx sleep?' she asked.

'Upstairs with us,' Eleanor said. 'On the other side of the house. You know what he's like. He follows me everywhere.'

But, Mirabelle thought, Jinx hadn't followed Eleanor tonight. He loitered in the hallway even now.

'I miss Nina,' Niko said sadly. 'I feel her here.'

'We're all very sorry, old man.' Bruce paused and made his way to the door where Eleanor slipped her hand into his. Niko sighed and followed, back into the certainty of rooms lit by electric light.

Left behind, Mirabelle watched as McGregor turned, the moonlight catching his white shirt, stark against his black jacket. A jagged shadow fell across one side of his face so he looked like a charcoal drawing. 'I'll speak to the police tomorrow,' he said. 'I'll see what I can find out.'

Mirabelle got up. 'I'm tired. Let's pack it in.'

He draped his arm around her shoulder. 'We should say goodnight to the others.'

In the drawing room, Eleanor and Bruce were lounging on the sofa. Niko had already gone upstairs. 'Are you two all right?' Eleanor asked.

McGregor kissed Mirabelle on the cheek. 'Better than this morning,' he said.

Bruce grinned. 'Do you remember sneaking downstairs and sniffing the brandy in here? You must have been all of six years old.'

McGregor smiled back. 'The grown-ups were at dinner. We made it to the drinks trolley and the fumes just about knocked us out. You wanted to taste it.'

'I did taste it,' Bruce said. 'Twelve years of age and a con-noisseur. It made me sick as a dog. I still can't drink the bally stuff.'

At the fringes of Mirabelle's mind, something niggled. A detail that wouldn't fall into place. Something about Nina.

'Who were the other couple?' she asked.

'What couple?' Bruce said.

'At dinner the other night. The last time you saw Nina. It was Nina and Tash, you two, the Dougals—'

'And the Walkers,' Eleanor cut in. 'They live in the other direction. Almost in Inverness. They're nice – a pudding of a couple.'

'And might Nina have upset them?'

'I doubt it. It was a pleasant evening. Gwendolyn was better than usual. Better than tonight.'

'Now, dear . . .' Bruce admonished her.

'Well, she's a witch.' Eleanor sighed. 'Shame they don't burn them any more.'

McGregor laughed. 'That seems quite extreme, though I take your point. Poor Willie Dougal.'

'Perhaps Willie likes it,' Bruce said, and everybody laughed.

'Tomorrow we have to do something – we can't just sit around,' Eleanor sounded decisive. 'It's not good for Tash, or for any of us.'

'Right you are,' Bruce agreed. 'Keep calm and carry on.'

Mirabelle was suddenly struck by the memory of a tattered poster flapping in the breeze on the side of a shop that had been bombed. It had always felt strange when it was sunny the morning after a bombing raid, she thought. What had she been doing there, watching two women trying to salvage their things from the rubble before the Home Guard arrived? She couldn't remember, but it was not a promising image.

'Time for bed,' McGregor suggested, also thinking about the wartime maxim. Mirabelle nodded.

'Goodnight,' she called, and slid her arm around his waist as they made for the stairs.

Chapter 8

We must take our friends as they are

It was raining again when she woke, but today the drops fell half-heartedly through an unrelenting sheet of thin grey cloud and the fire in the grate lay unlit. Mirabelle crept across the cold carpet and tossed a match into the kindling. In the distance the telephone was ringing. She checked her watch and wondered who was on the wire so early.

Eleanor met her on her way down the stairs.

'It was bound to happen,' she said.

'What?' Mirabelle enquired airily.

'What Kenzie said the other night. The press picked up the story,' Eleanor hissed and, right on cue, the telephone sounded again. Bruce stormed out of the dining room into his study, looking as if he might explode. He slammed the door behind him. The women hovered at the foot of the stairs. The sound of Bruce bellowing into the handset penetrated the closed door.

'Good morning, miss,' Gillies said as she swept up the hall.

'Good morning, Mrs Gillies,' Mirabelle replied as the housekeeper disappeared again. 'She seems happy this morning.'

'I managed to engage a temporary maid through the

employment agency in Aberdeen,' Eleanor said. 'Now she's got somebody to boss around. We could use the extra pair of hands, let's face it, what with Susan off the deep end and six of us in the house.'

Bruce opened the study door, but no sooner had he done so than the telephone rang again. His face was livid. 'Good morning,' he nodded at the women and retreated. Behind them, Tash descended. 'I can't be bothered with breakfast,' she said. 'Especially as there's no coffee.'

'I'm sorry, honey.' Eleanor sounded sympathetic. 'Mrs Gillies is immovable. No coffee until eleven.'

Tash stared at the closed door to the study. 'The press have picked up the story, I'm afraid,' Eleanor said. 'They've been calling every few minutes.'

They could hear the bell chiming as Bruce slammed down the handset. The women waited in silence until he came out. 'They know your uncle's arrived,' he said to Tash. 'I've taken the bally thing off the hook.'

McGregor did not materialise. Niko had jet lag and slept in, so it was well after ten by the time everyone appeared downstairs. McGregor loitered at the long windows, peering down the driveway.

'What are you looking at, old man?' Bruce interrogated him.

'There's somebody down there.'

The men walked into the field beyond the drive to get a better view.

'I was a terrible hostess yesterday,' Eleanor announced, 'but today we must do things.'

Tash got up and walked towards the window. McGregor and Bruce were having some kind of altercation on the grass.

Together they turned and walked purposefully back into the hallway. Eleanor sighed. 'What is it?'

'There are three photographers at the gates,' McGregor said. 'And Murdo Kenzie.'

'Apparently, there's nothing we can do,' Bruce spat.

'It's a public road, Bruce,' McGregor said. 'Stay away from the front gates. You've done the right thing taking the phone off.'

'At home—' Niko started.

'You're not at home,' McGregor cut him off. 'They have the right to be there and the right to telephone. What we do at our end is our responsibility.'

Eleanor folded her arms. 'I'm not going to be trapped in my own house by Murdo Kenzie, damn it. We'll go for a walk,' she declared. 'Up the back road. Come on everybody.'

Outside, Eleanor put Jinx on to a lead. 'Might as well bring the old chap,' she said.

Arrayed in thick coats and sensible shoes, she led the way with Niko as the group turned on to the lane, Bruce bringing up the rear, his shotgun over his arm. 'If I can get a potshot at a rabbit, I'll take it,' he said, but Mirabelle wasn't sure that was why he had brought the weapon. The press intrusion had disturbed him and, for Bruce, she thought, his gun was a comfort that he wasn't entirely defenceless. She hoped the newspapermen hadn't sent anybody in the other direction. McGregor hovered beside his cousin, ready to intervene just in case. 'I love the cold when it's like this,' he said cheerfully. 'Clear and razor sharp.' He laid his hand on Bruce's shoulder.

On the laneway beyond the staff quarters, two small boys in brown jackets and shorts passed them. The children kept their eyes on the ground and cut so close to the hedge that they almost disappeared through it as they shied away from the group. As they passed, one whispered something to the other about the Green Lady and they broke into a run, clattering down the hill, squealing. Bruce turned as if he might shout after them, but McGregor shook his head. 'They're only kids,' he said.

'Do you think there's any truth in the story?' Mirabelle asked. 'The Green Lady, I mean?'

Bruce grunted. 'The poor woman died young, but as to the circumstances . . .'

'That's all we need – a ghost story in the papers,' Eleanor said. 'Hopefully those kids won't say they saw us when they pass the photographers, otherwise they'll walk up to hound us, I suppose.'

'At least the press care,' Niko commented. 'The fact they're there will put pressure on the police.'

'They don't care, Uncle Niko. They just want a story. They're ghouls.' Tash sounded bitter.

'Now, now,' Eleanor's tone was upbeat. 'Come along.' She picked up the pace.

Tash linked her arm through Mirabelle's as the countryside slowly swallowed them. After ten minutes, Eleanor turned on to a trail through the bracken that led to a steep incline. Three sheep stared at the party from a distance as they emerged, single file, at the top of the slope. 'There's a great view from the summit,' Eleanor promised cheerfully. 'It'll be good for us.' As they climbed, the sun came out. They were out of breath by the time they got to the top. The air smelled different up here, as if it was drawn around the hillside like a cloak. Tash opened her coat and turned to take in the view of the glen, which unrolled for miles to the south of the house in a lush wash of green. 'It's beautiful, isn't it?' she breathed.

'The valley was formed by glaciers millions of years ago – huge blocks of ice carving up the landscape – the whole of the Highlands, the lochs, all of it. People go on about the hills and glens, but what I love is the colours,' Bruce said. 'Every day it's a different view. I'll never get bored of living here. We had a visitor last year who called it "epic". I thought that was rather good.'

'He was a poet, wasn't he?' Eleanor said. 'A friend of a friend.'

Bruce spotted a rabbit and let off a shot, setting off down the hill purposefully to pick it up. 'Jinx is a hopeless gun dog,' he said.

'Poor Jinxy,' Eleanor petted the dog. 'Poor boy.'

'Epic,' Niko repeated, as if he was considering the word. 'It's invigorating up here. I'll say that. And impressive. No poetry about it.' He pulled out a magnesium-blue Fabergé cigarette case, a snake inlaid in diamonds curling around it, and offered it round, lighting up after everyone had refused. A gust of wind blew the smoke away as it changed direction, and Jinx barked.

'It's too late now, old boy,' Bruce said, as he returned with the rabbit's hind legs jutting from the game pouch slung over his shoulder. Jinx barked again. He strained, pulling Eleanor downhill into the wind.

'He's had enough of the scenery, apparently,' Eleanor called over her shoulder. 'Maybe we should go on. There's another outlook further along. It's a good spot for twitchers. There is a pair of eagles that nest on the crags, though it's too early in the year to see them.'

'We should have brought binoculars,' McGregor chimed as Eleanor disappeared down the slope with a determined Jinx ahead.

The others followed. It was pleasant in the sunshine, though the wind was bracing. Mirabelle held McGregor's hand. 'Our land stretches as far as the largest Munro over there,' Bruce pointed out. Jinx was now barking so loudly that it was difficult to make out what Bruce was saying. 'Whatever has got into that animal?' he snapped. Eleanor struggled to control him. 'Jinx!' she berated, but it was useless.

At speed the descent was difficult. Mirabelle couldn't help thinking of a John Buchan book she'd read where the hero had escaped, running miles across this kind of terrain, disappearing into the heather. Running would be dangerous – the ground was too uneven. Though not for Jinx. He dragged Eleanor across a bank of shale, on to the track and into a ditch, beyond which the land dropped into a long field planted with potatoes.

A moment later, Eleanor screamed, mud spattering her overcoat as she dropped the animal's lead. For a moment, both Eleanor and the dog disappeared out of sight on the lower ground. Then Jinx barked again. Behind them, everyone broke into a run, Bruce loading his gun as he went. Then Eleanor's face appeared above the line of the track. Her skin was pink, her mouth open in a quivering, uneven slash.

'Are you all right?' Tash shouted.

The sound Eleanor made in reply was not related to speech. It was a high, keening note.

'What is it, darling?' Bruce called.

Eleanor stopped dead. 'It's Susan,' she said weakly.

McGregor and Mirabelle moved forward as the others fell back. It was telling, Mirabelle thought, people's first reaction. There was no time to consider – you simply did what you did. Together she and McGregor climbed across the trench. The mud splashed cold on their ankles as they dropped on to the thick earth on the other side. The girl's body was soaked. Wet hair covered her face. Her legs were spattered with mud. Mirabelle crouched and felt, hopelessly, for a pulse. She brushed Susan's mousy tresses across her cheek and scanned the body for some kind of wound. There was nothing. McGregor put his arm around Eleanor, holding her back as much as comforting her. 'It's a nightmare,' Eleanor shouted and started to cry. He managed to pull her away, and with Bruce's help guided her on to the track. Then he turned towards Mirabelle, who had completed a rudimentary examination of the body.

'It's a hangman's fracture,' she pronounced.

'What's that?' Tash squealed.

'Her neck's broken,' McGregor explained.

'Did she fall?' Tash babbled. 'I mean, maybe she cut across the field and fell.'

Mirabelle stood up. 'No. If that was the case, she would have tried to break her fall. She'd have gone down with her hands ahead of her. This is a professional job,' she said. 'Someone broke her neck from behind. This wasn't an accident. This woman was murdered.'

'You mean, someone . . .' Tash's voice tailed off. 'God. This place.'

'I'll stay with her,' Mirabelle took charge. 'You should all go back to the house and alert the police.'

'You can't stay alone,' McGregor sounded concerned. 'He could still be nearby. Anything could happen.'

'My guess is that she died yesterday. I doubt whoever did it will still be here. We can't just leave her, and you're the best one to talk to the officers,' Mirabelle replied. Bruce looked as if he was about to speak. 'You need to look after your wife,' she added. She was right. Eleanor was crying silently, her knuckles white as she clenched her fists, as if she had something to hold on to when, the truth was, there was nothing to grasp. Niko had his arm around Tash, who looked as if she was going to be sick. 'There's nobody up here – not now,' Mirabelle said steadily. 'I'm just securing the scene. Like a policewoman.' McGregor nodded curtly.

'I can't believe she's just lying on the ground,' Eleanor said. 'Like roadkill or a dead cat. An animal out in the fields.'

'Hush,' Bruce murmured.

'Are you sure you will be all right?' McGregor checked.

'Yes. Go,' Mirabelle said.

Mirabelle watched as the group disappeared ragtag down the laneway, Tash crying as Niko guided her. Eleanor seemingly limping, and Jinx trailing his lead through the puddles. The sky above them was clear blue for miles, like a postcard. McGregor looked back and she limply raised her arm.

Once they were out of sight, Mirabelle turned to the body. Susan was still wearing the apron she had on when she'd brought the coffee to Eleanor's office the day before. She wasn't dressed to walk home – no coat, no hat. She would never have come up here in her day clothes – a good quarter of an hour away from the house as the crow flies – in the driving rain. Mirabelle checked the girl's pockets, which contained only a safety pin and a handkerchief. She inspected the obvious places on her skin, looking for defensive wounds but, she concluded, it was most likely Susan hadn't even known someone was attacking her. The killer must have taken her completely by surprise, in or near the house. Had he come from behind, she wondered? It was a quick and more professional hit, Mirabelle realised, than the one on Nina Orlova. It was almost as if the killer had taken her advice the day before – to remove the body somewhere it was less likely to be found or perhaps to kill the girl elsewhere. Was it even the same person, or were there two murderers, here in the middle of nowhere? She shuddered at the thought and wondered what the girl had wanted to say to Eleanor when she'd interrupted their conversation in the office. 'What happened to you?' she whispered to the silent, muddy corpse.

After about twenty minutes, an elderly constable appeared, cycling towards her on a rickety bicycle. She stepped away from Susan's body, instinctively – aware that he wouldn't appreciate her checking the girl's pockets. The mud at the scene was churned up, what with her footprints, Eleanor's and McGregor's – all of them squelching about, and the dog too. It was impossible to see if there had been an earlier set of prints – the murderer's. She cursed herself that they hadn't thought of that.

The policeman laboured up the slope. He tipped his hat as he propped the bicycle on the hedgerow. 'I can take it from here, lass,' he said, and offered his hand to help her over the ditch. 'The team are on the way from the station. The laird said it was the housemaid?'

'Her name was Susan,' Mirabelle blurted. 'She was from Inverslain. We thought she went home. Someone either killed her at the house and dumped her here, or kidnapped her and brought her up the hill to execute her.'

The policeman eyed Mirabelle with dubiety.

'She's not wearing a coat,' Mirabelle insisted. 'She wouldn't have come up here voluntarily without one. Especially not yesterday – it was freezing cold and raining heavily. She was a good girl.' She wasn't sure why she was so set on defending Susan's honour but, even though the policeman was there, she didn't want to leave the girl.

'Will you be all right walking back?' the man checked.

Mirabelle sighed. She had to remain rational. He would be able to watch her descent towards the house at least half the way, and she could be of more use, now, down there. 'Yes, officer.' She kept her tone crisp.

Unwillingly Mirabelle turned back down the lane. Crows swooped across the line of the hill as she wound towards the house, peering back to check the figure of the policeman standing next to the body. She suddenly felt she was going to be sick. She stopped, her stomach heaving, while she collected herself. Up till now it hadn't felt as if there was a killer on the loose – it had felt as if Nina's death was a mistake, or if not exactly a mistake, then at least a crime of passion. Susan had been dispatched more coldly. Two bodies in three days. Two days, really – Susan hadn't been found straight away.

By the time she reached the house, an ambulance had pulled up and a police car was parked at the door. Another officer was immediately dispatched up the laneway. It felt good to get inside. In the vestibule, Bruce's game pouch was dumped on the floor, the dead rabbit spilling on to the oak boards like a gruesome warning. The door to the dining room was open a crack and, through it, Mirabelle could see Gillies sitting at the table with Eleanor opposite, breaking the news. The housekeeper clasped a glass of whisky in her hands. Her face was streaked with tears. She turned away shamefaced, as Mirabelle opened the door.

'Mrs Gillies, I'm so sorry. You must have known Susan better than anybody,' she said.

'Thank you, miss. I'd best be getting on.' Gillies got to her feet and placed her glass on the tray. At the door, she turned. 'Susan MacLeod was a good girl,' she pronounced.

'I told the officer that,' Mirabelle said. 'Can you think, Mrs Gillies, who on earth would want to kill her?'

Gillies sniffed. 'Of course not.'

'Jesus, Mirabelle,' Eleanor cut in. 'Give it a rest. The police are going to be bad enough.'

'I best get back to the kitchen,' Gillies pronounced.

'If you're sure,' Eleanor replied.

With Gillies gone, Eleanor scrabbled around in the sideboard for a cigarette. Her hands were shaking and the flame quivered in mid-air as she lit it. Mirabelle couldn't blame her. 'Come on,' Eleanor said. 'We should go back into the drawing room with the others. The police will want to speak to us.' She rolled her eyes. 'God – I sound like a professional witness.'

Across the hallway, Bruce, Tash and Niko sat on the sofas. 'Where's Alan?' Mirabelle asked.

'Talking to the police in the study,' Bruce said. 'They wanted him first.'

Eleanor paced, agitated, in front of the fireplace. 'I was going to visit the McCrossans this afternoon. They called their baby Heather and I got a blanket for her from the mill and some Pear's soap,' she said.

'Darling . . .' Bruce started.

'Well, what were you going to do?' Eleanor spat. 'Go for a ride? Head out with your shotgun?'

'We've got to eat.' Bruce sounded sheepish.

'I'm sorry,' Eleanor apologised. She sank on to a chair. 'I didn't mean to get at you.'

Niko, standing at the window, pulled back. Outside, a bevy of men with cameras and notebooks was heading towards the house. Smartly, Eleanor jumped up. She closed the curtains and snapped on the lamps.

'Don't answer that,' she said as the doorbell rang. 'They've seen the police are here is all – nosey parkers.'

Everyone froze for a second. 'This is ridiculous,' Niko said. 'Leave it to me. Those goddam sharks. If we just give them a statement they'll go away.' The room shifted as he left and everyone listened while he answered the door and talked about his sister's death. Eleanor peered at the men through a gap in the curtains. Niko did a good job, Mirabelle thought. He remained dignified, asking for the family to be left alone. 'No photographs, please,' he finished, but the men took a couple of him standing with the door half open anyway. One journalist framed a couple of questions, which made it clear he did not yet know about Susan's body. 'And the man they've arrested,' he snapped. 'What can you say about him?'

'Arrested?' Niko asked.

'The coloured fellow.'

The words hung in the air. Then Niko recovered his composure. 'I can't make any statement about the enquiry. You need to ask the police,' he said and closed the door.

Mirabelle's mind raced. Gregory had been Bruce's first instinct. He had the strength needed to kill Susan, but then, she thought, why would he want to? And what had changed – McGregor had said that Gregory's alibi was sound. Eleanor peered through the gap in the curtains. 'They're leaving,' she said, holding out her arm as if conducting an orchestra. Everybody stayed silent until she pronounced the men gone and drew the curtain to let the light back in.

As Niko rejoined them, Tash got up from the sofa. 'The police have arrested Gregory!' she said. 'That's what they said, right?'

'I thought he had an alibi,' Niko replied.

Tash punched her uncle's arm. 'He does!' she insisted.

'Gregory wouldn't harm Nina and you know it. Nor some little maid neither. Those bastards. We have to bail him out. Come on. Get your coat!'

This time Mirabelle held up her hand 'Hang on. Just because a journalist says someone has been arrested, doesn't mean it's true. I can't see why they'd do that.'

Tash's fingers fluttered across the buttons of her jacket. 'Isn't it obvious? Because he's black. You have to help,' she said. 'It's monstrous. We can't let these dreadful things rob us of our humanity.'

'Perhaps they've only brought him in for questioning,' Mirabelle said.

'They didn't bring in any of us for questioning,' Tash snapped. 'They asked all the white folks questions right here. But they've taken Gregory to prison.'

'For heaven's sake, Tash,' Niko cut in. 'Nobody said anything about prison. Panicking isn't going to help.'

'He didn't do anything,' Tash insisted.

Mirabelle considered this. 'I agree. It's highly unlikely Gregory is the murderer.'

'It's not unlikely. It's impossible.'

'Why?'

'Because I know him. He just wouldn't. God! It's as if nobody cares.' Tash was on the cusp of bursting into tears of frustration. 'Doesn't anyone read between the lines? The papers at home are full of it – the right ones, that is. The easy answer for the police is always the black man.'

The girl's rant was interrupted by the sound of the police emerging from the study. Tash stopped and they all listened. McGregor's voice sounded comforting, Mirabelle thought. 'I feel as if I'm caged here. Jesus!' Tash burst out. Then, fired by fury and desperation, she took off through the double doors. 'What have you done with him?' she shouted up the hall at the group of men around McGregor.

Alan stepped forward. 'What do you mean? What happened?'

'They've arrested Gregory. You have, haven't you? When the hell were you going to tell us?'

'Gregory was taken into the station this morning, Miss Orlova,' the officer said. 'We don't have to keep you informed about our enquiries.'

'What the hell's he being charged with?' Tash snapped. 'You racists! Nazis!'

The officer was taken aback. 'Well that's something to say. To be frank, miss, most of the men here risked their lives fighting the Nazis not long ago, so we don't take kindly to that sort of talk. As far as I'm aware your steward was only being questioned when I left the station – a normal procedure and nothing to do with his colour. Now, if you'll excuse me,' he motioned to the ambulance driver and the doctor, 'we need to attend to the new victim – the young lady—'

'Why don't I phone the station and see what's happened?' Alan cut in. He locked eyes with Mirabelle as she came into the hallway. 'Help Tash, would you?'

'Jesus Christ,' Tash said, shrugging off Mirabelle's arm.

'We should sit down.' Mirabelle realised she sounded like a nanny. Still, Tash followed her into the drawing room and perched on the edge of a chair, ramrod straight, while McGregor went to make the call. 'We'll sort it out,' she promised.

Tash looked as if she might cry. 'It's important to stand up for what you believe in. Gregory never would have hurt Nina and I can't see why he'd bother killing the maid. We've been here a week. We don't know anyone. The police have to pin it on somebody, that's all.'

'You're very loyal.' Mirabelle thought of what her friend Vesta would say. Tash was right – the police hadn't taken anybody else into custody. From the other side of the room, Niko was watching her carefully. 'Tash enjoys a demonstration,' he said. 'It's a hobby of hers.'

Tash drew herself up. 'I can't bear people being picked on, especially for something as stupid as the colour of their skin.'

'You're right, darling,' Eleanor cut in.

Encouraged, Bruce joined her. 'I've heard it's difficult for coloured people in the States.'

'Difficult! Are you kidding!'

'It's not quite the same here,' Bruce continued.

'Yeah.' Tash's tone was loaded with irony. 'Everyone in this country is equal. I can see that.' She looked around the room pointedly.

Eleanor laughed. 'You know me, honey. This isn't where I come from. It's what I came to this country to write about. Class.'

'I don't know if we have class any more. Not like we used to,' Mirabelle said, and cursed herself for sounding prim.

Eleanor and Tash as good as erupted. They squealed and giggled, while Bruce looked confused.

'Take it from me, you definitely have class,' Tash said. 'The way you all know each other. It's a club. What the hell is the difference between a drawing room and a sitting room anyway?' The sound of guns being fired wafted up the hill and Tash flung her hands in the air. 'God, I wish we hadn't come.' Mirabelle felt sheepish. She had a sneaking suspicion the girl was right. She was about to say something when McGregor returned.

'They're holding Gregory for questioning, but they haven't charged him,' he reported. 'They said if I come in about an hour, they'll know more, but Susan's body has complicated matters. Once her time of death is established, they will have to deal with a second set of alibis. I'm going down to the station.'

'I'm coming with you,' Tash said.

'No.' Niko put his foot down.

'You can't stop me, Uncle Niko.'

'It's all right. I'll take her,' McGregor cut in. 'We'll be fine.'

'Oh, all right,' Niko said. 'Use the hired car. It's round the back. I had Gregory bring it up yesterday.' He picked up a fresh glass and poured a whisky from the decanter. 'The key is in the ignition.'

McGregor kissed Mirabelle on the cheek and disappeared with Tash. Niko watched them go. 'I'm going to make a call, if that's all right?' He checked his watch. 'It's time to start business in New York and I have to speak to people.'

'Have the study, old man,' Bruce offered. 'Please.'

'Goddam awful day,' Niko said. 'May I?' He lifted the decanter of whisky from the trolley.

'Take it,' Bruce directed.

Outside, Mirabelle watched the car emerge from behind the house, turn in a wide sweep, and disappear down the drive, running the gauntlet of the photographers.

'Tash is under a huge amount of pressure,' she said.

The Robertsons sat shell-shocked on the sofa. 'Gosh.' Bruce sighed.

Eleanor cocked her head to one side. 'You handled that well, Mirabelle,' she said. 'My bet is, Alan's not the only one with secrets.'

Mirabelle leaned against the cushions. 'I told you, I signed the Official Secrets Act,' she said.

'Well,' Eleanor replied. 'What are we going to do? We can't just sit here eyeing the cocktail shaker.'

'Why don't you visit the McCrossans?' Bruce suggested. 'That's what you'd planned.'

Eleanor looked at Mirabelle. 'Would you like to come?' Mirabelle shook her head.

'I'll go with you, darling,' Bruce offered. 'We can go round the back. Avoid the press. We might as well do something positive.'

With the Robertsons dispatched, Mirabelle sat alone. She stared at the cornicing that skirted the ceiling. The difference between a drawing room and a sitting room seemed obvious to her. Did that make her a hopeless snob? She got up and walked through to the orangery where she sat disconsolately on the wicker sofa and stared blankly out of the window. From far off, another gun blasted, the sound carrying up the hill through the clear, clean air. It had been an awful morning. She shivered as if Nina's cold fingers had run down her spine. As if Susan was whispering to her. It felt as if the house was hiding a secret.

Chapter 9

Make perseverance your bosom friend

When Gillies disturbed her, offering lunch, Mirabelle declined. Guiltily she slipped into Niko's room and retrieved Nina's diary. Then she fetched a saddle. She needed to clear her head. The house felt oppressive. She told the policeman she wouldn't be long and he instructed her to keep away from the crime scene. 'Are you sure you'll be all right, miss?' he checked. 'I'll be fine,' she insisted. It had been a while since she'd ridden but she'd be safer on a horse.

The air was chill and the horse's breath clouded ahead as she mounted and set off across country. From a distance, she watched the pressmen at the gate huddled around a brazier. They were playing cards on an upturned bucket.

She steered the horse north along the glen and headed upstream to a clearing, where the water bubbled from beneath the granite, flowering into a graceful waterfall and disappearing below ground again before emerging as the burn near the village. She wondered if Alan had thought there were fairies here too when he was a boy. Dismounting, she let the horse drink. It was surprising how quickly the world disappeared here – all signs of civilisation obscured by the majestic landscape. Resting on a rock, she took the diary from her pocket and scrambled for a hairpin to pick the lock. It took only seconds to peel back the strip of leather that acted as a bar.

Nina's writing was tiny and she had used several different pens, in shades of blue ink. Between the text she had drawn sketches. One of a New York brownstone with brimming window boxes, another of a pair of shoes with elegant stiletto heels, and one of Gregory leaning over a handsome-looking car, with the hood up, as he tinkered with the engine. At the back there were two tiny scraps of blood-red silk, pinned to the notebook's endpaper.

Starting at the end, Mirabelle began to read. The last entry was a list of items Nina had ordered at the cashmere mill. '12 × Ivory 4-ply cashmere cardigan with Peter Pan collar' and '24 × Caramel 2-ply cable-knit cashmere scarf'. Beside each description was a calculation of how much Nina bought the piece for and the price she'd sell it at in New York, followed by the mark-up – in most cases over 500 per cent. She had been meticulous. The page before the list contained a note of Gwendolyn Dougal's telephone number and address. The women had evidently hit it off. 'Send note', Nina had scribbled. Then a cryptic 'Tweed collective. Red?' standing apart from the rest of the text. Perhaps, Mirabelle thought, Nina had intended to buy tweed as well as cashmere while she was in the Highlands. One thing seemed sure – there was no indication that she felt her life was in danger. The book was mundane – a list of journalists who wrote for fashion magazines followed a list of vintage wine with marks out of ten and random reminders to buy Christmas lights and stockings. The murder, it seemed, had come out of the blue. 'Who were you meeting in the orangery in the middle of the night?' Mirabelle asked in a whisper.

Taken up with this window on to Nina's world, she jumped when a sheepdog burst through the undergrowth on the other side of the burn and barked in her direction. Her horse startled and she put her hand on its neck to calm it, slipping the notebook back in her pocket. 'Shush, boy,' she said soothingly to the dog, which wagged its tail. A moment later a slim woman with a short bob of flaming hair appeared. She was wearing an ochre plaid skirt and a thick red sweater that was far too big for her. 'Pearce!' she said. 'Hush.'

'Hello,' Mirabelle offered her hand across the water. 'I'm Mirabelle Bevan.'

'The laird's cousin?' the woman checked.

'Yes.' They shook. 'Jennifer Fraser,' she introduced herself. 'I was sorry to hear about the trouble.'

'I know,' said Mirabelle. 'I never met Miss Orlova . . .'

'And Susan MacLeod now too,' Jennifer added.

'Were you acquainted with either of them?'

'I knew Susan from the village and I'd met Miss Orlova. She came to the distillery. I work there. Mrs Robertson got me the job. They were looking for an apprentice distiller. They said it should be a man, but she made them take me anyway. Most of the lads have left the village.'

'Eleanor's marvellous, isn't she?'

Jennifer grinned. 'A lass has to know what she wants and Mrs Robertson wants to make gin. She's been at Angus, the master distiller, but he says there's no art in it. Mrs Robertson reckons there might not be art, but there could be money. So I've set up a still for her. To try it.'

'Eleanor has an eye for business.' Mirabelle smiled. 'Tell me, what are they saying about the deaths in the village?'

The woman hesitated. 'You can tell me,' Mirabelle assured her.

'Well . . . first it was the curse of the Green Lady, but the last couple of hours since word came down about Susan, it's a sex maniac on the loose. At least the dog can protect me from the latter. I'm sorry. I shouldn't be flippant. People are superstitious – it's always either the kelpies or the church down there – and women are in trouble either way.'

'I don't think it's either of those things.'

'They say Mrs MacLeod, Susan's mother, fainted when they told her.' Jennifer crossed herself. 'It's such terrible news.'

'I'm sorry.'

From above, the face of Murdo Kenzie appeared at the head of the brae. 'Miss Bevan,' he said delightedly.

'Did you follow me?'

Kenzie looked shamefaced. 'A little,' he said. 'I saw you mounting up and I borrowed a bicycle. Hello Jenny.' Pearce let out a low growl but Kenzie ignored the warning and continued to edge down the bank towards the women, moving awkwardly. 'I wondered, Miss Bevan, if you'd be interested . . .'

'I'm definitely not interested, Mr Kenzie.'

'But I understand you were there. The second victim. You found her. Is that right?' Kenzie took out his notepad.

'Murdo Kenzie, you can put that away,' Jenny said, her hand on the dog's collar. 'You can turn around too. It's a police matter and you shouldn't be harassing two ladies out for a walk.'

Kenzie grinned. 'Jenny,' he said, not taking her seriously.

'Pearce,' Jenny raised a finger and pointed straight at the journalist. Pearce growled and began barking. 'I'll let him have at you. Don't think I won't,' Jenny threatened. Kenzie looked nervous. He began to back off. 'I just need a quote,' he said. Jenny kept one hand in the air and the dog continued barking. 'Be fair,' Kenzie whined. 'Go on now,' she said. The dog strained.

The journalist disappeared back up the brae. 'Thanks,' said Mirabelle when he'd gone. Something about the girl taking no nonsense heartened her. Everyone in the house was some kind of victim. Not Jenny Fraser. 'Imagine your father was a respectable man. A schoolteacher. And you get a job for a scandal sheet instead of doing something worthwhile.'

'You know, I'm on the market for some whisky,' Mirabelle said with a smile. 'And potentially some of that gin of yours. A case of each?'

Jennifer blushed. 'You don't have to, Miss Bevan . . .'

'But I want to.' Mirabelle mounted the horse. 'It was a pleasure to meet you, Miss Fraser. Get in touch with the house and we'll sort it out?'

On the ride back, the sun was shining and the light cast a pure, pale yellow across the fields. The hills were dotted with sheep. If it wasn't so cold, Mirabelle would have thought it was summer – only patches of snowdrops betrayed the time of year. She loved that the cold made her skin sting – a sign of being alive. In the paddock at the front of the house, the other horses raised their heads, as ahead of her the old ambulance snaked down to the main road. This meant the police had removed Susan's body. As it passed the gates, the pressmen scrambled to take photographs. They clustered, discussing whether there might be something of interest left up the back road – if they'd be able to identify the scene of the crime. One of them began to walk along to investigate. Mirabelle dismounted, giving the horse a sugar cube from her pocket and throwing a blanket over him. Then she walked to the side of the house to put away the tack.

As she did so, the hired car McGregor had driven to the police station drove through the gates and the remaining pressmen mobbed it, their shouts carrying up the hill as they barked questions at the vehicle. McGregor didn't slow more than a fraction as he turned into the drive. Murdo Kenzie, back at his post, ran after the car a little way up the drive but gave up quickly – he was having a bad afternoon. Mirabelle grinned, watching from the hut around the side of the house as Gregory got out of the vehicle and held the door for Tash. He was out.

She followed them inside, catching the front door as it closed behind them. Ahead, McGregor and Tash disappeared into the drawing room. Gregory headed towards the kitchen and, in a split second, on a whim, Mirabelle decided to follow him. The door was ajar and the smell of baking bread billowed into the hall. She stayed on the blind side as Gregory greeted Mrs Gillies.

'Have you eaten, son?' Gillies asked.

'I could do with something.'

Gillies brooked no more discussion with Gregory than she did with anybody else. Instead Mirabelle heard the sound of plates and cutlery being arranged. 'Tea.' She made it sound like a fact of life. 'You didn't tell them anything?'

'No, ma'am. There didn't seem any point making trouble.'

'You did right,' Gillies said. 'Discretion is the mark of good service. I checked in the village with my sister in case there was any chatter, but you kept your nerve and quite right too. It was nothing to do with the murder. That poor dead woman deserves some privacy. As do we all.'

Mirabelle cocked her head while the sound of cutlery on porcelain betrayed Gregory's hunger. She shifted from foot to foot before making the decision to enter. 'I wonder if you might send some tea into the drawing room, Mrs Gillies,' she said airily. 'Gregory, I'm glad to see you back.'

'Ma'am,' Gregory got to his feet. He was wearing a thick black jumper. It looked as if it was cashmere.

'Please, eat your meal.' Mirabelle gesticulated at the vivid constellation of boiled eggs, ham and mayonnaise. 'I'm glad they released you. Tash was terribly concerned. We all were.'

Gillies put the kettle on to boil. 'If you need anything, you can just ring, miss,' she said coldly.

'I'm somewhat disoriented today, I'm afraid. Gregory, I hope you don't mind, but I wanted to ask exactly what the police wanted with you?'

Gregory remained calm. 'Ma'am,' he said, 'they asked me about Miss Orlova and my alibi is all.'

'Tash was worried they had picked you up because of the colour of your skin.'

'They have a right to ask me questions.'

Mirabelle sat down at the table. Behind her, Gillies clattered a pan in protest. 'They kept you a while. A few hours by my reckoning.'

'Well, they had a lot to ask in the end, what with Susan's body turning up.'

'It doesn't sit right with me, all this,' she said, as if confiding in him.

'Two murders? I should think not.'

'One expects a narrative.'

Gregory's face split in a grin. 'Pardon me, but are you saying Miss Nina's death has disappointed you with its lack of story? And the girl too?'

'There's clearly information missing.'

'I don't know.'

'That's strange.' Mirabelle turned in her seat. 'Because I

could have sworn I heard you and Mrs Gillies, before I came in, saying that there was something you hadn't divulged.'

Gillies's expression was flawless. For a moment, Mirabelle thought that neither of them was going to crack, but then Gregory slumped in his seat, abandoning his cutlery. 'It was nothing,' he said.

'I'd still like to know.'

'You're something else, miss.'

'That's a compliment in America, isn't it?'

'Kinda.' His dark eyes were still as he made the decision to tell her. 'It's only that I saw Nina with the other woman. The neighbour,' he said.

'I thought you were in Glasgow.'

'I don't mean the night she died. I saw them the day before.'

Gillies let out a low tutting sound. 'I never thought I'd see the day when we'd have guests of the laird eavesdropping.'

Mirabelle didn't reply. 'Which neighbour?' she pressed.

'The one with the title. Nina had the king-sized hots for that kind of thing. She said they were her people.'

'You mean Gwendolyn Dougal?'

'Yeah. The two of them were thick as thieves. Nina was getting bored, I guess, in the country. They cracked a bottle of champagne at the lodge and they were talking, you know, like they were long-lost friends. Just the two of them.'

'When?'

'In the afternoon.'

'So they knew each other? Nina and Lady Dougal?' Mirabelle remembered the diary entry – the card Nina had noted to send.

'It looked that way. She shooed me off. I had only gone to see if there was anything she needed.'

'And you withheld this information from the police?'

Gillies couldn't restrain herself any longer. 'It would cause gossip in the village. I asked Mr Gregory not to say anything out of respect for the dead.'

'But I don't understand.' Mirabelle was genuinely confused. 'What kind of gossip were you thinking of, Mrs Gillies?'

Gillies's lips pursed. 'It's a small village.'

A smile played around Gregory's eyes. 'Lady Dougal has a reputation,' he added.

'Champagne in the afternoon. It's hardly necessary.' Gillies sounded furious.

Mirabelle caught Gregory's eye. Her forehead creased. She was about to push him further, but he shook his head a fraction and she decided not to. It seemed a strange association. Tash loathed Gwendolyn and, if Mirabelle was honest, she had as well. But Nina it seemed hadn't – quite the reverse. 'Did Susan know about this meeting?' Mirabelle asked.

'I don't think so,' Gregory said.

'Do you have alibi for Susan's death?'

'Yes, ma'am. All day yesterday. The police questioned me for a while. Then I was with Mrs McCrossan and then helping one of the farmers down in the village.' His eyes flashed. 'Do you have an alibi?'

Mirabelle got to her feet. She certainly wasn't going to let him ask questions. 'I can take that tray, if you like, Mrs Gillies,' she said.

Outside, she lingered a moment in the hall. The sound of Gregory resuming his meal was the only noise in the kitchen. Then the door pulled back and Gillies stood brooding. 'I'm going,' Mirabelle said.

She set off with the tray, hoping people might be glad of some tea. She could use a cup anyway. As she rounded the corner into the main hall, she felt a pair of strong hands around her waist. 'What?' she said out loud, and upturned the milk jug as she was pulled into one of the alcoves. Her heart pounding, she took a deep breath, ready to use the tray as a weapon as she swung it round. 'Shhhh,' McGregor put his fingers to his lips. Then he kissed her. 'Are you the new maid?' he asked.

'You gave me a fright!' she snapped.

'Sorry. They aren't bringing any charges,' McGregor said, 'before you ask.'

'Yes, I ascertained that, thanks. Did they actually arrest him?'

'Well, it was difficult to get much out of them because Tash was almost hysterical,' he said, with a glimmer in his eye. 'But no. They would have kept him if they'd had grounds, but they probably let him go as quickly as they could to get her out of the way. She's a firebrand.'

He took the tray and placed it on a ledge outside the day room, righting the now empty milk jug and dabbing at the milk with a napkin. 'No use in crying over it,' he said good humouredly.

'They've removed Susan's body,' Mirabelle told him. 'The ambulance went down as you were coming up. And it turns out Nina and Gwendolyn Dougal knew each other before dinner the other night. They were firm friends.'

'Busy afternoon?'

Their eyes met for a moment. She found his nonchalance provoking. He wasn't usually like this on a case. 'If you aren't going to take it seriously . . .' she started but, before she could complete the sentence, the front door cracked open and Eleanor and Bruce arrived, noisily stamping their boots.

'God, that was awful,' said Eleanor as she hung up her coat. 'What are you two doing wedged in together?' she exclaimed as she noticed them in the alcove. 'Or shouldn't I ask?'

'I need a drink,' said Bruce. 'A large one.'

They all trooped into the drawing room. Bruce poured whiskies and downed his straight away.

'We're all anyone can talk about, of course,' Eleanor said.

'It's too too maudlin. We need some good news, that's the ticket,' Bruce chimed.

'Sheesh. And then some,' Tash agreed from the sofa. Niko put down the magazine he was reading and turned to watch.

'Well, when are you two going to tie the knot?' Bruce said with a smile. McGregor coughed. Mirabelle felt her colour heighten. 'I mean, snogging in the hallway alcove is all very well but it's not respectable. Best time for us is around June, old man,' Bruce continued smoothly. 'If you want us in attendance, that is. Eleanor and I always spend a week at The Ritz in June. We're building Eleanor's jewellery collection. You love Hatton Garden, don't you darling?'

'I'm learning,' Eleanor said. 'But you shouldn't put Alan and Mirabelle on the spot like that. It's not fair.'

'Not at all. We need to come down to Brighton.' Bruce ignored his wife's objection. 'There's a decent hotel, isn't there?'

'The Grand,' McGregor said, 'though it's not up to The Ritz.'

Niko eyed Mirabelle across the low footstool that separated the sofas, like a cat watching a goldfish in a bowl.

Eleanor pressed the bell and the new maid arrived. 'Ah. Good,' she said. 'Elizabeth, isn't it? Could you bring ice?'

Mirabelle wondered if the girl regretted taking the job. Between being engaged and taking the position, her predecessor had been found dead. In fairness, she ought to be getting danger money. There was a tang of desperation in the drawing room – a metallic smell, like sweat tempered by the sting of London gin. They'd come on holiday to get away from it all and instead trouble had run ahead of them.

'It's hardly time to—' she said.

'Oh, it's exactly the time,' Eleanor cut in.

Everyone waited. 'June,' she said. 'All right.' She told herself it would give them a few months to buy a house and get things organised. When she got home, she'd enlist Vesta's help.

'Marvellous! We ought to mark this.' Bruce's tone was celebratory. Mirabelle wondered if he'd pushed this on them out of boredom or out of guilt – he'd brought on their fight with his faux pas over breakfast, maybe now he was trying to make it right in a blunt kind of way. He rushed out of the room.

'What's he up to?' McGregor asked.

Eleanor shrugged. He returned a minute later with a portrait in an unwieldy ornate gilt frame. 'This is for you,' he announced. 'Consider her an engagement present.' He swung the picture round.

McGregor peered. 'It's Mother,' he said. 'Oh, that's lovely. But there's no need to be so generous, Bruce.'

'You should have it for your new place – wherever it is you settle. You and I lost touch for a while and you weren't at our wedding, but we'd be pleased and proud to be there for yours. Family. If you'd like that.'

'Thank you,' Alan said.

Mirabelle stared at the woman in the picture. The figure was in her mid-twenties, slender with a long, dark plait, wearing a ballet outfit, one foot *en pointe*, as if about to spring into a pirouette. Her face wore a melancholy expression.

'Was it painted here?' she asked. 'In the house?'

'That's the day room before Eleanor redecorated it,' Bruce

said. 'It was pale pink. I suppose it must have been done around 1910. The year before she married. The story goes that the pose was considered too racy and Aunt Deidre had to hide it from Granny. It hung in the West Wing for years – the old girl hardly ever went up there. I don't suppose she had the space for it in Edinburgh.'

Mirabelle wondered if the woman in the portrait had yet met Alan's father, and if she knew she would be leaving the estate where she had been born and brought up for an entirely different kind of life.

'I think you have her eyes, Alan,' she said. 'Did she paint? I noticed the landscapes upstairs.'

'She did,' Bruce enthused, glad to have something uncontroversial to talk about. 'In the summer she'd take her easel and disappear for hours. Perhaps we should give you a couple of her doodles of the old place? Matching set.'

'Thanks,' said Alan. 'It's a generous present, isn't it darling?'

Mirabelle nodded. 'Yes,' she said. 'Thank you.'

Bruce propped the painting against the chiffonier. It looked as if it belonged there. Mirabelle wondered if Deidre had made a mistake moving to Edinburgh and marrying her Mr McGregor.

Niko stood up. 'This is all very nice,' he said, 'but it feels as if everyone is trying to ignore the fact that there's every likelihood of a madman on the loose. Until we know who's responsible for my sister's death and for the maid's, there could be another attack.'

Mirabelle felt her skin creep. He was right, of course. If there was another murder, the odds were that the victim would be one of the people sitting in this room. There was a momentary stillness as everybody thought the same.

'Sorry,' said Bruce. 'I only meant—'

'Well, with that in mind, I've been thinking I'd like to borrow a gun – as a priority,' Niko cut him off. 'We should be considering protection. Don't you think?'

Bruce seemed taken aback. 'I don't know, old man. The police are here. Besides, we keep our guns under lock and key.'

Niko pushed him. 'I don't think the normal rules apply now, to be frank. Police or not. We're clearly in danger and we're stuck here. They won't release Nina's body for another day or two – perhaps longer in light of the girl's murder. They made that quite clear to me.'

'The police will be concerned you might skip the country. That's what's on their minds,' McGregor said.

'I'd love to skip the bloody country.' Niko sounded furious. 'But we can't leave Nina. We're not barbarians.'

Outside the light was failing. 'All right,' Bruce decided. 'I'll look out a gun for you. Do you know how to use it?'

Niko stiffened. 'How hard can it be?'

'I don't like it,' McGregor sounded definite. 'This isn't some Wild West border town. We can't have everybody armed to the teeth.'

'It's not your sister that died,' Niko pointed out. 'It's pitch-black here at night. I want to be able to look after Tash. What if somebody comes into the house?'

'Even if they do, you can't shoot people just because they're indoors,' McGregor said. 'Get it wrong and you'll do ten years. You need to know there's a threat to life.'

Niko turned his attention back to Bruce. 'What if it's Eleanor next? What about that?'

Bruce nodded. 'All right,' he said, and disappeared into the study to emerge with three shotguns – one for each of the men.

McGregor bristled. 'We have to be careful,' he warned the others. 'Do you understand?'

'Don't I get one?' Tash objected.

'No,' Niko cut in. 'I'm in the room next to yours.'

Tash didn't remonstrate. Instead she walked out.

'Her temper today . . .' Niko said. 'It's the pressure.'

Later, at bedtime, the fires had been lit and the beds warmed. Elizabeth had been busy. Mirabelle sat at the dressing table in her nightgown, turning round on the stool as she brushed her hair so she could see the painting of Deidre McGregor, which had been brought up to Alan's room. The shotgun was propped next to it. Dinner had been stilted and they had all come up early.

'A lass has to know what she wants,' she whispered and felt foolish. 'I hope Niko doesn't go overboard, now he's armed,' she said louder, so Alan could hear her.

'I've warned him.' He appeared behind her in the mirror, still in his dinner suit, tie undone, top button opened casually. 'I think my mother would have liked you, Mirabelle.'

Mirabelle did not say that her family would almost certainly have disapproved of him. Though now it had transpired that McGregor had this place in his background, they might not have disapproved quite so much. It saddened her to think her parents were snobbish; that they wouldn't have liked her life in Brighton, the agency she ran or the people she associated with. Times had changed. They were still changing. Tash was proof of that.

'Bruce railroaded you into a June date, didn't he?' McGregor said, falling back and sitting on the end of her bed.

Mirabelle nodded. She put down the hairbrush.

'Is it OK?'

She nodded again. 'Yes. I want to marry you. I do.'

'I'm so relieved,' he said.

She didn't know what more to say. If they were going to get through this, they weren't going to do it by talking. They watched each other for a moment. It was different now that she understood more about him. She beckoned him with her finger. 'Come here. I think I want you on your knees again.'

McGregor dropped his gaze. 'Hold on,' he said. He picked up a towel and draped it over the portrait of his mother.

Mirabelle laughed. 'Would she distract you?'

Lasciviously, McGregor ran his eyes across her body as he fell to his knees in front of her. 'Actually, I'm not sure anything could put me off.' He drew her close, pulling her down next to him and kissing her neck as he dropped his jacket on to the floor. She tugged the buttons on his shirt, staring at him as his body emerged – the definition of his arms, the wide expanse of his chest and his pale skin with its stray, dark hairs. She unfastened the waist of his trousers. 'Are you blushing?' she asked.

'It seems too much.'

'I want to see you, Alan. All of you.'

She reached out an elegant finger and ran it across his stomach, looking down towards the patch of twisted flesh that was the cause of the trouble. This was a man who had lived with the full weight of his guilt. He had tried to make amends by righting other wrongs. He was some kind of hero, albeit a flawed one.

'Are you sure?' He sounded nervous.

She laughed. 'I'm stripping you naked here on the floor.' His breathing became heavier, his hands on her skin now, caressing her from her waist to her thigh. 'You've punished yourself enough, don't you think?' She wound her leg around his so she could feel the rough flesh on his calf, and stroked the damaged skin with the side of her foot. McGregor's eyes filled with tears.

'Jesus,' he said.

'Do you want me to stop?'

He shook his head. He smelled of sweat and of the river-bank and of somewhere green and on high ground. Of police stations and paperwork. Of all the confusion he seemed to prompt in her. She kissed him once more, his chin scuffing her with its five o'clock shadow, and then they began to move.

Chapter 10

To be prepared is half the victory

The next morning it was clear they had all drunk far too much. The dining room at breakfast time felt like a library – as if you had to whisper. Mirabelle rather liked it.

'Did you say something to Gillies?' Eleanor hissed as Mirabelle and McGregor entered the room. 'She's in a horrible mood. She asked when you were leaving.'

Mirabelle poured the tea. There were no newspapers. She wondered what had been written about the murders. 'Your housekeeper has been withholding information from the police,' she said.

'What?'

Eleanor heaped jam on to toast and listened eagerly as Mirabelle explained. 'I didn't know Nina and Gwendolyn knew each other,' she said when Mirabelle had done.

'How did you meet Nina?' Mirabelle asked.

'She was always around New York. I was starting out as a journalist and she asked me if I'd put together a piece saying I'd bought things in some dreary, overpriced shop she was stocking.'

'And did you?'

'I told her I didn't write about shopping.'

'Only about privilege?'

'I wanted to write articles about things I found interesting – the pay was terrible, of course.'

'It sounds glamorous – bohemian.'

'My life is different now. If you'd told me I'd end up somewhere like this, I wouldn't have believed you. Shall we go to the cashmere mill this morning? Girls' outing?'

'Are the police happy with us going out?'

McGregor put down his cup. 'I'll square it,' he said.

Mirabelle decided to push her luck. The tea was helping immensely with her hangover. 'Eleanor, if you don't mind, I have an idea for a spot of investigation . . .'

'Oh God. You want to go to the Dougals' place and visit that ghastly woman, don't you?'

Mirabelle smiled. 'I'm a terrible nosey parker.'

'She won't have coffee,' Eleanor complained. 'You mark my words. It'll be mid-morning tea and something awful made from oats.'

'I thought you admired the British quality of tolerance.'

'There are limits.' Eleanor rolled her eyes. 'Do you think Gwendolyn's involved in the murders?'

'I don't know.'

'So we're going to snoop.' Eleanor's laugh sounded percussive. 'Next you'll be telling me Lady Dougal strangled Nina in cold blood.' She paused. 'Actually, I'm quite looking forward to you telling me that.'

Half an hour later, with Tash raised from slumber, the women piled into the car. It was cold. Motherly, Eleanor fixed the angle of Tash's hat. 'Better,' she said. Alan and Bruce stood in the open doorway and waved as Eleanor switched on the engine and turned the car in an arc so wide that the left side slumped off the driveway on to the damp grass. She gestured defiantly at her husband, tooted the horn as she righted the vehicle, and set off at speed. Tash slipped her arm through Mirabelle's in the back seat and gave it a squeeze.

'Gorgeous morning,' she commented.

'Miss Bevan has been digging dirt, Tash,' Eleanor called over her shoulder. 'And has uncovered the matter of your godmother and Lady Gwendolyn Dougal.'

'Oh. That,' Tash sounded dismissive.

'You knew?' Mirabelle said.

Camera flashes sparked as they speeded through the estate gates, but Eleanor showed no sign of slowing as she swung the car on to the main road with more precision than she had managed at the top of the drive.

'Nina liked people,' Tash said. 'But she liked people with titles best of all.'

Nobody said any more as they hurtled along. The sky was so clear today that Mirabelle could make out every detail – a flock of rooks dotted a stretch of open farmland and, above them, a scatter of lapwings; they hung elegantly in mid-air, where the cloud thinned to gossamer revealing a giddy slash of blue.

Gradually Eleanor speeded up, following the road through a stretch of bad bends, until she swerved through a bank of trees which gave on to an unexpected lake. She stopped dead a few feet from the shore, more abandoning the car than actually parking it. 'Well, we're here. That's the loch-ch-ch,' she announced with vigour. 'Took me a long time to get that.'

The woollen mill stood on the water, through a patch of fir trees. It comprised a collection of rough stone buildings that fitted together into a small campus, like a steading surrounded by trees. Between the evergreens, bare branches jutted like skeletons. Behind what Mirabelle assumed were the older, original buildings, an area had been cleared and a tidy array of Nissan huts had been added, corrugated iron furred with thick, green moss. 'Storage,' Tash explained. 'They gave us the full tour when we came before.'

Eleanor abandoned the keys in the ignition.

'I feel sick,' said Tash.

Mirabelle had to concur. The bends were not compatible with the amount of gin she had consumed the night before. Eleanor was oblivious. 'Come on.' She led the way down a path into a small reception area. Inside, a worn wooden counter stood unmanned. Behind it, a sign outlined what to do in the event of a nuclear attack. Eleanor sighed, as if the staff ought to be in attendance, like the concierge in the reception of a grand hotel.

'There isn't even a bell,' she said, testily. 'I've told them a hundred times. There are the tourists to think of.'

Through the open door, Mirabelle regarded the deserted yard and thought of the route they'd driven without passing a single soul and only one small, handwritten sign pointing the way. She'd have been surprised if there was another living soul in miles and certainly no tourists. From the slate roof, two gulls eyed the women glassily and swooped over the water.

'Yoo-hoo!' Eleanor called and, when there was no reply, marched outside and knocked on another door, flecked with peeling paint. This yielded results. A nervous girl, rather younger than might be expected to be in full-time employment, emerged into the yard as if she had received an electric shock. She wore a green tweed skirt and a pale yellow sweater that certainly wasn't cashmere.

'Mrs Robertson,' she squawked, an HB pencil gripped so tightly between her fingers that her knuckles whitened.

'Good morning, Margaret,' Eleanor said kindly. 'Miss Orlova has come back to check on her order and I've brought Miss Bevan, who would like to do some shopping.'

'Right-o,' the girl said and, with a sense of purpose, she walked back into reception and smartly turned the key in a wooden door marked 'showroom' at the end of the desk. Inside, two fluorescent strips flickered into a harsh flood of light. Below them, spaced evenly, two plastic models sported cashmere polo necks over casual, tartan skirts. Behind these, row upon row of shelves, floor to ceiling, contained folded woollen items in a rainbow of colours. Propped up against the shelves were two large photographs of stiff-looking models wearing colourful V-necks. Margaret switched on a two-bar electric fire.

'Obviously, they could do better for display,' Eleanor commented. 'I mean, it doesn't make one want to buy, does it? But look at this.' She pulled a few sweaters off the shelf and laid them on a rickety trestle table that was erected to the side. 'You have to feel it. Good cashmere will last you a lifetime,' she enthused. The wool smelled raw – fresh off the loom. It draped beautifully.

Behind her, Tash fitted a cashmere tippet on to the model. 'That's better,' she said. 'And look at this,' she gestured as she picked a pale peach wrap from another shelf. 'It's for you, Mirabelle,' she declared. 'Orange is notoriously difficult to wear but you'll do it. That evening dress you had on the first night you were here was so chic. Oh yes, that's perfect.' She held the length of material up to Mirabelle's cheek and called over her shoulder to Margaret, 'Is there a mirror?'

'I'll see.' The girl ducked out of sight. Eleanor mimed shooting herself in the head at the idiocy of not having a mirror in the showroom. 'No customer service,' she proclaimed.

Tash smoothed the knit to Mirabelle's skin. 'People keep saying I should be a model,' she said, 'but I don't fancy it.' She struck a pose for an exquisite, frozen moment, arms outstretched. Then she smiled. 'Nina was indulging me this trip, you know. I want to be a designer. That's why I came along. She was having some of my designs made up, though she didn't approve.'

'I don't blame her.' Eleanor sounded startled. 'Modelling pays so well. Girls are earning extraordinary sums these days.'

'I saw the cashmere down at the lodge. On the table,' Mirabelle said more encouragingly. 'I was drawn to the turquoise.'

Tash's eyes lit. 'It's a wonderful shade. I chose it for next season – by the time we've had it made up, it'll be winter 1959, can you imagine? People think knitwear is about the collars, but actually it's about the fit on the body,' she said as she warmed to the topic. 'The length of the sleeve is the important thing. I like a flared sleeve. It's modern.'

'Oh yes. I can see that,' Mirabelle said.

'It takes more fabric but there's definitely a market at the top end for something unusual – fitted on the body and then . . .' She flicked her fingers. 'Something new.'

Margaret returned with an inadequately small, hand-held mirror in which, squinting to make herself out, Mirabelle could see that Tash was right.

'Nina could wear orange, but she never did,' Tash continued. 'Red. Boring red. I think these mid-pastels are wonderful, don't you?' She pulled out a cardigan with a Peter Pan collar the colour of heather and held it up to her cheek. The buttons were like tiny pearls. 'Oh god, I thought I was done, but I guess I'd better take this one too. They'd cost five times as much in New York.'

Mirabelle remembered the huge percentages in Nina's diary. She was about to ask something about mark-ups, when a woman wearing an ill-fitting brown tweed suit appeared in the doorway. Her jacket collar was edged with velvet, which made it stick out in an awkward V.

'Good morning, ladies,' she said as if the words were an announcement. 'Miss Orlova, I'd like to extend our condolences. We were all sorry to hear about your godmother.'

Tash put down the cardigan. 'Thanks,' she said, biting her lip. 'Oh gosh. I'm getting upset again.'

It must be difficult, Mirabelle thought, everyone talking about Nina. She knew from experience, grief came and went like a cruel game of hide and seek. Tash pulled herself together. 'I came to confirm,' she said. 'Nina was working on behalf of several boutiques, as you know. The orders still stand despite her death. I'd like to ship just as we arranged.'

'It's extremely thoughtful of you at such a difficult time, miss.'

'She would have hated to let anybody down,' Tash said sadly. 'And I'd like to add an order too. Those green hats with the bobbles we looked at? Do you know the ones I mean?'

'Certainly.'

'I'll take two dozen of those. Three-ply. They're just the thing for a New York winter.'

The woman shifted her weight slightly.

'Nina didn't like them but I do,' Tash continued. 'They'll sell well at this little place I know. And that'll be all, apart from this cardigan. I'll take that now. It's for me.' She handed it over.

'Right.' The woman handed the cardigan to Margaret, who now hovered in the doorway. 'Wrap that, would you, dear?' she said. 'And would you like to take that peach stole, madam?'

'Oh, yes, please,' said Mirabelle. 'Tash has a frightfully good eye. Do you make all of this here?'

'Yes, miss,' the woman said. 'I can take you around the weaving sheds, if you'd like.'

Eleanor pointedly looked at her watch. 'Your call, Mirabelle, but we can't do everything.'

They paid, took their parcels and walked back to the car. Mirabelle slipped the stole out of its brown paper and draped it over her shoulders on top of her coat. 'You disagreed with your godmother about the order she made?'

'She could be old-fashioned,' Tash said. 'She was wrong about those hats. People will go wild for them, don't you think, Eleanor?'

'I can see youngsters wearing them next winter,' Eleanor enthused. 'Skating in Central Park.'

Tash loitered beside the car door. 'I suppose I can do what I want. Now that she's gone.'

'Is there something you would like to do, that you couldn't before?' Mirabelle pressed. 'Bobble hats notwithstanding?'

Tash stuck her hands in her pockets. 'I don't know,' she said. 'It's still sinking in. One minute I'm heartbroken and then I just want to get on. The hats are a start, I guess.'

Along the bank, vivid yellow crocuses peeked through the undergrowth like doubloons cast on the shore. The water was smooth as glass. Eleanor reached into her handbag and brought out a silver cigarette case. Mirabelle and Tash both declined. She leaned against the car and lit a smoke.

'Are those Capstans?' Mirabelle asked.

'I know. Terrible, right? I can't help it. Bruce has tried everything – he bought me a carton of some smart Italian brand but it turns out I have the palate of a sailor. He won't let these in the house.' She took a deep draw and put her arm around Mirabelle's shoulder. 'They learned to swim right here, our men. Can't you see them, two skinny kids splashing about for dear life? The water is freezing even in high summer.' She chortled.

Ahead of them, a bird dived for fish, falling from the sky like a stone and emerging triumphant with a squirming, silvery trout. Eleanor stubbed out her cigarette and slipped into the driving seat. 'Come on,' she said. 'Let's get it over with.'

'What do you mean?' Tash sounded perturbed.

'Gwendolyn. It's almost eleven and Mirabelle has questions she wants to ask the old bird.'

Tash raised her eyebrows.

'I like to be thorough,' Mirabelle said.

The Dougals' house was a castle. The road began to climb away from the loch-side as the women drove towards it, the gradient becoming steeper and the engine labouring. 'Wow,' Tash breathed as five storeys of hewn granite with two towers and a keep swept into view. 'Is that . . . real?'

'You have to go over the bridge.' Eleanor gestured towards a worn wooden drawbridge that spanned the shallow moat. A huge yellow and red lion rampant flew from the other side. 'It's real all right.' Eleanor sounded weary. 'It still looks like it did in the fifteenth century, inside as well as out. Medieval Scotland was neither warm nor comfortable. Brace yourselves.'

On cue, the moan of bagpipes started somewhere in the interior.

'Oh god.' Eleanor sounded annoyed. 'I forgot they did that.'

'Did what?' Mirabelle enquired.

'Porridge. Bagpipes. Dead stags,' she said dismissively.

The moat was mostly filled with mud that had frozen in

patches. A few gloomy-looking puddles had freshly formed on the surface after the heavy rain. A long tartan pennant ran down one turret. Eleanor led them through the archway and into a cobbled quad. 'The Dougals were Jacobites,' she said. 'That's how the story goes.'

Tash looked blank.

'It's just one set of royalty fighting with another,' Eleanor clarified. 'Kings against kings. Anyway, the Jacobites are sainted, pretty much, though they lost. The story goes that Bonnie Prince Charlie spent three nights here on his retreat from Culloden. That's where he lost,' she said, with a matter-of-fact air.

Before they reached the front door, it opened, and Willie Dougal appeared with two jaunty terriers at his heel. 'Ladies!' he called. 'What a lovely surprise. Welcome to Brochmor.'

They removed their coats in the hallway. Eleanor had not exaggerated. The hall rose over thirty feet and was decorated with spears and pikes that had clearly been there for centuries. Three tattered flags were nailed over a wide fireplace – two ropey-looking saltires and another lion rampant. On either side of the hearth, bashed-up suits of armour were displayed on stands and, above them, several stag heads mounted on dark wooden shields. Tash stared and then raised her eyes, transfixed by the wooden beams. 'It's a great old place,' Willie said jovially. Mirabelle shivered. It might be a great old place, but Eleanor was right – it was cold.

'We popped by to visit Gwendolyn,' Eleanor announced.

An expression flickered across Willie's face that betrayed the fact that this was unlikely in the usual run of things. 'She's in her chamber,' he said, and started to lead them upstairs, the dogs following obediently as the sound of the pipes receded. The hallway was dark despite the brightness of the morning. The castle had small windows set into its thick walls and they glowed like diamonds against the dark stone. Mirabelle noted that the sills stretched three feet deep.

'What're the bagpipes for?' Tash asked.

'The men always practise at this time of day,' Willie said. 'When we have guests, they're woken by the pipes. It's the best alarm clock. At Christmas we host a ceilidh and they play there too. You'd love it.'

The day room was at the end of the corridor. Behind the heavy oak door, several freestanding lamps blazed and the walls were lined with tapestries in yellow and burnt orange. Gwendolyn was stationed at an oak writing desk by the fire, a cigarette burning in the ashtray beside her and her terrier at her feet. The room smelled of dried lavender and the faintest whiff of damp dog.

'Oh,' Gwendolyn said, 'how lovely.' She rose and pulled sharply on a long piece of fabric that hung beside the mantel. 'I'll have them bring us tea.' The terrier growled and Gwendolyn ignored him. She kissed Eleanor on the cheek, gave Tash a hug and held out her hand to Mirabelle. 'Will you be joining us, darling?' she asked her husband, who loitered uneasily in the doorway.

'No, no. You ladies enjoy yourselves,' he said.

As he left, the women arranged themselves in the old chairs around the fireplace. On the mantel, several highly polished, silver-framed pictures contained photographs of the couple – Gwendolyn sticking a rosette on an enormous prize bull, Willie hunting with a gun over his forearm, and the two of them dressed for a Highland Ball, a showy diamond brooch pinned to a tartan sash over Gwendolyn's shoulder. Mirabelle shifted in her seat.

'To what do I owe this honour?' Gwendolyn asked.

'I thought Tash and Mirabelle might like to see the castle,' Eleanor replied.

'It is such an attraction, isn't it?' Gwendolyn sounded smug. 'Bonnie Prince Charlie stayed here for three nights on his retreat from Culloden and Queen Victoria and Prince Albert spent a night in the same bed in 1856.'

'I do hope it wasn't exactly the same bed?' Tash giggled.

'Brochmor has a long and illustrious history,' Gwendolyn continued drily. 'Willie's family has owned everything for miles around for generations. He's still the clan chief, though these days it's more an honorary title. He's just a simple farmer, really.'

The door opened and a maid in a traditional black and white uniform brought a tray laid with tea things. Mirabelle noticed oat biscuits – just as Eleanor had predicted; four on the plate, which seemed a touch exacting. Mrs Gillies, for all her faults, doled out food lavishly. Gwendolyn poured the tea, brushing off the maid as if the girl was an annoyance. 'I can show you around,' she offered. 'Everybody says the view from the ramparts is extraordinary. Did you hear the piper? We live our traditions here.'

'It's so important,' Eleanor said, her tone absolutely flat. Mirabelle thought it was game of her to play along because she definitely wasn't enjoying herself.

'Yes,' Gwendolyn enthused, seemingly unaware. 'It means the world up here because Scotland is essentially still tribal. Willie's people, the tenants, I mean, appreciate his leadership. Tash dear, how are you coping? It must be a comfort now that your uncle, the baron, has arrived.'

Tash bit into a biscuit and found she couldn't speak. She chewed noisily before managing to swallow. 'Not for me. I ate a huge breakfast,' Mirabelle said as Gwendolyn swung the plate towards her. 'We're trying to figure out Nina's last hours,' she continued. 'That's the thing. And we wondered if she mentioned anything to you, Gwendolyn? Anything she might have been worried about?'

'To me? Why ever would she mention anything to me?' Gwendolyn put down the plate.

'I just wondered if anything had come up when you two met. For champagne. Before dinner the other night.'

Gwendolyn looked uncomfortable. 'Who told you?' she asked, and then answered her own question, 'Ah. Her black man.'

Mirabelle's skin prickled. 'Gregory did mention it,' she said, trying to keep Gwendolyn talking. 'What did you talk about?'

'This and that. People we had in common. The state of the world.'

'What was Nina's view on the state of the world?'

'Very much the same as mine,' Gwendolyn said with a smile. 'She was a sensible woman. She understood we need to keep control of things in the West – that we need to work together.'

'To keep out the Reds, you mean?' Tash demanded.

'Exactly. They can't threaten us. Now, more than ever, it is up to the Allies to stick together.'

'The Russians, as I recall, were our allies during the war,' Mirabelle said.

Gwendolyn looked outraged. 'That's hardly relevant. There's no excuse for what they're doing. Bloody backward Communist bullies – our local schoolchildren are undergoing drills, you know. In the event of—'

'Honestly, Gwendolyn,' Eleanor couldn't bear it any longer. 'It's not so black and white. The West has done its fair share of bullying. Britain isn't what it was, let's face it.'

This riled Gwendolyn. 'What nonsense!' she muttered. 'Look at the way the Russians behaved over Suez. Bloody cheek! Anyway,' she struggled to control herself. 'We should go up to the ramparts. You know what the Scottish weather is like. If we don't get up there while the sun is out, it'll be tipping down before we know it. You can't come to Brochmor and not see the view.'

They abandoned the tea things. The dog came with them. As they climbed the stairs, he wound between their legs, almost tripping them up. Mirabelle caught Eleanor's eye and they smiled like naughty schoolgirls. From the ramparts the view was as extraordinary as Gwendolyn had promised. Bagpipe practice over, they settled into the thick silence, which was only broken now and then by the sound of the birds and the wind. Gwendolyn began a commentary that she had clearly given several times before. 'This part of the castle is thirteenth century – built by Lord Fraser Dougal and completed in 1275, and over there is a later addition, built in the early eighteenth century. Johnny-come-lately,' she laughed at her own joke. 'We have a ghost,' she added. 'Not as sad a story as your Green Lady.'

'I didn't know you believed in ghosts.' Eleanor kept her tone measured – quite a feat.

Gwendolyn continued with relish. 'The castle is haunted by Lord Fraser Dougal's son, Robert. He died at the battle of Stirling Bridge in 1297, fighting alongside William Wallace. They say he couldn't bear to leave Brochmor. Occasionally someone sees him here on the ramparts. Sweet, really. It must be awful to have an unhappy ghost – I mean the Green Lady is so tragic.'

Eleanor's slim smile strained. 'We manage.'

'He walled her up, didn't he? The husband. When she

locked herself in her room? Starved to death, poor thing. Now, let me see, that must be Bruce's great-great-great-great-grandfather. I heard someone saw her in the village on Wednesday night. They say she appears if the laird hurts a woman.'

'Oh, for heaven's sake. There's no such thing as ghosts, Gwendolyn. It's just a stupid story,' Eleanor snapped.

There was some weak warmth in the sun. Mirabelle turned her face towards it. She worked out the direction of the railway, though you couldn't see it from the castle. Old habits, she chided herself, always figuring out how to get away. The tracks were close, she realised, though whoever had been the laird when the railway was laid clearly had a hand in keeping the steam trains out of his line of vision. At a glance, nothing much had changed here in centuries. Bruce was right, she thought, the biggest shake-up the place had seen since the Jacobites was probably Eleanor with her forward-thinking determination. She had taken on a lot – ghosts and all.

Gwendolyn continued her commentary as if nothing had happened. 'Do you see that little whitewashed bothy?' She pointed. 'Willie's grandmother had it built. She and her husband used to play at being crofters. They'd stay overnight and she'd make porridge. Silly but romantic. It's nothing like a real cottage inside, of course. They made frightfully posh crofters but it's a sweet story.'

'Do you and Willie ever stay overnight in the bothy?' Tash's eyes sparkled.

'Certainly not!'

Downstairs, in the great hall, the maid arrived with their coats. Gwendolyn continued playing lady of the manor, talking about the thickness of the walls and the horrors of the dungeon. 'It's full of wine now, and barrels of whisky,' she cooed. 'They say if you were incarcerated in the Dougal dungeons, you could scream for a hundred years and nobody would hear. The best of it is we don't need to build a fall-out shelter. I mean, if we had a new house like yours . . .' she drawled. Mirabelle smiled politely. Bruce and Eleanor's house had been built in the eighteenth century.

'Well, you must come for dinner one evening,' Gwendolyn continued. 'Are you free over the next few days?'

'We'll see about the arrangements for the Orlovs,' Eleanor piped up. 'The police have not yet released Nina's body.'

'Yes, of course. It's a time of mourning.'

Mirabelle wasn't quite ready to leave but it was difficult to get a word in edgewise, never mind find out anything useful. 'My, aren't you colourful?' Gwendolyn commented as Mirabelle pulled on her coat.

She took her chance. 'I can't help wondering, how did you meet Nina, Gwendolyn?'

Gwendolyn's chest practically swelled. 'She wrote to me,' she said. 'When she knew she was coming to Scotland. She'd heard about the castle and asked if she might visit.'

'And did she?'

Gwendolyn looked sad. 'She didn't have time. Her life was cut so tragically short.'

'So when you visited her that afternoon . . . ?'

'We had corresponded. I had seen pictures of her in the society pages – we take all the magazines at Brochmor, even the American ones. Willie has cousins across the pond. I knew Nina and I would get along like a house on fire.'

'Did she invite you over?'

'We were coming to the Robertsons' anyway. It's such a sweet little lodge, isn't it?' Gwendolyn slipped a sly smile.

'It must be so handy for you, Eleanor, when you haven't the room to accommodate guests in the main house.'

Again, Eleanor did not rise to the bait. 'Thank you, Gwendolyn,' she said. 'We'd best be going. Our menfolk will be expecting us.'

Gwendolyn stood waving at the door as the car disappeared down the hill. Tash sat back in her seat and laughed. 'God, she is awful, isn't she?'

'Well, she seems to have hit it off with your godmother. Do you know what Nina could possibly have seen in her?' Mirabelle asked.

'I do.' Tash turned in her seat. 'Gwendolyn told us herself – they would have agreed. Politically, I mean.'

'But Gwendolyn is a racist. I don't understand – for a start, Nina employed Gregory . . .'

'My godmother wasn't very . . . nice. That's the truth. Running her stupid errands was all Gregory was fit for as far as she was concerned. She treated him like a slave.' Tash fumbled with a button on her coat. Her cheeks flushed. Mirabelle realised this explained the girl fussing after Gregory, pouring him a whisky. She had been embarrassed by Nina's behaviour. She'd wanted to differentiate herself. Tash pursed her lips. 'Also,' she paused, 'I expect Nina and Gwendolyn had an arrangement.'

'What do you mean?'

The girl heaved a breath dramatically. 'Nina was *partial*, Mirabelle. Gosh, I'm not sure how you even put it here. She liked women. As well as men. She just liked everything, I guess. That's what they said about Nina and my mother. That is why she took me in. My mother was the love of my godmother's life. Not that her death stopped Nina, you know, with other people.'

Mirabelle cast a glance over her shoulder. Gwendolyn was still at the door, waving. From the driver's seat, Eleanor giggled, her eyes alight in the rear-view mirror. 'You look shocked,' she said. 'I guess that's what you get when you go poking around – you can't complain when you actually uncover something.'

'Oh. Quite right. But you mean that Gwendolyn is . . .?' Mirabelle couldn't quite finish the sentence. Gwendolyn Dougal seemed so proper. 'I mean, she's married,' she managed to get out, realising how naïve she sounded.

'It's not entirely a secret, poor Willie. Well, I say poor Willie, but as Bruce always says, perhaps he likes it,' Eleanor said. 'Who can tell?'

Tash seemed relieved to have got this off her chest. 'Gwendolyn was just Nina's type. She had a thing for rich and vicious.'

Mirabelle pieced it together. 'So when Mrs Gillies said she didn't want any gossip—?'

Eleanor cut in. 'She probably meant about a Sapphic love affair. She is protecting *your* honour, Tash. She seems to have taken a shine to you. Or maybe it's the honour of Scotland or Gwendolyn – I don't know. She's probably out-and-out shocked that such things go on, as if it isn't just the way people are. Your face, Mirabelle, is a hoot.'

Mirabelle sat back in her seat. 'It's not that it's shocking – it's a motive, don't you see? Do you think the police know?'

'There have been rumours for years about Gwendolyn Dougal,' Eleanor said over her shoulder.

'So, that afternoon, if they had fought or even if they hadn't. If Gwendolyn had become jealous . . . why, it could be key—'

'Gwendolyn left with her husband that night. I can attest

that she was so drunk she had to be helped into the car,' Eleanor cut in again. 'She can't drive anyway. It's far too modern for her. Are you suggesting Willie drove her back to our place the following night to an assignation with her lover that went wrong?'

'Or perhaps he drove back himself. He might have been overtaken with jealousy. Maybe it wasn't her, it was him.'

Eleanor laughed. 'I've known Willie and Gwendolyn for a few years now. The pair of them are the least passionate people I ever met. I doubt it, Mirabelle. Honestly I do.'

'Gwendolyn was pretty uncomfortable there.'

'That might not be on account of the murder. It takes a special kind of person to blame the Russians for the Suez Crisis rather than Sir Anthony Eden. She probably didn't want to admit her association with Nina. It must be difficult – I mean someone you've had relations with being killed.'

'She doesn't like you much.'

'Of course she doesn't. I'm everything she hates – a trumped-up colonial. I'm somebody who doesn't agree with her about black people and Jews and, well, anybody who isn't like her. She's a snob – she lives in a medieval castle; she'd still have serfs if she could. The best she has to deflect from her secret is to slander Bruce – the Green Lady rises when the laird hurts a woman.'

'I knew Gillies sounded too outraged for it to be about them drinking champagne.'

'Well, at least you know now,' Eleanor said. 'Nina was a lesbian.'

Tash stared out of the window. 'Technically I don't think she was a lesbian. I mean, she liked men too. Back in New York she has quite the following. I'm going to miss this place when I go home,' she said. 'Imagine Gwendolyn sitting there serving tea and biscuits and thinking that we didn't know.'

'I didn't know,' Mirabelle said, sheepishly.

Tash slipped her arm through Mirabelle's once more. 'Maybe it would be best,' she said, 'if you left the investigation to the police.'

Chapter 11

If Heaven had looked upon riches as valuable,
it would not have given them to such fools

The newspaper men blocked the gates. Murdo Kenzie stood in the middle of the drive so Eleanor had to stop. She honked her horn and he grinned at her. 'Two murders on your property, Mrs Robertson,' he shouted when she refused to roll down her window. 'It's only fair we hear your side.'

Eleanor kept honking while the photographers took pictures. When Kenzie finally stood aside, she accelerated. Bruce met them at the front door. 'The police are in the orangery. They want to speak to everyone,' he said.

Inside, the figures were obscured by plants. 'Ah, Miss Bevan,' the inspector greeted the women through the foliage. 'Miss Orlova. Mrs Robertson.'

Next to the senior officer, a uniformed policeman stood to attention. Bruce took a seat on a wicker chair. Niko and McGregor stood side by side next to the stove.

'There's nothing missing,' Niko said, inexplicably.

'It must have come from somewhere,' the detective objected. 'Are you sure it didn't belong to Miss Orlova?'

Niko shook his head. 'Nina wasn't interested in jewellery.'

McGregor put a hand on Niko's back. Looking more closely, Mirabelle could see the baron had a tear in his eye. She was reminded of Tash's story of White Russian women festooned in Fabergé they couldn't sell.

'Jewellery?' she asked, slipping into a seat. 'What do you mean?'

'We found a gemstone. An amethyst.'

'And you think it was Miss Orlova's?'

The policeman looked uncomfortable. McGregor shifted. 'It seems Nina swallowed the thing shortly before she died,' he said.

Tash looked distressed. 'God. That's weird,' she burst out.

Niko made a dismissive sound – a kind of grunt. 'So you cut her?' he said.

'I'm sorry, sir, but under the circumstances . . .'

'It was necessary. I understand.'

'I'd like you to look at these.' The officer removed an envelope from his inside pocket, took out three small square photographs and passed them round. The image was a purple stone on a piece of dark velvet. A wooden ruler lay beside it showing the stone measured half an inch or so, square. 'We're having an expert look at it today in Edinburgh,' the detective continued. 'To see if there is any clue as to where it came from. It's a substantial piece.'

Niko examined the photographs carefully. 'Well, inspector, I think your expert will tell you that isn't an amethyst.'

'Isn't it?'

'It's a large piece of alexandrite,' Niko sounded triumphant.

A ripple of interest shuddered across the room. 'What's alexandrite, Uncle Niko?' Tash asked.

Niko stared at her as if he couldn't believe she had asked the question. 'It's rare, I suppose. Why would you know?

It's Russian. Only found in the Ural Mountains. In daylight it looks green, like an emerald, but in artificial light it appears purplish-red. This picture has been taken under a lamp – hence your error.' He handed back the photographs. 'This stone is worth a lot more than an amethyst – tens of thousands of dollars, I'd say. There's very little of the stuff for sale outside Russia.'

The policeman scribbled notes. 'And you're sure it didn't belong to Miss Orlova?'

Niko lit a cigarette. 'I told you – Nina wasn't interested in that kind of thing. As currency, gemstones aren't popular with my people – not any more. The point is, when I said the Reds were implicated in my sister's murder, everyone thought I was crazy, but now you've found this. A Russian stone. Don't you see?'

Mirabelle noticed the merest flicker of annoyance cross the policeman's face. It must be tiresome, she thought. Murders of women were generally the result of a fight with a man, usually a lover, or at most a dispute over money, and yet here was the victim's brother, repeatedly implicating a hostile state. The officer handed the photographs to Tash.

'It's not hers,' Tash confirmed. 'She didn't even like purple.' Mirabelle thought about the cardigan that Tash had just bought – a paler version of the colour of the stone.

'But it's progress,' Bruce said. 'Somebody is bound to report something that valuable missing. It's a motive, isn't it? Almost a relief, in fact. At least we know what the whole thing is about.'

Orlov looked as if he might hit Bruce. 'My sister was not a jewel thief,' he growled. 'If that's what you're hoping to imply.'

'Not at all, old man.' Bruce sounded shocked.

'So far we've had no report of a robbery, sir,' the detective said. 'Well, if that's all, we'll speak to the staff briefly,' he continued. 'Then we'd best get back to Inverness.' The policemen left the room.

Niko waited until they were gone. 'He wants to accuse Nina of being a thief,' he spat. 'And then he can say she deserved to die for taking the stupid thing.'

'Investigations don't work that way,' McGregor said. 'He's a good detective, that man. He held back the pictures so he could measure our reactions.'

'So he thinks it's one of us?'

'He thinks it might be,' McGregor said. 'Of course.'

Everyone lapsed into an awkward silence, only broken by Bruce rubbing his hands together. 'I could do with a sharpener,' he said. 'Who's with me?'

Niko and Tash fell in behind him. The others stayed where they were. Eleanor seemed stunned and, like Mirabelle, just stared, this time in daylight, at the spot where Nina Orlova had been found.

'Do you think this is related to the murder?' Mirabelle broke the silence.

'Well, it would be weird if it wasn't,' McGregor said. 'Though I can't see how.'

'She must have been hiding it.'

'Probably. But from whom? And why? And where did she get the stone? Niko is determined it wasn't hers. Tash confirmed it.'

'A lover's gift maybe?' Mirabelle suggested.

'A lover?'

'This morning I found out that Nina had formed a connection with Lady Dougal.'

McGregor couldn't help but smile. '*The* Lady Dougal?'

'Yes. Gwendolyn.'

'I say. Well, perhaps it was a gift.'

Eleanor shook her head sadly. 'I've known Willie and Gwendolyn since I first came to Scotland. If Gwendolyn could save half a shilling on the Highland Ball, she'd do it. I'd lay a pound to a penny that it was Nina who stumped up the champagne they were drinking the day they met. I doubt Gwendolyn gave Nina a present worth, what was it? Tens of thousands of dollars.' Eleanor got to her feet. 'Bruce's right. A whisky would help.'

They were well matched, drink for drink, those two, Mirabelle thought. 'We'll be through in a minute,' she said.

They waited for her to leave. Mirabelle got up. She checked through the open door and, finding the hallway empty, closed it.

'What are you doing?'

'I eavesdropped yesterday, on Gillies and Gregory in the kitchen. I'm just checking there's nobody outside to eavesdrop on us.'

McGregor's face split in a grin. 'So, you're a snoop and you're checking nobody else can snoop?'

'Exactly. I think Gillies hates me,' Mirabelle whispered.

'Gillies disapproves of everybody,' he said. 'You can't blame her for not wanting to talk about it all. Highlanders are very tight lipped.'

'What was she like when you were a child?'

'She was a maid in those days.'

'And just as gruff?'

'Actually, she gave me a toffee once.'

'And Mr Gillies? What happened to him?'

'I have no idea. The Great War, I imagine. I suppose this affair you've discovered explains why Nina never married.'

Mirabelle nodded and thought that, if Nina Orlova hadn't married because of her feelings for other women, what

177

might be Niko Orlov's reason for remaining single. Though, the same question, she realised, might be levelled at her and McGregor. Maybe they all had secrets, which had made it more difficult to settle. At least until now.

'This stone looked around six carats. Bigger than your engagement ring.' McGregor lifted Mirabelle's left hand to inspect the pink diamond and then kissed it. 'Mirabelle, there is more. I didn't want to say it in front of the others – well, not the Orlovs.'

'What?'

'It's about Gregory. The detective ran a check with the New York Police Department and Gregory isn't actually Gregory's name. It's Wilbur – Wilbur Jones. That's what it says on his passport. That's why they took him to the station the other day.'

'People go by different names.' Mirabelle shrugged.

'Sure. He might be using an alias for any one of a hundred reasons. He could be hiding a criminal record. Or maybe he's hiding from someone. Or, it could be a stage name, for a particular kind of work.'

'Is that likely?'

'The detective did some digging and found that Gregory boxes semi-professionally. It turns out the Orlovs are not his only source of income. He's good, apparently. He competes locally in New York. He won four knockout fights last year.'

'And he calls himself Gregory?'

'Gregory the Grim. In the last eighteen months he has won a couple of good-sized purses – hundreds of dollars each.'

'Hands-on violence,' Mirabelle said, thinking of the two corpses.

'Strangulation is a piece of cake for a boxer. They're used to fighting up close – skin on skin,' McGregor nodded. 'And there's something else. His alibi isn't holding up or, weirdly, it's turned out to be too sound. It seems he was in Glasgow all right. He drank in a bar near the Clyde – the Scotia – until closing at ten.'

'Do you know the place?'

'Let's just say I wouldn't take you there. But it's a city institution. He was seen, of course. The place was busy.'

'And after that?'

'He went back to his hotel where he ordered more beer in the guest lounge at ten thirty, and then went upstairs. The hotel staff can account for him up until eleven, or just after. Then the maid at the hotel walked into his room at seven a.m. She was under the impression that he had checked out and the room needed to be cleaned. And there he was in bed. Naked. The officer said he made quite an impression on the girl. Of course, that means he couldn't have killed Nina. There's no way he could have got up here, committed the murder and then got back down again for seven. It's over four hours each way, even driving like the clappers.'

'So, he's off the hook?'

'Not exactly. The officer went on to check Gregory's assertion that he went to Greenock that morning.'

'And did he?'

'First thing. He was in the harbourmaster's office looking for a shipping clerk at seven thirty, which is impossible.' McGregor spread his hands, as if he had completed a magic trick. 'Gregory couldn't be naked in a hotel room in central Glasgow at seven and then in Greenock by half past. It's a forty-five-minute drive, perhaps an hour. It's fishy as hell. The man has two alibis and there's definitely something wrong with one of them. That's why they kept him so long.'

Mirabelle considered this. 'Maybe the witnesses got the time wrong.'

'Maybe, though they think it unlikely. They're cross-referencing where they can, but the black man doth protest too much. There's something wrong. They grilled him for ages but he didn't crack. I think they only let him go because they know they can take him back in, any time.'

Mirabelle got up and stared out of the window. A flock of ducks flew overhead in a V formation. McGregor joined her. 'Do you know why they fly fanned out like that?'

'No.'

'Geese do it too. They take turns at the front so the birds behind don't have to struggle through the wind. Geese migrate thousands of miles. That's only possible because they pull together.' He put his hand on Mirabelle's shoulder. 'Like us.'

She leaned into him. Alan McGregor on holiday, or perhaps Alan McGregor in Scotland, seemed to have acquired a smattering of poetry. It was beginning to feel as if they belonged together.

'Do you mean work together?'

'Yes. You are always butting into my investigations . . .'

'Helping, you mean?'

'Look, this isn't my case and it isn't your case either. The police are getting nowhere. We've been frittering about at the edges of it, but maybe we should team up and solve the damn thing together – as a present for Bruce and Eleanor, if nothing else. You take the front. Then I take the front. And we'll get further, faster.' He kissed her shoulder, biting her skin through her silk blouse. She considered his proposition. Everyone said marriage was about teamwork. 'All right,' she said. 'Obviously you're going to have to up your game substantially . . .' She pulled a cushion off the sofa and batted him. McGregor laughed. She took off and he chased her around the orangery as if they were teenagers. In fact, Mirabelle thought, she had never done this when she was a teenager. Not once.

He caught her beside the electric fire and they kissed, springing apart as the door opened and Eleanor wandered in with Jinx at her heel. The dog bolted to Mirabelle's side and nuzzled her hips.

'Don't mind us,' Eleanor said. 'Bruce sent me. He's getting jumpy. They're sitting through there, talking about Susan. Can't keep off it. It's terribly grim. We thought we might visit the MacLeods – the girl's parents – but I can't face it. So we're going shooting. Niko needs some practice and this whole thing has rendered Tash positively murderous. Can I be honest?' Eleanor did not wait for an answer. 'When I first met you, Mirabelle, I thought you were cold. I didn't see what you saw in her, Alan. But having you here, I have to say, it's lovely to have family around.'

'Thanks,' said Mirabelle.

'She's just English,' McGregor chipped in. 'What you're taking for coldness. It's just people over the border.'

Mirabelle hit him again with the cushion. 'That's enough,' she said.

But it wasn't her Englishness, she thought, as Alan took her hand and they followed Eleanor into the hall. It was all those years of the war, living through the Blitz and ending up in Brighton, of all places. Not that she minded Brighton. But when you'd lost everyone and were truly alone, you couldn't be warm. She'd spent more than a decade, she realised, in a cold kind of coping. Being happy again had felt like a betrayal of the people who'd died. As they slipped into the drawing room, she realised she felt warmer in this cold place than she had in all her time in Brighton. McGregor and his family were heating her through. The room smelled of wood smoke and tobacco. Jinx settled on the rug. Bruce poured drinks.

'I was thinking we could ring an agent down south and see what they have on their books. They might send photographs,' McGregor announced brightly. Mirabelle looked blank. 'Houses,' McGregor continued. 'I mean, we'll need somewhere to live.'

Eleanor clapped Alan on the shoulder. 'That's progress,' she said.

Progress, Mirabelle thought. But her mind wasn't on houses and weddings any more than it ever was. That wasn't the kind of teamwork she was interested in.

Nina Orlova had gone to the orangery to meet somebody and it was something to do with this gemstone, or the money it was worth. That's why she had been killed. And that meant the murderer couldn't be a prowler. It had always been unlikely, but today's developments made it impossible. Mirabelle heard Tash's voice from the night before, as if it was an echo. 'That means it's one of us,' the girl had said, but that wasn't necessarily true. It simply meant the murder hadn't been entirely random. Whoever they were, the murderer had either been buying, selling or stealing a large piece of alexandrite.

Chapter 12

Dreams are the touchstones of character

The pressmen looked rattled, and quite rightly. From the roof terrace it would have been easy to pick them off. Bruce clearly relished the possibility. He took aim carefully and fired a potshot at one of the large fir trees close to the gate.

'Darling!' Eleanor chided him.

'I thought there was a pigeon,' he lied.

'Now, now, old man,' McGregor said. 'Not even in jest.'

The entrance to the terrace wasn't grand. A door in the upstairs hallway led to a small vestibule, like a cupboard, and up a set of steep stairs that were only just better than a ladder. At the top, cold air kissed their skin and the sky played out its panorama.

The terrace was larger than Mirabelle had imagined when she saw it from the road. She and Tash sat languidly on a wooden bench that was weighted down with bricks so it wouldn't tumble in high winds. They spread out the velvet cushions they'd brought from downstairs, and half a dozen thick cashmere rugs that Mrs Gillies had passed up to them. 'This is much more glamorous than when I went shooting in Montana,' Tash said, her breath clouding in the cold as she settled into a nest while Eleanor set up a picnic of several small pies propped up by a large pile of pickled onions and a bottle of Tio Pepe.

Bruce laid the guns against the slated incline. 'We should try to bring everything down over the back field. It'll be tidier for picking up the kill, what with Jinx being a useless hunting dog.'

Mirabelle wondered about the fate of the ducks that had flown overhead. She hoped they hadn't lingered. The season was coming to a close. If they made it to the end of the month, they'd survive the summer. Eleanor put a pickled onion in her mouth. 'Pigeons and rabbits,' she said. 'Let me,' she motioned towards her husband's gun. Bruce helped her to aim and fire. 'Oh yes, it makes you feel better, doesn't it?' she said, 'even if you don't hit anything.'

Bruce was a passable teacher. He fitted each gun and took turns to tutor them individually. Mirabelle declined. Tash was, as she had intimated, a natural, bringing down several pigeons and, in error, one crow, whooping whenever she hit anything as if, Eleanor said quietly, she was in the audience at an American football match. Niko found it more difficult to bag his shot, though in the end he had the best kill – a deer that wandered out of the wood behind the house.

'May I?' he checked before firing.

'If it's on our land, we can shoot it,' Bruce said, and patted Niko on the back when he brought the animal down.

'Bruce shot a deer from our bedroom window once. It was just after we got married,' Eleanor said fondly. 'It was eating the saplings we planted because I wanted to be able to see blossom from my window. The trees would have died if he hadn't. He leaned out of the window and kaboom! I thought, "Wow. That's macho!"'

Bruce's colour heightened. 'Deer are a menace,' he said.

They swigged Tio Pepe to keep them warm.

Around four o'clock the pressmen began to move off and Bruce, Eleanor, Tash and McGregor went to bring in the kill or, as Bruce called it, 'Go for a walk.'

'The last time we went for a walk it wasn't so great,' Niko smirked when he was invited, so he and Mirabelle stayed on the roof to dismantle the picnic and stack the guns.

'I'm sorry about Natasha yesterday,' he apologised once they were alone. 'She's very passionate.'

'Not at all. I'm fond of her.'

'I hope she didn't offend you with that snob stuff. Where were you brought up? London?'

'Yes.'

'Fewer guns,' Niko commented. 'And no need to hunt rabbits.'

'Hunting has never been my bag. You and your sister were brought up in town too?'

'The bright lights of New York, New York.'

'I'm fascinated by your sister.'

'Nina was an original. You couldn't shove her into a kitchen and expect her to conform. I could see you two getting along.'

'I still can't figure out why she came up to the house that night. I keep getting drawn back to what she was doing here?'

Niko tipped the ash from his cigarette into a green glass ashtray on the picnic table. With his shirtsleeves rolled up, he regarded her slyly from beneath his lids.

'Aren't you cold?' she asked.

'I like cold. I like the sensation.'

'What do you think your sister was doing up here?' Mirabelle pushed him.

'You know who I think did it.'

'The Communists.'

'Sure. They ruined our lives. If the Revolution hadn't happened, by the time she was twenty-one, Nina would have married a minor aristocrat, and so would I, and we'd be living in St Petersburg with tons of children. Winter in town – balls and parties, summer at the dacha, swimming in the sea.'

'Would you have preferred that?'

Niko smiled. He was, she thought, extremely handsome. 'Tash tells me you aren't keen on marriage. Are you having second thoughts about your hero the hunter? All these displays of . . . togetherness . . . I don't find them entirely convincing.'

'Your niece is observant.' Mirabelle tried to stay relaxed. 'But on this occasion she's wrong. I love Alan.'

'So what's your problem with tying the knot?'

'What's your problem, Baron? You haven't married either.'

Niko laughed. The sound seemed to ricochet off the chimney and disappear into the stack of cashmere rugs. He stared at her lazily, his gaze frank. 'I almost married once. It's difficult. I know it sounds crazy, but what happened to my family has scarred our souls, Miss Bevan. It's terrible to not have a home. It brings to your attention, shall we say, that the real treasures are people. That's why Tash is so loyal. So fierce. The truth is that giving someone my absolute trust might be beyond me. We lost everything.'

It struck Mirabelle that a certain kind of woman would love this sort of talk. Niko was a potent mix of American, well-to-do businessman and tortured Russian aristocrat. She wondered if Nina had been as dramatic. He leaned in. 'There's something almost Russian about you, Miss Bevan. Ice and fire.'

'My grandmother was French,' Mirabelle tried gamely, stepping back. 'Perhaps it's that.'

Mirabelle stared at him, sensing that there was more. The silence lay between them. Niko held out for about a minute. He lit another cigarette. 'When the Orlovs came to the States, people thought we'd too much money or we had it easy. They gossiped about whether our family should have retained our title. They questioned if we had betrayed people. Done some kind of deal. The fact that we got out and were OK somehow made us suspect.' He blew air through his lips to demonstrate the hopelessness of such debate. 'People judged us. They made assumptions. They thought Nina was flippant. She worked in fashion. She spent her life in and out of shops – the byways of filthy lucre. And then there was her personal life. A single parent, in effect. A woman of . . .' he paused, clearly considering how to phrase it, 'varied tastes. So much of her life was inconsequential. Sinful, even. But my sister knew right from wrong. Since we were children. I suspect that you, Miss Bevan, are more alternative than either she or me when it comes down to it. So, I feel defensive of her. She was misunderstood in life and now—'

Tash appeared at the head of the stairs. 'Oh god, you aren't pulling that routine, are you, Uncle Niko? Leave Mirabelle alone,' she said, stepping on to the terrace. 'Two unsolved murders and all you can do is flirt!' Her frame disappeared behind the pile of colourful cushions which, balanced precariously in her arms, wobbled as she swept back downstairs. A trail of lily of the valley lingered in her wake.

'Have I embarrassed you?' Niko asked.

Mirabelle shook her head. 'I don't normally talk about relationships, that's all.'

'You think that was talking about relationships?' Niko's gaze softened. 'Well, he'd be a lucky man, your policeman. If he isn't going to be lucky, come and see me, won't you?'

Mirabelle felt herself blush. Niko clicked his heels. Then he lifted the guns in their cases and made for the stairs.

A minute later, Mirabelle flopped on to the bench. She pulled one of the cashmere throws over her coat. Below, the others were returning to the house, the random route they were taking across the field attesting to their drunkenness. She reached for a cigarette and was still smoking when McGregor returned to the terrace.

'What do you think?' he asked.

'I think the Robertsons are cracking up,' she said. 'It's probably sinking in that they have to live here once the crime is solved and we've all gone home. They're thinking of pulling down the orangery. Eleanor can't face visiting Susan's family. Have you any ideas who did it yet?'

McGregor sat down next to her. 'Is this whole thing just a jewel robbery, do you think?'

'A robbery that nobody has reported?'

He pulled her on to his lap, one hand caressing her hip, the other curled around her waist. They sat like that for a while. The light began to dim. It got dark early this far north, but the sunsets were worth it. A peachy glow began to burn on the horizon as a black van drove up the back lane from the gates where the newsmen had finished packing up. The sound of its engine carried on the breeze. Inside the house, lights went on along the first floor as people went up to dress for dinner. Mirabelle was about to suggest they went down. She would have liked a bath. Then a movement at the back of the house caught her eye. A figure shrouded in black came out of the kitchen door and disappeared behind the staff quarters. She got to her feet. 'Look,' she said, flicking the butt of her cigarette into the gutter.

McGregor joined her at the railing.

'Who is it?'

It was difficult to tell from above. Part of the view was obscured by the roof. Mirabelle pulled herself over the barrier and clambered up the slated incline to get a better view. Behind, McGregor let out a loud tutting sound, but he followed her. 'Is this how you solve crimes at home?' he asked.

'Sort of. I look for the things that don't fit.'

'So in this instance . . .'

Mirabelle sighed. 'Who the hell is that?'

They waited. The figure must have stopped somewhere near the staff quarters, exactly in their blind spot.'

'What else doesn't fit?' McGregor asked.

'Apart from the gemstone in Nina Orlova's stomach? It's bothered me from the beginning, actually. Her clothes.'

'Clothes?'

'Nina's outfit. She and Tash had dressed for dinner. Cocktail dresses, Tash said. They stayed up late, they'd eaten and played cards. Then Tash went to bed and Nina got changed. Fair enough, but if I was going rambling up a hill in the middle of the night, I wouldn't choose a red wool suit. I'd wear trousers and sensible shoes. Feel how cold it is now, never mind at three a.m.'

'Did Nina ever wear trousers? I don't recall any in her wardrobe.'

Mirabelle considered this. 'You might be right. Perhaps she didn't own any, or at least didn't pack them. But still, that suit was the kind of outfit you'd wear to a smart lunch. And with heels.'

A worried expression flickered across his face. 'Really? When you've been solving my cases – is this the kind of thing you've been concentrating on?'

'Well, how do you do it?'

'Police work. I work my way back from the murder. I follow the final movements of the victim. I interview everyone they came into contact with. Most times it's the most obvious person.'

'Most times,' she said, her tone betraying her scepticism. 'So who's the most obvious person here?'

'Annoyingly, the most likely murderer was Nina Orlova, don't you think? She was the one with the most complicated life. She was the one with the secrets. It feels as if she was aggressive. And yet, she ended up the victim.'

Mirabelle was about to say something about the alexandrite being a secret – someone else's secret – when the figure emerged from the back of the house on to the lane. It was Gregory. They could both see that now, his distinctive rolling gait, the way he held his shoulders. 'What's he doing?' McGregor asked. He was running – sprinting, in fact, up the lane towards where they'd found Susan – to the spot where the black van had parked in a passing place cut into the hill. The passenger door opened and Gregory got in. Mirabelle and McGregor waited a split second for the engine to start, but it didn't. 'Come on,' McGregor offered his hand to help her down. 'Our friend Wilbur is up to something.'

The two of them rushed inside, down two flights of stairs and through the hallway. Mrs Gillies was working in the kitchen as they burst in. 'Sir!' she objected, but there was no time to explain. They crashed through a second hallway at the rear, past the laundry where a whiff of soapsuds hung on the air, past a rack which, Mirabelle realised, still held Susan's coat and hat, and out of the back door.

'That van belongs to one of the newsmen. He's selling his story,' McGregor panted. 'Bastard.'

Mirabelle's mind raced. Of course. The red tops would pay for an account of what was happening inside the house. She wondered if Gregory knew about the alexandrite. He must – surely the police had questioned him about it. Tash would be furious or, worse, heartbroken when she found out he'd sold her out, Mirabelle thought as they hammered up the lane in the twilight, coming to a halt as McGregor put out his hand to stop her a few yards behind the van. Both of them were out of breath.

Then they heard it. The sound of a struggle. The acoustics weren't normal because of the trees and the way the land cut away to one side, and at first, eerily, Mirabelle thought the sound was coming from behind them, but then she realised it emanated from the van itself. McGregor pressed his finger to his lips. He flicked his head towards the low stone wall that ran around the passing place. Together they climbed over the copings and he pulled her down behind a tangle of roots where a tree had been removed. Then, the two of them peered over the top. Inside the van, Gregory and another man were fighting. The sound of one of them banging against the side made her pull back.

'Should we help him?' she whispered.

McGregor shook his head. 'Gregory the Grim can take care of himself. Let's listen and see if they say anything.'

Another bang emanated from the van. Then it began to rock. Mirabelle stood up. 'They're not fighting,' she said.

'Well what are they . . . ?' McGregor didn't finish this question as the answer came to him. 'Oh, god. Well I'm not arresting them. That's a whole can of worms. It's a bit cold out here, isn't it?'

Mirabelle grinned. During the war, London's parks were famously the haunts of homosexual activity at night. Churchill himself once expressed his admiration for men braving the icy winter weather. 'Makes you proud to be British,' he'd said. She'd heard that the American troops were just as bad. There had been some excitement in gay circles, what with the influx of American soldiers, including black regiments. Mirabelle remembered one upper-class queer referring to them as 'fresh pansy blood' at a party.

'Oh God, that's it,' she hissed. 'Of course.'

'What?'

'Gregory's alibi. It was another man. In the bed, I mean. In the hotel.'

McGregor shook his head. 'The maid identified him.'

'You think she was looking at his face?' Mirabelle smiled. 'You think anyone even thought there might be two black guys. In Glasgow. Both homosexuals? But it's a port, isn't it? Like Bruce said. Gregory got lucky – good for him. And it means he probably *was* in Greenock the morning Nina's body was discovered, just as he said – even further away from the scene of the crime. He left the hotel while the other guy was still asleep.'

'Maybe,' said McGregor as he worked it out.

'Should we tell the police?'

McGregor shook his head. 'It's illegal. I don't know how they view that kind of thing up here. If we say anything, they might arrest him. But at least we know. I'll check with him, discreetly, later. If you're right, it means we can count Gregory out.' McGregor screwed up his face. 'Come on.' He motioned her to head back in the direction of the house as the sound of a loud grunt came from the van.

Mirabelle giggled.

McGregor helped her back over the low wall and they were about to sneak off when the vehicle's back door snapped open and Gregory jumped on to the track. 'Hey,' he said, looking up the empty road and back at the two of them.

Mirabelle squirmed. McGregor stiffened. 'Is there a journalist in that van?' McGregor asked.

The engine started and Gregory slammed the door, stepping to the side of the road. 'Photographer,' he said.

'You realise,' Mirabelle smirked, 'that's doubly inappropriate. Really, Gregory. You shouldn't be consorting with those people. However, as it happens, it lets you off the hook.'

The van took off. Gregory looked sheepish. 'Off the hook?' he said.

'Your alibi in Glasgow. You had a man in your room. And you couldn't tell the police that for obvious reasons.'

'Oh that. Yes.'

'And now, of course, you owe us one.'

Gregory looked grim. Mirabelle wondered if that was where his boxing moniker had come from. His expression was stony. 'I didn't tell the photographer anything. He asked. You know, about the body of the maid and the gun. I'd never say anything. I'm not a grass.'

'How did you know about the gun?' McGregor cut in.

Mirabelle turned to him. 'What gun?' she said. 'I thought we were supposed to be working together.'

It was McGregor's turn to squirm. 'I meant to tell you. I'm sorry. The police told me about it the same time as their concerns over Gregory's alibi, but I skipped over it. We went back to the drawing room for drinks.'

'Skipped over it,' Mirabelle repeated. 'For drinks.'

'Sorry. Yes. They found a gun. In the ditch. Near Susan's body.'

'A Russian gun,' Gregory said. 'I heard about it at the police station when they were questioning me. It made me think, perhaps Niko is right.'

'What? And the Russian secret service are now picking off maids to get at the Orlovs?' Mirabelle stared at the darkening landscape before her. It seemed highly unlikely. 'God. What a mess.'

'I don't know,' said McGregor. 'I mean people bring guns home, don't they? From service. However it got here, whoever owned it, it looks like they took Susan up to the field at gunpoint and then broke her neck. Which is an odd thing to do when you have a gun. Perhaps it was quieter. Perhaps she tried to fight and they dropped the gun in the affray.'

Mirabelle considered this. Susan hadn't seemed the kind of person who would put up much of a fight, but then, you never could tell. 'Either way, it means her death was premeditated – professional, in fact,' she said.

'Someone with a service background,' McGregor added.

Gregory shivered. 'Can I go?' he asked. 'It's getting cold up here.'

'Yes. Go on,' McGregor dismissed him.

'You won't tell Natasha?'

'No need to upset her,' Mirabelle said. 'But be careful, Gregory. You need to pick your liaisons more wisely.'

They watched him head back down the road towards the farm where he was lodging.

'You're nonchalant, I must say.' McGregor sounded impressed.

Mirabelle shrugged. It was becoming increasingly apparent that when it came down to it, McGregor had had a tame kind of war amid the tragedy.

'Sex and death cannot be news to you,' she said. 'Not in your profession.'

As they swung through the back yard, Bruce was in one of the outhouses. The deer carcass was hanging from a hook on the main beam. He was covered in blood, gutting it, steam rising from the animal's body. 'Hello!' he called. 'Where have you two been?'

'Romantic walk,' McGregor replied.

'Good. Good,' said Bruce, and returned to plunging his hands deep inside the dead animal's belly.

Chapter 13

Murder: the killing of a person without valid excuse

The next morning, when Mirabelle woke, McGregor was, for once, ready before her. As she opened her eyes she tried to focus on him putting on his jacket in front of the mirror and running a comb over his hair. 'Good morning,' she said sleepily.

Alan pulled open the curtain. 'I was going to let you sleep on.'

She hauled herself on to her elbows and glanced blearily through the window at the view of the hills. 'It looks like a lovely day.'

McGregor checked his watch.

'Are you going shooting?'

He grinned. 'I wish I was,' he said. 'It's Sunday.'

Mirabelle blinked. Then she realised what he meant and cocked her head. 'Alan McGregor, are you going to church?'

'We always go to church here.'

'Wait. I'm coming.'

It was nice, she thought, to do things together like this. She scrambled out of bed and pulled on clothes, choosing the suit she'd arrived in – smart but not too showy. She lingered in front of the mirror only long enough to apply a creamy slash of lipstick and check that her hair looked passable before she doubled back to the wardrobe to pull out her hat, pinning it in place as she gestured for him to get going. 'Is it because it's a family tradition?' McGregor asked.

She eyed him with dubiety. 'Not at all,' she said. 'It's because we might find out something.'

Downstairs, however, it became apparent that the Robertsons were not intending to go to church, or, at least, not Eleanor. The two of them were at the breakfast table, she wearing clothes wholly unsuitable for worship – a pair of check trousers and a short-sleeved cashmere top. 'Oh God,' Eleanor exclaimed seeing the two of them in their Sunday best. 'If you want to go, take the car.'

McGregor picked up a sausage from the sideboard and ate it with his fingers. 'It's only habit,' he said. 'I mean, we always went to church when Bruce and I were kids. Mirabelle and I don't bother in Brighton.'

Bruce stood up. 'Well, I have to. I feel bad enough about not going to see Susan MacLeod's family yesterday.'

Eleanor looked hollowed out. Mirabelle wondered if she had slept. 'Why don't you two go,' she said kindly. 'We girls can stay here.'

After McGregor and Bruce left, Gillies replenished the toast. The clock on the mantelpiece seemed to tick particularly loudly this morning. Eleanor peered over her shoulder to check the housekeeper had closed the door. Then she got up and opened the sideboard, taking out a newspaper. 'Bruce cancelled ours but I managed to get this sent up from the village,' she said. 'I miss the news, don't you? I like knowing what's going on – the Cold War is still headlining, I see.'

It was a *Sunday Telegraph*. 'Shadow of the Bomb', it

pronounced. 'It was the only paper left,' Eleanor explained. She split the copy into two and offered Mirabelle half.

Neither woman spoke until Tash came down. As the door opened, Eleanor jumped like a schoolgirl caught with contraband. 'Oh, it's you,' she said.

'Uncle Niko still has jet lag,' Tash declared. 'It's the worst.'

Mirabelle poured the girl a cup of tea and set the paper aside. She had been wondering about a few things – now the facts had had time to settle.

'Tash, do you have any idea if there was a link between Susan and your godmother? Anything at all?'

'I think we've all had enough questions,' Eleanor objected. 'I mean, there are policemen in the shrubbery and pressmen at the gates and really, enough is enough.'

'It's all right, Eleanor,' Tash said as she picked up her cup. She leaned across the table. 'There's no point pretending we aren't thinking about it the whole time. So, the answer is . . . I doubt it. Nina wasn't one for befriending the staff.'

'Did you ever see them speak?'

'Yes. Susan did our laundry.'

Eleanor gestured, rolling her hand in the air as if to ask what the point was of having this conversation.

'And apart from that?' Mirabelle pressed the girl.

'I've got nothing. I'm sorry.'

Mirabelle turned to Eleanor. 'And Susan had no connection with Russia that you're aware of?'

Eleanor snorted. 'Russia? Susan?'

'The police found a gun. A Russian one. Near the field where Susan died.'

Eleanor's brow crinkled. 'That doesn't make sense,' she said. 'You met her. She was just an ordinary girl. If you're thinking she was somehow involved with the KGB – well,

198

KGB agents don't recruit maids, at least not in the Highlands. If she'd been placed in service to someone in the SOE—'

'What's the SOE?' Tash enquired.

'The British secret service, as was,' Mirabelle replied smoothly. 'It's not called that any more.'

'Well,' said Eleanor. 'If she'd been in the household of a senior secret service officer, I'd say maybe, but why would the Reds place Susan MacLeod here, in this old place with Bruce and me?'

'Had she worked for you for long?'

'She started before we got married.'

'Who took her on?'

'Gillies knows her mother. I honestly don't think the girl had ever been further from home than this house. It doesn't make sense.'

'So, she would have been . . . fifteen or sixteen when she first came to work here?'

'Around that. Poor kid. God, I feel like we're living in a rat trap. God knows who's next.'

Mirabelle decided against pushing Eleanor further. She was obviously finding it difficult. 'What were you doing at fifteen?' she asked.

Eleanor smiled. 'In New York? I was still at school.'

'Tash?'

'Same. What about you, Mirabelle?'

'We lived in London. I was about to be sent to be finished.'

Eleanor leaned forward. 'I've always wondered what exactly girls are taught at finishing school.'

Mirabelle smiled. Eleanor was a strange mixture this morning – both forthright and vulnerable. 'Household management and etiquette – how to address the royal family and senior clergy. Deportment. Elocution—'

'I thought you went to Oxford?' Eleanor interrupted. 'Alan told Bruce that you had a degree.'

Mirabelle smiled. 'I do. Languages.'

'Do you speak Russian?' Tash asked.

'I can say a few words – I picked those up later, during the war. But I studied French and German. Women at Oxford were expected to get married – that's what we were there to do, really. Find a husband, though I failed that particular assignment.'

She recalled her student room in Lady Margaret Hall. Everybody knew what had happened to her parents. There had been a couple of young men who had taken a particular interest and it had been painful to realise that it was the money she'd inherited that had brought her to their attention. After that she played her cards close to her chest. It had taken her a long time with Jack to show her cards, and as long again with McGregor and, even now, if she was honest, she was holding an ace or two up her sleeve. Like Niko, though for entirely different reasons, trust was not her strong point.

'Didn't you want a husband?' Eleanor seemed interested.

'That took a bit longer.' Mirabelle smiled. 'I made friends, though. Did you study at college?'

'I didn't,' Eleanor admitted. 'My family didn't have the money, and when I was seventeen I started writing for the newspapers. I guess I was lucky – there was a vogue a few years ago for the female point of view.'

'Oh, that's ongoing,' Tash said sagely. 'I got a commission last year from Harpers to write a piece about not being interested in domestic life.'

'How did it go down?'

Tash smiled. 'Let's just say, the magazine got a lot of mail.'

'You speak Russian, don't you, Tash?' Mirabelle brought them back closer to the point.

'*Da*. I grew up with it in the house.'

'But you don't hanker after . . . the old life?'

'*Nyet*. Unless by the old life you mean living on the Upper West Side. I guess that's the old life to me.'

'Will you stay there when you get home?'

'I don't know,' she said, swirling the tea around her cup.

Eleanor stared at the clock. 'I'm going to let Jinx out,' she said, and pulled the dog from under the table as if he was a magic trick. Jinx, Mirabelle thought, was the quietest animal she'd ever met – except the time he scented Susan's body on the hill.

Tash watched Eleanor go. Then, when she spoke, the words came in a rush. 'Mirabelle, I think I know what they might have in common. Susan and my godmother.'

'What?'

'It's something Nina said. She said Bruce was quite shocking. I didn't think anything of it at the time and then last night I remembered and I've been thinking about it ever since.'

'What do you think she meant?'

'Two women dying in his house? I am beginning to wonder if what they had in common was, you know, Bruce's attention.'

'Bruce?' It seemed unlikely to Mirabelle. Bruce was far more interested in shooting than he was in people, and more interested in whisky than he was in shooting, if it came to that. Besides, Nina was one kind of woman, a particular kind of conquest; Susan quite another. Tash might be extending the kind of behaviour she suspected Niko of indulging in, to all men.

'Are you sure that's what she meant?' she said. 'He's never so much as looked at me.'

'Me neither,' Tash admitted, 'though it makes sense, doesn't it? As a cover-up, I mean. He doesn't want his wife to know what he's been up to. It's a helluva lot more likely than Uncle Niko's obsession with the Communists. And Eleanor is so upset. I mean, she was quite gay when we first arrived but yesterday and today she's been on edge. I suppose we all have, but perhaps it's because she suspects something? It would be awful, wouldn't it? I mean if it was your husband.'

Mirabelle considered this. Bruce had been her first instinct too. He was strong and not squeamish. She thought of him, elbow-deep in gore, gutting the deer at the back of the house. 'He seems so devoted to Eleanor,' she replied, parroting what McGregor had said. 'And the alexandrite, Tash? What about that?'

Tash stared miserably into the fire. 'Perhaps he gave it to her.'

'And she decided to swallow it?'

'Perhaps he gave it to her in exchange for her silence. So she swallowed it. Nina was dramatic like that – always on show.'

'And the Russian gun?'

'I don't know.'

Mirabelle's eyes darted. It still seemed strange to her that Bruce had cried over Nina's body. McGregor had dismissed the idea, but what if her gut feeling was right – Tash's too – and Bruce had killed these women because he couldn't bring himself to admit his infidelity? Susan had wanted to tell Eleanor something the morning she died. Perhaps she wanted to make some kind of sordid confession.

'Should I say something to the police?' Tash asked.

'No,' Mirabelle was surprised how emphatic her tone was

– a knee-jerk reaction. 'I want to think about it. And don't tell your uncle,' she hissed. 'For heaven's sake.'

The rest of the morning, they saddled the horses and Eleanor set jumps in the paddock. They took turns to sit on the fence and appraise each other's performance. Niko came down and joined in. He had, Mirabelle noted, a passable seat. 'You missed church,' she said.

'There isn't a Russian Orthodox church nearby,' he quipped drily.

'Do you normally attend on a Sunday?'

'Nina and I used to go together. We are a devout family.'

Tash looked as if she was going to say something but then thought the better of it. It occurred to Mirabelle that the girl didn't believe in God, and more – Niko didn't know.

The constable who had been left to monitor the premises paraded in front of the house like a guard at Buckingham Palace. It was almost one o'clock when the car drove back up the drive with another, smarter, vehicle following it. Mirabelle was just clearing the last vertical when McGregor and Bruce got out and came over, followed by a well-dressed couple who emerged from the other car.

'God, that was awful,' Bruce said, kissing his wife. 'It'll take me a while to get over this morning.'

Mirabelle dismounted and tied up the horse. 'It must have been difficult,' she said.

'Difficult? The MacLeods have seven children and somehow I thought that might make it easier for them. There are times when I am an idiot. The police had better find the damn fellow,' he spat. 'That'll at least help everyone draw a line under the whole sorry business.'

McGregor introduced the couple from the second car.

'Belle, these are the Walkers – Desmond and Valerie. This is my fiancée, Mirabelle Bevan.'

The Walkers were plump and pleasant, outfitted in perfectly tailored black clothes. Mrs Walker wore a Victorian jet brooch on her collar and a tiny hat with a veil that covered her face. Both the Walkers, Mirabelle noted, had red hair, which, in the instance of Mr Walker, was peppered with white.

'How do you do,' Mirabelle held out her hand. 'Was it you who came to dinner the night before the first murder?'

'We did,' said Valerie Walker, who, Mirabelle noted, had an admirable grip. Mrs Walker continued. 'Gosh – calling it the first murder. How awful, but then what else would we call it? I must say, it is shocking – the men at the gate.'

'Press,' McGregor confirmed.

'And on the Sabbath.' Valerie lifted her veil. Her expression was stony but her eyes sparkled with delight. She was thrilled by the murders, Mirabelle realised. Eleanor introduced the Walkers to Niko, who gave one of his stiff, military bows.

They moved inside, Tash receiving the attentions of Mr Walker, who was passing on his condolences. The corner of a pretty lace handkerchief emanated from her sleeve and she reached for it as she started to cry quietly. 'It seems to come in waves,' she said.

'We had to come,' Valerie Walker insisted as she perched on the edge of the sofa. 'I mean, the police questioned Desmond and me about going to dinner. I ask you! I said to Desmond, this is grim for us, darling, but can you imagine what it must be like for the poor Robertsons? And that beautiful child.'

Tash managed a smile.

'Now you're here, you must stay for lunch,' Eleanor insisted.

'It's kind of you but there's really no need,' Valerie Walker replied without conviction.

'Tosh. You came all this way.'

'Well, it only seemed right. Poor Miss Orlova. And your maid as well.'

Eleanor looked crestfallen. 'Yes,' she said. 'The *second* murder. It's a terrible thing.' That phrase again.

'What have the police said?' Mrs Walker asked.

Mr Walker cast his wife a glance, as if she had gone too far. 'Valerie,' he said. 'Poor Eleanor has been through enough. I'm sure the Robertsons aren't privy to the police investigation.'

Everyone shifted uncomfortably. After all, it was one thing to discuss matters among themselves, quite another to gossip. 'The police haven't told us much,' Bruce said.

'How do you know each other?' Mirabelle chimed, hoping to divert the flow of conversation.

'Desmond is in confectionery,' Bruce explained. 'His father was a friend of my father's. We were at school together.' It struck Mirabelle that Bruce, well into his fifties, talked about school as though he had only just left.

'That car of yours hardly makes a sound,' McGregor said, pitching in.

'She's a beauty, isn't she?' Bruce replied enthusiastically. 'Not like my old tin bucket. Desmond let me have a go last summer – she's a bit of a tank but she drives smoothly. I took her as far as Castle Dougal. I thought Gwendolyn was going to explode when she saw it.'

Mirabelle laughed out loud.

After lunch the Walkers insisted on seeing both crime scenes – first the orangery and then taking a long walk up the back lane to the field where Susan had been found. On the way back in, through the kitchen, Valerie Walker suddenly felt faint and Mrs Gillies looked for a moment as if she might slap the poor woman, but instead withdrew a bottle of smelling salts from her apron and insisted Valerie sit on the kitchen bench, with her head between her knees. No matter how stridently Mrs Walker objected, Gillies kept her there a full five minutes. Mirabelle liked her for that.

By five, the Walkers had left. 'We may have to start charging for guided tours,' Eleanor said. 'I bet the church was aflame with people dying to come up here and poke about.'

Bruce shrugged. 'It's only natural,' he said.

Tash excused herself, to go for a bath. Niko sat reading.

'Do you think there's anything we can do?' McGregor asked.

'Do?' Bruce leaned forward. 'What could we do?'

'It feels as if we've overlooked something. We must have.'

Eleanor sighed. 'You're just those kind of people,' she said. 'I mean, you and Mirabelle – you want to put the world to rights. Help yourself. Search the place.'

Niko looked up. 'Damn Reds,' he said under his breath. 'That's what I keep coming back to. I should have made Nina send somebody else to buy the cashmere. I should have put down my foot and none of this would have happened.'

'And Susan?' Mirabelle ventured. 'I mean, you think the Russians killed Nina and we've been through why that might be the case. But the maid?'

'She must have known something.' Niko was insistent. 'Or perhaps they'd come back for me. Or for Tash. Perhaps the poor girl disturbed them. Who knows? I guess we'll find out more when they've done her autopsy.'

'Her neck was broken,' Mirabelle said.

'That's enough,' Bruce said. 'The last thing we need is everyone getting worked up, and please, no more about the post-mortem examination. Susan was a good girl. She wasn't interested in politics.'

'Don't you read the newspapers?' Niko said. 'The space race. The rocket launches. The threats. That's the kind of people those pinko bastards are. They infiltrate everywhere. It's impossible to say who is and isn't interested in politics any more. A man was killed in Berlin only last week – a commuter. I read about it. They used poison.'

'We should dress.' Eleanor stood up. 'It's almost time for the gong.'

Upstairs, Mirabelle perched on the edge of the bed. McGregor leaned on the door frame. 'Dinner is going to be fun,' said Mirabelle.

'Sundays in the country are usually dull,' he replied. 'Niko might not be as wrong as we all thought, though. I had a word with the inspector this afternoon, on the telephone. They're thinking of passing the file on.'

'What do you mean?'

'Kicking it upstairs.'

She looked blank.

'To the Foreign Office. The local police force is jumpy – what with the Russian gun and the alexandrite. And today a woman in the village came forward with a sighting of a man wearing what sounds like a naval jacket on the morning it rained. She thought he must be a poacher and didn't want to grass him up, but she told a friend on her way to church and they convinced her it would be best to come forward. There aren't many strangers round here and he was distinctive.'

'What did she mean "naval"?'

'Sounds like a donkey jacket – the kind of thing a subma-riner might wear. At first they thought it must be one of the journalists, but they organised an identity parade in the back room of the pub and the woman swears the fellow was darker and taller than any of those chaps. None of them has a navy jacket either. It puts a stranger, possibly someone military, in the vicinity, though only one woman saw him – she was out on her bicycle and visibility was limited, but she swears he was heading north of the village, into the woods.'

Mirabelle lay back on the mattress. 'God,' she said. 'I've been thinking that it might be Bruce.'

McGregor put his head to one side. 'I can't see it, Belle. Can you? Really?'

Mirabelle shrugged. 'We need more information,' she said. 'Or we aren't going to get anywhere.'

Chapter 14

To do a great right do a little wrong

After dinner, everyone went to bed early. Mirabelle watched McGregor, naked under the covers, his breathing smooth as the moonlight seeped around the edges of the bedroom curtains like waves lapping at the fringes of the shore. The air was chill. It was, by her estimation, three in the morning, but she couldn't sleep. When they had come upstairs, the sound of distant music had emanated from Tash's room – she was playing gramophone records. Tab Hunter singing 'Young Love', with a descant of Tash's reedy voice out of tune, had reverberated along the hall. It hadn't seemed right to complain.

Now the house was silent. Mirabelle pulled on her dressing gown and went to the window, reaching through the curtains and cooling her hands on the glass. It was beautiful outside; the moon-washed fields stretched for miles. Then, in the hall, she heard a floorboard creak; her heart lurched at the thought of the Green Lady. 'Don't be silly,' she chided herself quietly, though she eyed the dressing table to see if anything on it could be used as a weapon. Her heart slowed when the figure of Niko appeared in the open door between the two rooms. He wore a thick silk dressing gown and his shotgun was slung across his arm – in a way quite debonair. McGregor turned over and snored. The tiny silver carriage clock on the bedside table showed a quarter past three.

'Go away! This isn't appropriate,' she hissed.

'It's Tash,' he whispered. 'She isn't in her room.'

'Have you checked downstairs?'

'Of course I have. Help me. Please. God knows where she's gone.'

'Hang on.' Mirabelle scrambled into her slippers and, gesturing for Niko to follow her, they sneaked through the second bedroom and down the hallway. 'Did you talk to the policeman on duty?' she asked.

He nodded. 'She didn't pass him but it's a huge house and he walks around the perimeter every half an hour. I'm scared she's gone on some damn-fool excursion like my sister did. I heard the police had a report of a man – a sailor – the day the maid died. Did you know?'

Mirabelle nodded solemnly.

'Anything could have happened with a Russian agent on the loose,' Niko insisted.

Mirabelle was about to object – nobody had established that the mystery man was Russian, but then Niko had a right to be jumpy – there had been two murders. 'Let's be logical. We'll start in her room,' she said.

There was nothing obviously missing. Tash's walking shoes were stowed in the wardrobe, along with an array of cashmere cardigans and sweaters. The evening dress she'd worn to dinner had not been replaced on its satin hanger, and the shoes she had been wearing were not on the shelf. 'She didn't get changed, then,' Mirabelle commented. She led Niko back into the hall and downstairs.

'I've looked down here,' he objected.

Mirabelle ignored him and perused the coat rack. 'Her coat is gone. Did you notice that?'

'No,' he said. 'Oh God.'

Mirabelle opened the cupboard where the wellington boots were arrayed tidily. 'It's hard to be sure, but she hasn't left her heels here. I think it's safe to say she won't have got far wearing a satin evening dress and a pair of stilettos, though she must have gone outside. I mean, that's presumably why she's taken her coat.'

'She promised she wouldn't leave the house.' Niko sounded angry.

'What do you mean?'

'She was talking about it earlier. The little fool had some damn notion about Nina going out under the stars the night she died. As if it was romantic. I mean Nina. A woman who never walked when she could drive and never drove when she could fly. She didn't give a fig for stars or a nice view. Tash knew that.'

Mirabelle took this in. 'Well, she must have gone somewhere,' she said.

With the idea that perhaps the girl had gone to find Gregory, she led Niko into the kitchen but there was nobody there. Continuing, she unbolted the back door. Outside, the windows in the staff quarters were dark over the old stables. The silence hung heavily in the air, resonating like a long, clear note.

'She's not out here,' Niko pointed out. 'She couldn't have bolted the door on the inside if she'd left.'

That was true. Mirabelle looked up. She squinted. High above the main house, the orange tip of a lit cigarette glowed in the sky. 'Oh!' The thought occurred to her in a flash. 'She promised you she wouldn't leave the house and she didn't,' she said. 'Come on.' The soles of her slippers clattered back down the corridor, through the kitchen and up the staircase. Niko followed. At the rear of the first floor they climbed the wooden stair to the terrace.

Mirabelle put out her hand and steadied herself. As she stepped outside, the freezing air hit her skin, so cold up here it almost took her breath away. The sky was cloudless. Ahead, the roof was empty, but she swivelled to check in the other direction and, sure enough, lying on the slates on a cashmere rug, Tash lay smoking. Swaddled in her coat, her breath clouded into the wide, starry sky.

'Mirabelle,' she said. 'Isn't it marvellous? You can see for miles. I swear the sheep look luminous in the dark – it's the most amazing thing. I keep seeing shapes moving in the trees and I can't quite make them out.' She put on a comedy voice. 'Maybe someone is coming to get us.'

Mirabelle moved towards the bench and Niko followed, with his shotgun still over his arm. 'It's three o'clock in the morning,' he spluttered.

Tash sat up. 'At home it's barely time for dinner. You can't make the house into a prison, Uncle Niko. Things are bad enough and it's glorious out here.'

Mirabelle shuddered. She surveyed the view. Tash was right. It was extraordinary at night. The trees were silhouetted on the ridge above the house in such detail they might have been minutely painted by hand. Looking up, there was nothing for miles as the land rose and fell, mountain and glen, the animals lying still in the darkness. Below, she could make out the glassy outline of the orangery, like a ghost-room, haunting the house with its glossy darkness. The constable walked up the back lane, the badge on his cap glinting in the moonlight. A single streetlight gleamed in the village, miles away, down the hill. Beside her, Niko stood peering at the vista, as if he couldn't understand it.

'I can't see anything,' he said.

Tash got to her feet. 'If it was summer, I'd want to camp up here. Still, perhaps you're right. It's time to go down.'

In the hallway, she disappeared obediently into her bedroom with a cheerful 'Goodnight.'

Mirabelle and Niko loitered. 'Did you tell your policeman?' Niko said. 'About the war? Did you discuss your relationship?' Mirabelle didn't move, didn't say a word. Niko smiled. 'OK. It's none of my business. Thanks for helping me find Tash. This place has me spooked. They're out there, you know. I can feel them.'

Mirabelle gave a slim smile. Places in which there had been a murder were always inhabited by the dead. For a while at least. It had taken her years before she could face walking up the street where Jack had died. Niko was bereaved. He had lost his sister. But that didn't mean there were Russian agents in the shadows. 'Try to get some sleep,' she said gently. 'Goodnight.'

Back in bed, she slipped cold limbs beneath the sheets. The house creaked. She thought about the view from the roof and then, just as she began to close her eyes, there was an unholy bang. It sounded like an explosion.

McGregor jumped out of bed, stubbing his toe and cursing. Mirabelle snapped on the light. 'Jesus!' McGregor scrambled for his dressing gown. Already awake, Mirabelle grabbed hers and made it to the bedroom door ahead of him, starting down the hall.

Bruce was at the head of the stairs, staring along the corridor at Niko, who had abandoned his shotgun against the wall and was on his knees over a man's body. He was

213

alive, whoever it was. He was moaning. McGregor strode past his cousin and pushed Niko out of the way. Mirabelle gasped. It was the policeman who had been on duty. The poor man moaned once more, a wide, red rip in the sleeve of his greatcoat dripping blood as he turned, yelping in pain.

'Fetch Mrs Gillies,' McGregor directed over his shoulder.

Mirabelle took off down the stairs and through the kitchen. She crossed the courtyard and met the housekeeper at the entrance to Eleanor's office. Elizabeth stood beside her. The girl's eyes were frantic. 'This place is cursed,' she said.

'Hush, lass,' Gillies berated her.

'We need you, Mrs Gillies,' Mirabelle cut in. 'Please. The constable has been shot.'

The women set off. Back upstairs, McGregor had procured a pair of scissors and was cutting away the man's uniform from around the wound. Instinctively everyone stood back to let Mrs Gillies in. 'Go down and boil a kettle,' she snapped at Elizabeth. 'I need hot water and antiseptic from the first-aid kit. Miss Bevan, please fetch towels from the linen room. Don't worry, son,' she reassured the officer, 'you'll be fine.'

Niko looked away. McGregor pulled him aside roughly. 'What the hell were you doing?'

'I heard someone in the hallway. I thought it was an intruder.'

'Are you mad? He's in uniform.'

'It was dark,' Niko spluttered. 'I thought he had broken in. He had taken off his hat. He was just a man I didn't recognise, in a dark overcoat. I thought it was the man from the day the maid died.'

'Don't you think you should have checked?'

'Tash had been on the terrace and he was heading up there . . . she said she thought she'd seen someone in the trees. I thought he was looking for her.'

McGregor was furious. 'And you didn't ask him? This is exactly what I warned you about.'

Niko stared at the carpet. 'I overreacted,' he said. 'It was a mistake.'

Gillies cast the men a look that silenced them. Then she turned back, staunching the bleeding with a towel. 'You're only winged,' she said. 'You've been lucky. I'll clean and dress it.'

Mirabelle's eyes moved to the area behind the constable. The skirting board was shattered and the plaster above it pockmarked with shot. Mrs Gillies was right. The policeman had had a lucky break. Niko had mostly missed him. Elizabeth arrived upstairs with a steaming bowl of hot water, which she laid on the carpet. She withdrew a bottle of TCP from her pocket and Gillies set to work, bandaging the wound, the antiseptic scenting the air. 'Thank God for you, Mrs Gillies,' said Eleanor.

Mirabelle turned. 'Were you downstairs?' she asked.

Eleanor pulled her dressing gown around her. 'Don't be silly. I was in bed.'

The policeman let out a moan. 'Now, lad. Dinnae fash,' Mrs Gillies comforted him.

'You better get dressed, Niko.' Bruce put his hand on Niko's shoulder.

'I'll ring the police,' McGregor offered.

Gillies put the constable to bed in one of the guest rooms. In the kitchen, Elizabeth made a pot of tea and everybody sat around the table staring at the cups in front of them. Eleanor fetched a decanter from the drawing room and one by one they passed it round, spiking their drinks. 'Sit with us, Elizabeth,' Eleanor said kindly, and the maid, who had retreated to stand beside the crockery cabinet, shakily sank on to the bench and did not raise her eyes from the table.

They listened to the sound of Mrs Gillies's footsteps as she approached. She looked annoyed as she put the bloody bowl in the sink and switched on the tap.

'I don't know what we would have done without you, Gillies,' Bruce said. 'Would you like some tea? Or a brandy perhaps?'

'Please, sit down,' Eleanor implored her. In the hallway, the clock struck four times, the tension palpable until Gillies switched off the tap and sat. Mirabelle held McGregor's hand under the table. She found quite suddenly that she did not want to let go. He had held off the police until the morning, nothing to be gained from a middle-of-the-night sortie to the house. There was nowhere for Niko to go and the injured man was cared for. 'What will they do to Niko?' Eleanor asked.

McGregor put down his cup and turned towards the baron. 'You'll be charged. I'm sorry – I think it's inevitable.'

The expression on Gillies's face betrayed the fact that she thought the baron certainly ought to be. 'That lad is only twenty-three,' she said. 'He's all the man he'll ever be, and now he'll be scarred for the rest of his life.'

'Damned bad luck,' said Bruce.

There was the scrape of a chair across the kitchen tiles as Niko got up. 'I'm going upstairs,' he announced.

Tash got to her feet in a gesture of solidarity. 'Yes,' she said. 'Me too.'

'I know you think I'm a fool,' Niko said. 'I just panicked. It's felt as if we're trapped here, just waiting for one of us to become the next victim. I honestly thought . . .' There was silence. 'Well,' he said, unable to finish the sentence. 'I'll be in my room.'

Nobody spoke for what seemed like a long time once he'd left. 'Will he be sentenced?' Bruce asked.

'You don't shoot a policeman and get away with a fine, Bruce,' McGregor replied.

Eleanor sounded impatient. 'He should serve a sentence. That poor kid might never recover. A young man like that, disfigured . . . Oh. Sorry,' she said, remembering McGregor's scar.

'I never thought I'd see the day. Guns in the bedrooms,' Gillies uttered, as if she was a soothsayer. 'Gentleman firing in the hallways. I don't know what has become of this house.'

McGregor turned towards her, respectfully. 'I know my uncle and aunt would be grateful to you for managing things so well for Bruce, Mrs Gillies.'

Bruce got up. 'I think we should all get to bed now.'

McGregor followed his cousin, pulling Mirabelle by the hand.

She fell into the bed, propping herself up on the pillows.

'He's just terrified of the Russians,' Mirabelle said. 'That woman seeing someone in the woods has spooked him. Still . . .'

McGregor got in next to her. 'There's something, isn't there?' he said. 'I need to think.'

She felt the same but she was tired and there were so many details. Eleanor had lied, for a start. In the hallway, she had appeared behind Mirabelle, which meant she couldn't have come from her room. She must have been downstairs. But why didn't she say so? She wondered how quickly Bruce had got to the scene of the shooting. Had he already been awake? Were the two of them downstairs together and, if so, why?

'McGregor,' Mirabelle started.

'Shush,' he snapped sleepily.

Mirabelle turned over. She bit her lip and wondered what it must be like for Niko, in his room, knowing in the morning he'd be arrested and charged.

The sun came up in a burst of rosy light that felt too optimistic. Mirabelle had been dressed for ages. She thought she'd be the first downstairs, but Eleanor was already at the table, in an almost sheer cashmere sweater, a tweed skirt, riding boots and a double row of creamy pearls.

'Good morning,' she said, raising a slice of toast. 'I can't believe I'm hungry. Gillies said it was the pressure. And look, she's actually made coffee. Would you like some?'

'Yes please,' Mirabelle said. 'Alan is still asleep. I thought it best to leave him.'

'This will perk us up,' Eleanor replied enthusiastically, as she refilled her cup and poured a fresh one for Mirabelle, as if nothing had happened three hours ago. Mirabelle perused the hot plates but decided against eggs. Eleanor, she noticed, despite what she had said, was more toying with her toast than eating it.

'Are you going riding?' she asked.

Eleanor looked down at her outfit. 'I thought I might. I felt like being practical this morning. Tweed is always more practical, isn't it?'

'Have you checked the constable?'

'I put my head around the door. He was asleep, poor man. Gillies is going to take him tea and toast and check his dressing. He won't get as good attention in hospital.'

'Gillies really is amazing,' Mirabelle enthused.

'I'm not sure what we'd have done without her.' Eleanor

looked at her watch. 'I expect the police will be here soon. It's about an hour from Inverness. I'd guess nine, wouldn't you say?'

Mirabelle nodded. She sipped some coffee.

'They call it the gloaming.' Eleanor gestured expansively out of the window. 'The half-light. It's rather beautiful this morning.'

'I think the gloaming is at dusk,' Mirabelle corrected her. 'But it's the same kind of light, I suppose, whether the sun is coming up or going down.'

'Oh.' Eleanor sounded disappointed. 'Don't they have a special name for it in the morning?'

The door opened to reveal Niko and Tash. The women murmured their good mornings. There was the sound of more coffee being poured. Mirabelle shifted in her seat. 'Oh God,' Tash said, 'this is torture. It's like waiting for goddam Godot.'

Niko laid his hand on the girl's arm. 'I shot the guy,' he said. 'I have to take the heat.'

Tash pushed her plate away. 'I told him to just go. Run. You'd have made it to Glasgow before the police got here. You could catch a ship or a plane or something. At least you'd be safe. I can bring Nina back.'

Niko sighed. 'Well, you'll have to, honey. Won't you? Either way. Gregory will help you.'

Tash's eyes clouded. 'I don't know what you came for,' she said.

Mirabelle grasped Tash's hand. 'Don't worry. We'll help,' she reassured her.

'Of course we will,' Eleanor chimed in.

A single tear drifted down Tash's cheek. 'All of this,' she said, 'has just been awful.'

McGregor appeared in the doorway and surveyed the

situation. 'Come on,' he gestured to Niko. 'Let's sit in the drawing room. I can't imagine you want to eat.'

'I need a lawyer,' Niko said.

'I can ask around. Bruce will have a family firm, but they might not have the expertise.'

'I'll plead guilty of course. I mean, Jesus, the kid could have died.'

The men left the room. Eleanor looked glassy eyed. 'I think this is the worst house party anyone has ever thrown,' she said. 'And we were so looking forward it. We only wanted to welcome you to the family.'

The police arrived sharp, and with them an ambulance wended its way up the drive to pick up the injured constable. When the man came downstairs, Niko rushed forward. 'I want to say I'm sorry, old man.' He held out his hand.

The constable looked nonplussed. Then he smiled. 'I'm not able to shake your hand, sir.'

Niko looked sheepish. 'Of course,' he replied hurriedly. 'I panicked when I saw you. The last few days – the pressure you see. I can't believe that I actually let off a shot. And I want you to know that I'm sorry. Genuinely.'

The policeman nodded. 'The housekeeper told me I'd heal,' he said, and walked out of the house, draped in a grey blanket. Eleanor waved from the front door as if the ambulance was a cruise liner leaving the dock in a frenzy of flags and champagne. Then a policeman arrested Niko and the inspector ordered one of the constables to drive him to Inverness.

The house seemed suddenly silent. Everybody congregated in the drawing room with shadows under their eyes as the detective inspector lingered in front of the fire. He had not removed his coat. 'It's all go today,' Eleanor said cheerfully. Nobody laughed.

'I think it's best if none of you leaves the house from now on,' the inspector said. 'I'm not putting you under house arrest, but that's my advice.'

Bruce eyed the drinks trolley, but forbore suggesting whisky. 'Has there been any progress with the murders?' McGregor asked.

The inspector shook his head. 'We're bringing up more men.' He turned to Bruce. 'I have to ask, what were you thinking, sir. Giving guns to your guests?'

Bruce looked sheepish. 'He asked and we were all afraid. It's isolated here and we had two women dead. Everyone has been on edge.'

'But what good could it do to arm everybody? And with shotguns?'

Tash stared at the man. As far as she was concerned, this wasn't the point. 'What about my godmother?' she asked. 'Isn't there any news?'

'I have it on good authority that Miss Orlova's body will be released tomorrow,' the inspector said.

'Then. I'll need Gregory.' Tash was insistent. 'If Nina is coming home, I'll need him. Could he move up to the house, Eleanor? I'd like him by me.'

'Of course, dear,' Eleanor replied. 'I'll have Gillies send for him.'

'The staff at the morgue will organise an undertaker,' the inspector offered.

Tash nodded silently. 'The irony is not lost on me that you're letting my godmother go just as you take my uncle away.'

'Miss . . .' the inspector objected.

McGregor held up a hand. 'Miss Orlova is understandably upset,' he said. 'I assume you'll be charging the baron?'

'We'll take statements from all of you and from Baron Orlov. I'm confident there will be charges. I'm sorry, miss.'

Tash waved her hand with hauteur, as if dismissing him.

The constables started in the kitchen with Mrs Gillies and worked their way through everybody. Even Eleanor was becoming adept at giving statements. After they had finished, Mirabelle and McGregor slipped outside, as far as the paddock, to lean on the fence and stare at the horses. The light was flat and grey now and the view obscured. McGregor put his arm around Mirabelle's shoulder. Through the long drawing-room windows they could see Eleanor and Tash in conversation on the sofa, their faces rosy in the warm light from the lamps. The inspector watched them from the other side of the room.

'He didn't want us to go outside,' Mirabelle said.

'He didn't. But we're close enough. Walk round with me?' McGregor prompted her.

He led her up the side of the house, on to the lane and through the gates to the courtyard. 'This way,' he directed, opening the door, bypassing Eleanor's office and taking the stairs up to the staff quarters.

There was nobody up there, though the air smelled of toast. Eleanor was right. It was cosy. The curtains had a tiny repeat pattern of roses. The carpet was the colour of rope. In one bedroom, Elizabeth had unpacked. A jam jar of fragile-looking snowdrops sat on the windowsill, a knitted teddy bear on the bed, three library books on the table as well as a crossword half completed and a piece of cross stitch that appeared to be a picture of a small cottage surrounded by summer flowers. It nestled in a workbasket full of colourful embroidery silks and small curls of wool. Beside the bed a half-drunk glass of milk smelled as if it was about to turn. 'You think Mrs Gillies had something to do with it?' Mirabelle asked him.

'I can't put my finger on it and it's driving me crazy,' McGregor said. 'But something is wrong.'

'You sound like me,' she smiled. 'What happened to being logical?'

'I don't know. Maybe you've given me some kind of virus.'

They both jumped guiltily, hearing a movement downstairs – a shuffling noise on the ground floor. They didn't want to get caught. McGregor brought his fingers to his lips and together they moved quietly to the head of the stairs, from where they could see Eleanor in her office, setting up her desk for Monday morning, fetching files from the cabinet. Jinx had followed her out and settled on the floor as Eleanor fiddled with something in a drawer. She drew a silver lighter from her pocket and placed it on the desktop, then, across the courtyard Mrs Gillies's voice called, 'Madam!' and Eleanor abandoned what she was doing.

'Yes?' she called back.

'The inspector is asking for you.'

Eleanor disappeared across the cobbles and Mirabelle and McGregor slipped down the stairs.

Inside the office, Jinx got up and, with Eleanor gone, jumped on to her chair behind the desk. Then he let out a yelp, clattering to the floor with a thump. McGregor opened the door. 'What's up boy?' he said gently.

Jinx whimpered. He sounded as if he was trying to bark but he couldn't. Instead he let out a strangled whine as he staggered to his feet and then keeled over, yelping once more as he landed next to a leather briefcase tucked underneath the desk. McGregor got on to one knee and put his hand on the poodle's pelt. The dog was quivering, heaving for breath. 'What is it, boy?' McGregor asked again. Jinx panted and then slumped like a huge rag doll.

'What's wrong with him?' McGregor sounded mystified. Mirabelle placed her hands low on the dog's chest. She felt sick. There was no heartbeat.

'I think he's dead,' she said.

McGregor jumped. 'Jesus! We should fetch somebody.'

Mirabelle put her hand on his arm to slow him. Her eyes flew around the room. The painting on the wall. The row of books. An old almanac on Eleanor's desk. 'Hang on,' she said slowly. She followed Jinx's journey from the door to the desk, her eyes falling on Eleanor's chair. She squinted as she noticed the tiniest dot out of place. Embedded in the thick, tweed upholstery was a point of the wrong colour – it was too pale. Looking round, Mirabelle picked up a leather bookmark from the desk and carefully, protecting her skin, she used it to press down the fabric, exposing a small needle sticking through the tweed. She stared at Jinx's prone body.

'Someone planted that. Someone must be after Eleanor,' she said.

It took a split second and then they moved together, clattering in a rush across the courtyard and through the back door, shouting as they went, 'Eleanor! Eleanor!'

Outside the laundry, Elizabeth jumped back to let them pass. In the kitchen Mrs Gillies let out a 'what the blazes . . .?' but pointed in the direction of the hallway as she realised their panic must have good reason. As they rounded the corner they shouted again 'Eleanor!' And there she was at the front door beside Bruce, seeing off the inspector.

Mirabelle and McGregor rushed across the boards and pulled Eleanor out of the open doorway and into the safety of the house. McGregor began to gabble, trying to explain. 'It's the dog. The dog is dead,' he said. 'Somebody put a pin in the chair in Eleanor's study. Jinx climbed on to it. It must have been poisoned,' he managed, realising as he said it how mad it sounded.

Bruce reeled. 'Jinx is dead?' he said as the inspector stepped back into the hallway. 'Who the hell would want to kill a dog?'

'It wasn't aimed at the dog,' McGregor repeated. 'It was in Eleanor's chair. It was meant for her.'

'Oh,' Bruce said. 'Poor Jinx. He didn't deserve that.'

Eleanor was about to sink on to the chair in the hall, but Mirabelle grabbed her. 'No,' she said. 'There's no saying where else they might have been.'

Beyond the open door to the drawing room, Tash jumped to her feet. 'Why would anyone be after you?' she said.

Eleanor shrugged. She rubbed her arm where Mirabelle's fingers had dug into her skin. Her face crumpled and she began to cry. 'Jinxy,' she burbled. 'Poor boy.'

'What are you going to do?' Tash snapped in the direction of the inspector. 'I mean, you can't expect us just to sit here with a madman on the loose. Not so crazy now, is it, what Bruce did handing out the guns? We're sitting ducks. It's like some kind of murderous roller-coaster and you don't have a clue.'

The inspector returned to the front door and called one of the policemen inside. 'I'm going to take a look for myself,' he announced.

Bruce hugged his wife, who was rocking backwards and forwards, a handkerchief pressed to her face. McGregor motioned that he was going to follow the inspector and Bruce nodded. 'Me too,' he said, handing Eleanor to Mirabelle, as if she was a crying child. Tash put her hand on Eleanor's back. 'I don't want to sound like Uncle Niko, but poisoned pins?' she said.

'I know,' replied Mirabelle. 'It sounds like KGB. I mean, those are the stories you hear. Men killed in the street with darts. Umbrellas that fire bullets.'

'Don't be ridiculous!' Eleanor snapped, heaving for breath. 'What would you know about the KGB?'

'Did Susan talk to you the other day, Eleanor?' Mirabelle asked. 'Before she died?'

Eleanor sniffed dismissively and let out a sob. 'She wanted some time off. I said we'd talk about it after the houseguests had gone.'

Mirabelle put an arm around her friend's shoulder. 'It's all right,' she said, and then felt foolish because obviously it wasn't.

'Why would they want to kill Jinx? I want to see him. Don't let them just take him away.' Eleanor began to cry again.

'Someone wanted to kill you, Eleanor,' Mirabelle said gently. 'That's what it is.'

'Well, damn them,' Eleanor spat, her sorrow turning to fury. 'Damn them all to hell.'

Chapter 15

Every man is a piece of the continent

It took a while for the women to calm down. They stood in the middle of the hall for ten minutes as if they were marooned. 'I'd go and lie down but there's probably a snake in my bed or an assassin in my closet,' Eleanor said.

Eventually, one of the police officers appeared in the doorway. 'The inspector told me to stay with you for safety.' He stood as if to attention.

Tash laughed. 'I think the safest place may be the kitchen. I can't see anyone getting past Mrs Gillies and there's no . . .' she paused, 'upholstery.'

The kitchen lights were burning bright and it was warm by the stove. Gillies stirred a pot, scenting the air with the smell of barley soup. The radio was on, the announcer reading the news; something about a clergyman calling for nuclear disarmament. 'Sorry to disturb you, Mrs Gillies,' Eleanor said.

'It seems so calm in here,' Mirabelle chimed.

'There's nothing else to do, is there?' Gillies said stoically. 'We've just got to get on.'

'Well, it smells delicious.'

Gillies, unsure how to respond to praise, returned to stirring the soup.

The rest of the morning passed in a succession of pots of tea and a rush of police officers, who drove from Inverness. Eleanor fussed. 'I can't see how we are going to face food,' she said. 'I mean with all of this going on? Perhaps Mrs Gillies could just serve us in the kitchen?'

Gillies did not reply, but went to the pantry and brought in a large chicken, which she placed in a roasting tin. Elizabeth was sent to the scullery to peel a bucket of potatoes. 'It's easier to serve you in the dining room, Mrs Robertson,' Mirabelle said eventually.

Mirabelle thought it must be the shock. Perhaps it was good she had something to focus on. 'Best to lay on sandwiches for lunch and people can help themselves? Make some for the police officers,' she directed, suddenly very much the lady of the house.

'Yes, ma'am.'

Mirabelle wished she could help, but Mrs Gillies would entertain no offers. She sounded so resentful that her kitchen had been invaded that it seemed churlish to push the point.

Almost at lunchtime, an ambulance arrived to remove Jinx's body, which was being sent for a post-mortem examination. Bruce stridently objected until, eventually, he was quieted by McGregor.

'He's more upset about the dog than anything else,' Eleanor snapped. She was upset too. 'You won't cut him up much, will you?' she entreated the ambulance men as they placed the dog's body on a stretcher.

The man smiled apologetically. 'They need to know what killed him,' he said gently. 'We'll be as careful as we can.'

After a team of three men had searched the drawing room, the women returned to the front of the house. Tash and Mirabelle stood at the long window and watched as

Gregory walked up the hill, carrying a small suitcase. He was challenged no fewer than half a dozen times as he approached the house. Tash went to meet him at the front door. 'Sit with us,' she said.

'Shouldn't I be helping with something?'

'I'll feel safer with you here,' Tash insisted.

'The village is in uproar,' Gregory reported. 'People can't believe it. Journalists are offering people a fortune for information. They're searching outbuildings for this guy – the one with the navy jacket,' he said.

'Was there a sighting?' Mirabelle asked.

But Gregory just shook his head.

An uneasy silence settled on the drawing room, broken only by the sound of officers moving around the rest of the house. It was an eerie feeling. The team who had taken over Eleanor's office stripped the chair and dusted it for fingerprints. Upstairs, they took Eleanor's bed apart. Her bathroom and dressing room were as good as dismantled though nothing was found. By four o'clock, the rooms were cleared for use, and Eleanor announced she was going for a soak. Everyone else remained on the sofas, sipping whisky and playing cards quietly.

Outside, Mirabelle noted, the men changed shifts as darkness fell. Closer to the house two uniformed officers flanked the front door but, further away from the house, she noticed more men were setting up for the night. Before the dinner gong, a van arrived with a pack of three dogs on wide leather leashes, barking as they sniffed the air. 'What on earth do they need dogs for?' she asked.

McGregor, recently returned to the civilian group, watched from the window. 'They'll be more effective than men at night if anyone approaches the house. It means they're taking it seriously.'

The clock on the mantelpiece struck half past six. 'Should we dress?' Tash asked.

Bruce nodded. 'Why not? They dressed for dinner on the *Titanic*.'

Mirabelle and McGregor changed upstairs in silence. It was so quiet that, when she sprayed perfume in the air and stepped into it, she noticed the sound of the pump. At seven they came back down. Bruce dispensed malt – iced for Tash and with a dash of soda for everyone else. One of the policemen and Gregory stood guard on either side of the fire.

'This is terrible,' Tash said.

Everyone else murmured agreement.

'I've been thinking about where to bury Jinx. We don't have a proper pet graveyard but there are some family dogs interred near the lodge,' Bruce announced. 'Poor old thing hardly went that far away from the house when he was alive, but there's a clearing and we can order a stone.'

Tash's eyes filled with tears. 'Eleanor was right. You're more concerned about the dog.'

'It has to be done,' Bruce objected.

'I've been waiting for my godmother's body for five days.'

'Of course. I apologise,' Bruce cut in. 'I didn't mean to upset you.'

'I hope the poison tells us something.' McGregor's voice seemed to calm them. 'I mean, whatever killed Jinx is potentially a clue to the other deaths. Not that any of the clues make sense.'

'Murders. They were murders.' Tash finished her whisky and rattled the ice cubes in her empty glass.

'Are you sure you want more?' Mirabelle asked. None of them had managed to eat anything much all day.

'I'm positive,' Tash answered. 'Hit me.' Bruce poured her an uncharacteristically stingy measure but she didn't complain.

Then Bruce checked the clock on the mantelpiece. 'It's been such a terrible day. I can't blame Eleanor for not facing food,' he said vaguely.

Tash shifted in her seat. Mirabelle's eyes met McGregor's. The policeman made to move but Mirabelle put up her hand. 'Perhaps I should go up and ask her,' she offered. 'I can have Gillies send up a tray.'

The air in the hallway felt fresh on Mirabelle's skin and the pressure of having to say something to fill the horrible gap that had constituted the day was lifted now she was alone. She took the stairs slowly, in no rush. Turning to the front of the house, she knocked on the door of Eleanor and Bruce's bedroom. There was no answer. Feeling only mildly perturbed, she knocked again. 'Eleanor?' Still no reply so she turned the handle.

Inside, bedside lamps cast golden light around the room. The walls were decorated in pale peach paper set off by a thick white carpet. A huge bed was set against the right-hand wall with a tall, buttoned headboard in glistening pink silk. The effect was glamorous. Casting around the room, Mirabelle realised that it was empty. The curtains had not been drawn on the long windows to the front of the house, which were sheer, black voids. A smaller, single window overlooked the side, and must, she thought, be framed to show off the trees that Eleanor had wanted to see in blossom. Mirabelle moved into the centre of the room and called again, 'Eleanor?'

The door to the dressing-room suite was open and she continued. Eleanor's clothes were heaped in piles where the police officers had searched the wardrobes. At the dressing table, the upholstery had been removed from the stool and the horsehair pulled apart.

Trembling now, Mirabelle knocked on the bathroom door. 'Eleanor?' Silence. She turned the handle and felt a wave of nausea. The bathroom was empty. The bath was pristine. The towels lay folded, unused, on a freestanding oak rail. The bar of soap was dry on the washstand and the air was scented with washing powder and vinegar, not with bath oil, soap or scented cream. Nobody had used this room in many hours, perhaps not at any time today.

Mirabelle's skin felt suddenly clammy. Beginning to panic, she returned the way she had come, back into the hallway, checking the rooms as she went and calling Eleanor's name. She scaled the steps to the roof terrace but there was no one there. Slipping down the main staircase, she checked Bruce's study, the orangery and the kitchen, where Gillies was tipping vegetables on to silver platters, ready for service. 'I can't find Eleanor,' Mirabelle said. 'She isn't in her room.'

'Perhaps try the office?' Gillies suggested.

Mirabelle continued through the back door, where another policeman stood smoking. The Alsatian beside him jumped to his feet, as if to attention. The dog's ears pricked up as she spoke. 'Have you seen Mrs Robertson? Is she in the office?'

The man shook his head. 'There's been nobody out in the last hour,' he reported. 'Not even our lads. Me and Sassenach here are on guard till first light.'

'It's time for dinner,' Mirabelle replied, and cursed herself for sounding petty. 'I'll check she hasn't come down in the meantime,' she said and closed the door.

Back in the drawing room, Tash had started a game of solitaire. 'Is Eleanor all right?' Bruce asked.

'She's not in her rooms,' Mirabelle said. 'I checked the orangery and the office. When did you last see her?'

Bruce put down his glass. 'When she went up to bathe.'

'Wasn't she upstairs when you got dressed?'

'The bathroom door was closed. I thought she wanted time on her own. I got changed and came back down. I assumed she'd hear the gong.'

There was a beat – just a second as everybody took this in. Then McGregor gestured towards Gregory and the policeman. The three of them burst through the double doors into the hallway followed by Bruce. Tash put down the cards. 'Oh God,' she said.

'Eleanor!' McGregor shouted, opening every door as he made his way through the house. 'Eleanor!' A cacophony of men's voices ensued. 'Mrs Robertson! Eleanor!'

Mirabelle sank on to the sofa next to Tash. The girl's hands were quivering. 'I hate this,' she said. 'Nina would have hated it too. She was never a victim. Never till now.'

McGregor came back to the drawing room. 'Gregory has gone to alert the officers. We'll search the place inside and out,' he said. 'You stay here.'

'Can't we help?' Tash asked.

'Honestly, you won't make much difference – the main thing in the dark will be the dogs. It would make me feel better now, knowing you were somewhere together. Safe,' McGregor said, with a nod at Mirabelle, who leaned over and took Tash's hand.

Outside, the men were called together, and Bruce fetched some of Eleanor's clothes so the animals could track her scent. Tash and Mirabelle watched as the dots of light from two dozen torches fanned across the landscape. It would look picturesque, Mirabelle thought, if it wasn't so awful. She ran through the crimes one by one. Nina Orlova, killed by strangulation in the middle of the night, Susan MacLeod with her neck broken in daylight, Eleanor narrowly missing being poisoned and now disappeared. She hoped it was kidnap because that at least meant Eleanor had a chance. She felt nauseous at the thought her body might be out there, in one of the fields, just like Susan's.

Tash paced in front of the fire. 'Back in Russia when people were trapped on their estates because of the Revolution, there are stories about all kinds of debauchery. Naked hunts, orgies, feasts and crazy parties. People knew the end was coming so they lashed out and grabbed life. But I don't feel that way. I'm just terrified.'

Mirabelle felt more mystified than anything else.

'Do you think Eleanor simply couldn't hack it and ran off? I wouldn't blame her for wanting to get away,' Tash said.

Mirabelle shrugged. 'That would be the best-case scenario,' she said. 'I don't see how she could have got away. The house has been surrounded all day. There must have been a dozen men here this afternoon. More.'

'At least we know it can't have been Bruce,' Tash continued. 'I mean, not this time. He was with us.'

After a few minutes, the women decided to go up to the roof terrace so they could follow the proceedings from a vantage point. Grabbing their coats, they took the stairs. Outside, their eyes adjusted to the darkness. Neither wanted to sit on the bench so they took up a position at the farthest edge of the terrace, leaning over the rail. Tash pulled a cigarette case from her pocket and lit up. Mirabelle withdrew a pair of binoculars. 'Where did you get those?' Tash asked.

'On a hook in the boot cupboard,' Mirabelle said as she squinted.

After a few minutes the door opened, and Gregory stepped on to the terrace.

'How did you know we'd come up here?' Tash asked.

'Intuition.'

'Really?'

'I followed your perfume.'

Tash seemed satisfied with this. Mirabelle wondered if she was flirting with Gregory, and if she was doing so because she knew she had no chance with him. Childlike, the girl sniffed in Mirabelle's direction. 'You smell nice too.'

'L'Air du Temps,' Mirabelle said. 'Gregory, have you given up searching?'

'It occurred to me, ma'am, that you ladies were left unprotected.'

'Very gallant.'

'It also occurred to me that there is little chance of success for a man on his own. It's dark out there. I was just walking alongside one of the guys with a dog. I'm better placed here.'

Mirabelle nodded. She was going over everything that had happened, hoping something might spring to mind. A solution. A clue. Eleanor had said she was going for a bath, but the bath remained unused. This meant she might not have gone upstairs. If she hadn't, Mirabelle wondered, where could she have headed instead? Or if she had gone up, had she been abducted in her bedroom, before she could run the bath? There was no obvious sign of a struggle, but the place was such a mess after the police search that it was difficult to tell. Tash must have been thinking the same thing. 'Do you think she was kidnapped?' the girl asked.

'That's one of many questions,' Gregory replied.

'What questions?'

'Well . . . what did Nina, that maid and Mrs Robertson

have in common?' Gregory spoke slowly, weighing his words. 'That question for a start.'

'Exactly,' said Mirabelle. 'While everybody is out looking for Eleanor, maybe we should do some investigating of our own. It seems likely – 50/50 I'd say – that Eleanor didn't go upstairs after she left the drawing room, so maybe we should check her other room – the office.'

Mirabelle slipped back down the wooden stairs with the two of them behind her and together they cut through the main hallway and the kitchen. A perfect roast chicken dinner was laid on the table, almost cold on its silver service. Gravy congealed in a Victorian silver sauce boat. At the back of the house, the lights remained on in the servants' quarters. Mirabelle put her finger to her lips, and continued into Eleanor's office where she clicked on the light. The chair behind the desk had been removed and, Mirabelle noticed, the area where the dog had slumped in death had been cleared. The leather briefcase was gone from underneath the desk. Apart from that, it looked exactly as it had earlier – Eleanor's silver lighter sat on the desktop where she'd left it. The newspapers and books were all in place. She began to search the desk drawers. 'What are you looking for?' Tash whispered.

Gregory smiled. 'Miss Bevan doesn't know.'

'No,' Mirabelle admitted. 'But you can never tell what might help. I found a diary in your godmother's things when I looked there.'

'You went through Nina's things?'

'I'm sorry.'

'What was in the diary?' Gregory asked.

'Nothing connected to her death. Some drawings. Profit calculations on the cashmere. Nothing about jewellery of any kind. No notes about an assignation in the middle of the night.'

'Did you give it to the police?'

Mirabelle shook her head. She kept her eyes on what she was doing but the drawers yielded nothing but a sheaf of receipts, Eleanor's bottle of vodka and a few colourful sample books of tweed and cashmere. There was nothing taped underneath and no secret drawers or compartments. Mirabelle leaned against the desk, perusing the books behind her. One by one, she took them off the shelf to search for hidden papers, notes on the flyleaf. Anything. Then she ran a palm under each shelf. 'There's nothing here,' she pronounced.

From the hallway, the sound of footsteps descended. 'Can I help you?' Mrs Gillies peered through the door.

'It's OK,' Gregory replied. 'We were just curious.'

'It seems disrespectful,' Mrs Gillies sniffed.

'Are you done for the night?' Gregory ignored her objection.

'Elizabeth took the mistress's disappearance badly. She's talking of leaving and I can't blame her. You shouldn't be in here.'

'We're trying to help, Mrs Gillies.' Gregory's tone was admirably calm.

She sniffed again as if to dismiss the notion. 'I'm sure the inspector wouldn't be happy about you taking matters into your own hands. The police officers have already searched the office.'

'Perhaps you're right,' said Tash. 'We didn't find anything, anyway.'

Gillies disappeared up the stairs. Mirabelle cast her eyes around the room once more, lighting on the Patrick Heron Eleanor liked so much. On a whim, she examined the painting. 'Bingo!' she said as she pulled it away from the wall. 'Look.' Inset behind the frame, a khaki metal safe was flush against the plaster, the legend 'Schwab Safe Company' painted on it in gold.

Tash sighed. 'God,' she said. 'I wouldn't know where to start with that.'

Gregory pulled a soft pack of cigarettes out of his pocket and flicked his finger against the bottom so that a cigarette jutted upwards. He pulled it out with his lips and smoothly lit it with the lighter from the desk. All Americans behaved like film stars, Mirabelle thought. It was just in them, somehow.

'I have an idea,' he said. 'But I don't think you'll like it.'

'Try me.'

Gregory lowered his voice. 'I could crack it.'

'The safe?'

He nodded.

'Afterwards,' she said, 'can you put it back so it looks as if you were never there?'

'Sure. It's worth a try, right?' Gregory checked his watch.

Tash stood by the door, on guard for Mrs Gillies as much as the police. Gregory crouched down. 'Back home it's the Jews who are the safe crackers,' he said. 'Luckily my friend Maurice Klein taught me.'

Mirabelle smiled. 'I have a friend in Brighton who'd like you.'

'Really?'

'She's married to an American.'

'Black guy?'

'He's a musician.'

'That's brave.'

'Marrying a musician?'

'A white girl marrying a black fellow.'

'She's black.'

'That's enlightened of you, Miss Bevan,' Gregory said. 'The more I know you, the more I like you. And your friends.' He picked up one of Eleanor's vodka glasses and pressed it to the door of the safe, listening as he turned the dial. He smelled of tobacco and something sweet – vanilla or orange.

Mirabelle sank on to a chair. She wondered what she might say if they were caught and how often Gregory might have cracked a safe, and why. Gregory's expression fixed as he concentrated on making minute movements, turning the dial back and forth. It was excruciating. After about three minutes, he pulled the lever to open the door and Mirabelle found she could breathe again. 'There,' he said.

Inside, there was a large, old-fashioned accounts book. Mirabelle opened it. The pages were lined, predictably, with figures – they seemed to refer to the distillery and the cashmere mill and the tweed collective. Stuck in the back, between thick endpapers, she found a tiny stack of letters tied with a thin, turquoise ribbon. Mirabelle took these out. 'Go on,' said Gregory.

Almost unwillingly she tugged the ribbon. The letters were from Eleanor to Bruce at the time they first met. It seemed they had written to each other often when she was still in London and he had gone up north. 'Looks like Mr Robertson is a romantic,' Gregory commented.

'I'm not sure we should read these,' Mirabelle replied.

Gregory raised his hands. 'Put them back if you want.'

Tash peered as Mirabelle laid the letters in order. There were perhaps a dozen. Gingerly, she lifted the first. Eleanor's handwriting seemed confident, the words well spaced on the page and the ink thick where she had pressed on the paper. 'Dear Bruce,' it started, 'I visited the National Portrait Gallery today as you suggested.' Mirabelle read the missive quickly and then refolded the page. She moved to the next, where Eleanor had visited the public gallery in Parliament and vowed she had been so transfixed by the surroundings that she had found it difficult to focus on what was being said. She must have managed, though – she reported Nye Bevan's words in some detail and then chastised Bruce for supporting the Liberals rather than the Labour Party, who, after all, had instituted the National Health Service. The couple had, it seemed, debated politics early in their relationship. By the third letter, Eleanor had visited Scotland and thanked Bruce for a lovely weekend. She casually called him 'darling', as if this was now normal.

'Anything?' Gregory asked.

Mirabelle shook her head, turning over the next paper, which was encased in a pale blue envelope upon which Eleanor had written her return address. 'Eleanor McCrory. 15 Dean Street. Soho.' Mirabelle knew Dean Street. Just off Oxford Street, it comprised a stretch of small Georgian brick-and-stucco townhouses and shops, one or two of which had been bombed during the Blitz. She tried to imagine number 15 but couldn't place it. It would have been an exciting place to stay, she thought, for a young American girl – close to the theatre district with lots of coffee houses and bars nearby. A far cry from The Ritz. 'It's hopeless,' she said.

'They always say "follow the money" but I can't see any money to follow,' Gregory replied. 'I mean, these folks have got money but it's weird, it just doesn't seem relevant. Is it a British thing? Money just not sticking?'

Carefully Mirabelle stacked the letters back in order and tied them with the ribbon, placing them where she'd found them at the back of the accounts book. 'At least we tried,' she said.

'Done?' Gregory checked.

'It was a good idea. But yes. Done.'

Gregory replaced everything and closed the door.

'I can't wait to leave here,' Tash sighed. Mirabelle realised suddenly, once Tash and Gregory had gone, it would just be her and McGregor with the Robertsons, which, she thought guiltily, would seem a relief. Just the family. If only they could get Eleanor back. 'There are too many whys,' Tash continued. 'I mean, I guess we'll never know why Nina came up to the house the night she died.' She sounded sad. 'Or what really happened to Susan. It's such a tangle.'

'Oh, we do know,' Mirabelle said, suddenly passionate. 'We must by now. That's the frustrating thing.'

In another hour most of the men had returned. The dogs had picked up a trail and the handlers were continuing with them, but the decision had been made for the bulk of officers to turn back. The house, it seemed, was the centre of everything. In Gillies's absence, Gregory brewed huge pots of tea in the kitchen and cut rounds of chicken sandwiches, which were doled out on wooden trays. A line of three braziers was lit to help the men on guard stave off the cold.

'We searched down to the village,' Bruce said sadly. 'The outhouses. Farm buildings. Steadings. Even outdoor privies. There's no sign of her. My poor darling,' he stumbled over these last words as his voice broke and McGregor laid his hand on his cousin's shoulder.

'Did the dogs find anything?' Mirabelle asked.

'They lost the scent but the handlers thought they might pick it up again. It's often better at night, the chap said, but there's an area of rock she passed over that has made it more tricky,' McGregor said.

'So she was definitely out there? She left?'

'They think so. If they can pick up her trail again, they thought they stood a decent chance.'

'So either she left alone or someone took her.'

Bruce's eyes were edged with pink. 'Someone took her,' he said. 'My wife wouldn't just walk out.'

'Right now, the main thing is to find Eleanor,' McGregor's tone was firm. 'The longer it runs, the more likelihood—'

'I know,' Mirabelle cut him off. 'I know.'

About one in the morning, Tash retired to bed. Gregory was going to sleep in Niko's old room and he held the door of the drawing room for her, to escort her up. 'Thanks,' the girl smiled.

'You don't have to thank me,' he said.

'I do,' she insisted. 'I don't want to be like Nina, taking you for granted. When we get back to the US, things are going to be different, Gregory.'

'What do you mean?' Mirabelle asked.

Tash hesitated. 'Nina wasn't a good person. You know that, right? I mean, I loved her but she was awful. Her politics, and she was such a snob. That's why it's so hard, you see. I miss her but she behaved terribly. Every morning I cry when I remember she's dead and that makes me feel worse because she was so awful. I mean, Gregory, do you remember that time it was snowing and she sent you to the Lower East Side to pick up her order from the tailor? There was a blizzard and the whole city was at a standstill. You could have died of hypothermia.'

'But I didn't,' Gregory said.

'And there was the time she caused that rumpus outside the Stork Club and just got into a cab and left you? Those guys broke your nose.'

'That's my job, Miss Natasha. To take the heat. I took it for Nina and I'll take it for you, if you want me to stay on.'

'I don't know what I would do without you.' Tash leaned against the door frame and pulled a handkerchief from her pocket. 'This whole thing has been a nightmare.'

After they went up, Mirabelle wondered if Nina had chosen Gregory's name. Maybe Wilbur hadn't seemed macho enough for her so she'd given him a new one. America was mired in its history of slavery, still. Vesta told stories about Detroit where Charlie had grown up. People had separate buses, different entrances – Britain might have its class system but there was no apartheid, at least.

In the drawing room, Bruce lingered until half past the hour when he fell asleep on the sofa, snoring as he keeled over and then waking guiltily. 'You should go up,' McGregor said. 'It isn't doing anybody any good for you to sleep down here. If they find her, she'll need you rested, old man.' Bruce was unwilling but McGregor was right and eventually he bid them goodnight. Outside, the men huddled around the braziers, taking it in turns to sleep in the vans. Mirabelle and McGregor were left alone in front of the fire.

'I don't want to go to bed,' Mirabelle admitted as she drew the curtains.

McGregor hugged her. 'Me neither,' he said. 'We're the watch, aren't we? The last ones. It would feel like giving up on her.'

They pulled cushions off the chairs and made themselves comfortable on the floor. McGregor put up the fireguard. Lying in the dark, Mirabelle couldn't say how long she dozed, but when she woke McGregor was asleep. Her mind kept returning to Eleanor's office. To the moment when Eleanor had said she was going for a bath. To Tash saying her godmother had never been a victim before. To Susan MacLeod's room, which now contained

Elizabeth's sewing box. It always seemed strange to her when someone died and their place was taken. There was something in that, she thought, but the details were making her head spin.

Then, through a chink in the curtains, there was a sudden flash of light. A police van pulled up at the paddock and the man guarding the door moved towards it. As the van door opened, Mirabelle got up and squinted through the velvet folds of the curtain. It was dark, but . . . she thought the silhouette looked like . . . no, it couldn't be.

She moved smoothly to the hall, watching her hands as she opened the front door, as if she was in a dream where the two worlds she inhabited had come together like a surrealist painting. The air was damp with a fine mist of rain and her bare feet were freezing as she stepped across the portico and on to the gravel. 'Eddie!' she said.

Eddie Brandon stood beside the paddock, immaculately turned out in a four-button jacket with generous shoulders and a mean waist, a lapelled waistcoat and a pair of high-cut trousers. He hadn't changed, she thought. He was still the kind of man who ate well, drank a lot and never had a hair out of place. If anything, his looks had improved as he aged. He had a few grey hairs these days. They suited him. 'Good lord,' he said. 'What happened to you?'

'I slept on the floor,' Mirabelle replied.

'Well, you shouldn't be out here.' Eddie kissed her on the cheek and led her back inside. 'I wasn't referring to the disarray in your . . .' He gestured to indicate her outfit, then he picked up her hand and cast an eye over her engagement ring. 'I meant this,' he said. 'It's lovely. To whom do I direct my congratulations?'

'He's in the drawing room.' Mirabelle thought how strange

it was – the immediate intimacy of old friends. 'What are you doing here?' she asked.

'I haven't seen you in a while,' Eddie continued, as they wandered into the hall. 'It was in Paris, I recall. That must be four years ago. When that English policeman took a bullet for you.'

'He's Scottish.' She indicated the drawing room.

'Ah. It is he, is it? He took his time proposing.'

'Sir . . .' one of the policemen who had been guarding the house tried to cut in.

Eddie stopped him dead. 'I'd get hold of the ranking officer on site if I were you,' he instructed. 'I'll be taking over.' The man looked worried. 'Well, go on. I'll need to speak to him.' Eddie never brooked any argument. He turned back to Mirabelle. 'I have been trying to telephone you since the information came through. In the end I thought, hell, I'll just go up there.'

'We took the telephone off the hook. The press kept ringing.'

Eddie cast her a glance that made it clear this was not acceptable. 'Well, I'm here now,' he said, and pushed open the drawing-room door.

Alan raised his head sleepily. Eddie snapped on the lights.

'Congratulations, old man,' he held out his hand and peered at McGregor. 'Mirabelle is a catch. You'll never be bored, that I can promise you.'

'Alan, this is Eddie Brandon,' Mirabelle said as Alan got to his feet. Strange, she thought, this was closest she had to her own family, Vesta aside.

'Have they found her?' McGregor asked.

Eddie shook his head. 'They found this, though,' he said, and pulled a thin diamond strip from his pocket. 'About two hours ago. I stopped at Inverness police station before coming here. So many ruins on the way – the clearances, I suppose.'

Mirabelle took the sparkling strip from Eddie's hand. 'This is Eleanor's evening watch,' she said. 'Where did they find it?'

'To the west of here. It's definitely hers?'

'Yes . . . But . . .'

'What?' Eddie pressed.

Mirabelle couldn't quite put her finger on it. 'Oh nothing.' The men's eyes met in a kind of frustrated understanding. Extracting information from Mirabelle could be tricky.

'What a lovely house,' Eddie commented as he looked around. 'Whoever decorated the place has a great sense of colour.'

McGregor straightened his clothes. 'I'm sorry – I feel as if I've missed something? How do you two know each other?'

Eddie caught Mirabelle's eye. Her palms were sweating. She laid her hand on the marble tabletop. 'Lord,' Eddie said, 'she hasn't told you anything. That doesn't surprise me. Well done, old girl.' He clearly wasn't about to explain things to somebody else's fiancé. Instead he sat down on a comfortable chair. 'Let's get on, shall we? Debrief me, Belle. What do you know?'

Chapter 16

The only evil is ignorance

Mirabelle paused, collecting her thoughts. 'Long story, short,' she started. 'There have been two deaths. Three if you count animals.' Eddie raised an eyebrow. 'First, Nina Orlova was killed by strangling. The day after, the maid, Susan MacLeod, was killed – a more professional hit. Her neck was broken and her body dumped in a field. A Russian pistol was retrieved at the scene and a woman saw a stranger in the area – a man.'

'The naval jacket,' Eddie said.

Mirabelle nodded. 'Then yesterday the owner's dog was poisoned, though the poison was definitely intended for Eleanor Robertson, now missing, who is Bruce's wife, the lady of the house. (She, as I understand it, chose all the furnishings on this floor.) Eleanor is American. She disappeared late this afternoon. I don't know if she has been kidnapped or . . .'

Eddie rolled his palm to hurry Mirabelle along to the point of his journey north. 'The alexandrite,' he said. 'Found in the first woman's stomach.'

'Ah, that's what you're interested in?'

Eddie nodded.

'I wondered. Why?'

'You are supposed to be debriefing me,' Eddie objected. Mirabelle cocked her head. If she understood what he wanted, it would make the whole thing quicker, and he knew it. 'Oh, very well. It seems this alexandrite is useful stuff,' he said.

'Useful?'

'Do you know what a microwave is?'

Mirabelle shook her head.

'Our boffins are currently extremely excited about them. Last year the Yanks developed a machine called a maser. Heard of it?'

'No.'

'It stands for, now let me get this right, Microwave amplification by stimulated emission of radiation. Quite a mouthful. It keeps time in atomic clocks.' Eddie clapped his palms. 'For bombs, Mirabelle. Or rather, The Bomb. The only one that counts.'

'And alexandrite?'

'Refracts light or energy or something. Inside the maser. I'm not a scientist.'

'Ah,' Mirabelle said. The police thought they were kicking the case upstairs when they found the Russian pistol and heard about the mysterious stranger in the woods, but Eddie had been on it well before that. 'So when alexandrite turned up . . .'

'It came to me.'

'Would that be at the Home Office?' McGregor asked.

'A bit higher up than that, old chap.' Eddie sounded testy. 'So who was the woman exactly? The one who swallowed it. Did you meet her?'

'She died before we got here. All I know is that she was a visiting Russian American. She'd been here about a week when she was killed. A fashion buyer. Right wing, I'd say. Very,' Mirabelle filled him in. Eddie's gaze made her wonder if Nina might be more than she seemed. If she was what Jack had always referred to as 'connected'.

'She's not one of ours,' Eddie read her expression. 'Do you think this woman wanted alexandrite for the Russian government?'

'Oh no. Nina was a White Russian. A civilian. A fascist sympathiser, in fact. She got into an affray and, let me see—'

'This isn't at all clear,' Eddie snapped. 'Where did the woman get the alexandrite? And why? What is the Russian involvement – were they set to buy it?'

'I can't see that they would need to buy it. I mean, it's from Russia. They have the source.'

Eddie sighed. 'Yes. Well if they aren't buying it, they're either supplying it or selling it. Either way we can't have that willy-nilly. And I need to find out why it's up here at all. We have our work cut out. What have you been doing with your time? And where is the telephone?' he asked.

Mirabelle indicated the door to the hall. 'There's one out there. Or, if you prefer privacy, next to the dining room there's another in Bruce's study.'

'I'll report what we have. And then we'll get on, shall we?' Eddie left the room.

McGregor turned to Mirabelle. 'Well?' he said. 'Maybe you should debrief me too.'

She felt sick. McGregor coming clean about his secret had ultimately made her feel closer to him, but she wasn't sure that returning the favour was going to have the same effect on his emotions. As she took a deep breath, she thought of Niko, encouraging her to speak up. 'I want to tell you that

I had a difficult war,' she started. 'I'm like you. I failed too. People died because of me and the truth is there were more than fifteen of them. I never told you any more than you told me so really there's no reason for you to feel guilty about what you did.'

'You always said you were a secretary during the war.'

'I was. I worked for a man called Jack Duggan. I was in love with him. He was a senior naval officer working in intelligence and he was married – the same man I told you about before. I was assigned to his office because I could speak French and German. While I was there, I learned Spanish.'

'Spain was neutral. You pointed that out yourself when Bruce said it. Do you remember?'

'Nominally. Yes, it was neutral.' Mirabelle arched her eyebrow. 'Jack operated several of our people in the field and worked closely with Resistance cells in France and Germany. We had escape corridors through Spain,' she admitted. 'I signed the Official Secrets Act. I've never told a soul. I probably still can't – tell you the details, I mean.' She felt tears welling. 'Jack and I . . .'

McGregor took her hand. 'I know you were in love, Belle,' he said gently. 'A woman like you . . . how could I be the first? I have no regrets that you have a past. How could I? But who's this man? Brandon?'

Mirabelle felt her tears subside. 'Eddie worked for Jack,' she explained. 'I've known him since 1940. He's highly competent. There was a lot of pressure during the war. Sometimes we made the wrong decisions. I probably had more input than I should have. Jack used to take me everywhere. But I was good at it. When we debriefed, we realised some of the men responded better to a woman, so they upped my security clearance so I could work with returning escapees – you know, from the POW camps. And with couriers. And with Germans,' she added. 'Double agents. Nobody ever talks about those.'

McGregor seemed to take the revelations in his stride. 'I bet you were good at getting people to talk.'

She nodded. 'A cup of tea and just listening can work wonders. Jack was the stick. I was the carrot. Eddie was something in between. He's a devious bastard. That's not me talking – that's what Jack always said about him. Hard as nails. And queer. And clever. I have never seen him with a hair out of place.'

'Queer?'

'As Gregory. Anyway, I'm not perfect either. That's the point. For us, I mean.'

'What you're talking about is different from my case,' McGregor cut in. 'What you did isn't negligence. In fact, it's the opposite of negligence.'

'It still feels like guilt. Jack took difficult decisions. Quite often we wouldn't sleep afterwards. We used to walk around London for hours. In the blackout. One night during the Blitz we stayed out all night. I think we were waiting for some kind of divine retribution in the shape of a Luftwaffe bomb. Four brave people died that day. Actually, it's worse than that. Jack let them die. We all did.'

McGregor's eyes softened. 'We're some pair, aren't we?'

'Niko said I should tell you. That I was hopeless at talking about, you know, relationships.'

'Niko?' McGregor stiffened. 'You told Niko this?'

'I didn't tell him anything. But he's right. Knowing about you has brought us closer. Maybe it would be good if you knew more about me. Eddie seems OK with you being here.

251

He didn't have to keep you in the room just now. That means we can work on this together. If you still want to. I'm only a civilian here.'

'A civilian,' McGregor repeated.

'Yes,' Mirabelle said, considering the word and realising that, clearly, some people weren't civilians. Somebody had been working for the Russians. One person at least.

'Well, if you're a civilian, I guess I am too. And I'm less concerned with the alexandrite than your friend is. The main thing is that we get Eleanor back,' McGregor said.

Mirabelle was deep in thought. 'Her diamond watch,' she managed to get out. 'That's the thing. I can't quite put my finger on it.'

Within half an hour, the staff were up. Elizabeth set the fires, replacing the pillows scattered across the drawing-room floor on the sofa frames and opening the curtains. The sun was rising across the glen. The policemen gathered in the kitchen, where Mrs Gillies dispensed fried egg rolls and sweet tea as they chatted. 'It's not summer out there, Davey,' one said.

'I've heard the Russian winter is worse.'

'Aye. That'll be why they're here, the Russians, in our balmy temperatures, trying to snatch the laird's wife. Three below zero is a holiday for them.'

The dining room was set for McGregor, Mirabelle and Eddie, who had requested tea and thin slices of buttered toast. 'You've searched the house, I take it?' Eddie checked with Mirabelle. 'Because, if not, we need to tear the place apart in case there are more stones.'

'I went through Eleanor's office last night,' Mirabelle admitted. 'There was nothing. And the police went through her private rooms yesterday. The day before I checked in here and the drawing room.' McGregor looked at her. 'While you were out . . .' Mirabelle answered his unspoken question.

'And Eleanor?' McGregor said. 'What about her?'

'The police are still looking,' Eddie replied. 'We need to turn our attention to this. It's a matter of national security and it's connected.'

'You think both murders were because of this alexandrite?' McGregor added.

Eddie hated explaining. He bit into a slice of toast and sipped his tea. 'Yes. Of course,' he said.

Mirabelle stepped in. 'Obviously Nina's was. I mean, she swallowed a stone. We don't definitely know what happened to Susan. But it seems likely now we know the value of alexandrite – that there is more than monetary value, I mean. She must have found out, somehow.'

'So who do you think killed them?'

Eddie put down his cup. Mirabelle stiffened. This was generally the precursor to somebody getting a rollicking and McGregor was being dense. Before Eddie could speak, though, a constable came into the room. 'A telegram, miss,' he said, and handed a slip to Mirabelle. 'From Inverness.'

'Thank you.' She opened it.

On way, it said. *EB*

Mirabelle turned it over. 'Looks like you're on your way, Eddie.'

They laughed. 'Faster than a speeding bullet,' Eddie said. 'Well, it was only polite to give you notice. So, first, I need a plan of the house and estate.'

'There's one framed upstairs, in the hallway,' McGregor offered.

Eddie put down his cup. 'Let's fetch it.'

From the doorway, Mrs Gillies cleared her throat. 'Miss Bevan,' she said, 'I wondered about lunch.'

Mirabelle waved her off. 'I'm sure the policemen would like soup or something, Mrs Gillies, but I don't have the heart. Just do whatever you think is best.'

Mrs Gillies lingered. 'There are a couple of other household issues, miss. Might I have a word?'

Mirabelle wasn't sure how to explain. She was hopeless at anything domestic. Gillies was treating her like the mistress of the house, and, as the top-ranking woman, perhaps that was right, but honestly, the housekeeper would probably get more sense out of Bruce. The men disappeared up the hall to fetch the plans. 'Please, miss,' Gillies was insistent. 'If I could see you privately. Only for a moment.'

'Perhaps Mr Robertson can help . . .' Mirabelle started, but Gillies came further into the dining room and closed the door. 'Forgive my dishonesty, miss, but I think I might be able to help with your investigation. That is to say, there's something you ought to know.'

'Really, Gillies?'

'It's only . . .' The housekeeper crossed herself. 'It's Robertson business and for the women alone.'

Mirabelle felt her fingertips tingling. 'What is it?'

'The Green Lady, Miss Bevan.'

'The ghost?'

'Oh, she's not a ghost. Heaven's sake, that's only chatter in the village. What do they know? The thing is, I can't tell the officers about it. You mustn't either.'

'We can't withhold information, Mrs Gillies. There's too much at stake.'

'This is the Highlands. We've been withholding information from the authorities for centuries. If I show you, and it's relevant, we'll have to think of something.' Mirabelle considered this momentarily. She wanted Gillies to tell her. 'Very well,' she said.

Gillies led her through the hallway and up the main staircase into the dressing room of the main suite, where she carefully locked the connecting door to the bedroom in which Bruce lay sleeping. The place was in disarray. The policemen hadn't been careful. It would take hours to put the room back. Uncharacteristically, Gillies ignored the mess and instead opened the doors of the large mahogany wardrobe, which had been filled with Eleanor's clothes. She muttered a short prayer, pulled out one of the drawers and twisted a knob hidden beneath the lip. Then she pushed back the clothes the police search had left to reveal the back of the wardrobe as it slid to one side.

Mirabelle peered inside. Lit by a tiny skylight, the ward-robe concealed a room. It was only six feet square, and inside stood a worn wooden statue mounted on a plinth, of a woman in a green robe, the paint long flaking. 'Is this a priest hole?' she asked.

Gillies shook her head. 'There was a priest hole in the old Robertson house. That was many generations ago. By the time the family built this place, the killing times were over and the lady of the house had this hidden chamber installed, almost in memoriam. I understand it came in handy after Culloden when Charlie Robertson was on the retreat. His sister hid him here for several weeks in 1746 before they could smuggle him to France. There were redcoats everywhere, running amok.'

'And Eleanor knew this was here?' Mirabelle checked.

'Only Mrs Robertson knew, apart from myself.'

'Not Bruce?'

'The Robertson women pass the secret from generation to generation. Mother to daughter. I suppose Katrine Robertson must have shown her brother when she saved his life, but the secret died with him, in the male line. When you marry Mr McGregor, you'll be a Robertson, Miss Bevan, and you'll be entitled to the knowledge. I didn't want to withhold this place, but I couldn't bring myself to tell one of the policemen. The Robertson women have kept the Green Lady safe all the years; I couldn't throw her open.'

The little room felt eerie. As Mirabelle climbed through the wardrobe, Gillies stood guard like a gorgon. Briefly Mirabelle imagined hiding in this room for weeks, maybe months on end. It was like a cell. She ran her hands over the plinth and up the Green Lady's robes. Her fingers quickly searched out a tiny button on the reverse of the wooden book the saint was holding. She clicked it and behind the plinth a second concealed door opened. 'What's this?'

'The tunnel,' Gillies said. 'It comes out down behind the lodge. Nobody has used it for centuries as far as I'm aware. Is it a help, miss?'

Mirabelle peered inside. The tunnel was low – perhaps only four feet high. A set of steps ran down, between what she realised was the back wall of the drawing room and the front wall of the day room. She used her fingers to check the walls at the top of the stair. They were solid. Then, as she turned, she inspected the back of the door. People forgot doors once they had passed through them. The fronting was lined with four pine panels. As she tapped she realised one was hollow. An examination of the edging revealed how to open it so the panel swung out. Inside, there was an old bible. Mirabelle removed it. 'Mrs Gillies?'

'I don't know, miss.' Gillies said. 'I didn't know that was there.'

There was nothing inside the book beyond the printed text. Mirabelle noted the date on the flyleaf – 1790 – such a long time ago. In spidery writing at the front, somebody had drawn a Robertson family tree going back to the 1640s. She felt momentarily as if she was being pulled by a long thread, anchored centuries ago by a clever woman. 'Miss,' Gillies said, 'I can hear Mr Robertson stirring.'

Mirabelle nodded. She replaced the bible and it was only then she realised that the old book wasn't dusty enough. The rest of the crevice was coated in a thick layer, but not the cover. Something had sat on top of the book and had been removed.

'Was Mrs Robertson devout?' she asked, as she closed the door and climbed out of the wardrobe.

'Not especially,' Gillies said doubtfully.

'I didn't think so. Thank you, Mrs Gillies.' Mirabelle thought for a moment. 'If this is somewhere the Robertson women keep to themselves, did Alan's mother know about it?'

'Oh yes, miss. Miss Deidre was the one who showed me. She knew once she was gone there would be nobody to keep the secret, what with Mr Bruce and Mr Alan both being bachelors. She hoped one of them would marry. I showed Mrs Robertson when she first came to the house as Mr Bruce's bride. She was delighted.'

Mirabelle grimaced. 'I'm sure she was,' she said. 'And nobody else knows?'

'You and I, Miss Bevan, and I for one will take the lady's secret to the grave.'

The room smelled of dust now. Both women stopped as they heard Bruce leave the main bedroom and pad along the hallway towards the stairs. At least he'd managed some sleep. 'I shall tell them we were discussing dinner, if they ask,' Gillies said. 'Do you have any instructions about what to serve?'

'I wouldn't dream of issuing you with instructions, Mrs Gillies. You fire ahead with whatever you think best. Mr Brandon will probably be joining us. Before you go, can I ask, do you like Mrs Robertson?'

'Like?' Gillies looked for a moment as if she was considering if she had ever liked anybody.

'Yes,' Mirabelle persisted. 'I mean, Eleanor's fun. Lively. Good for Bruce. She was a breath of fresh air around here, wasn't she?'

'I was glad that Mr Bruce married,' Gillies allowed herself to say.

'And politically she was quite a change. Do you support that change?'

'I'm not a Communist, if that's what you're asking.'

'But I'll bet you're glad Eleanor is your mistress and not, say, Gwendolyn Dougal.'

Mrs Gillies sniffed. 'Our boys died,' she said simply. 'And Nazi sympathisers like Lady Dougal never paid for what they did – they encouraged the Germans for years before the war started.'

'I think Gwendolyn Dougal would be more accurately termed a conservative,' Mirabelle said.

Gillies's eyes sparked. 'That's what they call it now. But let me tell you, the Earl of Erroll had a sporran with a Nazi insignia – his valet told me. The Duke of Buccleugh was an appeaser. In 1939, the Duke of Hamilton wrote a piece in *The Times* about Germany's right to take Poland. We all read it. And they got away with it. Every one of them. And our boys died fighting. Those people sided with the enemy and kept quiet about it afterwards – they can call themselves whatever they like now, it makes no difference to me. I know who they are.'

'Our boys?'

'My nephew,' Gillies said.

'So you lost your husband to the Great War, and your nephew in the second? I'm very sorry.'

Gillies gave an almost indiscernible shrug. 'I recall serving at table in this house and a guest remarking that the first war was necessary,' she said. 'To keep the power on the right. To stop Britain becoming a Communist state – as if that was ever our way. Afterwards I was sick. All those lads dead and it was for nothing. General Haig should have been strung up. None of us want it to be pointless, but it was and that's the truth.'

'I take it, you'd heard Eleanor talk about politics and you'd agreed with her, more or less?'

Gillies acquiesced. 'You asked me if I like her. I'd say she's a good woman, at heart. Better than most.'

'And the current situation, Mrs Gillies? The Cold War?'

'The rockets, you mean? My sister says the hills will act as a shield if the Russians launch a strike. One thing's for sure, they're not aiming at old women like me, Miss Bevan.'

Mirabelle nodded slowly. 'Thank you for trusting me, Mrs Gillies, I won't say a word.'

Mirabelle headed back to the drawing room. It would never have struck her that the Highlands was so political or, for that matter, principled. In Brighton, morals had become more lax since the war. There was no doubt of that. Young people didn't care as much as her generation had – they wanted something new. Something more free. If anything, that's what they'd fight for. She'd had the expectation that up here it would be the same as Brighton, but this was a different country. If many people thought like Mrs Gillies, Macmillan and his government wouldn't be able to count on Scotland's vote, she thought. Not that that kind of thing was her business any more.

Bruce had joined McGregor and Eddie in the drawing room and was giving a short lecture about the estate's layout. Eddie had lit a cigarette. 'It's not a kidnap,' Mirabelle announced. 'It's not what we thought it was. None of it.'

'Do you know where she is?' Eddie asked.

'I know she left of her own free will.'

'What makes you say that?'

'The watch,' Mirabelle replied, because that made sense now. 'No kidnapper lets you don jewellery before he takes you. Eleanor only ever wore it in the evening. It's a dress piece. It wasn't on her wrist when she left the drawing room yesterday afternoon – she had her little gold strip – so if she dropped the diamond watch once she'd left, it means she fetched it before leaving. She knew she was going to go.'

'It wasn't a kidnap.'

'I realised when I was upstairs. She went up there. She changed – probably into suitable clothes to travel. She removed her valuables – the watch and who knows what else, but certainly any alexandrite there might have been. And then she ran.'

'Look here,' Bruce started to object.

McGregor put a hand on his cousin's arm. 'We need to figure this out to find Eleanor. Go on, Mirabelle.'

'But she wouldn't leave me,' Bruce said. 'She couldn't.'

Everyone ignored his comment and Mirabelle continued. 'We don't know what Eleanor was running from, or indeed what she might be running to. But if we know it wasn't kidnap, it makes her marginally easier to follow. She's working to her own agenda and people generally run to somewhere they know. There are no cars missing. The horses are in the paddock. That means it's likely Eleanor's on foot. Bruce, could you fetch the walking maps?'

Bruce hesitated a moment and then disappeared out of the room.

'Should we pass on this information to the men looking for her?' McGregor asked.

'Not yet,' said Eddie. 'You know more, don't you, Belle? Does she have the alexandrite? Do you know that?'

'Not for sure,' Mirabelle admitted. 'But she definitely took something she was hiding. I don't know what it was but there was a package of some sort concealed in her room.'

'How do you know?' McGregor asked.

Mirabelle felt her cheeks colour. She hoped he wouldn't notice. 'Dust moved on a surface,' she said. 'In an alcove. A hiding place.' It was always better to tell the truth – just, in this case, maybe not the whole truth.

McGregor seemed to accept this. 'So, did she know who tried to kill her?' he asked.

Bruce returned with the walking maps and behind his back Mirabelle shrugged. They were all aware they couldn't talk freely in front of McGregor's cousin. Instead, Mirabelle helped him to lay out the map.

'Where did they find the watch?' she asked Eddie.

Eddie examined the map efficiently. 'West of here and north.' He pointed to the moor beyond the mountains that overlooked Brochmor.

'On foot she might make four miles an hour. She'd be lucky at that – it's difficult ground,' Mirabelle said. Bruce looked at her with a shocked expression tempered with admiration. 'She started here.' Mirabelle pointed at the location of the Robertson estate. 'By the time she dropped the watch, it must have been three hours later. She was set on a course. I mean, we can guess the broad sweep of her direction from that information, and actually, it's a strange one.'

'Yes,' Eddie mused as he perused it. 'What's a clue but a mistake given another name?'

'What's strange about it?' Bruce stared at the map.

McGregor nodded slowly as he took in the information. 'It's illogical, Bruce. I mean, if you want to get out of difficult territory you make for transport. As your wife, Eleanor can't just turn up at the local railway station – or anywhere local, in fact. Everybody knows who she is. She'd be recognised in a heartbeat. Logically she should make for somewhere she won't be recognised, and her best chance at that is on the coast.'

Eddie nodded. 'It's a long coastline,' he said. 'Look at it.'

This was certainly true. The line intruded inland a long way, taking in the inlets of a sea loch which Eleanor had seemingly passed by. McGregor continued. 'She could steal a boat, or even hire one, if it was far away enough. She'd be less likely to be recognised, wouldn't she? Either that or she ought to make for as large a town as she can – she might get away unnoticed at Inverness Railway Station, for example, or Aberdeen. But she hasn't gone in that direction. Actually, she hasn't gone straight for the coast either. She's headed inland to the Highlands. Away from the coast and away from the main towns. I mean, what's she playing at? There's nothing there.'

'I wouldn't say that, old man. There's got to be something,' Eddie laid a finger on the land to the west of where the watch was found. 'They lost her scent over rock – that has to be somewhere here,' he mused. 'Mr Robertson, what's in this direction? This twenty-mile stretch, say?' He drew a circle with his finger.

Bruce put his hand to his chin. 'There are a couple of places – friends with estates,' he said. 'Small villages. Are you sure she isn't heading for the coast – the west coast, that is?'

Mirabelle considered this. 'It's a helluva walk,' she said. 'Across hills too. Why would she do that? She doesn't have to, just to get to the sea. Is there anybody in this area she likes, Bruce?' Mirabelle refocused Bruce's attention on the circle Eddie had drawn. 'Anyone she might feel close to?'

'Quite the reverse, I'd say. And they mostly live in London. They come up for the shooting, that kind of thing. Not at this time of year. A lot of that area is forested, actually. There are a few climbers' huts. Some academics from time to time – mostly in the summer.'

'Academics?' Eddie's voice sounded casual. Mirabelle stifled a smile. He was very good. Bruce continued, getting into his stride. He wanted his wife back, after all. They all did.

'The geology is interesting, apparently. And the archaeology. St Andrews brings students up during the breaks – not at this time of year, though.'

Eddie grinned. 'We've found the boffins,' he said. 'Do you know where they live while they're here?'

'They bought a place,' Bruce replied. 'On Michael McGregor's estate. He couldn't believe what they paid.'

'And where is that?'

Bruce squinted at the map. 'There,' he replied, pointing. 'West of Struy.'

Eddie picked up the chart and left the room. 'Sergeant,'

he shouted as he passed through the doorway and headed towards the kitchen.

Mirabelle sank on to the sofa.

'Will they find her now?' Bruce asked. 'I mean, if she ran, she must have been terrified. Someone tried to kill her yesterday and she didn't feel safe here, in her own home. My poor El.'

Mirabelle's heart sank. She wasn't sure what to say. Eleanor almost certainly had the alexandrite. And that meant she was involved in something unspeakably shady. Government lists of potential spies included a high proportion of academics and journalists. Eleanor had been in the second group before she got married and this might link her to the first. 'Bruce,' she said, trying to break it to him gently. 'The thing is, Eleanor might be with somebody.'

'What do you mean?'

'She might not be . . . alone.'

'I don't care about anything like that. I mean, this is more important. Poor El. After everything that's gone on, she's afraid for her life. And frankly, the police have been bloody useless! Until your friend turned up, nobody had a bloody clue.'

Alan laid a hand on Mirabelle's shoulder. He knew Mirabelle wasn't referring to an affair but there was no point filling Bruce in. 'We'll know soon enough,' he said. 'Let's not worry about it till then.'

Chapter 17

Trust: belief in someone or something

The police brought Eleanor back just after ten o'clock. Bruce burst out of the front door, launching himself at his wife as she approached the house, flanked by two officers who had parked their vehicle at the top of the drive. He flung his arms around her as she stepped on to the portico. 'Oh thank God! We've been so worried.'

'The dogs found me,' Eleanor said.

'It wasn't only the dogs, darling. Mirabelle has been a marvel. She figured out where you were, from those old maps in the cupboard and your bally watch,' Bruce enthused.

Eleanor cast Mirabelle a cold glance as she stood in the doorway. Then Eddie stepped forward and introduced himself. 'A word, Mrs Robertson?'

'We can talk later. I'm exhausted. Is it all right if I go to bed?' Eleanor said, pushing past him and into the hall.

'No,' Eddie replied. 'It is not.'

Eleanor cast a glance up the stairs. 'If I could only wash and change my clothes—'

'That's out of the question, Eleanor,' Mirabelle stepped in. 'You won't be going up to your room,' she said with finality. Bruce looked taken aback. Denying a woman the right to freshen up was an unthinkable discourtesy. Eleanor played on this. She hadn't given up on being able to sneak off through the wardrobe. Or, Mirabelle thought, perhaps just hide in the secret room until it was safe to escape again.

'First I was kidnapped . . .' she started.

'Kidnapped?' Eddie snapped. 'By whom? Did you arrest somebody with Mrs Robertson?' One of the police officers behind Eleanor shook his head.

'I was bound. Hand and foot,' Eleanor hissed.

'And yet you were alone when the police found you, Mrs Robertson. Who was this kidnapper? Can you describe him? What was his name?'

'I don't know. He didn't give me his calling card. He was Russian – a tall chap with dark hair. He grabbed me. Gagged me.'

'Where?'

Eleanor sighed. 'He bundled me out of the back door. Gillies was in the laundry.'

Mirabelle shook her head. 'We know you weren't kidnapped,' she said. 'We know that, Eleanor.'

Quite apart from the watch, Mirabelle noticed that Eleanor was wearing two cashmere sweaters and a thick jacket. She had known she was leaving. She had dressed for it.

'I have to sleep. I just have to,' Eleanor continued, insistent. 'I think it's the shock.'

'The dogs are still looking for the man, sir,' the policeman chipped in. 'So far they haven't picked up his scent. We have a team searching the cottage where we found Mrs Robertson.'

Eleanor was swaying on her feet as if she might fall. It was a convincing act, Mirabelle thought, but she wasn't about to let her disappear through the wardrobe again.

'And you found Mrs Robertson constrained?' she checked with the men.

'Yes, miss.'

'How was she constrained exactly?'

Eleanor shot further daggers in Mirabelle's direction. 'I was gagged,' she said. 'And tied up using rope.' She held out her hands to show Mirabelle the marks.

'And this person, this tall, dark man, just left you? In a cottage. In the middle of nowhere?'

'Yes!' Eleanor snapped. 'I was terrified.' There was fury in her eyes but also, Mirabelle noticed, tears welling. Bruce noticed too. He produced a handkerchief.

Mirabelle's mind swam, trying to figure out how much of what Eleanor said was true. Although she hadn't been kidnapped, it was possible she had an accomplice – probable, in fact. Still, in any conclusion everything would have to fit into place, like a lock opening. Like Gregory cracking the safe. She considered the evidence that they had accumulated – the life Bruce and Eleanor had built, Nina's character, the discarded Russian pistol on the back lane, the alexandrite and Eleanor's face as she arrived home only a few moments before. She smiled, remembering Gregory trying to follow the money, and then her attention returned to Eleanor's diamond watch and the way she was dressed. The ideas became a flood, more than she could focus on. But, she realised, if you thought about it, there was money. Right there, at the nub of things. 'I need to talk to Mrs Robertson alone,' she announced. 'You have some questions to answer, Eleanor, and it's best we do that privately. In the day room, perhaps?'

Mirabelle gestured up the hallway towards the gothic room next to the orangery. It would be the best place, she thought – to the rear of the house, relatively easy to guard, and small enough for Eleanor to feel constrained if she played it right. 'We need a policeman outside the window,' she said.

Eddie nodded. 'All right,' he agreed. 'I'll sit in.'

'Give me five minutes,' Mirabelle's tone was flat – she was telling him, not asking. 'On our own.'

Eddie looked at his watch. 'Five minutes.'

Ahead of them the maid disappeared into the back room, carrying a zinc bucket of kindling and a small brush and shovel, ready to set the fire. The niceties, Mirabelle thought; still it would be cold in there. The girl left the door slightly open and Mirabelle followed her. A constable appeared outside the window. Mirabelle gestured to him to move away. He was only there to stop Eleanor breaking out. She curled her finger, miming for him to turn round. Then she closed the lower shutters to block out the bottom of the window. She locked the door to the orangery, slipped the key into her pocket and snapped on the overhead light. They would need privacy.

Inside, accompanied by one of the officers, Eleanor sat down. The electric light was unforgiving. Dark circles under her eyes made it clear she hadn't slept. The officer closed the door behind him as he left the room and Elizabeth stood up, the curl of flames kindling in the grate. 'Thank you, Elizabeth,' Mirabelle said, considering where to start – perhaps telling Eleanor she knew how she had got out, to make it clear there would be no escape, and her best bet was to come clean. But as she was about to speak, the maid reached into the bucket, drawing a gun with a distended barrel from underneath the kindling. It had a silencer. She pointed the gun at Eleanor.

'Look out!' Mirabelle snapped in warning.

At these words, Elizabeth turned towards Mirabelle, her eyes hard. She clicked off the safety catch. Without thinking any further, Mirabelle launched herself at the maid, catching her arm so that she let off two shots that hardly made a sound and thankfully missed both Mirabelle and Eleanor, embedding themselves in the door. 'Move!' Mirabelle called to Eleanor as she tried to grab hold of Elizabeth, who immediately let off another two silent bullets.

Mirabelle cried out. Her arm suddenly flared with pain as one of the bullets penetrated her flesh at close range. Her legs gave way and a wave of nausea turned her stomach as blood dripped down her forearm on to the carpet. Breathing deeply, she managed to regain her footing, clasping her injured arm.

'Oh shit,' Eleanor said, moving towards the door, but she wasn't quick enough and Elizabeth once more turned the gun towards her mistress. Eleanor froze, raising her hands. 'What are you doing?' she asked.

'What does it look like, madam?' Elizabeth sneered.

'You?' said Eleanor. 'They'll come in here, you know. They'll catch you.'

Mirabelle knew this wasn't true, not immediately. Eddie would give her a full five minutes – that was the drill. The men would have returned to the drawing room. Any officers in the house would have been told not to enter no matter what. Eddie knew what asking for time alone with a witness usually meant. Any noise and he'd assume Mirabelle was applying pressure of a particular kind. They needed to make it to the door, she thought. And, unless they could disarm the girl when they did so, they'd have to be careful in case there was an officer standing in the hallway. She didn't want anyone else getting shot.

She ignored the pain that was blossoming along her arm and attempted to focus. Using her other arm, she shoved the maid hard. The girl stumbled and fired another two bullets in rapid succession. One disappeared into the carpet and the second hit Eleanor in the foot. To her credit she didn't howl, instead gasping in pain. Elizabeth moved smartly. Furious at missing her shot, the girl turned once more towards Eleanor to finish the job, but Mirabelle launched herself in the maid's direction again, this time knocking the gun hard so that it fell to the floor. Quick as lightning, Eleanor picked it up as Mirabelle held Elizabeth back. 'If I don't get you, one of us will,' the girl snarled at her mistress. 'You're a dead woman. You're a traitor and a thief. Where are the stones? Where have you hidden them?'

Behind them the door opened. It wasn't Eddie, though. It was Bruce. Thank God, Mirabelle thought. Someone who doesn't know the way things work. 'I say . . .' he started, 'is everything all right?'

'Fetch the police,' Mirabelle snapped. 'We need to arrest this girl.'

'Of course,' Bruce bumbled. 'Sorry.'

'Stop.' Eleanor's voice was clear as a bell. Mirabelle loosened her grip on Elizabeth, who pushed her away as if she had freed herself. Slowly, Eleanor raised the gun.

'Don't!' Mirabelle sounded horrified as she realised what Eleanor was about to do, but Eleanor didn't stop. Instead she hit the girl hard on the head with the butt. Elizabeth crumpled on to the carpet, a thin trickle of blood seeping through her hair.

'My God!' Bruce said.

'Be quiet,' Eleanor directed her husband. 'Come in, Bruce.'

'But darling . . .'

'Come in now and close the door properly.' Eleanor raised the gun as if she would use it. Silently, Bruce entered the room, his expression pained, as if he simply couldn't understand what was happening. 'Well, this is a mess, isn't it?' Eleanor gestured.

Mirabelle checked Elizabeth – relieved to see the girl was breathing. She rolled her on to her side for safety but there was no time to apply first aid. 'Eleanor . . .' she started, standing up again.

'Oh you're all I need. I mean, this whole thing is twice as bad because of you,' Eleanor snapped. 'When did you realise?'

'Just now,' Mirabelle admitted. 'Some of it. Gregory said follow the money and I thought there wasn't any but then it dawned on me . . .'

'The alexandrite.'

'Yes—'

'What are you talking about?' Bruce asked, confused.

'Quiet!' Eleanor sounded increasingly irritable.

Mirabelle waited a moment before continuing. 'You can't get away,' she said. 'There are policemen all over the grounds.'

'I'll find a way,' Eleanor replied. 'I did before.'

Mirabelle's eyes flicked to the window. 'You won't get far,' she said. 'Green is not go, Eleanor. Not this time. That won't work again.'

Eleanor sighed. 'I didn't take you for an extremist,' she said.

'You're the one making deals with the Russians. You are, aren't you?'

She noticed Eleanor's hand quiver. It was a small movement but it demonstrated that the shock of being shot was settling in. The shock of hurting Elizabeth too, if it came to that. Adrenalin was unpredictable. Mirabelle made to move, but Eleanor pulled herself together and raised the gun once more. Mirabelle took a measured breath, her heart fluttering.

'Stop right there,' Eleanor directed.

Mirabelle took one more step and Eleanor fired, pointedly, into the skirting, past Mirabelle's leg.

'I said stop,' she said.

Mirabelle complied. She took a deep breath. She'd talked her way out of worse, though her hands felt clammy as she started. She just had to engage Eleanor, that was the thing.

'Nina was your first problem, wasn't she?' she said, keeping her tone smooth – almost soothing. 'She made a link that set this whole thing in motion. Brought it to a head, I mean.'

Eleanor let out a puff of air, as if to blow Mirabelle's words away. 'God, she was awful. She always had been. A bitch with a bone.'

Relief flooded Mirabelle's limbs – Eleanor wanted to talk. That was good. 'That's why you accommodated her in the lodge.'

'I couldn't refuse her – I mean, she was buying stock for some great places. But I wasn't going to have her here. I hoped she'd just pay for her cashmere and go home. I mean, that's what she came to do. But she had a nose for money like you wouldn't believe. I'd forgotten. I should never have let her stay.'

'She realised about the alexandrite, then?'

'I was unlucky. She walked into my dressing room while I was sorting things out. An absolute fluke. She recognised it immediately, of course.'

'More than just that one stone?'

Eleanor laughed. 'Yeah. She was delighted.'

'And what were you doing with it? The alexandrite, I mean?'

Eleanor ignored the question.

'Darling,' Bruce cut in. 'I don't understand.'

'Of course you don't,' Eleanor shot in his direction. 'You're a sweet man, but you have no idea.'

'Give him an idea, Eleanor. He deserves that. We all do.' Mirabelle encouraged her. 'Seems like extremism is the thing you dislike the most. Am I right?'

'Yeah – McCarthy and his witch hunt back in the States. I've seen what extremism does. What it leads to.'

'And that's what you liked about Britain? Our more level-headed approach?'

'At first it seemed more tolerant here.'

'But recently?'

Eleanor sighed. 'People get scared. All this warmongering. Both sides are as bad as each other. When people are scared they look for black and white and stop seeing grey. They can't see that we've done bad things – just as much as the other side.'

'And you wanted to stand up against that?'

Bruce still wasn't getting it. 'But we won the war, darling. We're the good guys.'

Eleanor looked as if she might cry. 'Really? People don't realise what's going on in front of their eyes – not least you, Bruce. The famine in Bengal in '43 was down to Churchill. He as good as said the Indians deserved it. Hitler killed six million and he was a beast. But about half that number died in India at the hands of your leader – the guy everyone seems to revere. I mean, the Nazi death camps were terrible, but they were an extension of a British model. You're the *better* guys, not the good guys, darling. That's what I've come to realise.'

'I agree. Churchill isn't the god the papers make him out to be,' Mirabelle said, hoping that Eleanor didn't detect the personal experience in her tone.

'No. He isn't,' Eleanor continued. 'He's a grey figure. And Stalin was a monster, that I will allow, but Khrushchev, I don't know yet. It seems to me that instead of gearing up for war, with both sides locked into a race to develop the best bomb, for Christ's sake, shouldn't we open dialogue? Be brave enough to look at the grey in what we did, and in what they're doing. But that's considered too dangerous. You can't have sympathy for the grey areas. It's a capital offence, and they give all kinds of nasty names to people who want to be honest about the bad as well as the good. They call us traitors and name what I did treason. They insist we're 100 per cent fantastic and the other side are devils. It's just nonsense. I have to get out of here.'

Mirabelle stepped into Eleanor's path. 'Move,' Eleanor said.

Mirabelle shook her head. 'I'll speak for you,' she offered. 'Let me testify on your behalf. Whatever you've done.'

'You think they'll let me off on your say-so?'

'I don't know. You still haven't been clear about the detail of it, Eleanor.'

Eleanor shrugged. 'I built bridges.'

'Alexandrite bridges?'

'I passed stones to people they wanted to support – for research, for science. I helped them sell some of it – it's worth a fortune but they can't trade on the open market. The Brits are not going to let me off with a caution for either of those things.'

'No,' Mirabelle said sadly. 'They won't. What did they pay you?'

'Pay me?' Eleanor seemed genuinely bemused at the

notion. 'I wasn't doing this for money. I was doing it because they aren't all bad and we aren't all good. You'd better get out of my way.'

'No,' Mirabelle repeated.

Eleanor nudged the muzzle of the gun into the soft flesh of Mirabelle's stomach. But before she could make a decision about whether to fire, both women were distracted by a loud sob.

Behind them tears spilled down Bruce's cheeks. 'Is this why you married me? Because you're a spy? Have you always been a Communist?'

Eleanor didn't turn her head. 'I'm not a spy, darling,' she said. 'I've never been a spy. Or a Communist. I married you because I love you, you idiot.' Eleanor moved sideways but Mirabelle continued to block her path. 'Jesus!' she burst out in frustration. 'Do you want to be shot?'

'I don't think you're going to shoot me.'

'Oh no?'

'I want to know what happened, Eleanor, and so does Bruce – we deserve that. You know why Nina was killed, don't you? You said she caught you with the alexandrite. What happened then?'

Eleanor snorted. 'She tried to blackmail me. For her silence,' she said. I gave her one of the stones but she wanted more. That was what she was like. I said she could have what I'd offered and stay quiet or I'd take the damn thing back and she could hazard her chances trying to prove what I had been doing.'

'Could she have proved it, Eleanor?'

'She didn't have any real intelligence beyond me having a quantity of alexandrite that could only have come from one place. I wasn't going to end up beholden to her for ever. I knew if I didn't draw a line in the sand, she'd just keep going. So I figured it was better to draw the line early. I didn't mean for what happened to happen.'

'Do you mean you killed her?'

'I know you won't believe me, but I didn't intend to. I lost my temper. I'm sorry for that. But, for the record, if she wasn't black and white, that woman was a very dark grey. A proto-fascist. An authoritarian.'

'What happened?'

'I did what I said I'd do. I tried to take the stone back. We fought. At first we were like girls in the schoolyard. She grabbed me by the hair. Honestly. Then it got out of hand.'

'She swallowed the stone?'

'Russian aristocrats know a hundred places to secrete valuables. Yeah, she swallowed it. She smiled and said I couldn't get it back now, and that we were doing things her way. She wanted more before she left.'

'So you strangled her? Jesus, Eleanor!'

'It wasn't like that. I was furious. It was a cat fight. I grabbed hold of her stupid silk scarf. I thought it would tear but it was stronger than I reckoned. She was a fucking Nazi, Mirabelle. You were at Nuremberg. If anyone should understand, it's you.'

'You'd never killed anybody before?'

'Of course not. The balmy days before I was a murderer? Last week.'

'An assassin more like.'

'She's the assassin.' Eleanor nodded towards Elizabeth, still unconscious, lying between Mirabelle and the door. Mirabelle thought it was a good thing Eleanor hadn't killed the girl. Apart from anything else, Elizabeth trying to kill her backed up her story. 'What happened to Susan MacLeod?' she pushed.

'That wasn't me.'

'Was she a blackmailer too? What did she want to talk to you about that day in your office?'

'I don't know. Poor kid. She never came back. I've been trying to figure it out. I guess it was her.' Eleanor gestured towards Elizabeth. 'Or someone with her. I mean, they had to get Elizabeth into the house, to get rid of me and retrieve their goods, I suppose. So they removed the existing maid. They don't call it the Cold War for nothing.' Eleanor was right, Mirabelle thought, or close at least. That sounded right. It explained the Russian gun that had been found near Susan's body. Dropped in the retreat. Those frantic moments after a kill. The tall, dark man in the navy jacket.

'But I went to see the MacLeods,' Bruce murmured in disbelief. 'I sent them your condolences.'

Neither woman replied. 'So it wasn't planned,' Mirabelle said.

'God. No. It's been hell. Does it seem as if all this was planned?'

Mirabelle shook her head. 'And then you were trapped. Stuck in this house with Tash and Niko who were mourning the woman you murdered. When it came down to it, no wonder you couldn't face visiting the MacLeods. God, it must have been awful. And then someone came after you. Elizabeth, I suppose with that pin in the chair. The Russians. The real Russians. The ones you think are so reasonable.'

'People get scared.'

'Scared?'

Eleanor shrugged. 'Great cover. I mean, who suspects the maid?'

'It's usually the butler. The murderer, I mean.' Mirabelle smiled.

Eleanor shook her head. 'On stage. Women are a far more intelligent proposition, don't you think? I mean, we're less likely to be suspected because men underestimate us all the time. Anyway, Jinx took the poison for me. Poor Jinxy.' She began to cry. It was odd, Mirabelle thought, that it was Jinx that seemed to have broken her. Jack used to say murderers often cared more for their animals than for people.

'But why would the Russians want to kill you if you'd been helping them? And when you ran, where did you think you were going? Back to Moscow?' Mirabelle asked. Tears flooded down Eleanor's cheeks now. She shook her head. Mirabelle's brain was whirring. No – that was wrong. The Russians had wanted to kill Eleanor, so, of course she couldn't head into their territory. 'I don't understand, if you were loyal, what went so wrong?' she continued.

'I've never been to Moscow,' Eleanor sniffed. 'That's the ridiculous thing. I would have liked to see it.'

'And who tied you up? Because these people want you dead, clearly,' Mirabelle gestured towards Elizabeth, grappling with the parts of the story she hadn't figured out.

A carriage clock on a side table chimed the half-hour and Mirabelle started. Eleanor used the moment's distraction to regain her sense of purpose. She surged forwards and Mirabelle tried to block her. Eleanor raised the gun, as if to shoot, and in that split second Mirabelle's heart missed a beat as she launched herself towards the other woman. She anticipated a shot, but the gun didn't fire – not even the dull thud of the silencer. There were no bullets left. Mirabelle tackled Eleanor to the ground. The weapon went flying. Eleanor landed a punch on Mirabelle's cheek as Mirabelle tried to pin her to the floor. In desperation, Eleanor sank her teeth into Mirabelle's injured arm. Mirabelle heard herself scream, saw her own blood on the other woman's face. She kicked Eleanor's injured foot, then manoeuvred her body round and finally managed to hold Eleanor in place.

'I have to get out of here,' Eleanor snarled.

Bruce picked up the gun. 'Bruce,' Mirabelle said, 'could you fetch Eddie, please?'

For a moment she wasn't entirely sure what Bruce was going to do. Then, slowly, he moved towards the door. 'I still don't understand,' he said.

'Well, I don't either. Not entirely. But do you think I could explain what I know afterwards?' Mirabelle tried to smile.

'If you love me, Bruce, you'll knock her unconscious,' Eleanor snarled.

Bruce hovered between the women and the exit. Mirabelle held her breath. When he disappeared through the frame, Eleanor let out a frustrated growl and Mirabelle made sure to keep her grip steady. She couldn't remember ever feeling so grateful.

Chapter 18

*No one can confidently say that he will still be
living tomorrow*

Detective Inspector Cameron seemed exasperated by
the morning's events. It was, in fairness, something of
a turnaround. He arranged for Elizabeth to be taken to hospital under guard – the girl regained consciousness, but she
was woozy and incoherent. The medics said it would take
some time before she could be usefully questioned. Eleanor
had hit her hard. The ambulance attendant examined the
gunshot wounds and left Mirabelle in Mrs Gillies's care.
Because Eddie refused to allow Eleanor to be taken out of his
orbit, the man prescribed a strong painkiller and performed
a swift field operation on her foot. The leather of Eleanor's
walking boots had held the wound tightly, which meant she
hadn't lost much blood. 'You'll have a limp,' he pronounced,
'but I got the bullet out.' Eleanor simply shrugged.

Then Inspector Cameron, under Eddie's instruction, formally arrested her. She remained detained in the day room,
recovering. Two men were posted to guard the window and
two more on the door – what Eddie described laconically as
'policemen to watch policemen'. 'Just until we can remove
her somewhere more secure,' he promised. 'I'm not finished

with this house yet,' he said as he disappeared into Bruce's study to make some calls, muttering something about Khrushchev, which Mirabelle didn't catch.

In the kitchen, Mrs Gillies dressed Mirabelle's wound. 'There, lass,' she said, stony-eyed. 'Just a graze. Not as bad as the mistress.'

'It's not my fault,' Mirabelle said.

Gillies nodded, but didn't reply, and Mirabelle realised the old woman was processing what had happened. She had liked Eleanor, after all. And so had Mirabelle, it dawned on her with some confusion. Eleanor was right. The world was too black and white, even if the best way to counter that wasn't to collude with the Soviets.

Gillies made tea but Bruce was the only one to drink it, sitting at the table like a child, both hands clutching the cup for warmth. He kept staring at Mirabelle and then at the floor. The police were still working. They removed the shotguns from the study and rummaged through Eleanor's bedroom again but didn't find the Green Lady who, after all, had eluded discovery for centuries. It was a clever kind of catch, Mirabelle thought, and wondered if her own fingers would have found it, had she searched the room without knowing.

Around half past eleven, Gregory slipped into the kitchen and took his place at the table. 'What's going on?' he asked.

'We got some answers to our questions. Is Tash all right?' Mirabelle checked. In the confusion, she had almost forgotten about the Americans, still upstairs, sleeping.

'She's not awake yet,' Gregory replied, 'but the cops say they're going to release Nina's body today. At last.'

That made sense. Mirabelle drained her cup. The tea warmed her, though her arm had started to ache horribly now the adrenalin of the fight had subsided. Her brain felt as if it was working too slowly and that was frustrating. There were still matters to consider.

From the direction of the yard, McGregor came into the kitchen, carrying the account book Mirabelle had last seen in the safe. It surprised her that she hadn't wondered where he had got to. 'Where did you get that?' she asked.

'I cracked the safe,' he said, 'the one in Eleanor's office – behind the painting,' and then, as he realised his cousin was there, added, 'Sorry, Bruce.' He put the book on the table. 'I think I've figured out what Eleanor was doing. I mean, where it went wrong. The alexandrite was just money, wasn't it? I mean, if you consider it that way, it's quite clear.' He flipped open the book, indicating the columns of figures. 'The accounts for the distillery make absolute sense. So does what's entered for the cashmere mill. But here,' he said, 'Eleanor's tweed enterprise. How much did you give her, Bruce, to start that?'

'I put in two hundred guineas,' Bruce said sullenly, raising his hands in surrender. 'For a couple of looms. I didn't think it was wrong.'

'Not at all,' Mirabelle said kindly. 'Oh Bruce.'

'That's what I thought.' McGregor removed a pencil from his pocket and jotted down some figures in the margin. 'Not counting your two hundred guineas, the place has received a lot of investment.'

Mirabelle sat up. She forgot how badly her arm hurt. 'Go on,' she said.

'It's had more than a thousand pounds, in fact. It's currently highly unprofitable. The money has been run through in round figures – large round figures. Not the kind of sums you get from crofters investing their savings. They don't seem to be selling much of their product, either. Anyway, this shows how Eleanor has tried to hide what she did – by showing the investment as if it was income from sales, but then over here,' he flipped a page, 'she hasn't adjusted the stock. Almost everything they've made is still in the warehouse. They take a tally monthly. So I had to ask, where did the cash come from? She didn't have any of her own, did she Bruce?'

Bruce shook his head. Mirabelle's eyes narrowed. She remembered the note in Nina's journal – the tweed collective, she realised, was what had raised her suspicions. She was in the rag trade – she'd spotted it wasn't making money. Her cryptic note that just said 'Red?' wasn't about red fabric. She had realised something was going on. Beside her, Mrs Gillies sank down at the table as McGregor continued. 'You said Elizabeth called Eleanor a thief?'

'And a traitor.'

'This must be why. Try this for size – Eleanor is evangelical in her beliefs. She set up the tweed collective because she wanted to change the world. Not a bad notion. But she needed more money than she could take from the estate to get it going. Bruce told her to stop spending from his account and she was determined to get the investment she needed from somewhere – she wanted the tweed collective to work. In fact, I think it will work – eventually. The production is efficient and once the investment is made, they only have to buy wool. Where they've made sales, the mark-up is excellent. Long term, they will be able to pay off the capital if they can sell goods worth, say, a hundred and fifty a month. And when you look at what the cashmere mill is taking in, that's entirely possible. Eleanor wasn't wrong. It's only a matter of where she got the money to set the place up and keep it going until the profits roll in. And that's shown here – deposits in cash.'

'Go on,' Mirabelle encouraged him.

'So where did she get the cash? Well, like all evangelists, Eleanor thought people would agree with her because she believed herself to be right. So to keep this enterprise going, she borrowed money from the Russians – or, rather, the way they looked at it – she stole it. She has admitted they were already using her to bring in the alexandrite and I can see that's entirely possible. The coastline here is long and difficult to police. It would be relatively easy to arrange a drop – a good old-fashioned case of smuggling. You said that Eleanor put her hand up to supplying the stones to other people and also to selling it. On the international market, no dealer would buy from the Russian government without attracting a lot of adverse attention, but an upper-class woman is a different matter. I'm sure Eleanor lied and said she was selling the alexandrite for White Russian friends. Or that they had been in her family for years. Both plausible stories – White Russian assets are mostly in artefacts. Anyway, whatever Eleanor was doing for the Russians, she took some of the stones (or the money from the stones) for herself, or rather, for her pet project, and her comrades at the Soviet Socialist Republic weren't pleased when they found out.'

'You think she was a fence?' Gregory asked.

'That would fit, wouldn't it, with what she said to you, Mirabelle?'

Mirabelle nodded sadly.

'So basically a thief and a traitor,' Bruce said disconsolately. 'As the maid said.'

'That's harsh, Bruce,' McGregor told him. It seemed wrong to make it worse than it had to be. 'The Russians recruited Eleanor, that's true, but there's no sign she was being paid, apart from the money she creamed off to support the collective – Mirabelle said she was shocked at the very idea. I think she was naïve. We have no reason to believe that she lied to Mirabelle when she said she was fencing the jewels to forge links. A sort of appeasement. In the scheme of things she didn't take a huge percentage – far less than a professional dealer would have pocketed – and, in her eyes, it was probably merited all the more because it wasn't for her – it was for what she considered a good cause. She did a good job, actually, as far as I can see.' He tapped the accounts book. 'It must have been going on for the last three years, at least.'

'How could she?' Bruce said weakly. 'I just don't understand who'd want to buy alexandrite up here? It's hardly . . . Hatton Garden,' he finished, realising as he said it that he had answered his own question.

They all stared at each other. 'June,' Mirabelle said. 'She did it in London, every June.'

McGregor opened the book again and struck his pencil off the page. 'Yes, she did. Large deposits and capital purchases made in July and August of last year and,' he turned back a few pages, 'the same the year before. Maybe she thought the Russians wouldn't notice or maybe she thought they'd support what she was doing. It was a collective, after all.'

'Can you prove any of this?' Bruce snapped. 'It sounds like nonsense to me.'

'The evidence is here, Bruce,' McGregor said. 'I trained as an accountant. Don't you remember?' Mirabelle allowed herself to smile. Their eyes locked. 'It's solid police work, that's all,' McGregor added.

Gregory let out a low whistle. 'Are you saying . . .' he started.

'Gosh, yes. Sorry, Gregory. I'm afraid Eleanor confessed to killing Nina. Not a premeditated murder. Nina, it seems, was blackmailing Eleanor and they got into a fight. Eleanor won that fight.'

Gregory got to his feet. 'God,' he said. 'I'd better tell Tash.'

'Do you want me to do it?' McGregor asked.

Gregory considered. 'No,' he said. 'Leave it to me.'

After he'd gone there were a few moments of silence before Bruce nodded, acceptance dawning. 'Eleanor was never normally interested in shopping,' he said. 'But she loved Hatton Garden. She'd pop over on her own while I was catching up with the chaps from my regiment.' He looked as if he might be sick.

In due course, Gregory brought down Tash, Niko and Nina's bags and piled them by the front door. They looked like some kind of leather cairn, built in memoriam. Mirabelle and McGregor retired to the drawing room while Bruce poured his first whisky of the day. He sat on the sofa alone, his expression hollow, and looked, by Mirabelle's estimation, at least ten years older than he had when they'd arrived.

'Tash is coming down,' Gregory said, loitering by the door.

'You'll have to look after her,' Mirabelle told him.

Gregory saluted. 'I know. But once she's settled and the funeral is over, I think I might come back.'

'Here?' Mirabelle sounded perturbed. It seemed odd he would want to.

Gregory shook his head. 'Britain. London. Brighton maybe. Despite all this, your country feels kinda enlightened. And I'd like to meet your friend and her husband. What are their names?'

'Vesta and Charlie.'

Mrs Gillies brought in a tray with coffee. There seemed little prospect of anyone facing lunch. She was pouring inky black cupfuls when Tash came into the room. She had dressed hastily in mourning clothes, ready to retrieve her godmother's body, but she was not a woman enmeshed in grief, rather one inflamed by anger. She stared unrelentingly at Bruce, who put down his whisky and got to his feet, but couldn't quite meet her eye. 'How could she?' Tash managed to get out.

'I'm so sorry,' Bruce said. 'I didn't know.'

Tash's lips pursed. 'But you were married to her. That bitch. And all the time she's been saying "Tash dear, this" and "Tash dear, that" and she'd murdered Nina in cold blood. My godmother.' The girl's voice broke as she started to cry. 'This house is a killing zone,' she spat. 'Susan MacLeod. And that poodle. What the hell did she think she was doing just ruining people's lives?'

A single tear ran down Bruce's cheek. He wiped it away. 'Say something!' Tash demanded.

'Eleanor didn't kill Susan. That was the Russians, as I understand it,' Bruce said, and Tash broke, rushing towards him, hitting him ineffectively as she cried like a child in the grip of a tantrum. McGregor moved to help but Mirabelle waved him off. It was better to let it out. 'I don't get it,' Tash sniffed as her passion subsided. 'Eleanor was a Red? A real Red?'

Mirabelle nodded. 'At least, she was on their side.'

Bruce looked as if he was going to cry. 'My wife,' he spluttered, 'is not some pinko Communist. I can't let you say that.'

'Perhaps not in the doctrinal sense,' Mirabelle agreed. 'She suffered from reasonableness in a strange kind of way. That's the thing I can't quite seem to get a hold of.'

Tash's eyes burned. 'It wasn't reasonable to kill my godmother.'

'No. Absolutely not. But I have no doubt that she was trying to be reasonable. Eleanor was passionate in her views. She found Gwendolyn Dougal deeply offensive – more than most of us – more even than you, Tash. I can't say I entirely blame her. Think of her comments about the Russian involvement in Suez or how she reacted to Khrushchev's recent one-upmanship. I feel I know more about what she was against than what she stood for. Other than just some general sense of fairness. I don't think she was right. But it does explain what she did.'

Bruce looked flummoxed. 'Fairness is a good thing,' he said.

'So you're defending her – a murderer,' Tash sneered.

'It's easy to become hysterical about political affiliations,' Mirabelle insisted. 'Things aren't always cut and dried. We'll get it out of her, Tash. I promise. A full confession. And she'll go to prison. I'm sure of that.'

Tash blew her nose. 'This whole thing,' she said. 'It's just horrible.'

Mirabelle continued. 'I should say, we wouldn't know as much as we do if it wasn't for Gregory. He was the first to say follow the money, and that was the lynchpin of the whole thing. I should have known as soon as your godmother's post-mortem results came in. I mean she had swallowed the stone – that's a kind of transaction in itself.'

'Nina was blackmailing Eleanor, that's what Gregory told me,' Tash said.

'I believe that,' Mirabelle confirmed. 'Though obviously Eleanor shouldn't have killed her.'

It was to the girl's credit, Mirabelle thought, that she could see Nina as she really had been. Death was a great romancer of reputations, but Tash hadn't fallen into that trap. That said, it was better not to tell her that Eleanor was still in the house, only a few yards away. She'd find it too difficult.

'The main thing now is that you get your godmother home again,' Mirabelle said smoothly.

'Niko arranged the church.' Tash gestured vaguely, her beautiful eyes moist. 'An open casket – orthodox. Back home. And he got a lawyer, so I guess I'll leave him to that. But this has to be taken into account when they try him – he was living in a house with the person who killed his sister. It's too weird.'

Mirabelle wasn't sure what to say. She gave Tash a hug. The girl clung on to her for a moment, like a kitten digging in its claws.

Then, Gregory loaded the luggage into the hired car and they gathered in the hall to say goodbye. The house was emptying of police officers, and only the men hand-picked by Eddie were allowed to stay. It would take days before Tash would be back in New York with Nina's body. 'Write to me?' Mirabelle scribbled her address on to a card. 'Make sure you look after her, Gregory,' she instructed.

'I promise.'

Tash hugged McGregor and even Gillies, but she couldn't bring herself to shake Bruce's hand. Outside, the air was biting cold as they waved at the retreating car. At the gates there was a policeman now, rather than the pressmen.

'At least that's one good thing,' Bruce said. 'They've lost interest.'

Mirabelle thought the Robertsons were a well-matched pair – always thinking the best. 'I expect Eddie had a word,' she said.

'I must thank him,' Bruce said vaguely, as if it had been done for his benefit and not a blackout of classified information.

As they turned inside, Eddie appeared from the study. 'Good,' he said. 'The Yanks have gone.'

Mirabelle found, with surprise, that she was, after all, considering lunch. She hoped Mrs Gillies might be able to rise to something tasty. It felt as if things had come together, however troubling. Bruce, she realised, had retreated to the fireside alone. They'd need to look after him but, essentially, they'd figured out what had happened.

When she raised her eyes, she was surprised to see Eddie and McGregor standing as if they were waiting on something. 'This way, old girl,' Eddie said, ushering her into the dining room and closing the door behind her.

'Well? Do you know who it was?' McGregor asked Eddie as they grouped around the mahogany table.

'Who?' Mirabelle's mind was blank.

The men's eyes met. 'Did Mrs Gillies give you a painkiller?' McGregor checked.

'There's no time,' Eddie cut in. 'This is too important. We need to focus fast. I know who it is and the last thing I want is another bloody Burgess and Maclean on my hands.'

Mirabelle withheld from asking what was going on. McGregor put his hand on hers. He pulled a couple of sheets of paper from his pocket. 'OK. Here's what I've got. I found more circumstantial evidence – a loose end. Apart from the accounts. Here,' he pointed at one paper, 'this is the police inventory from yesterday – from Eleanor's office. When Belle and I were there earlier in the day, there was definitely a leather briefcase under Eleanor's desk. Do you recall? Burgundy, with her initials embossed on it? It isn't on the police inventory for the room. I assumed they'd taken it as evidence, but it's not noted here either – in the stuff they took away. And that's because it was gone.

I think Eleanor took it when she bolted. I think it contained the stones.'

'What's the second sheet?' Mirabelle peered.

'That's today's. Cameron let me have a copy. The leather case wasn't in the cottage where they found her. It's not in this house either. I had a man double-check – everywhere we could think of. It's gone. So the question is: what did Eleanor do with it? There are two real propositions, I think.'

'Three,' Eddie corrected. 'Either she delivered it, she hid it, or somebody took it from her – this Russian she talked about.'

'But she wasn't kidnapped,' Mirabelle said. 'She couldn't have been. She left of her own volition. Besides, the Russians wanted to kill her, not tie her up and leave her in a cottage.'

'Fair point,' Eddie said. 'But somebody did tie her up. I confirmed with the men who found her, she was bound and gagged all right. She can't have done that to herself. And she was in the cottage that belongs to St Andrews University. I rang them. I started at the physics department – I mean, we're looking for somebody who is interested in alexandrite's applied properties. It wasn't difficult. Dr Peter Dunn is on leave,' he raised an eyebrow. 'Or that's what the department thinks. He left yesterday afternoon. He said he had to visit an aunt who had fallen ill. I mean, really! He isn't on any of our lists – or nothing at a high level, anyway. No previous interest or affiliations that we'd consider suspect. I got a description. He's in his late thirties. Ginger hair. On the small side.'

'The opposite of how Eleanor described her kidnapper when we brought her back,' McGregor said as he thought it through.

Eddie's stare communicated his frustration. 'Quite,' he added. 'Your cousin's wife is a slippery customer.'

'And was he working on these, what do you call them? Masers?' Mirabelle asked.

'Well, almost. Something called a laser, apparently. Similar theory – different application. This is our man. Something happened between them. He tied Eleanor up. And he probably took the stones. In her case.'

Mirabelle's mind raced. 'But then why would Eleanor protect him? I mean, she could have given us a description. She could have told us who he was.'

'A bloody traitor is who he is,' snapped Eddie. 'We can worry about the motive later. I've put out an alert. So far, Eleanor hasn't said anything that would help us narrow down where the man might have gone. She's insisting that she isn't – what was it now? – a "snitch".' Eddie lit a cigarette. 'We'll see about that. But as far as I can reckon it, she left here on foot yesterday late in the afternoon and made to meet this chap either at the cottage or somewhere on the way. She had the stones with her. Yes, she had sold some down south, but Dr Dunn was to be the recipient of whatever was left. She was supplying him – had been supplying him, most likely, for the last two or three years, on behalf of the Soviets.'

'But I thought she left on the spur of the moment,' Mirabelle said. 'She only realised the seriousness of the situation when Jinx died. She knew they were trying to kill her after that. Up till then, presumably, she was hoping to just wait it out and trust that Nina's death wouldn't be pinned on her, which was a fair assumption. I mean, none of us suspected her – not me or you, Alan.'

Eddie took an elegant draw from his cigarette. 'One way or another, she summoned the doctor. On the spur of the moment, it seems. Visiting his aunt, my foot. I don't know if they were lovers, of course . . .'

McGregor cleared his throat. 'Poor Bruce,' he said under his breath.

'One way or another,' Eddie continued, 'Eleanor thought she could count on the guy's help. Maybe she thought they were going to run away together. Maybe she thought if she delivered the alexandrite, the Russians would allow her some kind of reprieve. But Dr Dunn was having none of it. He didn't turn her in to his comrades and, thankfully, he didn't kill her either, but he took the alexandrite – in the leather briefcase – and left her behind.'

'So he's out there,' Mirabelle said. 'But he knows she'll be found, right? And he couldn't possibly trust her to stick to her views, about snitching. I mean, he can't go back to St Andrews.'

Eddie shook his head. 'No.' He rolled his hand to encourage Mirabelle to continue the line of her logic.

'That's why you mentioned Burgess and Maclean. You're worried he's going to defect, taking the alexandrite. Because that's his only way out now.'

'Him and his research,' Eddie said. 'Don't forget that. We're so focused on bloody Oxford, I mean, it's my own fault.'

'Oxford?'

'Never you mind.' He stubbed out his cigarette. 'I have all ports being watched. Airports too. The navy is on alert. But Dunn will know that, besides which we have a long coastline – in that respect the odds are in his favour. So my question for you two is: how's he going to get out? Can we narrow his window of opportunity? Can we mine your cousin for local knowledge? Or is there anything else here?' He gestured around the room. 'And what is the best way to get something out of Eleanor? You know her.'

Mirabelle pushed back the mahogany carver she'd been

sitting on and walked to the window. 'There is one thing you've missed,' she said. 'The maid must have had an escape route. She couldn't expect to get away with killing Eleanor. So how was she going to get out? Maybe these two things are related.'

Chapter 19

Goodness is the only investment that never fails

A phone call to the hospital ascertained that Elizabeth was making no more sense than she had earlier, so, to Mrs Gillies's chagrin, they cut through the kitchen and up to the servants' quarters, into the tidy room where the girl had slept. They knew they had to be careful now. Mirabelle laid her hand on McGregor's arm. It was too easy to destroy evidence. To miss things. He was only a policeman and wasn't used to this kind of search.

Elizabeth had been furnished with a convincing amount of possessions as cover – clothes from a selection of shops in Inverness and books from the local library on the bedside. There was something meditative, Mirabelle thought, about a fingertip search. It had rhythm.

McGregor took a seat in the comfortable chair. 'All right,' he said, 'show me how you do it.'

They started in one corner and fanned out, touching the walls, checking for loose floorboards or wainscoting, for anything secreted underneath the furniture, in any crevice. Mirabelle ran her fingers along the seams of Elizabeth's clothes. Eddie took the library books apart and, when he found nothing, searched the bed and opened the tiny sash and case window to see if there was anything secreted in the rope space.

Mrs Gillies, meanwhile, hovered uncomfortably at the door. 'What exactly are you looking for?' she asked after about twenty minutes.

'We don't know, Mrs Gillies,' Mirabelle said. 'But you mustn't come in.'

Gillies sighed as Eddie carefully emptied Elizabeth's work-basket on to the table. A jumble of threads and a few cards studded with pins and needles. Mirabelle sank down next to him. 'It's too new,' she said, indicating the pristine lining paper at the bottom of the box. 'Bad practice. The rest is very convincing.'

McGregor picked up yesterday's newspaper, shoved down the side of the chair. He might as well read it while he waited. Watching the others search was dull after the first few minutes. 'She took the *Telegraph*,' he said. 'Some Communist!'

Eddie raised his eyes. 'Mrs Gillies,' Mirabelle piped up, 'did this newspaper belong to Elizabeth? Or did it come from the house?'

'Mr and Mrs Robertson take *The Times* and the *Inverness Courier*, miss. Not the *Telegraph*.'

'Do you read it yourself?' McGregor asked. 'Below stairs?'

Gillies shook her head. 'No, sir. Miss Bevan is right. It must have belonged to the girl. Mrs Robertson wouldn't have the *Telegraph* in the house, as a matter of fact. Mr Robertson used to take it when she first moved here but she objected.' She sniffed. 'Mrs Robertson called it insupportable.' Gillies reported Eleanor's comment, as if she was trying out the word for size.

'You're not keen on the *Telegraph*, Mrs Gillies?'

'Not by choice, sir. No.'

'And Susan MacLeod wasn't either? Or could this have belonged to her?'

'Susan didn't take a paper and, even if she had, that's yesterday's from what I can see, so she couldn't have bought it.'

McGregor smiled. 'You're right. And I agree with you,' he said. 'The *Telegraph* is too conservative by far.'

They crowded round the low table and laid out the paper carefully. Eddie inspected it as if it was a delicate baby and he a doctor charged with diagnosing a potentially fatal illness. He checked each sheet but there was nothing concealed inside. It was, as it appeared to be, a copy of the *Telegraph* newspaper from the day before. There were thousands exactly like it across the country. He turned to the crossword. Mirabelle smirked. 'You think the KGB have infiltrated the puzzle section?' she said.

'Oh they did,' Eddie replied blithely. 'We let them. But the notification of it is clear. The same every time. And not in this issue, I see. There's something else, though. We had one of these before.'

'A Russian assassin?'

'An extraction. And on that occasion,' Eddie flipped back a few pages, 'what we needed was in the notifications column. The *Telegraph* is full of strange notifications. It took a team of three mathematicians, as I recall. We had to send men to several christenings and funerals just to cover all eventualities.'

'You're not a codebreaker, then?' McGregor said. Eddie's nonchalance could be difficult to take.

'Not in the modern sense.' Eddie grinned. 'I learned some decryption techniques from my aunt Florence. She was a suffragette. The suffragettes used the classified pages in *The Times*.'

Mirabelle giggled. 'That's enough, you two.'

Eddie carefully perused the paper. 'Catholics are so delicious,' he said. 'Apologies Mrs Gillies, but they are.' Mrs Gillies nodded her assent. They waited for a tense minute as Eddie carefully scanned the notifications, which ranged over two pages. 'This one,' he pronounced, getting to his feet. 'It has to be. *Thanks to St Jude for favours rendered. Seal the village at the hour of Christ and his disciples* – a cryptic place and a time – not as uncommon as you might expect, but in this particular issue of the paper, it's the only one that contains both elements. We need to examine the maps again and then I'll interrogate your cousin.'

Inside the house, Mrs Gillies peeled off at the stove as the men rushed ahead. She hovered momentarily. 'Are you all right?' Mirabelle checked.

The housekeeper nodded. There was clearly something on her mind. 'He reminds me of Colonel Blimp,' she whispered.

Mirabelle smiled. She knew what Gillies meant. It felt as if Eddie was gearing up for a Highland dash – very John Buchan. Or very black and white, as Eleanor would have put it.

'The hour of the disciples is in the afternoon. At three.' Gillies cast her eye towards the clock. It was just coming up to two.

'I'll tell him,' Mirabelle said. 'Thank you.'

In the drawing room, Eddie pored over the map.

'Where did Bruce get to?' Mirabelle asked.

McGregor shrugged. 'Try his study?' he suggested, and joined Eddie scouring the coastline on the map for any sign of a sealed village.

'Mrs Gillies says the hour of the disciples is three p.m.'

Eddie checked his watch and grunted. Mirabelle waited

a moment. The house felt deserted after days of feeling claustrophobic. She crossed the hall and opened the study door but Bruce wasn't there. Then, on a whim, she went to the day room. An officer stood on either side of the door. 'The gentleman said nobody was allowed inside,' one said.

'I interrogated Eleanor,' Mirabelle replied stoutly. Absolute confidence was important in these situations and she had no time to argue. 'I have more questions and Captain Brandon is busy.' The policemen looked doubtful. 'He's in the drawing room if you want to check,' she said. 'I can wait, if you feel you don't have the authority.'

The man thought for a moment and stepped aside. 'We're here if you need us, miss,' he said.

Mirabelle slipped through the door. On the window seat in front of the shutters, Eleanor sat with her husband. They were holding hands. Eleanor's foot had been bandaged and an ebony Victorian walking stick was propped next to her. 'You shouldn't be in here, Bruce,' Mirabelle objected. 'Did the men let you in?' The couple looked at each other. Taking in the rest of the room, Mirabelle noticed a leather bag at Bruce's feet. It wasn't the missing briefcase, more the kind of luggage you might pack to go away overnight. 'What's going on?' she demanded.

Bruce took a deep breath – more of a sigh. 'It's family business,' he said.

'Not so long ago, we thought you were family, Mirabelle.' Eleanor gave a sarcastic laugh.

'What's in the bag?' Mirabelle asked.

Neither of them answered. Instead, Bruce got to his feet. 'I love my wife,' he said, then he turned to Eleanor. 'I don't care what you've done. You're my darling. My very own. Please come with me.'

Eleanor's eyes fell to the carpet. Streaks of blood obliterated part of the pattern. 'You're not cut out to be a fugitive, darling. You can't leave the house and the estate. You love this place.'

'There are other places,' Bruce said stoutly. 'There's only one you.'

Mirabelle walked further into the room. 'Don't be ridiculous. You can't go anywhere,' she said. 'You'd never get away.'

'Wouldn't you leave with Alan?' Bruce asked. 'Isn't being together more important than anything?'

Eleanor laughed again. 'Look at your face, Belle.'

'I don't know what you're talking about. There are two officers on the door and two more outside,' she said. 'And I have some questions. We think your friend, Dr Dunn, is being extracted, Eleanor. In less than an hour, potentially. Eddie has found some kind of announcement in the newspaper. Do you know anything about it?'

'If I tell you, will you walk out of here and leave Bruce and me to our impossible escape? The flight of two lovers?'

'Where do you think you're going?'

'Not into the arms of St Jude,' Eleanor said, with a smile.

Mirabelle sank on to one of the chairs. So Eleanor knew about it, whatever it was. 'St Jude?' Bruce said. 'What are you talking about?'

'The patron saint of Lost Causes,' Eleanor drawled. 'It's nothing darling, I was only joking.'

Bruce cupped his wife's face in his hands. 'This is serious, Eleanor. I know you've done some foolish things. It's like some ghastly nightmare. But whatever you've done, you were backed into a corner. That woman was trying to blackmail you. I want to spend my life with you. For better or worse, isn't that what we said? Whatever happens. So this is our way out. Let's go.'

Eleanor softened. 'God, Bruce, doesn't it bother you that I'm a murderer?'

'Of course it does,' he whispered. 'It's terrible that you killed Nina. I feel awful for Tash apart from anything else. But it's done. And they're going to take you and, at best, it'll be a sentence of years. Worst ways you'll hang. How could I live without you? Maybe this whole nightmare is just something we'll tell our grandkids. Let's make it that.'

Mirabelle felt unaccountably tearful as Bruce kissed his wife. 'Bruce,' Eleanor whispered and indicated her leg. 'I can't run now. Besides, what would we live on? Where would we end up?'

'I'll carry you if I have to, darling. Duncan McKay has a horse in the field at the foot of the hill. There aren't any officers down there.'

'And then?' Eleanor asked. Bruce cast a glance at Mirabelle. 'You didn't answer his question, Belle,' Eleanor continued. 'Are you a Robertson now? Would you forgive Alan anything?' She appeared to be enjoying this. 'If he'd killed somebody, would you forgive him. Oh, I forgot. During the war, he did.'

'That's different and you know it!' Mirabelle cursed herself for getting riled by Eleanor's goading. She was wasting time.

'Will you make the deal?' Eleanor continued. 'If I tell you about the . . . what did you call it? Extraction? If you think we'd never make it, there's no risk, is there? It's win-win. I begin to understand that you like that.'

Mirabelle looked round for a clue as to what to do. Eleanor laughed once more. 'God, you're lame,' she said. 'You're out of your depth.'

For a second, a picture of Jack Duggan flashed in front of Mirabelle's eyes. She'd have run away with Jack in a heartbeat. But he'd never asked her to.

'You're so black and white,' Eleanor jeered. 'It's like a child's game. *We have a bomb and you're the bad ones. No, we have a bomb and you're the bad ones.* All that does is keep people in thrall. Don't you get it?'

Jack wouldn't have been black or white, not in the current political crisis, Mirabelle thought. Eleanor was right – what was happening was permissible in wartime perhaps, but not once there was peace. Politics was a performance. If the war had taught them anything, it was that. Black and white was too simple by far. Not that Eddie would see it that way. Mirabelle cast her mind back over Eleanor's argument – so much of what she had said struck a chord. Churchill was both saint and sinner. The Nazis had studied British history and taken some of its worst excesses to the extreme. It wasn't that there was no right or wrong. But there was definitely no absolutely good or bad side. She was grey. So were most people. Most nations, if it came to that. 'All right,' she said. 'Tell me and I'll leave the room for five minutes. Five minutes, do you understand?' It had been enough time earlier in the day to nearly kill them all.

Bruce grinned. You'd have thought Mirabelle had offered him a biscuit fresh from the oven.

'Translate it into Gaelic,' Eleanor said crisply.

Mirabelle got up. 'Gaelic?'

'Like *Druim a 'Mhadaidh* – remember? Wolf Ridge. The day you arrived. Everything has two names here, sometimes more than two. So think of it as a crossword clue.'

'You don't speak Gaelic.'

'Nobody in the house does. I used to ask the chap who does the gardening to translate for me.'

Mirabelle burst out of the day room and back down the hall.

'I might ask your cousin,' Eddie was saying to McGregor. 'I can't see it on the map, can you?'

'It's Gaelic,' Mirabelle said. 'It's a translation. We need someone who speaks Gaelic. The sealed village.'

Eddie took this in, freezing for a second. Then he grabbed the map and dashed to the phone. The department had language experts. A few seconds later, she heard him barking down the line, then the click of the bell and him talking to the operator, making another call. She sank on to the sofa.

'Would you like a drink?' McGregor offered. She shook her head. 'I think I might.' He poured himself a whisky.

'Alan, do you love me enough to give up everything?'

McGregor took a sip. 'Do you want me to give up everything?'

Mirabelle shook her head. It sounded ridiculously soppy. She checked the clock and closed her eyes. When she opened them he was in front of her on his knees. 'Yes,' he said. 'Of course. I'd do anything for you. I've always felt that way.' She started to weep and he took her in his arms. 'What is it?' he asked. 'What's wrong?'

'I'm a terrible person,' she managed to get out. 'I don't love you like that. Absolutely. Without reserve.'

'Don't you?'

She shook her head.

'Would you give up a martini?'

'What do you mean?'

'I know you love a martini. So would you give up a martini? For me?'

She nodded. 'Don't be silly.'

'A big fat debt to collect? I know how you love those at that agency of yours. Would you give one up, if I asked you?'

She nodded again.

'A flat on the front in Brighton? Say in favour of a rather nice house further down the coast?'

She kissed him. 'You're ridiculous.'

'I'm not ridiculous. Would you?'

'I've said I would.'

'Would you, though? Really?'

'Yes.'

'Well, that's enough,' said McGregor. 'I don't require anything else. Besides, you're going to have a scar now,' he touched her bandaged arm gently. 'So you're not perfect any more. Which, of course, makes you perfect for me. More perfect, if that were possible.'

'It's been the worst holiday in the world,' Mirabelle said.

McGregor smiled. 'Terrible,' he agreed. 'There would have been fewer bodies if we'd stayed at home.'

Mirabelle thought about it. 'There wouldn't,' she said. 'We just wouldn't have known about them.'

'So why's all this on your mind?'

Mirabelle checked her watch. It was time. 'It's your cousin,' she said. 'He got into the day room and he thinks he's going to break Eleanor free.'

McGregor got to his feet. 'Jesus!'

'Would it be so bad if he did?' Mirabelle asked.

McGregor didn't answer. He turned slightly, as if he was about to go and check, when they both heard it – the crack of gunfire, two pistol shots, one after the other. As one, they ran into the hallway. Eddie was still on the phone. He motioned them ahead. The policemen were already in the room with Mrs Gillies, fresh from the kitchen, her hands covered in a dusting of flour. McGregor let out a howl. The Robertsons were lying in the window recess, the overnight bag open and the gun in Eleanor's hand – an old service revolver. Mirabelle watched in horror as their blood pooled on to the carpet, mixed together and trickled slowly towards the stains from earlier in the day.

Chapter 20

Nothing great was achieved without
danger

Eddie alerted the navy. The place name translated to Balanron or, as Mirabelle later learned to say it, Baile nan Ròn. Place of the seals – or Seal Village. A submarine commander called Michael Farquhar-Brown arrested two Russian seamen in the end, one of whom claimed asylum, but Dr Peter Dunn eluded Eddie's best efforts. For the time being, anyway. That night it was as if the house had been abandoned. The bodies had been taken to the morgue. The policemen had gone. Mrs Gillies walked down to her sister's for the night and Eddie had left for Inverness.

'What should we do if they drop the bomb?' Mirabelle asked him before he left.

Eddie stood absolutely still – like a statue of the perfect civil servant. 'The advice is to get under the kitchen table but I've read the projections. If they drop the bomb, Belle, the best thing to do is end it yourself, before it can incinerate you.'

'Do you think either side will fire their rockets?'

'I think they both would, if we don't get the balance right,' he said deliberately. 'Hitler played a terrible game of chess by comparison with the opposition we're dealing with these days. The alarm in the media is not misplaced.'

She was about to ask another question, but McGregor opened the drawing-room door and, instead, Eddie extended his condolences, kissed Mirabelle on the cheek and was off, like a knight on a crusade to get the night train back to London. It was late and he had bigger fish to fry.

Mirabelle watched him leave, the car lights receding down the driveway into the velvet darkness and turning along the road away from the village before the hill obscured them. She stood outside for a long time. The freezing air smelled of green things stirring and, she thought, of fallen stars – a metallic smell of great fires doused.

Gillies had left dinner in the kitchen but neither of them had the heart to eat. McGregor sat by the fire in the drawing room. This place was haunted now, she realised. It would be haunted for ever. All the deaths. Nina and Susan and Bruce and Eleanor. Even Jinx. It felt as if nothing would ever break the silence. When McGregor put a record on the gramophone, they let it play; once the music was done, they didn't put on another.

'I'm sorry,' Mirabelle said eventually. 'I didn't know Bruce had another gun.'

McGregor stared at his drink. 'How could you have known?' he asked. 'Besides, I'm not sure he meant them to die. That didn't seem to be what he was talking about from what you said. I'd like to have been a fly on the wall. Just that last five minutes. Why did they choose death? I mean, they could have run.'

'I don't even understand how he got in there,' Mirabelle said.

McGregor looked at his hands. 'There's a secret. A stupid family story.'

'What?'

'I don't know. A secret room. A tunnel. Maybe that's how he got in. He had hope, I suppose. The old fool.'

Mirabelle got to her feet. 'Come with me.'

She led him upstairs, picking a torch from the boot cupboard as they passed. McGregor objected when they entered Bruce and Eleanor's room. 'Belle, I can't,' he said as she snapped on the bedside lamps illuminating the suite in golden light. Tonight, the curtains had been drawn. In another story it might feel cosy. Mirabelle took his hand. 'Come on,' she said. 'You need to see this.'

The dressing room was still in disarray. She opened Eleanor's wardrobe. 'This is grim,' McGregor said. 'We'll have to sort it out but not tonight.'

'Give me a moment.' She opened the drawer and twisted the knob. The back of the wardrobe slid to the side. McGregor's face remained unexpressive. He moved forward. 'This is where she hid the alexandrite,' Mirabelle said.

Inside the hidden room, she sprang the catch on the wooden book and the door to the tunnel opened.

'This is how she got out the first time. When we thought she'd been kidnapped.'

'Why didn't you tell me?'

'Gillies showed me. She said it was a secret passed down the female line. But it seems like you knew, even if you thought it was only a story.'

'And you didn't tell Eddie?'

Mirabelle shook her head. 'Once I knew how Eleanor had got out, the fact she was wearing her diamond watch made sense and that was what mattered.'

'Come on,' said McGregor, taking the torch. He stooped, making his way down the rough stones of the staircase between the walls. When they reached ground level, they examined the stonework and found a small lever on the rough clay floor. McGregor pressed it with his foot and, with a click, a low door opened into the day room. On the other side, the opening was concealed by a chinoiserie cabinet inlaid with mother-of-pearl herons in flight. 'So they could have got away – why didn't they just click the switch? I don't understand.' Mirabelle slipped her arms around McGregor and hugged him. She suddenly felt so exhausted she couldn't even cry. 'Maybe Eleanor just gave up. The countryside was lousy with policemen and Bruce was determined to implicate himself. Perhaps he agreed to a death pact – he adored her.'

'She was like the alexandrite, wasn't she?' McGregor said. 'One thing in one light, quite a different thing in another.'

'I liked her,' Mirabelle admitted sadly.

Together they went out, into the hall. McGregor opened the front door and Mirabelle followed him outside. 'God's own country,' he said as the horses stirred in the paddock. It was cloudy now and no stars were visible. With the moonlight only just breaking through, the darkness seemed absolute. When Mirabelle breathed in, the air was so sharp she couldn't pick up the smell of the grass or the mud or the open sky. She stared at the hill ahead and found herself imagining Nina Orlova walking up the slope in the dark, only a few days before. Then, chiding herself for being gruesome, she gazed at the outline of the emerald-cut pink diamond on her finger, but all she could think was that she couldn't imagine swallowing it.

'Come on,' said McGregor. The two of them continued a little way down the drive. Ahead, the horses in the paddock moved and one came as far as the fence.

'They won't have liked it,' Mirabelle said. 'Having so many people around. Horses are flighty. They startle.'

They turned and looked back at the house, the lights from the drawing room illuminating the edges of the velvet curtains. 'I'm the heir,' McGregor said. 'Ridiculously. Mrs Gillies pointed it out. Not that I want the stupid thing. But I'm the laird now. Bruce's closest male relation. Tomorrow I'll have to contact the family solicitor in Edinburgh and I'll need to make a plan. Unless you want to be lady of the manor, Mirabelle.'

Mirabelle shook her head. 'Not in a million years,' she said. 'What will you do?'

'Sell it to pay the death duties, I expect,' McGregor said. 'It seems a waste – two hundred years of Robertson history. Not that it will sell easily – what with the murders. Who'd want such a big old house these days?'

Mirabelle imagined for a moment that Eleanor was laughing at her from somewhere far away. She pulled a sugar lump out of her pocket and fed the horse.

'I learned to ride here,' McGregor continued. 'Bruce and I learned together. There was a full stable in those days at the back, where Eleanor had her office.'

'What was your horse called?'

'It was more of a pony. Cabbages.'

'You didn't take it seriously, then?'

'Did you?'

'You are looking, Superintendent McGregor, at the Hyde Park Stables junior champion of 1928.'

'I might have known. And what was your pony called?'

'Bosco. He was magnificent and extremely badly behaved. I loved him.'

'I will take that as a lesson,' he said, and she could just make out his smile.

McGregor took her hand. 'This means I'll have to stay on. We were supposed to be gone by the end of the week, but there are the funerals to organise and the estate to wind up. I'll arrange for you to go back on your own. First class all the way.'

Mirabelle put her hand on to his shoulder and levered herself on to the fence. She wrapped her legs around him. 'I'm staying as long as you do,' she said. 'Even if all I can do is hold you. Or speak to an estate agent. Or help to choose a headstone. I'll be here. Whatever you need.'

'You're sure?' His voice wavered. 'You want to?'

'I'm your wife,' she said. 'And that's that.'

Epilogue:
Two weeks later. Edinburgh.

A beautiful woman must expect to be accountable

He got to show her his home town after all. Once the funerals were over, they left Gillies in charge of the house and engaged an estate agent to deal with the sale. Somebody daubed the gateposts in red paint – 'Commie bitch', it said. McGregor had it cleaned and hired a couple of guards to patrol the grounds. The night before they left, it snowed, as if the world was putting down dust covers.

In the end, it turned out there was more to Bruce's legacy than McGregor first realised – a portfolio of stocks and shares, a flat on Heriot Row in Edinburgh where they were now staying, and a sizeable sum in cash that was kept in a safety-deposit box in the Royal Bank of Scotland on the Mound.

Edinburgh was a darker version of Brighton – the familiar Georgian crescents and squares built in granite rather than stucco and a myriad of private gardens coming into bloom with the first of the daffodils, but only snatched glimpses now and then of the sea. In the morning, the haar slipped round the buildings like a sleek, white cat, obscuring the view. Mirabelle found she liked walking up to George Street to buy groceries at Willis's – milk and bread and butter – and a newspaper at Thin's. The headlines continued to be ominous, but then, she thought, headlines always were. 'Berlin Ultimatum' and 'Another D-Day for Europe' and 'Crucial Talks Continue'. Every time she read one, she heard Eddie saying the words.

Murdo Kenzie was writing now for the *Scotsman*, his work on what had become known as the 'Red Highland murders' winning him a job on the national paper. Mirabelle refused on principle to read his articles, no matter what they were about. On the way back down the hill she always hoped the mists would clear and she would catch sight of the Firth of Forth – a slash of vibrant blue. The days she did so, it seemed to nourish her. She missed the water, she realised. And she missed Vesta.

Her arm still ached but it was healing. She was doing better than McGregor, who kept waking in the night. Their second night in town she woke to find him in the drawing room, the long window wide open, with him perched on the sill, his legs dangling outside. 'I can't seem to cool down,' he said. The flat was freezing. Through the open window the thick tangle of the communal gardens stretched black, beyond the reach of the amber streetlights.

They got dressed and walked for miles through the grand, silent streets of the West End and out on Queensferry Road, past Valente's dress shop, the mannequins elegant shadows in the dark window. It took an hour to get to Davidson's Mains where McGregor grew up. The air smelled of fermenting malted barley, carried on the breeze from the breweries to the south. They watched dawn from the crest of a hill scattered with tidy, pale bungalows, and held hands. 'This one?' she asked when he hovered outside a house with a newly painted red door, and he nodded. It seemed a million miles away from the Robertsons' Highland home in all its isolation. A million miles from the bodies.

Daily, Mirabelle rang Vesta from a telephone box at the top of Dundas Street, and bit by bit explained what had happened. It was, she realised, a kind of recovery. Vesta took notes. Mirabelle could hear her pencil on the paper, could picture the office with its old kettle and chipped cups. The metal filing cabinets and frosted glass door. The gemlike glimpse of the sea that she could spy if she stood at the frame of the window. 'I picked up a lead,' Vesta announced, sounding chirpy, the third week Mirabelle was away.

'A lead?' Mirabelle was momentarily confused. This wasn't a case to her. Not any more.

'Your physicist. I rang the university.'

'In St Andrews?' Mirabelle's heart raced – anybody asking after Peter Dunn would be flagged. Eddie was good at his job – he'd had time to set everything up now.

'Not St Andrews. In Edinburgh. Dunn sat his primary degree in Edinburgh.' Mirabelle relaxed a little. 'I said I was his aunt and that he was about to get married. I was preparing a speech for my husband.' She laughed. 'Student japes – that kind of thing. I said I recalled something unusual had happened but couldn't remember the details and could they possibly help.'

Mirabelle fought her confusion momentarily. This is how it felt for other people when she breezed in and started asking questions when somebody they cared about died.

Vesta continued. 'Dunn was in an affray in third year. It was fairly serious – two students broke limbs. He was suspended. Well, they all were. He was relatively easy to find because of that. The lady kindly gave me his address – he lived at 34 William Street. I'm only passing on the details,' she said. 'But it might be worth having a look. It seems he was forgiven, by the way – he was quite brilliant, apparently, and people tend to forgive their geniuses. I thought you'd like to know.'

That afternoon, Mirabelle closed the front door on the drab hallway on Heriot Row while McGregor was at the solicitors. She walked westwards, cut up to Queensferry Street and beyond, on to the two blocks of squat Georgian granite tenements that made up William Street. The row accommodated a public house, a leather workshop and some offices. Sure enough, the bell plate announced Mr Dunn on the first floor. She rang but there was no reply, so she slipped her lockpicks from her handbag and broke into the stair. If the main hallway at Heriot Row was dull with its dusty Wedgwood green paint, the hall at William Street felt like a cave. A curving stone staircase led up to Dunn's door, of which Mirabelle also made short work, her heart pounding. Inside, the flat was empty – not a stick of furniture, not a scrap of clothing, only a pile of mail – two bills and a circular. Outside, the sun peeped from behind February clouds and brightened the cobwebby corners. He'd gone.

Downstairs, she loitered, watching the windows before turning back towards town. On the corner of the lane that led to the mews of the grander houses on Melville Street, she noticed a pawn shop – three brass balls mounted on the stone wall. Idly she wandered across the cobbles towards the window and there it was. Just sitting there on display behind the glass. Eleanor's burgundy leather briefcase. Quite distinctive. She looked around but the backstreets were deserted at this time of day. Only two blocks from Princes Street, you could almost hear the trams as they trundled along the main road. The closest place to his flat, she thought as she made the decision to go inside.

A bell sounded as she opened the door and a woman came out from the back, dressed in an ox-blood knitted skirt and sweater that almost matched. Her hair was swept up in a chignon – unfeasibly glamorous for the surroundings. Round her neck she wore a pair of tortoiseshell glasses on a chain. 'Can I help you?'

'I'd like to see the bag in the window. Is it for sale?'

'It is. It's monogrammed, I'm afraid. ER. The same as the queen.'

She fetched the bag. Mirabelle opened it and peered inside. It was empty. 'I'd like to buy it,' she said. The woman seemed pleased. It must, Mirabelle thought, be tricky to sell something initialled. 'Who did it belong to?' she asked casually.

The woman shrugged. 'An old customer. A nice chap.'

'Were his initials ER?'

'Well, no. He had it from his aunt, I think.'

'He lived nearby, I expect?'

'Just along the road,' she confirmed.

'Having a clear-out?'

'Going away,' the lady said. 'Emigrating, I think he said.'

'Somewhere nice? It's a terrible time of year for the weather in Scotland.'

'America.'

'Such a big place. I wonder where he ended up?'

The woman shrugged again, but warmed to the conversation. 'Are you ER, miss?' she asked.

'My cousin is,' Mirabelle replied, and a picture of Eleanor

316

standing by the loch came to her. 'But if the chap was emigrating, he might have cleared out more of his things. Did the bag come with anything else?'

'Nothing else monogrammed. Just some amethysts he had been left in an inheritance.'

Mirabelle's heart quickened. 'Do you have them?'

'They're going to auction. Lyon and Turnbull. Next week. Would you like to see?' The auction houses would be watched by now, Mirabelle thought, and wondered if Eddie would be clever enough to include in his alert description not only alexandrite but any stone that might be confused with it.

'Yes please,' she said.

They didn't seem enough to kill over. The one in Nina's stomach had been the largest. The scatter of sparkling violet cascaded out of a buff envelope on to a dark velvet tray. 'How much do you want for these?' Mirabelle asked.

'They're marked up to £321/10 shillings. So many of them, do you see? But they're off to the sale, madam.'

Mirabelle drew out her cheque book and pen. If the girl had known what they were, the price would have been ten times higher. More. 'Let me add on a little extra for the trouble,' she said.

Outside she prevaricated for a minute, wondering whether to call Eddie in London. But Dunn was gone. He had been, it seemed, grey as well. Of course he was – if he had been a black and white person he'd have killed Eleanor. She felt she owed him something for that. Reporting him to Eddie was stoking the fires. The very opposite of what she wanted. Dunn was welcome to his freedom. To continue his research in America or wherever he'd gone. Physicists were welcome everywhere – their skills endowing them with forgiveness for whatever they had done before. American laboratories were peopled with scientists who had helped the Nazis. The British, she imagined, were no more exacting.

Haymarket Station was a five-minute walk. She stopped for a moment, slipping into the rectangle of green beside St Mary's Cathedral, where she sat on a bench. An elderly man was walking a Highland terrier, the two well matched, short legged, and so old they almost creaked. Inside the cathedral somebody was practising the organ, the same piece over and over. 'The Day Thou Gavest Lord Has Ended'. She'd only ever heard it at funerals. They hadn't played it at Eleanor's and Bruce's, which had taken place in private with no service to speak of, only Mirabelle and McGregor holding hands over the grave and Mrs Gillies clutching a handkerchief but not, as far as Mirabelle could recall, actually crying.

When the old man left the park she picked up some stones at the edge of the grass – two reasonable-sized rocks to weight down the bag. Then she walked smartly to Haymarket and bought a ticket for Kirkcaldy. It was strange, she thought, just choosing a place like that. She could have opted to go to Burntisland or Rosyth, but Kirkcaldy seemed like the right place. The train had only four carriages. Mirabelle slipped into first class alone as it chugged out of the city, past South Queensferry. The bridge was spectacular – a draw for tourists, painted a strong rust colour that stood out against the misty blue sky over the Firth. She'd need to time it well, she knew, but there was a rhythm to the girders as they flew past. Mirabelle pushed down the window and counted. At the middle of the bridge she threw the bag, with all her might, out of the window and into the water.

Back in Edinburgh, a round trip later, she took a taxi to Heriot Row.

'Have you been to Scotland before, miss?' the driver asked as he started the engine and set off towards town.

'We're here on holiday,' she replied, 'It's my first time up north.'

As she let herself into the building, snow began to tumble out of the darkening sky. Flecks caught in the light from the streetlamps, which came on before it was dark here, late in the afternoon. Mirabelle smiled as the flakes swirled as if they were dancing. On the table, Mrs Gillies had forwarded two wooden boxes. McGregor came out to greet her as she took off her hat and gloves.

'Where have you been?'

'I have something for you,' she said. 'A gift.'

'This?' he asked, indicating the boxes.

They opened the first box in the small kitchen with a knife from the drawer. Inside, the bottles were lined up like soldiers, packed in straw. McGregor picked one up and squinted at the label. 'Nineteen twelve,' he said. 'When did you buy these?'

'I met one of the girls from the distillery. Our distillery now, I suppose. It's a wedding gift,' she said. 'I chose 1912 because it's the year you were born. Before the wars,' she pointed out. 'Before any of the trouble started.'

'Before the Russian Revolution,' McGregor confirmed.

'The other box is gin. For me.'

'Gin? From the Highlands?' McGregor made a face.

He went to the washstand and took down two glasses, lining them up on the edge of the sink and pouring a generous amber dram into each with a splash of water. In this light he looked handsome as his fringe flopped over his forehead. The glow of the lamp seemed to make his eyes bluer. It was McGregor she wanted now – no doubt in her mind. He handed her a glass. 'To you,' he toasted, raising his whisky. 'My wonderful wife-to-be.'

'I can't drink to myself,' she said.

McGregor sat back down. 'Why not? You've been amazing, Mirabelle.'

Mirabelle regarded her glass as if it was a crossword clue. 'Maybe we should toast the Robertsons. The Green Lady, even.'

'The ghost?'

'The legend,' Mirabelle raised her glass.

The taste took her back to the loch-side – standing with Eleanor by the car, talking about McGregor's childhood and the war and feeling that she might have found, if not a sister, at least a relation. That's what had happened. They'd become family. That was the tragedy of it, or one of them. Whisky could never only be a drink now; it was a feeling distilled into liquid form. But she didn't say that. Instead, she kissed McGregor, relishing the bitterness of the iodine and the hint of smoked peat that opened on his lips as the spirit rose to body temperature.

There was nothing for it in the end but to choose to live. She'd learned that with Jack in Nuremberg and had returned home determined to turn her back on all the death. And then Jack, himself, had died. 'We need to find a house, Superintendent McGregor,' she said. 'And a date. And a dress. I'm going to get Vesta to help me.'

'Is this what you think about when I leave you on your own?' McGregor teased. 'I like it.' She took another sip of the whisky. 'Let's go out for dinner tonight,' he said. At first they hadn't eaten at all, but now slowly their appetites were returning, outrunning Mirabelle's limited ability to cook. They had eaten out every night in the last week. The Pompadour restaurant at the Caledonian Hotel, with its hand-painted wallpaper and fancy French food, and the carvery at the George – meat and two veg. 'I heard they serve roast beef up at the bar at the Roxburghe,' McGregor said. 'It sounds chic. Italian waiters and glasses of champagne. I think you'd like it.'

'I'll get changed,' Mirabelle said. She'd bought a cocktail dress in Jenners the other day. McGregor had declared he liked it. 'Silver suits you,' he enthused. She'd wear that one tonight, she decided, though it wasn't silver, she insisted silently. It was definitely more of a grey.

Author's note

The quotations and misquotations used to open each chapter are taken from the following sources:

It is best to avoid the beginnings of evil: Henry David Thoreau. Courage is the quality that guarantees all others: Aristotle. There is nothing insignificant in the world: Goethe. The death of a beautiful woman is the most poetical topic in the world: Edgar Allan Poe. Better three hours too soon than a minute too late: Shakespeare. Happiness was born a twin: Byron. Belief is a wise wager: Pascal.

We must take our friends as they are: Boswell. Make perseverance your bosom friend: Joseph Addison. To be prepared is half the victory: Miguel de Cervantes. If Heaven had looked upon riches to be valuable, it would not have given them to such a fool: Jonathan Swift. Dreams are the touchstones of character: Henry David Thoreau. Murder: the killing of a person without valid excuse: dictionary definition. To do a great right do a little wrong: Shakespeare. Every man is a piece of the continent: John Donne. The only evil is ignorance: Herodotus. Trust: belief in someone or something: dictionary definition. No one can confidently say that he will still be living tomorrow: Euripides. Goodness is the only investment that never fails: Henry David Thoreau. Nothing great was achieved without danger: Machiavelli. A beautiful woman must expect to be accountable for her steps: Samuel Richardson.

Acknowledgements

Highland Fling goes out to the Lindley/McKenzie clan whose family home is the basis of the house in the Highlands that Mirabelle visits in this novel (though in real life it isn't in the Highlands and nobody has ever been murdered there). The book is dedicated particularly to the memory of Clive Lindley, my wonderful uncle, sadly missed for his advice, his ability to listen and his interesting take on just about everything. Thanks are also due to my parents, Kate and Ron Goodwin, who are staunch Mirabelle fans (I think they quite like me as well . . .), and a shout-out to my long-suffering editor, Krystyna Green, who knows what she likes and is usually right, goddamn it. She suggested rewriting part of the first draft of this novel, thus improving the narrative immeasurably, and is a star for that. To Penny Isaac, whose unwavering eye and dedication to the 1950s detail is always an inspiration and valuable support, and Amanda Keats who keeps us organised – thank goodness! To Alan Ferrier and Molly Sheridan, suppliers of elegant solutions of all kinds – thank you for your patience and kindness. Molly, you keep me exacting no matter what. And lastly, to Jenny Brown my brilliant agent, who dedicates herself to stories that change the world, even ones like mine, that hope to do so laterally.